PRAISE FOR NEW STAR

New Star ... *this book still delivers breathless, addictive stuff* ... *A solid post-apocalyptic/space war action tale for sci-fi fans* ...

—Kirkus Reviews

LIKE A NEW STAR

LIKE A NEW STAR

Clash of the Aliens

M. B. WOOD

WFP
WORDFIRE PRESS

EBook ISBN: 978-1-68057-055-7
Trade Paperback ISBN: 978-1-68057-054-0
Cover artwork by Michael J. Canales
Kevin J. Anderson, Art Director

Published by
WordFire Press, LLC
PO Box 1840
Monument CO 80132

Kevin J. Anderson & Rebecca Moesta, Publishers
WordFire Press eBook Edition 2020
WordFire Press Trade Paperback Edition 2020
Printed in the USA

Join our WordFire Press Readers Group for
sneak previews, updates, new projects, and giveaways.
Sign up at wordfirepress.com

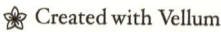 Created with Vellum

THE STORY SO FAR

In Book 1, Middle Eastern fanatics paralyze Western Civilization with massive EMPs, creating a post-apocalyptic world that is a sea of chaos and near-anarchy. Refugees create a society under a primitive rule of law. Proud, fierce, and free, Taylor MacPherson and a tight-knit group of survivors known as the Clan take their first steps to restoring law and justice... as a race of hermaphroditic aliens, the Qu'uda, arrives to find a post-apocalyptic Earth.

In Book 2, Taylor MacPherson witnesses a strange light in the night sky, which is a leftover missile-defense weapon that blasts the giant Qu'uda spaceship, stranding it in an unstable orbit. The Qu'uda send one of their own, "Billy," down to Earth to fashion parts necessary for repairs. A war among surviving human factions comes at a terrible cost to each, and Billy is abandoned by his race; he throws in his lot with Taylor and his refugees. The aliens leave the surface and plan to return and bomb the Earth into a new Stone Age.

Book 3 reveals the backstory of how the Qu'uda came to investigate Earth. Another alien race, the Hoo-Lii, has a rigid society ruled by Hive-Mothers, with a warrior class of mating males and a great underclass of "unripened," non-mating males and females. Wars between Hives are frequent, which are fought only with digit-held weapons or on a spine-to-spine basis.

An old Hive-Mother seeks to reverse societal decline. She ripens her daughter in defiance of the convention of bringing in a new female from outside to lead the Hive. The daughter, Suh-Joh, struggles with her unexpected role and builds a powerful military to force a facedown with the Council of Hive-Mothers. Despite her calls for change, new ideas are not accepted easily among the Hoo-Lii. Hive-Mother Suh-Joh now leads her once-decadent world.

Hoo-Lii religion, the Way-of-the-Mother, forbids weapons of mass destruction. Their society is in decline, slowly losing vigor and genetic diversity, though its priest-class possess a spaceship capable of faster-than-light travel, which can take them to interstellar settlements. One such settlement, Kamah, is an ocean world with three islands and is the destination for newly ripened Hive-Mothers. Another settlement, Chud-Loo, is a desert world where exiled dissidents eke out a precarious life under harsh conditions.

The alien Qu'uda send a spaceship of their own, the *Star-Seeker*, to investigate the source of the signals from Chud-Loo. Not recognizing the Qu'uda ship, the settlement's asteroid defense system blasts it with a powerful laser. The surviving Qu'uda crew seek revenge and plunge the ship into Chud-Loo, rigging their fusion drive to explode on impact.

The existence of the unexpected Hoo-Lii civilization alarms the Qu'uda. They build a deep-space radio monitor and pick up signals coming from yet another star system - Earth. This is the reason the Qu'uda sent their gigantic spacecraft to investigate the solar system, where the ship was stranded in an unstable orbit...

Back on their home world of Hool, Suh-Joh's scientists detect the faint EMP of a fusion weapon, which originated in the solar system. They send a faster-than-light ship to investigate, thinking this might be the race that destroyed Chud-Loo. When the Hoo-Lii reach the solar system, they set course for Earth, as does the Qu'uda asteroid ship. The Hoo-Lii are caught between the Qu'uda vessel and the human space station. The Qu'uda attack and damage the Hoo-Lii ship, making it lose much of its air and water.

Trying to open communications with the Hoo-Lii, the humans send a gift of water—which the Hoo-Lii consider a symbolic gesture of a species submitting to them as a servant class. The Hoo-Lii depart, promising to return ... to lead the humans.

CHAPTER ONE

Bilik Pudjata watched the long thin stream of blue-white fire etch its way across the night sky.

It was the fusion drive of the Egg-that-Flies fleeing from its orbit around the Earth. By the next night it had disappeared, lost among the stars.

Bilik had mixed feelings at the sight. It meant his former identity as an alien Qu'uda had truly died. From now on, he would be Billy Potato, a man of Earth, belonging to a new community, with a new home and a new identity.

ↄ

Mata ChaLik BuMaru felt the surge of acceleration—and something else. The ship—the Egg-that-Flies—was shaking.

"What is that vibration?" The memory of the catastrophic explosion that had stranded them in orbit came back. *No, not again.*

The holographic image bulged. The squat face and scarred head crest of KaLik DuGan appeared. He was the ship's engineer and its battle tactics master.

"I am analyzing the vibration." He bobbed his head in respect. "It's in the drive system. I am also investigating its impact upon structural members, whether it poses any immediate danger."

"Danger?" Mata ChaLik felt the claw of fear rip into his guts.

"What kind of danger?" He recalled how those savage dry-land vermin, the humans, had damaged the shuttle on its last trip to Earth, when it brought back the propulsion tube parts made on the planet's surface.

"Danger to the thrust transfer structure." KaLik referred to the large metal tunnel extending from the rear of the Egg-that-Flies through the fuel tank to the forward section containing their living quarters.

"We cannot shut the drive down while this close to the planetary body."

Mata ChaLik believed the propulsion system repairs would let them de-orbit this planet and go to the cold safety of the outer reaches of the system, to gather supplies and make repairs. During the stress and fear of the four long years they had been stranded in orbit, many of the crew had changed gender. "Can we maintain thrust?"

"I don't know. If only Bilik were here. He would know."

"He isn't. Just get me an answer as quickly as possible."

"Yes, Mata ChaLik BuMaru." KaLik wobbled his head crest submissively. "As soon as possible, leader of the Defenders of Qu'uda." His image vanished.

The course depiction of the Egg-that-Flies expanded. A yellow line paralleled the red course projection. A string of velocity parameters appeared.

If our drive system continues to work, thought Mata ChaLik, *we will get away from this cursed world, away from its savage natives.* "DalChik DuJuga," he called.

"Yes?" DalChik answered through the comm-net, her voice pitched higher than normal. She had dropped an egg, which had been sent to the planet below. She'd openly spoken of her worries of the fate that might have befallen her only chance for an offspring. "What is it now?"

"Retrieve plans and specifications for a Bird-of-War. That is an order. Once we refuel, we shall seek a source of materials to build weapons for our return to this planet."

Battle, he thought, *is more exciting than mating.* "We must exterminate those dry-land vermin, the humans."

"That has not been discussed by the Keepers-of-the-Egg,"

DalChik said. "You cannot run this ship as if it were a unit in the Defenders, not without the Keepers' consent."

Prior to departing Qu'uda, the crew had agreed important decisions would be decided in a meeting represented by all factions—including the Keepers-of-the-Egg—to ensure a consensus would be maintained in major decisions.

"During times of danger, when battle is imminent," Mata ChaLik said. "I do not need consent of the Keepers. The Earth creatures created a condition of war. Therefore, I am in command." He felt his head crest engorge and grow erect.

"We shall see about that." DalChik's image disappeared from the comm-net link.

~

KaLik DuGan looked at the analytical model. *Why*, he wondered, *does the propulsion tube vibrate? There was something within the drive system. Yet the fuel flow was constant without any pulsation, and the magnetic field ... Yes! There were variations in the magnetic field that contained the plasma.*

For a moment, the talon of fright touched him.

If the magnetic containment failed, the tremendous energy of the drive system would be released instantaneously to smash against the stern of their ship and leave them derelict, drifting in space.

Great Egg, he thought. *Please, not that again.*

"Magnetic containment system analysis, performance parameter comparison," he said.

Figures scrolled through the air before him; almost all were within normal bounds. The only one out of specification was the containment field itself, which meant the tube was the cause.

How can that be? Bilik Pudjata made all nine sections at the same time, in the same place, from the same material...

"Replacement propulsion tube material data," KaLik DuGan called to the computer. "Present data by each section of tube as received. Compare elemental analysis for minority components, organize by section." The numbers winked into appearance in nine columns.

KaLik DuGan stared at the data.

The iron in each section of the propulsion tube had slightly different magnetic properties. *Would that make the vibration?* As he ran the analysis, it became clear the magnetic field variation made the plasma expand and contract at slightly different rates during its passage through the propulsion tube. Further analyses showed the iron would, sooner or later, fatigue and fail.

After multiple analyzes, he felt confident it would last long enough to reach the outer cometary belt. His fear faded.

The prudent course of action was to replace the propulsion tube, KaLik DuGan thought.

"Mata ChaLik BuMaru," KaLik DuGan called. "I have answers to your questions."

Mata ChaLik's image appeared. He was in front of the trunk of a spindly Podu tree that trailed vines dripping water. It was like an erotic setting used for mating. "Yes?" he asked, head crest quivering.

"If this is not a convenient time." KaLik DuGan had heard rumors of Mata ChaLik torturing a crewmember into a gender change for mating. He had no desire to be part of that.

"Tell me," Mata ChaLik said. "What have you found out?"

KaLik DuGan explained the problem and his conclusions.

"Can you make a replacement tube?" asked Mata ChaLik.

"Yes," KaLik DuGan said. "As long as we have thrust to produce gravity, we can handle molten iron. We can set up a casting facility within the thrust transfer structure. Once we commence the casting operation, it will be isolated from the living area since it has to be open to the vacuum of space."

"Start at once."

CHAPTER TWO

"Mr. MacPherson." A horseman dressed in the familiar brown garb of a Clan soldier reined in his horse. "There's trouble out west. There's a rebellion in the Fed territories." He stood stiffly straight and gave a military salute as though Taylor MacPherson were still the Clan's War Leader.

"What's going on?" Taylor stepped off the sidewalk onto Front Street.

Taylor was a slender man, with gray hair and bright blue eyes set in a long face. He'd just left his laboratory in Marting Hall, a Victorian style building, three stories of ornate gray sandstone in the old Baldwin-Wallace University in Berea, Ohio. Mossy sidewalks beneath stately maples and oaks connected the widely scattered buildings of the campus. Taylor had resigned his position as War Leader to restore the university.

The horseman slid off his horse. "A mob marched into Fremont and caught the garrison by surprise." He paused to catch his breath. "The mob killed at least a half dozen. Then they marched to the center of town an' burned the courthouse an' strung up a couple of merchants. They claimed they was righting a wrong." The horseman straightened as he added, "Sir."

"You'd better get this to the Council right away." Taylor was conscious he no longer had a role in government. "Thanks for letting me know, but this is Council business." He pointed north to

River Road. "Go that way. The Hill is about two miles." He directed the horseman to the Clan's administrative center.

"Yes, sir." The horseman struggled to get a foot into a stirrup as the horse made a circle. Once mounted, he cracked his crop and the horse broke into a trot.

ॐ

It was less than a month later when Taylor watched five battle groups of Clan Horse Soldiers and militia—almost one thousand—clatter through the streets of Berea to the applause of its citizens. They had just returned from putting down the rebellion in Fremont. Only one Clan soldier had died in the encounter. Even as the Horse Soldiers conducted their victory parade, another group was on its way west.

Taylor felt a great unease as he walked away from the main street. *So, now we've become the occupier of the Fed instead of seeking to solve the problem. Nothing good will come of this. The union of the Fed and the Clan was supposed to be one of equals, even though we won the war. Somebody has to do something about this. But who and how?*

ॐ

Taylor headed home on the long walk from Berea to the Hill. It was a familiar path and his mind wandered back to his first arrival here. In the distant past, he and his wife, Vivian, had planned to grow their business and start a family. It hadn't turned out that way. A war in the Middle East, fueled by ancient hatreds and fought with modern weapons, had become global.

Fanatics had resorted to nuclear weapons, first attacking with massive high-altitude EMP bursts that paralyzed the industrialized nations. Afterwards had come the missiles and Vivian had been caught in Washington, DC, along with millions of others on the east coast. She'd been incinerated in the nuclear fire.

Ohio was untouched, for none of its cities had been targeted. Within days the financial system had failed, and anarchy became the norm.

Was it Margaret Thatcher who said the veneer of civilization is quite thin? She was right. As soon as credit cards, checks, and order entry systems—the financial mechanisms of society—had quit working, business transactions froze, stopping the distribution of goods. Food, medicine, fuel, everything had become scarce. Soon, the only law that existed came out of the barrel of a gun. It didn't take long for the lights of civilization to fade. The cruel night of anarchy—the Collapse—dawned. He'd almost given up, overwhelmed by events...

Taylor had fled in fear of his life. Hiding in the local metropark to wait until law and order was restored proved to be futile. It hadn't been long before the first of many refugees joined him. He remembered Franny, poor Franny, raped, her husband killed, and her daughter sodomized. He realized others had suffered more. He just couldn't leave them; he had to take care of them. He shook his head. Little had he realized what he had started by taking in those refugees.

It had forced him to organize, to build shelter and defenses. That was his salvation. The memory of the first settlement on the hill alongside the Rocky River in the local metropark came back. First, it had been a stronghold and then it had become home. It was there they'd fended off an assault by a large gang.

Lord, we took a lot of casualties. But those difficulties forged us into a strong group—an extended family which, he though wryly, *I named the "Clan" on impulse due to my Scottish heritage. I didn't think about its other connotation. Well, we aren't bigots. Never were.*

A breeze stirred the tall oaks and beech trees. The top of the mesa-like hill came into view. He turned onto the stone path that led up this mound called the Hill into the familiar warren of houses that was home.

Taylor paused on the steps of his house—a blocky sandstone two-story structure. *How different this is from the early years, especially the first winter. That was when Franny recovered from her shock and came out of her shell.* He smiled at the memory of how, during a Christmas celebration—a pale imitation of past seasons—Franny had learned of his loss. It was that night they'd become lovers.

Civilization had collapsed to a mediaeval level. Even so, the Clan had survived and that had gotten the attention of a gang controlled by Skid Vukovitch.

Taylor felt a wave of revulsion. *What a horrible enigma; a classical music-loving ex-motorcycle gang-leading psychopath. Skid, in his megalomania, appointed himself mayor of Cleveland and demanded a food tribute from the Clan.* Taylor shook his head and shuddered at the memory. *Naturally, we refused.*

Skid was brutal and totally uncaring. He'd conscripted an army of refugees and used them as shock troops, cannon fodder, in his siege of the Clan. In that battle a sniper had shot and killed Franny.

It was Chris—Franny's daughter, now a battle-hardened fighter, who had recognized Skid as the man who'd killed her father and raped her mother. She'd gone after Skid and killed him.

What a driven woman, he thought. *Fighting all her life against the evils that had preyed upon her and her mother.*

Then my neighbors, Fred and Maria, convinced me to take Noelle, a young, attractive widow as a housekeeper. What a pair of connivers. They were matchmakers and Noelle was in on it. Yes, she seduced me with her charms. It didn't take long for me to realize she didn't really love me and would do anything for a job and a home for her child. However, she is an excellent housekeeper, so I kept her.

CHAPTER THREE

"Billy," Kevin O'Neil said. "Can I talk to you?"

Billy Potato's head swiveled. "Kevin," he said. "Come in." He pointed to a chair in front of the desk.

Kevin sat down and glanced up.

Billy was an odd one; that was for sure. He was barely five feet tall. Still, he was larger than most of his fellow alien Qu'uda. He always wore a wide-brimmed hat and a long gray cloak that almost reached the ground. Beneath the cloak were legs that had one more joint than those of humans. It made his knee flex in the opposite direction, giving him an odd gait.

Kevin had learned Billy's pasty-white face, with its stiff, smoothed-over features had come from being altered to resemble a human. Each of his hands had three stubby fingers and an opposing thumb with extensible claws. His absence of shoulders and the way his head tapered into his body gave him a pear-like shape. Some said he looked like a potato, just like his name.

Billy's office, located in the heart of the new university, was bare, almost stark in appearance, free of paper and books. Sunlight filtering through the leaves of nearby trees illuminated the far side of the room and made a dancing pattern of light on the windows.

"Billy, our people out in western Ohio, in the former Fed, need help. It's all these newcomers from the Clan," Kevin said. "Y'see, they're taking over the place, running roughshod over them. People are talking about taking things into their own hands."

"What help do you need?" Billy asked, face impassive.

"Well, I know you Qu'uda have got some kind of radio." Kevin hesitated. "Can you communicate between here and Defiance? D'you know what I mean?"

Billy paused a moment. "I cannot grow a biocomputer for you, therefore I cannot set up a comm-link system."

"System?" Kevin stared into the distance as if a faded memory had grown sharp. "Y'know, we once had a system. I bet most of it is still in place. We need more than a communications system. We also need transportation." He paused. "Did y'know it took me three days to get from Defiance to Rocky River?"

"Yes." Billy sat motionless, barely visible behind the desk. The sun had moved, enveloping him in shadow.

"We might be able to use trains like we used 'em before, as well as the phone system." Kevin raised his eyebrows.

"What are they?" Billy asked. "Why do you need my help?"

Kevin pursed his lips. "If we could reactivate the phone system and got the trains running, it would help hold this danged federation together. It needs something, that's for sure."

"Explain these things," Billy said. "The phone system and the trains."

Kevin explained how the phone system and trains used to work.

Billy stared at him for a moment. "The steel rails—are they the same as those used at the iron furnace?" He referred to the tracks at the iron melting facility that had made the huge iron propulsion tube for the alien ship, the Egg-that-Flies.

"Right," Kevin said. "Only difference is these rail lines go all the way across the country. Coming here, I followed a rail line for some distance. 'Cept for the vegetation growing on the tracks, they still seem in good condition."

"What do you need to get this phone system and trains in operation?" Billy asked.

"My guess is that it'll take a lot of men and materials."

"The Council has the power to make them available. Therefore, I cannot help you with this problem," Billy said. "I will talk to

Taylor MacPherson about this phone system and trains. Perhaps he can help."

"Billy," Kevin said softly. "How did you come to Earth?"

Billy stared at him. "I came here, to Earth, which we call Kota, from Qu'uda, which is in the system you call Epsilon Eridani.

"That was long after our ship, the Star-Seeker, investigated a strange pulsing signal in the system you call 82 Eridani. Soon after the Star-Seeker arrived, planetary defenses crippled it. Facing certain death, the crew crashed their ship into the planet.

"When the Star-Seeker's message drone reached Qu'uda and told of its disastrous encounter, it provoked near panic. You see, we Qu'uda feared these aliens might look for those responsible. So, we set up a deep-space observatory to warn us of any approach.

"It was while working at the observatory I detected a faint video broadcast from a nearby star system. I learned later it was the resignation speech of a former human leader called Nixon. To us, these new aliens—humans—appeared primitive, thus exploitable. After much consensus building, we constructed an interstellar spacecraft. This craft, the Egg-that-Flies, was made from a small asteroid and fitted out for the trip to the humans' system. Desire to be close to the center drove me to seek a position on the ship sent to investigate this planet. Unfortunately, I succeeded.

"It took a long time to build the ship and even longer to make the trip, but we are a long-lived species and possess great patience. We are a hermaphroditic species whose gender change is a survival trait that evolved from living on a planet subject to periodic catastrophes.

"We Qu'uda underestimated the aliens—the humans—on Earth. We thought you to be primitive and perhaps, docile. That was a mistake. It was only when we were more than halfway to our destination we detected electromagnetic pulses, which could only come from nuclear explosions. Our society regards those who use such weapons as insane. There was no turning back, for we were locked on a course through interstellar space.

"I remember how fearful but curious we were as we orbited our ship about Earth to gather information. As we prepared to leave to get fuel from a gas planet, a human weapon damaged our ship's drive. The drive lost its coolant, which forced a shutdown. When I tried to restart the ship's drive, it exploded. Our ship went into an unstable orbit, destined to spiral eventually into the planet. The shock of the explosion and our perilous situation triggered gender changes in many of our crewmembers.

"Our ship needed a new propulsion tube. However, it could not be cast in zero gravity; it had to be made on the planet below. Our leader, Mata ChaLik BuMaru chose me, Bilik Pudjata, to go to the surface and make a new propulsion tube. The tube's size required it be made in sections. To make me less conspicuous among the aliens, our surgical staff altered my appearance to resemble the aliens. Later, I found that I looked strange to the humans, and even more so to my fellow Qu'uda.

"From planetary survey data, I selected a radiation-free area on the south shore of the southern-most inland freshwater sea, which you call Lake Erie. It had many iron-containing structures.

"Using a language learning program in my personal biocomputer, I learned enough of the aliens' language, which I later learned you call English. My first contact was a grower of vegetables. He called me Billy Potato, which I used from then on with humans.

"I had much difficulty understanding these humans: They do not run their society by consensus; they are cursed with excessive individuality and a propensity to violence. That led to a violent encounter that left me sorely wounded. In a confrontation, I killed several of them. That's when I realized humans only respected violence, so I killed those who opposed me, which made the others more cooperative. It took time to mobilize a local community to work on an iron casting facility. From the humans, I learned this group was a local city-state headquartered in Defiance, Ohio, which they called the 'Fed.'

"I used fusion drive units from a wrecked shuttlecraft to generate electricity to run the iron casting facility. Getting these humans to work together was difficult, almost like herding baby wrigglers. I had to kill several to encourage them to come to a consensus. Most difficult.

"It was while building the iron casting facility I encountered humans from the Clan who believed the iron casting facility was in their territory. I learned the Clan had once beaten the Fed in battle and viewed this incursion as hostile, and so they mounted an attack upon the iron casting facility. I had to call in the shuttle to evacuate the workers and the equipment. When our craft flew over the Clan's forces, their attack disintegrated—it was most surprising.

"For a while, the Clan was not a problem. Then they sent a delegation to meet me. Unfortunately, due to my poor understanding of English, I insulted them and they broke off negotiations. As I continued to work on the foundry to make the propulsion tube, I found everything took longer than planned. That strained my relations with the Qu'uda on the ship. They said I had adopted the ways of the humans. It was only later I learned I had become alien to my own kind. You see, Qu'uda are much more group-directed and conformist than humans.

"The Clan mounted another attack, this time against Defiance. Since I had persuaded Mata ChaLik to provide surveillance data from the shuttle, the Fed military ambushed the Clan's force. They fled and left many of their dead behind. At that time, I believed had solved the problem with the Clan.

"The orbit of our spaceship began to deteriorate faster than first estimated. Once again, fear and ancient survival instincts made many of the crew become female, and they mated and produced eggs. Mata ChaLik did not believe I could make the propulsion tube in time and started the evacuation. He sent four crewmembers to an island south of the mainland with all of the newly laid eggs.

"Yes, I know the crew on the ship were afraid; if the ship crashed into the surface—because of its size—it would destroy much of the life on the planet. When Mata ChaLik announced plans to blow up the ship to prevent this, I drove the human workers harder to make the last propulsion tube parts. Even though there were problems and further delays, I was sure I could make the parts in time to save the ship.

"The Clan attacked again. This time, the shuttle did not see them coming. As a result of the surprise, I had few guards in Defiance, but we held off the Clan long enough for the shuttle to pick up the last of the castings. Time was short; our spaceship had only days before it would fall from orbit.

"I was injured during the battle. A human woman, Joyce Vargas pulled me to safety and when she called for help, the Clan warriors who heard her captured me.

"About the same time, the shuttle, loaded with the parts and flying low across Defiance while building speed, was hit by gunfire. As a result of the damage, the shuttle could no longer descend to the planet. So, the Qu'uda had to abandon those left on Earth, the four crewmembers on Andros Island who had been left to guard the almost one hundred eggs, along with me.

"The Qu'uda installed the repair parts and departed for the outer system to get fuel and materials. It was then I learned from my biocomputer's communications module they had abandoned me because I had become too 'alien' for them. The human propensity to violence had angered those on the ship. They have vowed to make weapons and return to Earth to remove all technology from the humans whom they regard as insane.

"The fact they abandoned me was devastating. You see, Qu'uda *must* belong; if not, we go insane. I had no one. I was completely alone. Life had no meaning—it was the end. I was prepared to die...

"A most strange thing happened: This female human, Joyce Vargas, convinced me the humans would accept me. At first it seemed impossible. However, both Joyce and Taylor MacPherson, the Clan Leader, assured me it was true. They even honored me with the role of teaching their young—a position of great trust. So strange is the feeling, to be more accepted by aliens than one's own kind. Yet, I still don't understand your wild and chaotic society of individuals..."

Kevin nodded. "I knew some of this, but never knew the whole story."

CHAPTER FOUR

"Look, do whatever you must, but the classrooms must be ready by the end of this month." Taylor MacPherson turned toward Marting Hall, which was an ornate sandstone Victorian building.

Workers hauled loads of bird droppings, fallen plaster, and decayed leaves from the building to put them into horse-drawn carts. Pounding hammers echoed across the campus of Baldwin-Wallace University, which was now busy with efforts to remedy thirty years of neglect.

"Yes, sir." Mitch Doaks glanced at the building. Another load of debris thudded to the ground from a second story window. "It won't have any heat or running water. I'm not sure the floors are sound in this building."

Mitch still wore the uniform of a soldier with the patches he'd earned on the expedition to Perrysburg. He'd just been appointed assistant to Taylor at the new university.

"There's plenty of space. Move the students from one room to another as work progresses. We've got to have generators running by the time the classes get started. Understanding and using electricity is the key. We need facilities."

Mitch frowned. "Well, okay, I can do that."

"Good." Taylor nodded. "The students need hands-on experience with electricity. Theory is fine. However, our first students have to be practical engineers." He stabbed an index finger into the palm of his hand. "They have to know how to re-build pre-Collapse equipment."

Mitch waved his hand. "I hadn't realized how deteriorated these buildings were. They look all right on the outside. I guess I got fooled when I visited your lab."

Taylor nodded. "Right, I used the best building available."

"As long as you realize things are going to be a little rough at first." Mitch raised his eyebrows and shrugged. "I'll do my best to have them ready before winter sets in."

"It's Billy you've got to please. Him and his instructors. Otherwise, I'll get involved." The worry lines between Taylor's eyes deepened. "Is that clear?"

"Yes, sir." Mitch stood a little straighter.

ॐ

"Yes, Joyce." Billy looked up from the papers scattered over the large desk. He liked the way sunlight streamed in through the windows of his office. Books and equipment were stacked on the floor. "I want our students to cover this material by mid-winter."

"That's a lot to cover in such a short time." A frown flickered over Joyce's face. "Some will grasp it, most won't."

"We must find those who understand electricity." Billy pointed at the course outline. "Those that don't can build electrical equipment. We need both kinds of students."

"We'll have our hands full."

"I must get a fusion reactor and a computer working, as well as start classes."

Joyce said nothing.

Billy turned and peered at Joyce.

"Billy." Joyce paused. "Billy, I'm not sure how to say this." She looked away. "I mean, I really like you, but ..." Her voice trailed off. A touch of color bloomed in her cheeks.

"What is it you want to say?"

Joyce twisted her hands. "Well, I like you, but things are different now than they were before. Do you understand?"

"Ah." Billy forced his mouth into the shape these humans called a smile. He'd adopted it as he gained insight on the alien

Earth people's behavior and had learned it was an expected facial expression. "Now you know what I am, that makes things different."

The room grew still. In the distance, voices rose and fell. Outside, a warbler began to sing. *I miss the closeness of my own kind. I need ...* He put the thought from his mind even as a wave of emptiness washed through him.

Joyce slowly looked up. There was moisture in her eyes. "Well, yes. I still like you and want to work with you. It's just I don't think it would be right for us, you know." She hesitated. "To do it."

"Remember, I told you I wanted you to know what I am. There are many things, Joyce you have done for me that my own kind have not. You have honored me with your friendship. You have shown me your community regards me as a central figure."

Billy looked down at his desk for a moment before glancing up. *She is the only one who wanted to couple with me. Right or wrong, possible or not, that makes her special.*

"You told me I belong. All these things are true. If we do not couple, you are still the person who carried the message from your community that your kind accepted me. This, I will never forget." *Now when she looks at me like this, I know she thinks me different from them. Alien, different and untouchable.*

"It's, it's just I don't want to hurt your feelings." Joyce looked away from him. "It's just that I think of you," she hesitated. "On a different level. I'd tell you the same things again, because you're the most unusual person I've ever known. I want to work with you, there's so many things you can teach me." She took a deep breath and paused for a moment. "It's just I don't want to be your lover. It doesn't seem right."

Lover? Is that their word for coupling-partner? "We must work together." Billy paused. "You know more about electricity than any other ..." he paused. "human." *The only human who made me feel accepted. And now?*

༄

Billy peered around the edge of the door into Taylor's office. "I have a problem. We must talk."

Taylor leaned back and his chair squeaked in protest. "Sure." He beckoned for Billy to come in.

The room overlooked the center of the campus, now full of workers and students. The grass had been cut and used for hay, leaving stubble that many feet had pounded flat. Summer was fading but the leaves still seemed lush and green. The sun beat hotly on the window ledge.

"I must find a way to communicate to the Qu'uda left behind with the eggs." Billy removed a stack of papers from the chair by the desk, but there was no space on the desk so he placed them on the floor. "I received one message from them. Now I cannot communicate with them. I believe the satellite that relayed the messages no longer functions." He perched on the edge of the chair and leaned forward.

"Why d'you want to contact them?" Taylor asked. "Weren't they part of the group who abandoned you?"

"My biocomputer recorded a message from one who was left behind—a Qu'uda who at one time was a close friend—which tells me it was not their choice to stay." Billy's head swiveled toward Taylor. "I fear they may find this planet a difficult place to live. I want to help them. I need them."

"Okay," Taylor said. "I do have a ham radio. Do you know what frequency they use?"

"Frequency?" Billy asked. "What do you mean by frequency?"

Taylor sighed. It was a common problem; even though Billy quickly grasped their technology, there was always the problem of words he did not understand. "Why don't we get the radio and I'll show you how to use it. Then you can adjust it to transmit on a frequency your biocomputer can receive."

"Is this another piece of technology that requires careful adjustment?" Most Qu'uda equipment had internal biocomputer controls that made all the adjustments.

"Yes, it's easy to use." Taylor rose from his chair. "C'mon, it's downstairs. I'll show you."

He led Billy into the laboratory. "Show Billy how to use the radio."

A technician glanced up. "Which one?"

"How about the ham radio?"

"Okay." The technician hooked a Yaesu short-wave radio up to a power supply and an external antenna. "This is how you tune it." He showed Billy how to operate it.

"Okay. Now you know where we keep it. Feel free to use it anytime." Taylor turned to leave the cluttered room. "I hope you contact your friends."

Already Billy had his hands on the radio, staring at its digital keypad. "Thank you. I have work to do." He did not look up as he tapped in the first of many frequencies.

CHAPTER FIVE

Billy worked with the radio, getting the technicians to modify it. He installed a dish antenna to focus on the satellite left by the Qu'uda to bounce signals over the horizon. By the end of a week, he'd made contact with the four guardians of the eggs.

"This is Bilik Pudjata," he said in his native Qu'uda language. "Can you hear me?"

"Bilik? Bilik? Is that you?" came a faint response.

"This is Bilik Pudjata. I can hear you. Who is this?"

"Bilik." The voice paused. "This is Cha KinLaat DoMar. Where are you?"

"I am with the Earth people, near where I made the castings for the Egg-that-Flies. Mata ChaLik BuMaru, too, abandoned me. He believed me to be no longer Qu'uda."

"This I know, Bilik, for he told me. He left me and three others to raise eight squared plus four times eight eggs. I'm a failure, for I cannot protect them from the terrible creatures of this horrible world..." Cha KinLaat spoke at length of her problems, including how all had become ill. They found the native foods did not provide complete nourishment. And their food stores were almost gone.

Billy remembered his own experience and what it took to survive. "Cha KinLaat, I do understand and can help you. Listen carefully ..." He explained about the Qu'uda magnesium deficiency, which could be remedied by pulverizing rock and adding it to their diets. "Recognize I am using Earth people's equipment to communicate with you. My biocomputer cannot talk with yours to give it instructions on how to make the antibodies and hormones needed for survival. I shall talk with the Earth people to see if there is a way to communicate with you."

"You have no idea how terrible this place is."

"I do. I want you to survive. Listen and do what I tell you. I learned from my experience on this planet." Bilik went on to advise her of the things she could do to ease their existence.

In the course of the conversations with her, her hatred of Mata ChaLik came through. Bilik wondered if it were solely due to being abandoned.

ॐ

Tim Van Minh saw Taylor MacPherson enter his lab.

"How d'you feel, Tim?" Taylor asked.

"It's difficult to walk." Tim forced the words out, but they were still slurred. "I'm still adjusting."

Tim had received burns over one side of his body when the Bird-that-Soars had fired its energy beam weapon at him. He had learned he'd come close to death twice. First he'd almost died from the shock of the battlefield injury and then from an infection during his stay in the hospital. Upon recovering, he'd come to Taylor's lab to work with him.

"I have one project needing immediate attention." Taylor glanced at Tim's workbench covered with partially disassembled personal computers. "It's figuring out an interface between Billy's biocomputer and our electronic computers."

Tim caught Taylor staring at him. Every time he'd looked in the mirror, he had seen the damage done. Half of his face was scar tissue. It was the same down his entire right side.

"D'you think you can handle it?"

Tim attempted to smile, but only half his mouth opened. "I don't know. The only thing I've worked on since getting here are computers." He shrugged. "I've had a lot of time to read about them and work on them."

An interface for Billy? He felt a wave of revulsion. *That damn*

Qu'uda flying monster almost killed me. It left me a cripple. I'll never find a wife the way I now look. Can I even work with that alien?

"There are few who understand computers these days." Taylor stepped over to the bench and pulled a keyboard forward. "I'm sure you'll find it interesting."

"Well." Tim hesitated. It was something to do. "Okay."

"Let's start with the basics."

こ

A month later, Tim stopped at Taylor's office to talk to him about the interface between Billy's biocomputer and a personal computer. "Look, the problem is a basic incompatibility between electronic and biological systems. There's just no way for them to connect together."

"So?"

"So, if they won't connect, we've got to give them a common framework each understands."

"Sounds easy, but how do we do that?"

"I think there are several ways." The words came out of Tim's mouth even more slurred than usual. It was obvious he was excited about something. "We could use an audio link but the transfer rate is too slow. So, we've got to figure out a way to get Billy's bio to use something fast."

"Electrical—how about a pickup on Billy's arm?" Taylor suggested. "Y'know ..." He stopped when he saw Tim frown. "Okay, what've you got in mind?"

"Radio." Tim pointed to the radio transceiver. "You remember how Billy figured out how to use the radio to communicate with the Qu'uda down on Andros Island? That's the key. We know the frequencies the bio uses for communication. Now it's just a matter of learning the code."

"Y'think so?" Taylor's mind buzzed. "Yes, that gives direct access to an electrical signal. Once we understand how the biocomputer works, we can read it."

"No," said Tim. "Billy's bio is far smarter and faster than our PCs, so let's use that to our advantage."

"Run that one by me again."

"Teach it the programming system used on our PCs and then ask it questions in that code. When it responds, data will go directly into program files. For example, show it a graphics program for items that require drawings, y'know, like the fusion reactor. Then have the bio send an equivalent file directly to the computer. Teach it how to put data into appropriate file format."

"D'you think that'll work?" To Taylor, it sounded almost too simple, then again, he realized, Tim was very bright.

"Billy gave me the key when he told me his second bio had a language learning program." Tim's scarred face moved to give a half smile, revealing cracked teeth. "That's how Billy learned English. Only this time, it'll be easier because we can tell Billy the meaning of something the bio doesn't understand. It goes directly to the bio to use with its learning algorithm. Bingo, it understands."

"Okay, Tim, you're on. You're in charge of this project. If you need more help, come and see me. This is important."

"I'll need Billy to get this going." A trace of a frown flicked across Tim's face. "Once we've got it figured out, he can go back to his regular teaching schedule."

"Don't worry about that. Billy and I have talked about this. He understands the need—maybe even better than you or me. Well done, Tim," Taylor said.

Taylor felt a glow of pride, for Tim's concept proved correct. Once the biocomputer acquired the programming language, the flow of information became a torrent. The result was one personal computer could not keep up with the information flow. Tim assembled a multiplex receiver and connected it with a dozen computers. Data in the form of designs and plans grew at a rapid rate, including those for several types of aneutronic fusion reactors. The computers kept several people busy full-time until all of the information had been transferred. Understanding what had been retrieved from Billy's biocomputers would take years of effort.

He also knew Billy still needed to find a way to rescue the Qu'uda stranded on Andros Island in the Bahamas. For the present, there was no way to reach them.

CHAPTER SIX

"Okay," Taylor said. "Cheronoff sounds like a good addition to the university's staff. Even if we don't need a metallurgist at this moment, we will soon." He reached across his desk for a pen and signed the document. The day was drawing in and the office had grown dim.

Lights, he thought. *Soon we'll have electricity.* He looked up. "It's your responsibility to get him here. If you need an escort, talk to Mitch Doaks or Joe Del Corso—they're assigned to the university on special duty—they'll fix you up."

"I'll need an escort. This Charlie Cheronoff is no fighter an' the trip from Pittsburgh goes through some tough territory."

Pittsburgh Pete was a wiry dark-haired man who worked for the Clan in the Appalachian area buying oil and coal. He'd come across an older man who worked wonders with metals. After protracted negotiations, they'd come to an agreement—actually a payment in gold—to guide Charlie Cheronoff to the university.

"See Doaks, then." Taylor suspected Pittsburgh Pete was getting paid on both ends. It really didn't matter. *If Cheronoff wants to come to Berea that badly, so much the better*, he thought.

"Thanks."

"When d'you think you'll get him here?"

"Probably a week or so." Pete nodded and left.

"Taylor," said a woman's voice. "A moment, please?"

Taylor looked up. "Dr. Encirlik." He stood and offered his hand. "Always a pleasure to see you. Have a seat, please." He noticed that her olive complexion was pale, wan. Her spare frame seemed smaller, more fragile, but in spite of her obvious tiredness, her eyes were bright.

"Can't. I've got too many things to do. I just had to tell you there's a treasure trove of medical information in Billy's download." She referred to the data obtained from Billy's biocomputer. "It's amazing how long these aliens live. Almost a thousand years."

"Is that right?" Taylor leaned back in his chair, conscious of his sixty years. "Anything we can use?" He knew Dr. Encirlik had also complained about not feeling well lately.

"I'm not sure yet." She plucked her lips with a forefinger. "You see, their terminology is different from ours, never mind their biology. Certain principles appear common; after all, the laws of physics and chemistry are the same."

"So?" Taylor paused.

"They're wizards at culturing tissues, growing body parts and getting wounds to heal. That's why Billy recovered so quickly from his injuries. The age extension stuff just fascinates me..." She trailed off, eyes watching him.

"Dr. Encirlik," Taylor said. "Are you asking for more resources to investigate age extension?"

Doctor Encirlik smiled briefly. "Yes. I'm short on people. I think I have the same interest in it as you."

Taylor laughed. "I'll find you another assistant."

"Thanks." She smiled and quietly left.

Taylor sighed and stared at the pile of paper on his desk. *I was sure my workload would ease once I became an academic, but I'm busier than ever*, he thought.

"Hi, there," a feminine voice said.

Taylor looked up. "Joyce." His heart beat faster.

"Am I interrupting anything?"

"Just the usual administrative stuff."

"You treated me to supper; now let me treat you." Joyce hesitated. "D'you like Vietnamese cuisine? I found this charming little place called the Travelers' Inn that has Vietnamese food on its menu."

"Yes, I know it." Taylor nodded. "When did you have this treat in mind?" The Travelers' Inn was one of his favorite eating-places.

"How about this evening?" Joyce asked.

"Sure," said Taylor. "Can I meet you there, say six o'clock? I've still got a bunch of things to take care of."

"It's a date." Joyce paused at the door. She turned and winked. "See you then."

ౚ

Noelle Smith opened the door. "Yes?"

At the bottom step was a tall, sturdy man who wore the clothing of a Clan soldier with authority. "Er, is Mr. MacPherson home?"

"He's not here at the moment. Can I help you?"

"I'm Mitch Doaks; I've just joined the university to help Mr. MacPherson. I stopped by because I've been asked to go to Pittsburgh and bring a new member of the university's staff back to Rocky River. I wouldn't bother Mr. MacPherson at home, 'cept the man who I'm supposed to go with is, well, kind of disreputable-looking." He hesitated. "And Mr. MacPherson has already left his office."

Noelle shrugged. "Well, he's usually home for supper by six or so. Why don't you come in and wait for him? Shouldn't be long." She wore a high-waist dress that emphasized her bosom. Her hair was tied back with an embroidered ribbon. Even though she was in her forties, she was proud of her smooth and wrinkle-free face.

"Really, I don't want to bother you," he said.

"Nonsense. My name is Noelle Smith. I take care of Mr. MacPherson's household. Come in, please." She smiled. "He gets visitors all the time."

"Well, as long as it's no bother." Mitch stepped through the doorway and walked through a hallway of polished wood and oriental rugs. "Er, very nice." He gestured toward the hall and its furnishings. "Very neat."

"Thank you." Noelle pointed toward a doorway.

It led to the kitchen, which had windows lining one wall that reflected light off an adjacent building. Shining pots and pans hung over a counter with oak cabinets above. There was a double sink and a cast iron stove against a wall. In the corner was a round table with a vase of flowers and two chairs.

"You can wait here and keep me company while I finish preparing supper." Noelle opened an ice chest and removed cheese and a piece of cooked meat.

"I didn't intend to interrupt anything," Mitch said.

"Not at all. I recall hearing your name from Taylor. If I remember correctly, you were on several expeditions to the western territories." Noelle turned her head and smiled, raising her eyebrows to seek confirmation.

"Why, yes, that's right." Mitch's face showed the beginning of a flush. "We took a lot of casualties in that campaign. I'm glad the Fed joined us. I prefer peace to war."

"Weren't you injured on the expedition to Perrysburg, the one that encountered the alien flying machine?" Noelle looked up from slicing the meat and placing it on a platter.

"Ms. Smith, I'm amazed that you know these things," Mitch said. "I fell off a horse and hurt my shoulder."

"Please, Noelle." She looked up. "Taylor spoke highly of you." She opened a drawer and took out a loaf of bread. "I like hearing details of what happened in the campaign."

"Then call me Mitch," he said.

"Tell me, Mitch, how does your family feel about you spending so much time away from home? Don't you miss them?"

Mitch took a deep breath. "Well, when my wife was alive, it was a strain, but after she died, it became my profession."

"I'm sorry to hear about your wife." Noelle bit her lip. "That had to be quite a loss. Can I get you something to drink? We have beer, fresh cider, and cold sassafras tea?" *He's polite*, she thought. *And he has some class.*

"Cider would be fine." Mitch took a deep breath. "Thanks." He hesitated. "Noelle." He pronounced her name as though he was savoring it.

Noelle opened the ice chest and took out a tall carafe. She

poured a glass of amber-colored cider and brought it over to him. As she leaned over to place it before him, her left hand briefly touched his shoulder. "There." She glanced at the clock ticking on the wall. "I wonder where Taylor is?" It was almost six-thirty.

"Perhaps I should be going."

"Nonsense," said Noelle. "I'm sure he'll be here anytime. Have you plans for supper?"

"No—"

"Good. Then join me while you wait." Noelle pulled a chair away from the table and sat opposite Mitch. "Sit." She pushed the platter of sandwiches and a plate forward. "Eat." She leaned her head into her hands and smiled. "Now, tell me more about yourself and that campaign." *He'll be nice company*, she thought.

As they ate, Mitch related his personal history—slowly at first, almost reluctantly.

Noelle encouraged him several times, realizing he was reticent about what he'd been through, which, it seemed was quite a bit. There was a politeness, a reservoir of respect that was almost flattering. She felt herself drawn to this tall soldier.

"Why don't you tell me how you came to be here?" he asked.

"Oh," Noelle said with a laugh. "We should save that for another time. When you come back to see me." She smiled.

"I'd like that," Mitch said. The room had grown dim. He glanced at the clock. "It's almost seven. Perhaps I'd better come back in the morning."

Noelle checked the clock and a brief frown crossed her face. "I wonder where he is? Well." She sighed. "Perhaps you should." She stood. "Mitch, I do thank you for keeping me company." She guided him toward the front door. She found her hand had gravitated to his elbow with a feeling of quick familiarity. She felt a trace of surprise at how fast the time had passed. *I do hope I see him again.*

"Er, Noelle, I'm sorry I stayed so long. I didn't realize how late it had become." A flush appeared in his cheeks.

"Well, if I hadn't enjoyed your company, you'd've been long gone." Noelle glanced at him out of the corner of her eye. "Perhaps I'll see you tomorrow? If you can?" Her hand moved from his elbow to his shoulder.

"Er, yes, I guess so." Mitch offered his hand.

Noelle took his hand and enfolded it in hers. "Good night, Mitch." She had to force herself to release it.

ຊ

As Taylor walked home from the restaurant, he felt a glow from being with Joyce Vargas. He chuckled at the memory of introducing her to Nguyen Van Minh, the owner of the Travelers' Inn. That was when her face had shown she realized he had more than a passing acquaintance with Vietnamese cuisine. As they'd talked, he'd found she possessed a tremendous knowledge of electrical technology. No wonder Billy wants her to teach electrical engineering at the university.

There's more to it than that, he realized. *What am I doing with a woman who's twenty-five years younger than me? Just business, right? I must be imagining things; there's nothing to it. The memory of her kiss on his cheek lingered.*

"Where were you?" Noelle had her hands on her hips. "I was worried about you."

"I had dinner with ..." Taylor hesitated momentarily. "A friend who stopped by to see me at the university. I'm sorry. I forgot to tell you. I hope that you didn't prepare a fancy meal..." Somehow, he didn't want to say anything about Joyce to Noelle. That could be uncomfortable.

"Well, no, I didn't. I made sandwiches from the remains of the roast." Noelle sighed. This wasn't the first time he hadn't shown up for dinner. "Oh, a Mitch Doaks stopped by. Something about Pittsburgh. He'll stop again in the morning."

"Ah, yes," Taylor said. "That's about escorting a new academic back from Pittsburgh." He yawned. "It's been a long day. Care to join me in a glass of wine?" He knew she liked to have a conversation before turning in.

"Yes, I'd like that." She turned toward the kitchen. "I'll get it. There's half a bottle in the ice-box."

Later that evening, after Taylor had retired, Noelle came silently into his darkened room and slipped into his bed. As she drew close to him, he realized she was naked. Without a word, they reached out for each other.

Tonight, for some reason, they both responded quickly and their lovemaking was impassioned. While together, the image of Joyce's face flashed before him.

When they were done, Noelle vanished as quickly as she came.

༄

"Mr. Doaks is here," Noelle called.

Taylor finished a letter, got up from his desk and hurried to the front hall. As he descended the stairs he caught a glimpse of Noelle and Mitch talking intently. At his approach, Noelle vanished in the direction of the kitchen.

"Did Pittsburgh Pete come to see you about escorting Cheronoff?" Taylor asked.

"Why, yes." Mitch's eyebrows rose. "That's what I wanted to confirm with you. I didn't know who he was. His appearance isn't the most, er, reassuring."

Taylor chuckled. "Yeah, I know what you mean. I'm sorry I didn't send you a message. I could've saved you a couple of trips out here." He glanced at his watch. "D'you have any pressing items?"

"No," Mitch said. "I told Pete we'd leave tomorrow."

"Noelle," Taylor called.

"Yes?"

"Please make a pot of tea for Mr. Doaks and me."

"Certainly." Noelle's voice almost sang the reply.

"She seems to be a cheerful sort," Mitch said. "Is she always this way?"

"Oh, she's probably feeling good about something. Let's go to my study. I'll bring you up to date on what's going on at the university, and in particular, things that might affect you." Taylor guided Mitch toward his study. "Let me see."

He turned the conversation toward the internal workings of the university. Soon they were deep in discussion about the details of administration.

Later that morning, Noelle appeared at the door to the study. She had changed into an embroidered linen skirt and a blouse with a low-cut scalloped neck. "Will you be having lunch here?" Her eyes flicked toward Mitch.

"Yes, please," said Taylor.

When they came downstairs, Taylor saw Noelle had prepared a plate of dry-cured ham surrounded with fruit and cheese, with a loaf of fresh baked bread. He noticed during lunch she was in a good mood and quite attentive to Mitch.

CHAPTER SEVEN

"It is too cold for me to teach." Billy wore a down-filled coat under his long gray cloak, which gave him an oval shape. "My students cannot learn when they are cold."

After the trees turned golden, blustery winds sent leaves scurrying through the campus of the university. The unpredictable October weather worsened and an early cold front blew in from Lake Erie, dumping six inches of snow on the ground. The lack of heat in the classrooms had made heavy coats the normal academic uniform.

"I'm sorry," Taylor said. "I've been expecting a shipment of stoves for the classrooms from the Defiance ironworks. I just learned the wagon bringing them broke down." It seemed the more they tried to do; the more stupid things like this hampered them. "We need to get the rail system up and running."

"When there is heat, I shall resume teaching." Billy turned and waddled out of Taylor's office.

Damn, Taylor thought. *Another delay.*

His breath hung frostily white in the air. *Maybe I can catch O'Neil in his office.*

The walk from the campus to the old railway station in Berea took ten minutes. Students and staff at the university as well as construction workers had now begun to reoccupy abandoned houses and stores. People were moving into town, bringing it back to life.

Taylor poked his head into the first office inside the old train station. "Is Kevin O'Neil here?"

A tousle-headed young man looked up from a drafting table. He seemed barely old enough to have left his family. "Mr. O'Neil? Down at the barn by the tracks. D'you know where that is? No? I'll show you." The young man jumped off his stool and led Taylor through a maze of buildings. "See that new building over there?" He pointed at a large building constructed from rough-sawn lumber that straddled a rail line. "In there."

Within the building, bright lights focused on a vehicle that reminded Taylor of a truck, except it had steel wheels that fit the rails. People were clustered around the vehicle. Voices shouted and metal clanged. A motor chugged fitfully. "Hey," Taylor yelled. "O'Neil here?"

"Who's wants me?" A smudged face emerged from below the vehicle. When Kevin saw Taylor, he struggled to his feet, wiping his hands on a greasy rag. His short gray hair stuck out in all directions.

"This damn truck, every time I put a load on it, something else breaks. That's the problem of cobbling together stuff out of worn-out crap." He cocked an eye at Taylor. "I can guess what you want."

"Oh?"

"You want to know when this will be ready to roll, right?"

"Well, yes." Taylor paused. "I've got no idea what's going on. I'm not on the Council anymore, so I don't get any progress reports. I was wondering if you were at a stage where I might be able to help." It wasn't quite what he'd had in mind originally. He knew if he came across as just being nosy, he wouldn't be welcome; he just needed the trains running.

"Y'see," Kevin said. "We had the bright idea of using old diesel-powered trucks as prime movers on the rail lines." He pointed toward an office at one side of the barn. It had a large glass window overlooking the work area. Inside were two tables strewn with paper and greasy engine parts. "It was after we realized the old diesel-electric locomotives would be real bastards to work on. Most had sat outside and their engines were corroded to beat Hell."

Kevin dragged up two chairs. "Tea?"

"Sure." The office was cold so Taylor left his coat on.

"Jimmy," Kevin called. "Two teas and make it snappy."

"So you got some diesel-powered trucks?" Taylor said.

"We've scrounged up quite a few. Problem is they're old, too. So it was a case of trying to re-build something without spare parts. On top of that, fitting steel wheels in place of rubber tires wasn't so easy. We found some smaller steel wheel-axle combinations at an old rail yard in Cleveland." Kevin yawned.

"Can I back you up for a moment?" Taylor asked. "You keep talking about vehicles. What about the track system?"

"The rail lines?" Kevin shrugged. "I showed one of my construction types—Chip Wilson—what was required, y'know, clean out all the vegetation, replace rotted sleepers, straighten or replace the rails, etc., and he took over that job. The guy is good. Hell, that's the easy part. Did you know most of the rail system is still in half-way decent shape?"

"Well, that's a relief," Taylor said. "So, when will the line between here and Defiance be ready for traffic?"

"That's a different story," Kevin said. "Y'see, Crosby's people are using the railroad right of way for the phone system. Again, there's a lot of stuff that's still intact. As usual, the details are the killer."

"Okay, but when?" Taylor asked. "When do you believe the line to Defiance will be ready? Delivery from the ironworks is getting critical. I need those stoves."

"We should have a line ready by spring. We can work on and off through the winter. The rail line between here and Sandusky is already usable. The Islanders won't let us use the bridge across Sandusky Bay. So, we're looking at an alternate inland route that goes via Wellington and Fremont." Kevin looked up as a youth came in carrying two steaming mugs on a tray. "Gee, Jimmy, doing it all fancy like a waiter, eh?"

"Only the best for you and Mr. MacPherson." Jimmy glanced, head lowered at Taylor. "We don't get distinguished visitors often."

"Thanks, Jimmy." Taylor picked up a mug and sniffed. It was a blend of herbs and sassafras.

"Where were we?" Kevin asked.

"The inland route."

"Oh, yeah," Kevin said. "It looks like that'll be the way we go.

It'll avoid a problem with that group on the Portage River. Less trouble to go through Fremont."

"Are those rail lines okay?" Taylor asked.

"Yeah, I guess so." Kevin gulped some tea. "I walked a good part of it and it's all there."

"So, the vehicle is the main hold-up to get rolling?" Taylor said. "Something about reliability?"

"We keep breaking stuff in the drive train when we try to haul a half dozen or more loaded wagons." Kevin shook his head. "We don't have a way of making replacement parts. If we had a machine shop like they have in Defiance, it'd be easier."

"We have a machine shop at the university," Taylor said. "Maybe you should bring your broken bits and pieces over to see if we can do something for you."

"Really?" Kevin face brightened. "We're getting damn frustrated trying to find parts in junked trucks."

"I'll also set up a meeting with Tim Van Minh. He's a young man with real talent in engineering," said Taylor. "Bring your plans. He might have a suggestion or two on other ways to put things together. I'll let you know when the meeting's scheduled." He glanced at his watch. "Gotta go."

CHAPTER EIGHT

"You must work faster," Mata ChaLik BuMaru said.

"We have done our best." KaLik DuGan had supervised the casting of the new propulsion tube and moving it from within the thrust transfer structure. He'd had to cut an opening in the rear wall of the aft section. They'd discarded the old propulsion tube made from the nine sections cast by Bilik Pudjata. The Egg-that-Flies had passed the giant gas planet, for it had taken more time than expected to make another propulsion tube.

KaLik tested the new tube and found it free of defects.

"Make additional tubes," Mata ChaLik said.

Only after KaLik had made more tubes did the ship turn end-for-end and begin deceleration. It was destined to stop almost an eighth of a light year from the center of the system.

ↄ

"We must get fuel and after that, metal." Mata ChaLik found the resources in Kota's asteroids were rich but widely dispersed. It had taken more time than he'd expected to gather the metal for the new propulsion tubes and the warcraft.

Each time Mata ChaLik met with DalChik, their negotiations were acrimonious. "I am the center," he said, his voice raised, head crest engorged, and claws extended. "You will do as I say."

DalChik extended her claws. Being in the female form, her claws were longer and stronger than those of any male. "You threaten me on a personal level? You wish to meet me in combat?" She enjoyed a reputation for ferocity.

Mata ChaLik retracted his claws. "This is a military situation. I demand you submit to the Defenders."

"You are wrong." DalChik retracted her claws. "Again."

"The ship goes where I say," Mata ChaLik said. "It is further proof I am at the center of this ship."

"It is true your Defenders control the navigation and propulsion," DalChik said. "However, I control access to the information necessary to build your new craft."

As archivist, she controlled access to the information data banks. In addition, her idea to leave the Kota system and return to Qu'uda had attracted most of the crewmembers who were not Defenders.

"It is time for us to return home. Remember," she said. "There are other aliens out here who may find us."

She referred to the mysterious Hoo-Lii who had destroyed the exploratory vessel, the Star-Seeker, which had sought out the source of powerful radio signals. The Star-Seeker had been ravaged by a monstrously powerful fusion pumped laser as it approached an apparently barren planet. Even though crippled, the crew of the Star-Seeker located the source of the weapon and guided their craft to explode over the sole outpost of the Hoo-Lii on that planet. However, it was not the Hoo-Lii aliens' home world.

"Home-seekers," Mata ChaLik said with a sneer. "Those who fear the savages on the third planet."

"Yes, we do," DalChik said. "And we are the Home-Seekers."

"You and your 'Home-Seekers' would show these dangerous creatures from the third planet the way to Qu'uda. Or even leave tracks for the Hoo-Lii to follow," Mata ChaLik said. "To run from these savages will mean we may face them later when they are stronger and have access to space."

"We do not believe they will soon get into space. As for the Hoo-Lii, we shall never lead them to Qu'uda." Many believed DalChik's words rang true. "If they do, it is a long way to Qu'uda. Why would they pursue us there?"

Mata ChaLik refused to answer the question and continued to hold the astrogation data hostage. He would not release it until DalChik would give in and provide the plans for the warcraft.

DalChik's Home-Seekers, even though they outnumbered the Defenders, did not seek control of the Egg-that-Flies. Even if they did, they lacked the astrogation data to get home. However, Mata ChaLik's Defenders needed the plans to build the craft they sought to prosecute the war.

It was stalemate.

༄

A solution to the stalemate came when a long-range radar scan found a metallic asteroid. It was one-fourth the size of the asteroid from which the Egg-that-Flies was made. Ground penetrating scans showed the asteroid had a core of extremely homogenous iron-nickel.

"This asteroid is almost perfect for construction of space craft," said KaLik DuGan. "Not only does it have the right composition, but it is also free from voids and fissures."

Mata ChaLik's head crest erected. "What do you mean?" he demanded. "Build a spacecraft from something that large?"

"Yes," said KaLik DuGan. "A little Egg-that-Flies."

"That is what the Home-Seekers should do," Mata ChaLik said. "Build another spaceship and run home."

KaLik DuGan flexed as if in submission. Even over the comm-link he had found if he made the body gestures as he spoke, his communications were better understood and more importantly, more readily accepted.

"Mata ChaLik BuMaru, if it pleases you, consider the idea of the Defenders building their own space craft. That would allow us to build it strong and well-armed, the way the Egg-that-Flies should have been built in the first place, with a skin so thick it resists the claws of the mightiest weapons. One whose engine is buried deep within a thick layer of iron-nickel, and is impervious to the weapons of the creatures from the third planet."

"Do not reveal these thoughts to the Home-Seekers," Mata ChaLik said. "Let us approach them with the idea they build a ship to flee home and let them persuade us to accept their help in building a Little-Egg-that-Flies to our specifications." He outlined a negotiating strategy to get the craft they wanted.

ↄ

"Build a craft to return to Qu'uda?" DalChik asked. "That is not possible in the volume of this asteroid."

"Surely you have learned how to reduce the space requirements for living from our experience on this long trip?" Mata ChaLik said. "This gives you the opportunity to build it the way you want it."

"Perhaps," DalChik said. "Perhaps you should build the craft according to the austere conditions you and your Defenders subscribe." Everyone knew Mata ChaLik and the most central Defenders had created sumptuous quarters, eliminating rare food plants in the process, claiming they were not needed. "One where you grow just the necessary food."

"That is a possibility," Mata ChaLik said. "That would require help from the Home-Seekers and the plans you hold hostage."

"Hostage?" DalChik said. "You hold us hostage to your bloody desires for war with the aliens on the third planet."

"It is our duty, as Defenders of Qu'uda, to eliminate any possible danger to our home even if you do not have the same dedication to duty."

"We can enumerate our differences until the star goes nova," KaLik DuGan said in a humble fashion. "We could build a craft more suitable to the Defenders' needs from this asteroid. However, we do not possess the skills necessary to do it properly. So, if we give you the Egg-that-Flies for your return home, then you must help us build a Little-Egg-that-Flies. For if you do, then you will return home sooner." He flattened his head crest in a submissive fashion.

"True," said DalChik. "If we download all the plans for both Egg-that-Flies and the other craft, would that not be enough to build them?"

"Perhaps if we possessed all the needed skills," said KaLik DuGan. "However, we don't and for us to try, would condemn us to finishing our days in a vessel stranded far from any habitable planet. It is in your best interest to help us."

"If we do help you, do we get all the astrogation data needed to make the trip between the stars?"

"After we complete the construction of the Little-Egg-that-Flies and at least one warcraft, a Bird-that-Kills."

Work started on the Little-Egg-that-Flies. Mata ChaLik was pleased at first, for it went smoothly and much progress was made. It was only when the more complex work started the true difficulty of building an interstellar craft away from a substantial industrial base became apparent.

The task would take far longer than any had believed.

CHAPTER NINE

"What happened?" Duncan Boggs asked.

As Commander-in-Chief of the Lima-Findlay Alliance, he held absolute power. "The Clan's troops put down a rebellion in the old Fed territory?" Boggs was a big man, with a thick beard, black and tinged with gray. His once-powerful physique now bulged with the evidence of good living. His thin lips twisted into a smile. "Why?"

Boggs put his hands on the highly polished mahogany table and leaned forward to concentrate on Archie Beauvoir's answer.

Six men in dark blue military uniforms sat around the table. The wood paneling in the room matched the table. Heavy velvet drapes partially obscured the windows and thick carpeting on the floor contributed to the room's dark atmosphere. Boggs' headquarters were in the former Lima Memorial Hospital where he used its boardroom for important meetings.

"Well, General Boggs," Archie Beauvoir said slowly. "It seems the hucksters in the Clan abused some of the farmers in the old Fed. When the farmers didn't get justice, they formed a mob and took things into their own hands."

General Boggs enjoyed, no, savored, hearing about troubles in Clan territory. Boggs took any opportunity for revenge since his defeat by the Clan ten years ago. He also knew Archie Beauvoir held a grudge against the Clan. Ten years ago, Horse Soldiers had ridden rough shod over Alliance forces in a battle where Archie had lost the use of his left arm.

Last year, when the Fed came to Lima seeking sulfur to make gunpowder, Boggs had asked for weapons in trade and was surprised when the Fed agreed. He was even more impressed by the high quality of the guns.

Later, he sent spies into Defiance to find out who was supplying the Fed with guns, for he knew in the past, they were little more than a collection of farming communities. When the spies returned with the story Defiance had industrialized and now had a gun factory, he found their story hard to believe. After dismissing them, he sent a delegation of upper level officers posing as merchants seeking trade.

When they returned with more high-quality weapons and other metal goods, Boggs understood Defiance's metamorphosis. It had everything the Lima-Findlay Alliance needed to make them more powerful than other nearby city-states; it had a gun factory. But the Clan taking over the Fed had dried up the supply of weapons and put an end to thoughts of joining up with the Fed.

News of trouble in the former Fed territories triggered the idea in Boggs that Defiance might be his for the taking. "Why don't we help out these poor farmers?" He let a smile show. "Bid them welcome to Alliance territory. Let them rest up. Give them food, guns, ammunition and sympathize with them in their battle with the oppressors. Maybe even send some of our own troops to help them out from time to time."

Archie stared at Boggs for a moment. "Stir up a little trouble in the old Fed territories? Sure, I know how to do that. Is there anything else I should be doing?" Archie hesitated for a moment. "Such as getting an army together and moving it to the Auglaize River?" They had previously discussed an attack on Defiance, agreeing an amphibious attack down the Auglaize River was the best way into the city.

"I like the way you catch on, Archie." Boggs lumbered to a window and drew back a drape. "Yes, I think it's time to get serious about taking Defiance." He stared out of the window that faced north as though he could see the city. "Help out these farmers, make them our allies. Let the locals think we want to help them."

He paused. "In their, er, struggle for justice." He rubbed his hands together and laughed. He found Archie's knack for detail complemented his strategic thinking. *We make a fine team.*

"Just so." Archie stared at the wall as though he didn't see it. "We should move against Defiance in late spring, while the river has enough water to move boats and barges."

One-handed, he spread a map on the polished table, using two paperweights to hold it open. "We need to make it difficult for the Clan to send in reinforcements." He leaned forward and pulled on his lower lip. He pointed to the map. "First, we block roads here, and here, and here." Blue-clad men crowded around.

~

Boggs knew some of the Alliance troops had relatives in the Fed. That made it easy for them to cross back and forth from Alliance territory into the Clan area. During breaks in the winter weather, he sent troops north across the border with weapons and food for the dispossessed. They adopted the clothing of the locals and joined them in raids on isolated communities.

It pleased him to learn the raids caught Clan garrisons by surprise. News the area south of the Maumee River, east of Defiance to Perrysburg, had slipped from the control of the Clan gave him further encouragement.

Boggs ordered the Alliance forces to move further east to harass the communities along the main east-west connecting highway, old Route 20.

Maybe, he thought. *This will change the de facto boundary between the Clan and the Alliance, which had grated on him for the last ten years.*

~

As winter eased into spring, Boggs ordered more raids. Encouraged by their success, he sent more troops and planned larger attacks.

Boggs stared north out of a window in his headquarters at the road that lead to Defiance. "If we can take the area from Sandusky Bay through Fremont, we can prevent the Clan from moving reinforcements to Defiance."

"They still could send them by boat, via Maumee Harbor and then overland," said Archie. "My last estimate on boat capacity was about five hundred men per week, weather permitting."

"Exactly." Boggs slammed his fist on the table. "That won't be enough to relieve Defiance if we get there first." He rose and stabbed his finger into his palm. "They can't carry horses at the same time. Their strength is in their mounted bowmen."

"Maybe it's time to send more reinforcements to the border," Archie said. "Maybe now's the time to push the Clan forces out of Fremont." He nodded slowly.

Boggs smiled as he rubbed his hands together. "Do it."

CHAPTER TEN

As Taylor arrived at his office in Marting Hall, Kevin O'Neil and another man waited at the door.

Battered chairs lined the corridor and faded green paint peeled from its walls. Weak winter light leaked in through a grubby window at the end of the corridor.

There was snow on Taylor's boots and his breath steamed out like fog. "Come in." He opened the door. "Sorry about being late. The walk from the Hill took longer than I anticipated." *Winter just keeps hanging on this year*, he thought.

Kevin gestured toward a tall, well-muscled man in his forties. Gray flecked his short hair and lines filled a weathered face above a closely trimmed beard. "Taylor, this is Captain Kerr, formerly of the Fed guard in Defiance."

"I believe we've met."

Less than a year ago, Taylor had led the Clan to victory over the Fed guard commanded by Kerr.

Kerr gave a half smile and nodded. "Right."

"C'mon in and sit down. I need to get Tim." Taylor returned a moment later with Tim Van Minh.

Tim limped into the office and nodded at the seated men.

Kevin nodded to Tim and unrolled a sheaf of drawings and spread them on the desk. "This is how we're trying to modify an old truck to serve as a prime mover on the rail lines." He pointed at a drawing. "We figure rail transportation is the way to go, to move lots of goods through the Clan."

Tim bent his head to study the drawings. "If I understand this correctly, you're having a problem attaching steel wheels to the truck axles."

"Yes," Kevin said. "The axles snap and the truck brakes tend to lock up and slide."

Tim asked questions and over tea, he offered his opinion, "It seems to me a truck just isn't suitable as the prime mover; you really do need to use a locomotive."

"We tried to find one in working condition, but the diesel engines are corroded, probably from the high-sulfur fuel they used," Kevin said.

"Look," Tim said quickly. "How about using truck engines as the power source to generate the electricity for the locomotive? Replace the existing engine with one from a truck."

"That might work," Kevin said. "We'd need to take a locomotive apart to see how to do it."

"Billy's working on a simplified design for an aneutronic fusion reactor," Tim said. "It'll produce electricity directly without using a rotating generator. Once we get the bugs worked out, it could become the prime power source for all transportation vehicles."

Kevin stared into space for a moment. "That puts a different light on the problem," he said. "So, we should plan on having a big chassis ready, which can hold these fusion power units, right?" He folded his arms over his chest.

"Generators, yes." Tim nodded.

"Any ideas from what you've seen so far?"

"Cannibalize the existing locomotives. They've got everything needed for rail haul." Tim hesitated. "We can help you make replacement parts. Our foundry can make precision castings and some of our machinists are excellent. All we need is approval from the university's administration." He looked at Taylor with raised eyebrows. He referred to the new university at the old Baldwin-Wallace University in Berea that would spread the recently acquired Qu'uda technology.

"I see no problem in supporting rail development. It's technology." Taylor nodded slowly. "Once you know what parts are needed, we might want to transfer that work to Defiance. They've got a much larger foundry and more machine shops."

Kerr cleared his throat. "Before we can do that, we've got to solve a couple of problems."

"Which are?" Taylor said.

Kerr shifted in his chair. "We need men to re-build the rail bed in a couple of places. Since the troubles started with the farmers, we're short of workers." It was a common practice to use professional soldiers for construction when not required for military action. Even though the active rebellion had faded, the farmers still showed their resentment, sometimes in a violent fashion. Several battle groups had been stationed in Sandusky to keep the peace. "That's slowed things down."

"I thought that problem had been resolved." Taylor frowned.

"Well, troublemakers from the Lima-Findlay Alliance have been visiting the areas around Fremont," Kerr said. "They're stirring things up. Y'know, providing guns and stuff like that. If the locals had been treated fairly from the git-go, we wouldn't have this problem.

"The Lima-Findlay boys act like all the land south and west of Bellevue is theirs. The Clan doesn't have much of a presence between Bellevue and Maumee, no matter what you claim." Kerr frowned. "So, anything going through the area is at risk of getting picked off."

"What we claim," Taylor said. "You are a part of the Clan."

"Yeah, right, whatever." Kerr took a deep breath. "Anyway, the people there are reluctant to let us use the rail lines unless we can promise them protection. They know as soon as anything valuable arrives, the Lima-Findlay boys will show up and demand tribute."

"Have you brought this to the attention of Council?" Taylor cocked his head and stared intently at Kerr.

"Why would they listen to me?" Kerr shook his head. "I fought against them. More than one Council Elder got injured in that battle. They remember I'm the guy who led the Fed guards. They don't trust me."

Taylor steepled his fingers and chose his words carefully. "Captain Kerr, that has to be put behind us. You will have a chance to share your knowledge with people who'll listen. It may not happen right away, but I'll see to it you have a chance to express your concerns."

Joe Del Corso popped his head around the edge of the door. "Mr. MacPherson, a message for you." He waved a slip of paper. "The messenger's waiting downstairs."

"Thanks." Taylor opened the message that read: Lunch? If not, tell the messenger, otherwise I'll stop by at noon, Joyce. He smiled. The idea was appealing, in fact, he found that he thought of Joyce often. "No message."

Taylor looked up. "Let me put together a letter approving your use of the university's facilities for the rail project," he said. "I'll contact the foundry to let them know you're authorized to make castings. For that, I'll need an estimate as to the cost. Is there anything else?"

"Yes," said Tim. "I'd like to spend more time on this locomotive design. I'd like to make sure there'll be enough room for the fusion power plants when they become available."

"Certainly," Taylor said. "Just make sure Billy knows what you're doing."

CHAPTER ELEVEN

Joyce brushed snow off her clothes as she stepped into Taylor's office. "Have you any idea what the weather is like out there?"

She wore a long brown coat with embroidery along its sleeves. A raccoon fur hat on her head matched her coat's collar. Her cheeks had a glow that matched her full, red lips.

Taylor looked up. "Haven't checked." *There's something about her that I like*, he thought.

"I swear another six inches has fallen since first light."

"It took me well over an hour to make the walk from the Hill to the university this morning," Taylor said.

"It's getting colder," Joyce said. "Much colder."

"So, where do we go for lunch?" Taylor stood and reached for his coat on the back of the chair. "Nowhere far, I hope."

"The cafeteria is in the next building. There won't be many there today," Joyce said. "Most classes are canceled."

"Let's go," Taylor said without enthusiasm. It wasn't the food was bad; it lacked privacy.

Outside, the wind swirled around them, blowing snow into their faces. They high-stepped down the path, which had been cleared that morning but now had six or more inches of fresh, fluffy snow. The wind out of the northeast had a bitter edge. It took twice as long as usual to reach the student union building.

"Phew," Joyce said as they stepped inside the chrome and glass door. "It's getting worse." The heavy door banged shut.

"Damn cold, too."

The cafeteria was deserted except for one server on duty. "Only soup and bread today." The matronly woman frowned as though being asked a great favor. "The others left early. That's all I've had a chance to make." She clanged the pots as she moved them about.

"Well, Mrs. Postlethwaite." Taylor forced cheer into his voice. "What kind of soup is it?"

"Lentil with ham." She sniffed, staring down her nose.

"Sounds good."

They sat in a corner and ate quietly, catching up with each other's activities. The normal bustle of the cafeteria was absent, causing the room to feel even colder and emptier. Their voices sounded loud in the tall-ceilinged room and as they moved their dishes on the table, their clatter echoed.

As Taylor finished his soup, he realized they were the only people left in the cafeteria. Mrs. Postlethwaite had disappeared. "I'm not looking forward to the walk home this evening." He watched Joyce mop up traces of soup with a piece of crusty whole-wheat bread. His eyes found her face. *She isn't a beauty, but very attractive in a lively sort of way*.

"Mmm," Joyce mumbled and swallowed. "You shouldn't make that walk in this storm. Could be dangerous." She took a swallow of water. "Was the road cleared this morning?"

"Nope. Had to wade through the snow."

"You're not walking home tonight," she said with finality.

Taylor raised his eyebrows. "So, where do I stay?"

Joyce took a deep breath. "If there isn't a place at the university, you can stay with me." A spot of color appeared in each cheek. "What I meant was ..." She stopped and sighed. "This isn't coming out right. What I mean is, it could be dangerous for you to walk that distance through the storm. If you need a place for the night, I'm sure I can work out some kind of accommodation for you."

"I see." Taylor felt a sudden urge to grin. "Are you returning to your classes this afternoon?" The idea of a young woman inviting him to sleep over had a deliciously attractive, and perhaps, illicit flavor ... *Stop it, get hold of yourself*.

"I'm working on the fusion generator design this afternoon. Billy needs some of the electrical details worked out. It's a special connection facility. Nothing particularly difficult."

"D'you want me to stop by your laboratory?"

"No." Joyce paused for a second and fidgeted with her spoon. "Since I'm not sure exactly how long this'll take, why don't I stop by your office. It'll be about four or five o'clock." She looked up. The color had faded from her cheeks.

$$\mathcal{C}$$

A little after four, Joyce showed up at Taylor's office. "I didn't get finished. I need some reference books and I didn't want to go to the library in this weather." The wind had eased somewhat and less snow was falling. Frost had formed on the inside of the windows. "It's gotten very cold out there," she said. "If you've got extra clothing, put it on."

Taylor rummaged around in his closet and found a wool sweater he occasionally wore. He filled the stove with logs and damped its air supply. *That should last the night. At least it'll hold the chill off until morning.* "I guess I'm ready. Do we have far to go?"

"No," Joyce said. "My apartment is above a store just across from the Berea Commons. Normally, it's a five minute walk." She adjusted her coat. "Today, I don't know." She shrugged.

Outside, as they waded through almost a foot of snow, it squeaked underfoot. Fluffy flakes fell, obscuring all but the closest buildings. Light was almost gone.

Joyce led the way, gloved hand over her mouth. She made footprints in the snow for him to follow. It was almost as though they were in a silent, deserted world; as they crossed campus, only one other figure ghosted by on an adjacent path. It seemed like ages before they stepped out of the wind into the shelter of a doorway between two closed shops.

Joyce fiddled with a key in the lock for a moment before the door swung open to reveal a set of dark stairs. "Up here." She pointed. She held the door open for him. "Hurry up."

Up the stairs and along a dim hallway was her apartment.

Joyce unlocked the door and pushed it open. "C'mon in. This is it. Not much, but it's home."

A battered sofa, two armchairs, and an old wooden desk with a chair occupied a large room. Along the wall stood a bookshelf filled with tattered and worn books saved from the wars. A radiator hissed intermittently. "Ahh, central heating," Taylor said with approval as he examined the bookshelf, which contained mainly technical stuff, engineering texts. "It's nice to be out of that cold." He shed his coat.

Silently, Joyce took his coat and put it in a closet. "Why don't you come into the kitchen while I fix us something to eat." She went through a doorway.

Taylor followed her into the cramped kitchen, noting the chipped porcelain sink, ice chest, and a tiny charcoal cook-stove with its stack bent crookedly through a metal panel in the window. A saucepan and kettle were on the counter. A rickety table and two chairs squeezed into a corner.

Joyce opened the ice chest and studied its contents. "Well, it looks like a soup night." She looked up quickly at Taylor. "I'm sorry, I really wasn't expecting company." A trace of a blush appeared in her cheeks. "I don't have much to offer."

Taylor raised his hand. "Joyce, you didn't invite me here to demonstrate your culinary skills. Soup is fine with me. What can I do to help?"

"Are you any good at getting this contraption going?" She pointed at the charcoal cook-stove. "I always seem to have trouble with it. It'll be great when we get electricity."

"Yes, and yes," Taylor said. "I'll get it going."

"Good. I need to get into something dry."

Taylor bent to the task. After about fifteen minutes, the stove started to draw strongly and he shut its damper. "Stove's ready," he said loudly.

Joyce reappeared in the kitchen. She'd changed into a brown wool sweater and matching slacks. She had loosened her hair. "Thanks." As she poured the soup into a saucepan, she asked, "Can you turn the stove up, please?"

"Sure." As Taylor reached past Joyce to adjust the damper, he put his hand on her shoulder. "Excuse me."

Joyce laughed. "That's—that's all right." She turned and got two bowls out of a cupboard. "Would you put these on the table?" She handed him the bowls.

As they waited for the soup to heat, Taylor asked Joyce about her work and they quickly fell into a conversation about stories of life in the laboratory, which Taylor thought was forced.

When the soup was hot, she removed it from the stove and replaced it with a kettle filled with water.

"Have I had this soup before?" Taylor thought the creamy chicken-vegetable soup had a familiar flavor.

Joyce laughed. "When Mrs. Postlethwaite makes a soup I like, I buy some and bring it home."

"Good idea. This is just what I needed."

As they ate, their conversation slowed, for they had exhausted their usual topics—something was different. After the meal, they gathered the dishes with minimal conversation, using the boiling water from the kettle to wash and rinse them.

As Joyce put away the last item, she said, "Well, now what do we do?" She carried the oil lamp into the dark sitting room.

Taylor sat down on the sofa. "This, I assume, is my bed for this evening." He punched the pillows. "Yes, it'll do fine." Silence descended.

Now, he thought. *What do we do next?*

Joyce pulled a chair over and sat down. She stared at Taylor for a moment. The two spots of color on her cheeks reappeared. "Can I ask you a question? A personal question." She bit her lip momentarily.

"Sure, what d'you want to know?"

"Do you have a personal relationship with Noelle?"

"She's my employee. She takes care of my household."

"You didn't answer my question," Joyce said. "I asked you if you had a personal relationship."

"Why d'you think there's a personal relationship?"

"Because I don't think she likes me. Maybe it isn't just me. Maybe it's any woman who comes near you. I don't know. I get a feeling she considers you to be hers." She bit her lower lip.

"She's been with me for a long time." Taylor didn't know why he was being evasive. He almost felt guilty.

"Oh, God, what am I saying? How do I explain this?" She got up and disappeared in the kitchen for a moment, returning with two glasses. "Here, have some wine."

Taylor took a sip of wine. *Something from the Erie Islands*, he guessed, but held his silence. *What is going on?*

Joyce took a deep breath. "When I asked you if you had a personal relationship, what I meant was, are you sleeping with her?" She sighed. "Sorry, I don't know how else to put it."

Taylor took a sip of wine before answering. "Why do you want to know?" He wasn't eager to talk about Noelle.

"It's like this," Joyce said. "I don't know anyone here. Except Billy, of course. Before I knew he was an alien, I thought I was in love with him. Well, maybe I was in love with him. But he wouldn't ever let me get close to him. When I found out he was an alien, I was glad we didn't. God." She sighed. "Would that have been a shocker."

"I think I can understand that."

"You do?" Her laugh seemed brittle. "When I saw him without clothes, y'know, after the battle, and saw he didn't have the right equipment, it gave me a real turn. But that was nothing." She went to the kitchen and returned with the bottle of wine. She refilled her glass and topped off Taylor's. "Later, Dr. Encirlik, that bitch, told me his sex organ was a foot and a half long and shaped like a rapier. I had nightmares about it." She took another sip. "Skewered on an alien dick." She laughed like glass breaking. She went to the window and looked out for a moment. She turned and stared at Taylor over her wineglass. "Remember? That's when I met you."

"I think she was pulling your leg. Billy has a cloaca for a sex organ. Intercourse between Qu'uda and humans isn't even remotely possible. What does this have to do with the question?" Taylor said. "The personal relationship thing."

Joyce wrinkled her nose. "It seems so obvious to me." She shook her head then tossed down her drink. "Don't you get it?" She carefully set her glass down on the desk and straightened her sweater. She put her hands on her hips to stare down at him.

"No." *Maybe I do*, Taylor thought. *But what if I'm wrong?*

She sat down next to Taylor, reached out and took his hand. A flush suffused her cheeks. "When I first met you, back in Defiance,

I thought you were a real bastard. A ruthless, cruel warlord." She lowered her head, as though studying his hand. "After I saw the way you treated Billy, I realized you weren't a bastard, just a hard-nosed prick, a typical leader." She raised her head to stare at him almost defiantly. Reflections of the oil lamp flame glowed in her eyes, casting shadows on her sculpted face.

"Gee, thanks," Taylor said dryly.

"It was only after I got here and we got to know each other, I realized you're smart and tough, a real leader." Joyce hesitated. "But not a bastard. Even now, I'd bet everything I have that you and Noelle are getting it on, and you won't say anything about it." A tear glistened in her eye. "You still don't understand?"

Taylor stroked her hair. "Joyce, I've learned that it doesn't pay to talk about some things. There are things I feel that I have difficulty talking about." He took a deep breath. "For example, I find I look forward to seeing you. I think about you all the time. There's something about you that's familiar, something I couldn't put my finger on." He paused. "Tonight, I realized what it was."

Joyce's hand slipped to his knee.

"In my life, I've only loved two women." Taylor felt himself starting to choke up. *What am I saying? What am I getting myself into?*

"Is ..." Joyce bit her lip. "Is one of them Noelle?" Her grip on his knee tightened.

"No." Taylor shook his head. "The women I loved died a long time ago. In the wars. It almost destroyed me."

Memories of Vivian and Franny came surging back, memories of the feelings he'd had for them, memories of laughter, warmth, and love. The brief times he'd had a home and truly belonged. The memory filled him with its unexpected intensity: Love, rich, full, and rewarding. And when it was gone, the loss was almost unbearable. *Oh, God, I don't ever want to hurt like that again.* He took a deep breath and exhaled slowly.

Joyce lifted Taylor's hand to her lips. "I'm sorry. I didn't know. I shouldn't have said what I did." She sat up straight. "The familiar thing. D'you know what it is?" Her eyes glowed almost luminously. She licked her lips and took a deep breath.

"Yes," Taylor said. "You remind me of the women I loved. Not in appearance; but in the way you are." His heart began to pound and his mouth felt dry. It was like making a confession; but it wasn't guilt. "Maybe that's what I feel."

A trace of a smile grew on Joyce's face and she exhaled slowly. She stared intently at him, her hand rubbing her knee.

"You have to understand what happened," Taylor rushed to say. "Whenever I fell in love, something terrible happened. I'm afraid to love again."

He felt scared and excited at the same time. It was the closest he'd come to confessing love to a woman in years, and he wasn't sure how to handle it. *Do I love her? She stimulates me on so many levels; something I haven't felt in years. I'm afraid, too. And she's so young...*

Joyce stood up and extended both hands to Taylor. Her face was glowing and she began to breathe hard. Her nipples showed clearly through the sweater. "Come, it's time you found out you can love again, with a woman who loves you."

౨

The sound of shovels scraping on the sidewalks woke Taylor. Sunlight streamed through the window. Even if it had been cloudy and gray, he would've thought it bright and beautiful. He stretched and felt Joyce's skin against his belly. He touched her and she sighed.

"Taylor," she said, as if savoring the sound of his name.

"Yes, Joyce." His heart began to race.

"This is wonderful." She sighed again. "I've had such a difficult time keeping my hands off you. All this time, I thought you belonged to Noelle. I was so jealous of her."

Taylor took a deep breath. *How do I tell her*, he thought. *Should I?* He opened his mouth to speak, but hesitated.

Joyce turned in the bed and put a finger on his lips. "Don't say anything you don't mean," she said. "After all, I did drag you into bed. If it's a mistake, I'll find out soon enough. Just don't say anything this morning—it's too perfect to spoil." She closed her eyes and kissed him.

Taylor felt an immediate surge of desire and reached for her. Their bodies quickly became intertwined as they made love.

CHAPTER TWELVE

"Well, I've got good news and bad news." Kevin O'Neil stood at the entrance to Taylor's office and sighed. He had bags under his eyes and there were smudges of grease on his clothing. "Which do you want to hear first?"

"Give me the good first. Then we can go directly from the bad news to a course of action." Taylor leaned back in his chair.

Paper was stacked on both sides of the blotter on his desk. The early morning sun had begun to warm the room. Outside, water dripped past the window. Patches of pavement could be seen through the snow on the paths that sliced across the lawns.

"Crosby got some of the phone system working. That's the good news," Kevin said. "We thought we had a connection to Defiance, but a test call wouldn't go through. So he sent a crew out to check the line, it was okay to Sandusky and Bellevue." He took a deep breath. "The problem is around Clyde and Fremont." He shook his head. "They ran into trouble there."

"What kind of trouble?" Taylor asked.

"The crew was killed and the line cut. The Lima-Findlay boys were seen in this area, stirring up the local farmers. But we're not positive they're responsible."

"Were there any Clan soldiers with them?"

"No." Kevin came into the room and sat down. "God, those poor sods. They were good people."

Taylor stared into the distance for moment. "This is a security issue for the Greater Clan," he said. "We should talk with Chris Kucinski. This is her responsibility. She's in charge of security." Taylor stood and picked up his coat off the back of the chair. "Let's go see her." He made a face. "If it's a bigger issue than that, then we can talk to the Council Elders to get the benefit of their wisdom." Before he left, he scribbled a note to Joyce to cancel their lunch meeting.

ર

It took several tries to locate Chris Kucinski. She was a tall, thin woman with gray streaked auburn hair who wore a brown soldier's uniform. She had been busy mobilizing Clan soldiers to help with snow removal and other weather-related work. They caught up with her in the Oxbow area where she had just finished one project and was on her way back to the Hill.

"A line crew was killed," Taylor said.

"Why don't you tell me about it on the way to the Travelers' Inn?" she said, walking her horse alongside Taylor and Kevin. "I missed breakfast."

"Sure." Taylor realized he was chilled to the bone.

Inside the steamy restaurant, Nguyen Van Minh insisted they use the small back room so they could be by themselves. The room's high windows caught the sun, which illuminated the murals on the wall depicting life in a far-away Vietnam. Many regarded the murals to be a fantasy.

They dined on one of the restaurant's specialties—Canh Chua Thap Cam soup—which was a fragrant tamarind soup filled with chicken, crayfish, and mixed vegetables. They ate with noisy appreciation as Kevin told Chris what he knew about the line crew up to the time they were killed outside of Bellevue.

Chris quizzed him until satisfied that she understood the situation.

"We've got communications with Sandusky and Bellevue," Kevin said. "I could send another crew out, but if we lose more people, we won't be able to finish the system. Those people take time to train." Worry creased lines between his eyebrows.

Chris put down her cup of tea. "Most of the soldiers are in barracks during winter. Since we gave the Alliance army a good licking ten years ago, they haven't given us any trouble." She took a sip of tea. "We have an army group in Fremont that covers the area from Perrysburg to Norwalk along old Route 20." Old Route 20 was the unofficial border between the Clan and the Alliance about twenty miles south of Sandusky. The road was almost ruler-straight for fifty-five miles east-west between Perrysburg and Norwalk. "I'll spread them between Bellevue, Fremont, and Perrysburg and set up an active patrol. Their presence should send a message to the Alliance for their boys to stay out."

"Y'think so?" Kevin still had a frown on his face. "My people encountered more hostility from the local people the further west they went. Especially along the border."

"I can't promise anything. I have limited resources. Until I have proof there is an emergency, I won't get more." Chris leaned toward Kevin. "Look, if it makes you feel any better, I'll have a platoon ride with your line crew. That should give them some security."

Kevin nodded. "Good. I'll have the new line crew check-in every day. We'll know right away if there's trouble."

Chris stared at him for a moment. "How'll you do that?" she asked. "I know you have a phone link to Sandusky and Bellevue. D'you plan to have someone ride back with a message each day?"

Kevin smiled. "Oh, no, my line crew can call from anyplace on the phone line."

Chris frowned for a moment. "Oh, yes, now I remember that about phones." She stood. "Good. Now, let me use your phone to contact the battle group in Fremont."

"Well," said Kevin. "That's a problem. The line from Bellevue to Fremont never got completed. I can contact Sandusky. Maybe you could have a courier take a message to Fremont?"

"Fine," Chris said. "Let's do it."

ॐ

Noelle Sutton was frustrated. Mitch Doaks had stopped by for another enjoyable conversation. *He seems to want to make my acquaintance. Not only is he handsome and convivial, he also has a good position with the university; a man with a steady job. My,* she thought, *I haven't felt this way about a man in a while. Can I seduce him without appearing too forward? After all, I don't want him to scare him off; I'd like to have him around for a while.*

When Taylor had showed up after the blizzard, she'd felt a sense of relief. That night, Noelle went to Taylor's bed but couldn't arouse him. It was like trying to get a well-flogged horse to gallop. She felt insulted when some of her tried and true techniques failed. When she left, she was more than a little annoyed. *Am I losing my attraction to him? Is my job safe?*

ॐ

After being with Joyce, Taylor no longer had the strength, nor the desire for sex with Noelle. Besides, he was a little sore; he hadn't had that much sex in a long time. He'd forgotten how strenuous a night of love making with a vigorous young woman could be. When Noelle slipped into his bed that night, her soft hands and lips failed to excite him.

Over the next couple of days, even though Noelle said nothing to him about their failed evening, it was obvious she was upset. He also noticed she was absent more than usual from his home. It was sort of a relief.

ॐ

By early spring, the success of the Alliance's raids encouraged Duncan Boggs to send more troops to the frontier. "We've got to stop the Clan from sending overland reinforcements to Defiance." It was his recurring worry as they planned their attack on Defiance. "I don't think the Clan will be able to get reinforcements in by boat fast enough to give us trouble."

"It's possible they'd use the bridge over Sandusky Bay to move reinforcements west along old route two." Archie Beauvoir pointed to the map on the table. The weak sunlight penetrated the drape-lined room and provided enough illumination to read the map. "They'd have to figure out how to get past the Erie Islander's fort near the Sandusky Bay."

"By the way," Boggs said. "Send them a wagon-load of gunpowder and remind them of the agreement." He referred to the mutual assistance pact the Islanders had sought when the Clan tried to use the bridge the previous year. Boggs believed gunpowder was a cheap price to pay to get the Islanders to deny the shorter route to the Clan.

"We still need to get the boats to Dupont," said Archie. "It's slow going this time of the year."

Dupont was a small village due north of Lima on the Auglaize River where it widened and became deep enough to carry a barge. The freeze-thaw of late winter softened the dirt roads. It wasn't practical to haul carts laden with boats yet.

"Will the army be ready?" Boggs asked.

"Yes. I'm pulling together contingents in all the major towns. There's no need to move them to Dupont until the time is right." Archie let a trace of a smile flicker across his face.

Everyone knew Dupont, which lay about thirty miles due north of Lima, was too small to accommodate an army. Besides, a troop movement of that size would get the locals gossiping. It could tip their hand to the Clan. "It'll simplify logistics," he said. "Let the towns feed and house the troops. That way we won't have to haul supplies toward the frontier."

"Good." Boggs paced back and forth. "Have we forgotten anything?"

"I don't think so," Archie said.

They had hashed out plans for the assault on Defiance many times. The key to their attack would be to float an armada down the river under the cover of darkness, timing its arrival to Defiance at first light. Once the Alliance forces engaged the city's troops, a second force would attack from the south where they expected sympathizers would open the gate.

CHAPTER THIRTEEN

Taylor settled down to clear his in-basket. *I can't believe how paperwork proliferates*, he thought. *We're turning into a bureaucracy.* He glanced out the window.

The ground was bare except for the sodden grass newly emerged from under a blanket of snow. Naked branches waved forlornly at the heavens.

"Mr. MacPherson." An out of breath Joe Del Corso burst through the doorway. He handled many of the support service activities of the university. "Mr. O'Neil and Commander Kucinski want you at the communications building right away." He took a deep breath. "They said it was urgent."

"Sure. Can you deliver a message for me?" Taylor asked, busily scribbling a note. Dear Joyce, he wrote, forgive me, but an emergency has come up. I won't be able to meet you for lunch. Love, Taylor. He stared at the note for a moment. *Now I'm signing my notes with love*, he noted wryly. *My, this is the third date in a row I've broken. I wonder what she's going to think?*

Joe stood waiting, silent.

Taylor quickly sealed the note. "Can you take this to Ms. Vargas in the electrical engineering department?"

"Yes, sir." Joe smiled. He'd done this before.

"Thanks." Taylor grabbed his jacket and headed out.

The communications building was off-campus, a solid brick

building that previously housed a telephone exchange. The rusty steel door squeaked open after Taylor knocked several times.

Inside, wire cables snaked untidily across the floor to a desk where Chris Kucinski gingerly held a phone handset to her ear, a frown on her face.

"I see," she said. "How many got away?" Her frown deepened. "Where're you?" Her eyebrows rose. "Really? Good. If you learn anything else, please let me know." She handed the phone handset to Kevin who placed it in a cradle. Ed Kerr stood behind Kevin, a frown creasing his face.

"A sizable Alliance force raided Fremont. A few of our soldiers got away and warned Bellevue before it was attacked. Now the bastards are pillaging and looting. By nightfall, they'll be drunk, raping, and killing. There's too many of them for the platoon of soldiers to handle."

"How many soldiers would it take to give those raiders a good thrashing?" Kevin's eyebrows rose.

"A battle group could teach them a lesson they wouldn't forget in a while. It'll take several hours to get a group ready to travel," Chris said. "Even if the weather holds, the ride from Rocky River to Bellevue will take a full day. The earliest they could get there would be late tomorrow afternoon, with horses in no condition for battle." She sighed. "Damn."

Kevin took a deep breath. "If a battle group were ready by noon," he said. "I could get it to Bellevue by three."

"What?" Chris asked. "How?"

"We've got a hybrid locomotive running," Kevin said. "It should average at least twenty-five miles per hour on the run to Bellevue, including the slow section in Norwalk."

Taylor stepped forward. "Are you sure?"

Kevin nodded. "Yes. I figure it can haul eight or ten boxcars. That ought to hold a battle group. Yeah, it'll be a little tight, but it shouldn't take more than three hours."

"Tell me more," Chris said.

"We'd take the line to Vermilion, then branch off through Norwalk and stop short of Bellevue," Kevin said. "We'd have to pack the horses into the box cars so they don't fall over."

"It'd be the same as taking horses on a boat," Chris said. He referred to the practice of blindfolding the horses and pushing them tight together to keep them standing. It was messy, but the horses didn't get hurt that way.

Chris looked at Taylor. "What d'you think?"

"I'm guessing that Kevin is betting his career on this move." Taylor glanced at Kevin. "The trains have lukewarm support in the Council, and he sees this as a way to get additional support." He turned to Kevin. "Right?"

"Sort of." Kevin's face reddened. "I know what raiders do to small towns. It ain't pretty. Those people will have their lives ruined by a bunch of drunks." He beckoned toward Ed Kerr. "You know the condition of the track. What d'you think?"

Kerr sniffed. "The section between here and Vermilion is excellent. A train could go any speed on it." He made a face. "From there to Bellevue it's not so good. If we keep our speed down to twenty or less, it should be okay. Bellevue to Fremont is in the same shape."

Chris stared at Kerr for a moment. "Y'know this track?"

"Yes, ma'am," Kerr said. "I've walked it twice."

"Mr. Kerr, I'm giving you a temporary commission to lead a battle group to Bellevue." Chris's eyes almost closed as she took a deep breath. "I think the battle group from the western territories should take this on." She turned toward Taylor. "D'you see a problem with the Council if I do this?" The battle group she had selected was comprised mainly of former Fed guards.

Taylor chuckled without mirth. "There's always a problem with the Council if you do something without asking their permission first." He rubbed his chin. "In this case, time is of the essence. I'd recommend you do it now and explain afterwards."

"Don't I get any say in this?" A trace of a frown danced between Kerr's eyebrows.

Chris cocked her head to one side for a second. "Why, no. You're being drafted for the duration of this conflict. I don't know of a better person to lead this particular battle group." She shrugged her shoulders. "I don't know much about trains or tracks. I don't even know if those men are capable of this assignment. You do." A flicker of a grim smile crossed her face. "Of course, you could refuse."

Kerr stiffened into almost a parade position. "No, ma'am, I won't refuse." His face grew hard. "And they're good men."

"Fine, let's go. I need to get your commission in writing, and you need to get your battle group mobilized." Chris turned to Kevin. "Where should Captain Kerr bring his troops?"

ॐ

Several days later, Taylor asked Chris for a report.

"Well, the Clan battle group arrived on the outskirts of Bellevue at two o'clock. The train really got them there quickly. It took half an hour to get all the horses unloaded and mounted into formations."

"Really?" Taylor said. "That was quick."

"Once Kerr had his battle group ready, they rode into Bellevue and caught the Alliance raiders in the middle of a victory celebration. The battle group made short work of the raiders. However, some managed to flee into Alliance territory and the rest surrendered."

"So, who were these raiders?"

"Half of the prisoners wore the leather and linen uniforms of troops of the Lima-Findlay Alliance; the rest were farmers." Chris paused and stroked her chin. "Kerr told me the farmers were from the old Fed who had suffered at the hands of the new businessmen from the Clan."

"Hmm, we've got to fix that problem."

"Next day, at first light, Kerr used the train to take two-thirds of the battle group to Fremont. While on the train, they passed lines of refugees. The train stopped at the eastern boundary of the town. Once again, Kerr assembled the battle group ready for action.

"It turned out most of the raiders and townspeople were gone; the only ones left were either injured, in a state of shock, or drunk. The soldiers' barracks and the administrative center had been burned to the ground. Civilians and soldiers hung from old light poles; bodies littered the streets. Fremont's leadership was dead."

"Damn. We've got to put an end to these raiders."

"Kerr organized an evacuation, using the train, and brought the few remaining townspeople to Rocky River."

"Sounds like Kerr did a good job." Taylor shook Chris's hand.

ᘒ

"Captain Kerr." Charlie Ramsey looked over the crowded Council Chamber. "It pleases me to give you this public commendation for your service to the Clan."

Several persons in the public section of the Council Chamber started clapping. The applause swelled to a roar. It was a victory for the Clan that had been won by a former leader of the Fed army.

"Captain Kerr," Charlie Ramsey said. "The Council has voted to approve the conversion of your temporary commission in the Clan Horse Soldiers to a permanent commission. You now have command of the Ninth Battle Group." He barely cracked a smile.

Ever since Ramsey's son-in-law had died in battle with the Fed, he was reluctant to do anything for the former officers in the now-defunct Fed Guard. However, the vote of the Elders from the western territories combined with the vote from those Elders sensitive to public opinion carried the day.

"Your battle group will provide escort service for the rail system as it expands toward the frontier. Congratulations." He shook Kerr's hand.

"Thank you." Kerr bowed toward the Council of Elders. "I appreciate your vote of confidence in me and the soldiers of the Ninth Battle Group." He turned toward the public section. "I promise the Clan, your faith has not been misplaced."

Taylor stood with the rest of the people in the public section and joined in the applause. *I'm glad he got the position*, he thought. *It's time we learned to trust the former Feds.*

"Well, hello, Mr. MacPherson," a familiar voice said. It was Joyce. Her voice held a hard edge. "Haven't seen you in a while." She was calm in a controlled fashion. "Do you have time for tea?" she asked. "Or has another emergency come up?"

"Joyce," Taylor said. "Sure, let's go to the Travelers' Inn." *Damn*, he thought, *I deserved that.* "I'm sorry," he said. He took her elbow to guide her through the crowd leaving the Council Chambers.

She shook off his hand. "We have some things to talk about," she said over her shoulder and walked rapidly in front of him in the direction of the restaurant.

The sky was leaden gray and remnants of snow covered the ground with a dingy veil. The wet sidewalks were muddy, and Joyce's heels threw up drops of water at Taylor as he hurried to catch up.

"Joyce," he said. "I haven't been avoiding you." They approached the main road down from the Hill where it crossed the outer path. People crowded the sidewalks.

"Really?" Joyce glanced at him briefly. "Well, you've missed our last three meetings," she said. "I'm tired of being the one who suggests the next meeting." She sniffed.

Taylor saw her eyes water. "Joyce." He grasped her arm and pulled her to a stop.

She turned toward him.

"Joyce, please," he said. "I'm sorry."

The crowd flowed around them, faces glancing curiously at them. "I don't know how to say this without it sounding cold."

"Go on," she said. "Say it. I've been expecting it for some time." Her lower lip quivered, and a tear ran down her cheek. "You've probably gone back to that cow, Noelle."

"Stop it," Taylor said. "It's not that." He took a deep breath. "My priority is Clan business." He gripped her arms tightly. "Don't you understand the concept of duty?"

"Duty," she almost spat the word out. "Is that your excuse?" She shook his hand loose, turned, and strode away.

CHAPTER FOURTEEN

Taylor returned to his office and tried to bury himself in work, but he kept seeing Joyce's image. *If I'd said it differently*, he thought. *Perhaps she'd have understood.* A thought ran through his mind, *Maybe she didn't want to understand; she wanted him to give up all he'd worked for. That's not fair. I'm sure that isn't so. Look at the way she was with Billy and others. Perhaps I should let it die. Maybe I'm just too old for her.*

"Mr. MacPherson." Joe Del Corso popped his head around the door. "Mr. Billy asked you drop by his office."

Odd, thought Taylor. *Billy usually just stops in when he wants to see me.* "Are you going back in the direction of the Engineering building?" he asked.

"Yes, sir."

"Please tell Billy I'll be there about eleven o'clock." In spite of the distracting thoughts, there was work to be done. The paperwork never ended.

"Yes, sir." Joe disappeared down the corridor.

By eleven o'clock, Taylor had dealt with the most urgent items of the in-basket and he went to Billy's office.

Billy's head swiveled toward Taylor. "Hello," he said. "I have a problem." He gestured toward the seat before his large, almost empty desk. The office was large, and the light of a gray day barely lit its corners.

Taylor took off his coat and sat down without saying anything. The room was very warm. Billy liked it that way.

"I have established communications with the Qu'uda who were left to guard the eggs, which have now hatched."

"Right." *Nothing new here*, Taylor thought.

"I must bring them back here," Billy said. "One of the guardians has died. They have difficulty finding enough to eat. The stress of taking care of the wrigglers weakens them further. Wild creatures attack them continually." He rose to his feet and waved his hands in the air.

"Was it your special friend who died?" Taylor asked, frowning. "What was her name?"

"Cha KinLaat DoMar," said Billy. "No, it was another. We must rescue them."

"It's a long way from here," Taylor said. "To go overland to Florida and then get a boat to go to the Bahamas would be almost impossible." Almost like going to the moon.

"No," said Billy. "We need a craft that flies."

"We don't have any. Every aircraft we've found is damaged or corroded beyond repair."

Billy thrust a sheet of paper forward. "Read this. I asked Sinkton, the head of the scouts, to look for flying craft. He claims there are unused flying craft nearby."

Taylor studied the piece of paper. It was a report from a spy mission that told of a rumor about intact aircraft at the old Wright-Patterson AFB outside of Dayton.

"If this is true, we must send an expedition to get them," Billy said. "I must rescue my friends."

"That'd be difficult," Taylor said. "We're having problems with the Lima-Findlay Alliance, and on top of that, McFarland, the leader of the Columbus-Dayton Confederation, has a reputation for being difficult."

Difficult? Taylor thought. *More like the most brutally repressive leader in the Ohio. The majority of the Confederation's inhabitants were treated like serfs. Its military rulers acted like mediaeval nobility.*

"We must," Billy said. "Please."

Taylor stared at Billy. *He's alone here, knowing his people are wasting away. If we had aircraft*, he thought, *it would be an immense step forward for us, too.*

"We could send an emissary under a white flag." He hesitated, thinking how it might be done. "He would have to detour east through the Central Ohio Union to get to Columbus. It could be done. Still, it would be risky."

"It must be done," Billy said. "I need flying machines to rescue my people."

"All right," Taylor said. "I'll talk to the Council about this in case there are problems I don't know about. Once I've got clearance, I'll talk to Chris Kucinski to find out who's available for this kind of expedition." He frowned. "It'd better be someone with experience, someone with a high survival quotient, maybe Sinkton."

"Thank you, Taylor," Billy said in his grunting style. "There is one other thing." His head swiveled away. "Something is wrong with Joyce Vargas. She no longer works well. She seems unhappy but does not say why. Will you talk to her?"

"Okay." *Oh, Lord, help me get through this.*

Taylor stared down the gleaming steel rails that seemed to merge into a single line in the distance.

The late April sun felt warm on his back.

Sparrows chattered noisily in the sprouting willows growing in the ditch alongside the railroad track. A diesel engine rumbled then revved. A puff of black smoke drifted lazily away. Carriages squealed and clanked as they began to move. He stepped away from the tracks. A rusty black locomotive crept forward, pulling a clanking row of boxcars and flat cars.

"Well," Kevin said. "What d'you think of that?"

"I'm impressed." Taylor turned toward Kevin. "You're ahead of schedule. Now you've got Defiance and Berea linked by rail, what d'you do for an encore?"

Kevin looked around as though he was concerned someone might be listening. "I suppose it's all right to tell you." He lowered his voice. "I met with the Council in a closed session. They're planning to move against the Alliance."

He paused as the locomotive slowly rolled by. It looked like there were at least a couple of squads of militia on board and several boxcars held horses. "I guess they've had enough with the raids and troubles out west."

Yes, Taylor thought.

Over the last year, there had been more raids, each bolder than the last, with the Lima-Findlay Alliance taking possession of a large swath of land south of the Maumee River that had been part of the old Fed territories. The combination of public outrage and realization the Greater Clan had to grow must have fueled the Council's decision to invade the Alliance.

Sinkton brought a report of aircraft held by the Columbus-Dayton Confederation at the old Air Force base, which provided additional motivation. McFarland, its leader, wouldn't deal for them; he claimed he could get them operational.

Hah, fat chance, Taylor thought. Sinkton also learned McFarland had been talking about that for years but had done nothing about it.

"So, what's your role in this move against the Alliance?" Taylor wanted confirmation of what he already knew.

"I'll be working with Captain Kerr. It seems the Clan has a deal with the Central Ohio Union to fix their rail lines, ostensibly for trade." Kevin cupped his hand to the side of his mouth. "We'll use it to attack Lima directly. Won't that surprise them? There's a rail line running straight from Mansfield to Lima. Kerr's people have fixed that line." A hint of a frown crossed his brow. "All except for some vegetation on the right of way close to Ada, which is about fourteen-fifteen miles from Lima which is being handled now."

"Aren't you worried this activity will tip our hand?" Taylor was sure the Clan could defeat the Alliance, but he always worried about an ambush. He still remembered what had happened during their war with the Fed.

"Well." Kevin frowned. "There's no love for the Alliance in the towns on the way. At least, that's what I'm told."

Very few people lived between Mansfield and Ada. The area was the former agricultural heart of Ohio and had seen a loss of population after the Collapse. Mansfield was the capital of the Central Ohio Union and traded with the independent towns of Bucyrus and Upper Sandusky.

"Who's planning the campaign?"

"As far as I know, it is Commander Kucinski and Captain Elroy Stanek," Kevin said. "They've had me in to talk with them several times. They want all kinds of details on the equipment."

That was reassuring, Taylor thought. "When does this campaign start?" he asked. The Clan's strength was in its cavalry and the wet ground of spring would be a disadvantage.

"I need to get another locomotive running first," Kevin said. "It won't be for another week or so. So your guess is as good as mine."

"What about the phone system?"

"Crosby is going great guns on that. He figured out a way to use some of the old switching gear." Kevin spat on the ground. "I'm surprised it still works. I guess they built the equipment to last. His biggest problem is training people to do the hook-ups. Communications between here and Defiance, and points in between are fine. A cell phone system is beyond our current capabilities."

Good, Taylor thought. *Maybe that'll prevent any more problems in the small towns. Those greedy business-types almost wrecked our federation.* "Anything else I should know?"

"Well," Kevin said. "Did you know the foundry in Defiance is now making four-inch caliber field guns?"

"Field guns?" Taylor raised his eyebrows. For a moment he had a vision of modern artillery. "With smokeless powder?"

"Oh, no." Kevin raised his hands. "They use black powder. They're breech-loading single shot cannon with rifled barrels. The breech-loading feature speeds up swabbing and reloading. They're accurate up to a range of about a mile. They'll be sending six of them on the campaign against the Alliance," he said. "That'll surprise the Hell out of them."

Yeah, thought Taylor. *Just like Billy's improvised cannon surprised and killed Bray Grant and his men. We seem to have a talent for killing. It's the nature of our species.* "I suppose you're right." He stared down the track as the train disappeared from sight. "Thanks for the update."

Kevin extended his hand. "Thanks for putting in a good word for me with the Council."

"Anytime," Taylor said. He headed back toward the university. *Now,* he thought. *Here comes the difficult part. It was time to see Joyce.*

CHAPTER FIFTEEN

"Joyce?" Taylor put his head around the edge of the doorway to her office. "Can I talk with you?"

Joyce's head rose sharply. "Taylor. What d'you want?" She put a pen down on a desk cluttered with paper and reference books. Worry etched lines in her forehead and the circles beneath her eyes were dark. She ran fingers through her tangled hair. It was dull and untidy.

"I came to see you. I came to apologize."

Joyce leaned back in her chair to stare at him. "Isn't it a bit late for that?" The corners of her mouth turned downward.

"I hope not." Taylor stepped into the office and carefully closed the door. He took off his jacket and placed it on the chair alongside Joyce's desk. He turned his head to look at her directly. "I guess I said some things that just came out wrong." He took a deep breath. "Look, I'm sorry about what I said." He sighed. *Oh, Lord*, he thought, *this isn't coming out right, either.* "Please, try to understand."

"Understand? Maybe you should try to understand I don't like being treated like a one-night stand." She stood up and paced to the opposite side of the desk. "You send me love letters and then won't see me." Her face became pale. "You sleep with me, then avoid me."

"I wasn't avoiding you."

"Oh, really? Well, that's what it seems like when you don't show up three times in a row. Then you give me crap about duty. What do you think I am? An idiot?" She turned her back and folded her arms on her chest. She sniffed.

Taylor took a deep breath. He stood and walked to the window to stare out at the campus.

The grass had become lush and green. The maple trees' blossoms gave them a reddish cast. People walked along the paths, gesturing animatedly, with smiling faces.

They seem so happy, and in here, we're so unhappy. He turned back to the room. Almost absently he noted it lacked its usual order. Papers were piled up, even on the floor. *Billy was right*, he thought. *She isn't getting her work out.* "I deserved that. I should've been more considerate."

Joyce stood on the opposite side of the room and blew her nose. Tears trickled down her cheeks. "Oh, Taylor, what happened? I thought we had something special. When you didn't show up, I felt used, discarded."

Age, Taylor thought. *That should give me perspective. What do I do about this?* For an instant, he was tempted by the thought he had to solve the problem with Joyce for the benefit of the Clan, because she was a critical part of the team working on the fusion reactor.

How can I be so cynical? Is that what I've become? He looked at her. The memory of what he felt when he was with her came back, almost overwhelming him, like something long ago remembered. *Oh, God, I do love her.* "Joyce, you are special to me."

"Is that right?" Her voice faltered. "Then why do you treat me this way?" Her lower lip quivered. "Is it because you have to sneak out to see me, so that Noelle doesn't know about me? Or is it because I'm not good enough for your friends?" She still had her arms crossed in front of her.

Annoyance surged through Taylor. "Oh, for God's sake, it's not that. It was my stupid sense of duty that got in the way. There isn't anyone else." He moved to her and gently held her by the elbows. His fears rose to the surface.

"Look," he said softly. "I'm twenty years older than you. I worry ..." he hesitated, afraid of what was happening. *I'm losing her.* It was almost like staring into the face of death. "No," he said slowly and looked into her eyes. "Being with you is like a dream fulfilled." He took a deep breath. "You awakened feelings within me that have been absent for years. Feelings I never dared hope to have again." He released his grip on her elbows. "I didn't know how to handle them ... still don't."

He turned away. "I let Clan business become the reason I didn't see you. It wasn't an excuse. It was a fact." He took a deep breath and turned away. "God, I was stupid, insensitive." He turned back to Joyce. "Do you understand now? I'm sorry." He hesitated. *I love her, but I'm afraid to face it.*

"If you'll give me a chance, I'll show you how I feel about you." He dropped his hands to his side and sagged, deflated. He waited for her to speak.

Joyce said nothing.

He stared at the floor. Hope began to drain away. He felt his throat constrict and he tried to swallow.

Joyce was completely motionless, her face white. A tear trickled down her cheek. Her eyes were wide, staring. "Well, after all that, how do you feel about me?" She bit her lip. "Well?"

Taylor took a deep breath and held it. *It's now or never*, he thought. "I love you." He exhaled and waited.

Joyce cocked her head and looked at him. "Do you?"

"Yes, I do. I love you."

Joyce looked up. Her eyes were shining. "Really?" She took a couple of hesitant steps toward him.

Taylor raised his arms and stepped forward. "I do."

Joyce wrapped her arms around him and laid her head on his chest and quietly sobbed. She sniffled. "I missed you. I was so afraid I'd never be with you again."

Taylor stroked her hair. "Joyce, I missed you, too. I feel like a fool for treating you the way I did. I've put the Clan first for so long I let it come between us. I won't do that again." He felt her tears through his shirt.

She pushed him away to arm's length. "Okay, there's something you've been evasive about from the beginning, we've got to get it straightened out right now."

"What's that?"

"What exactly is your relationship with Noelle?"

"Since we first ..." Taylor hesitated. "Made love, I have not been intimate with Noelle."

"You are sleeping with her. I knew it." Joyce pushed him away and pounded him on the chest. "You bastard. You wouldn't tell me." Anger stormed across her face.

Taylor caught her hand as she tried to hit him again.

"You prick, you two-timing prick."

"Listen, please listen." He pulled her close and found she offered little resistance. "I've never asked you about who you've been with and I don't want to know. Understand?"

"It's different with her. She lives with you."

"True."

"I'll always think she'll try to sleep with you when you go home."

Taylor sighed. "Well, there's only one way to solve this problem. Will you have supper with me tonight?"

"How'll that solve the problem?"

"We'll have supper at my home." Taylor raised his eyebrows. "Bring your overnight bag. That'll solve the problem."

A smile slowly grew on Joyce's face. "I like it."

ꝏ

"Oh." Noelle's eyes widened in recognition. "Please, come in." She opened the door wide and stepped aside to let Joyce step into the cool, dim hallway.

"Thank you, Mrs. Sutton." Joyce switched the overnight bag from one hand to another. "Is Mr. MacPherson in?"

"He stepped out for a moment, but he said he was expecting you." Noelle's eyebrows arched as she glanced at the bag. "Would you come this way, please?"

She gestured toward a small room just off the foyer. Inside, the walls were lined with bookshelves. Two leather armchairs, shiny with wear, faced the door. One had its back toward a tall window in the sun and the other was in a corner. A Persian Bijar rug covered the polished oak floor.

"May I take your bag?" A trace of a frown creased Noelle's brow. She crossed her arms.

"Certainly."

"I'll put it in the guest room. It's the first room to the left at the top of the stairs."

Joyce cleared her throat. "No, put it in Mr. MacPherson's bedroom. Thank you."

Noelle's eyes widened for a moment. She opened her mouth, and then shut it. She swallowed hard, picked up the bag and left.

Noelle returned moments later. "Can I get you anything?" her lips were drawn tight and her face was pale.

"Do you have herbal tea?" Joyce asked. "Cold."

As Noelle returned with a glass of tea, the front door opened and closed. Noelle held still, head cocked, listening.

Taylor paused at the doorway of the room, a smile appeared on his face as he looked in. "Ah, there you are," he said. "Have you been waiting long?"

"Just a minute or two." Joyce rose to her feet and offered her cheek to Taylor.

As Taylor kissed her, his eyes swiveled toward Noelle standing silently in the doorway to the kitchen. "Ah, Noelle, we'll be eating in the dining room," he said. "Alone." He put his arms around Joyce and hesitated. "Also, Ms. Vargas and I will be having breakfast in the dining room tomorrow."

Noelle's eyes widened and her mouth opened. She swallowed hard. "Certainly, of course." Her eyes flashed from Joyce then back to Taylor. Her face paled and she looked down. "Yes, of course." She turned quickly and left.

"Well, fancy that." Joyce chuckled. "You all but told her you plan to sleep with me tonight. And then you told her she wouldn't be eating with us. That was rude." She laughed. "She'll probably poison you one of these days."

"Possibly," Taylor said. "D'you think she got the message?" He sat in the chair by the window.

Joyce dropped into Taylor's lap and put her arms around his neck. "Taylor, you're a bastard, but I love you." She kissed him on the lips and then laid her head on his shoulder. "In a way, I'm sorry for her." Joyce sat upright and looked at him. "Did you ever love her?"

"No," Taylor said without hesitation. "Let me tell you a story," he said.

He related how Fred and Maria Del Corso had tried to fix him up with Noelle and how he had come to realize both he and Noelle had gotten what they wanted from the relationship: He got a housekeeper and she got a secure place to raise her child.

As he finished the story, Noelle knocked on the door and announced in a voice dripping with ice, "Supper is ready."

CHAPTER SIXTEEN

The rhythm of the train had lulled Chris Kucinski to sleep. When she woke, she didn't know where she was for a moment. The train had left just before first light and she was tired from the early start and the mobilization effort of the previous days. "What time is it?" she asked. "Where are we?"

Elroy Stanek peered out of the opening in the boxcar door. "It's about eight o'clock," he spoke loudly over the clacking of the steel wheels on the rails. "We've just passed through Bucyrus. We picked up some volunteers."

The boxcar swayed from side to side. Distantly, a diesel engine rumbled. A draft from the door freshened the air.

"Volunteers?" Chris wasn't fully awake.

"Yes, we stopped for water and this group showed up." Elroy smiled. "We thought it was trouble." He paused to swat away a fly. "It turned out to be the volunteer contingent from the Central Ohio Union folks. Exactly as promised."

The Clan's relationship with the people from Mansfield, the Central Ohio Union, had been long-standing, dating back to the days just after the Collapse. The Clan had traded goods and provided assistance to the small communities as they got back on their feet during those difficult days. When the Clan had sought the right of passage, the Union had quickly agreed, and offered a contingent of troops.

As the cobwebs from her sleep cleared, Chris recalled the composition of her forces. *They should be enough*, she thought. *Two trainloads of troops and horses—about a thousand soldiers. And*, she calculated. *The trains would return with more provisions and material within the day. Yes, as long as the Alliance hasn't caught wind of this expedition, we should catch them by surprise.*

A part of the deal with the Central Ohio Union was a gift of two hundred black powder rifles—those made in the electrified factories of Defiance. The rifled field guns would not be revealed until used in the coming attack.

Chris worried the train might be ambushed, but Captain Kerr had assured her his scouts had kept the track under constant surveillance and operated its switchgear. Any word of movement by Alliance troops would reach them via a newly activated phone link. Thankfully, there was no sign of that.

"It'll be another hour before we reach the outskirts of Ada," Elroy said. "This train sure beats traveling on foot. Damn sight quicker, too."

"Yes," Chris said absently. *The horses will be fresh, too. Ada will be the first*, she thought. *Kerr had reported it had less than two hundred troops stationed there. Still, better to send in a couple of field guns to get it over quickly, with a minimum of casualties.*

The swaying became more pronounced and the train slowed. Outside, the land was flat and overgrown, almost a prairie. In the distance was a farmhouse—a rare sight in this empty land—which was slowly reverting to native growth. Inside the boxcar the temperature rose from the sun's heat. A door rattled open and air flowed in, fresh and cooling.

This, Chris thought, *is the way to travel.*

Outside, the train clattered through a cluster of red brick buildings with broken windows. "This was the town of Dunkirk," Elroy looked up from a tattered map. Weed-choked streets, empty buildings, a door or two swaying in the wind, was all that remained. "We're only eight or so miles from Ada."

"Send word to the gun crews to be on the alert," Chris ordered. "The closer we get, the greater the danger."

"Yes, ma'am." Elroy slipped into a more formal manner with the order. He sent a messenger forward to the front of the locomotive where a squad of soldiers armed with muzzle-loading rifles guarded the two field guns mounted on a flatbed carriage. If there was trouble, they would buy time until the remainder of the soldiers could be mobilized.

The rumble of the diesel engine faded. The train coasted onward, with the rhythmic clacking of steel wheels on steel rail now the only sound. The train lost speed as it coasted over flat, open fields. Much of the area showed signs of emerging forest, interspersed with patches under plow. Only occasionally did a farm building come into sight. Ahead, on the horizon, arose two water towers and a grain elevator over a cluster of brick buildings. The train's brakes squealed as it slowed down.

They had arrived.

CHAPTER SEVENTEEN

The train halted at the road crossing a half-mile east of Ada. The boxcars clanked one by one into stillness.

Weeds sprouted through numerous cracks in the crumbling asphalt road. To the north, a line of young willows marked the location of a ditch called Grass Creek. Even though the sun had not reached its zenith, it was already warm.

Across an open field dotted with scrubby vegetation to the west, lay the town. The two rusty water towers still had faint lettering spelling out Ada. The old grain elevator, which rose above the two- and three-story buildings dominating the small town, had a shack perched on top.

"Hyah," a Horse Soldier called as he cracked a whip.

A gun carriage's wheels rumbled. Pulleys squealed as a team of horses dragged the last field gun off a railroad flatcar. The gun carriage hit the ground with a thump.

"Whoa," a teamster yelled. As the horses halted, he removed the restraining lines and waved to the waiting officers.

Each gun had a six-foot black steel barrel perched on a wooden axle that lay between two five-foot diameter metal spoke wheels. Six horses pulled each gun carriage and a sturdy high-wheeled cart with ammunition and cleaning supplies. The crews lined up four of the guns and rolled them toward the assembled battle groups.

The last of the horses returned from the creek, water dripping from their muzzles. The brown-clad Horse Soldiers stood waiting for orders. Most carried the recurve bow that had served the Clan so well for over a generation, while the foot militia held muzzle-loading rifles.

Elroy Stanek climbed into the saddle and held up his hand. It grew quiet except for the rattle of tackle and horses nickering. "Group A and B, go north to old Highway 81, then head west into town," he yelled. "Group C and D, head south to the first two roads west and take them into Ada." He looked over the assembled warriors. "Group E and the Union volunteers, take the railroad track into Ada. Remember, don't harm the university on the south side of town."

He raised his hand. "Okay, move 'em out!" he called.

Earlier, a group of scouts and a platoon of mounted warriors had ridden out to the roads on the west side of Ada leading to Lima to ensure no one got out.

The brown-clad soldiers climbed on their horses, each with a foot militia mounted behind. Two battle groups were Horse Soldiers; the rest were foot militia, with the field guns at the rear. Doubled-up, the horse-mounted forces moved at a walking pace as they divided into streams.

At first, they flowed like heavy clots of molasses, thinning into thin brown strands. They moved with the melody of hooves thudding on soft ground and the jingle-jangle of tackle.

The rear locomotive rumbled and its wheels squealed, protesting against the track. As it backed up, its line of boxcars banged and clanked, gathering speed to disappear down the track. The second train remained, engine idling.

Commander Chris Kucinski led a battle group into Ada along the railroad track, with a line of workmen behind inspecting the rail bed. The locomotive followed, barely moving. As the battle group crossed over the creek, several dozen men with long-barreled guns emerged from behind two large storage tanks two hundred yards down the track and opened fire.

The Clan soldiers and their allies hit the ground.

Chris used her binoculars to examine the troops ahead. "Bring up the rifles. Give them a taste of our marksmanship."

A group of militia moved forward with their long-range and

highly accurate rifles. After several volleys, the defenders retreated to the cover of two large brick buildings overlooking the railroad tracks like the walls of a canyon.

The Clan advanced to the tanks. They were a part of an old wastewater treatment plant. Through the glasses, Chris examined the brick buildings. "Mr. Stanek," she called.

"Yes, Commander Kucinski?" Elroy said.

"Hold up the advance, I want to try something." She turned in her saddle and beckoned to a messenger. Blond whiskers were just starting to show on his chin and his bright blue eyes were wide with anticipation. "You, blondie, come here," she called. "Let's see if we can cut this short."

The messenger spurred his horse forward and reined it in sharply as he drew alongside Chris. "Yes, ma'am." He saluted.

"Take a white flag and go to those men." She pointed at the brick buildings, which were now quiet. "Offer them an honorable surrender—they can keep their guns and there'll be no looting." She made the messenger repeat the message twice before instructing him to advance.

"I hope this works," Chris said as the messenger walked his horse forward, holding a white flag up high.

The messenger advanced to within twenty yards of the buildings. As he started to dismount, a shot rang out. The messenger collapsed to the ground. His horse reared, backed up, then galloped off. The boy's body lay still.

"Fools," Chris said. "Stupid bloody-minded fools."

She turned in the saddle and pointed to the group of messengers. When she had their attention, she beckoned to a slender young woman and a freckled-faced young man standing together.

They advanced, faces white, lips quivering.

She pointed to the woman. "Take a message to our group A and B on the north side. You." She pointed to the man. "Go to group C and D on the south side of this town." She didn't have time to go through her message more than once before waving them off. "Now, Mr. Stanek, show me what your gunners can do."

Elroy hurried over to the field guns.

The gun crews unharnessed the horses from each gun and led them away. The crew rotated the guns to face the buildings. Within five minutes, the gun crews stood at attention alongside the field pieces. "Ready, sir."

"Fire at will," Elroy called.

The first gun boomed. A corner of one building exploded in dust. The second gun fired. More building crumbled down, scattering bricks and glass.

"Advance," the gun crew chief called.

The gun crews moved the guns forward about twenty yards. A squad of militia moved along with them. As soon as the guns stopped, the crew swarmed over them, rotating the rolling-block breech open and ramming a long swab up the barrels. In a dance-like motion, as soon as a swab was withdrawn, one man pushed in a stubby cylinder filled with metal balls and another followed with a bag of black powder. Two men rotated the breech plug into position and dogged it shut.

While this took place, the gun crew chief adjusted the guns' aim. "Ready," he called.

"Fire in the hole."

The field pieces boomed, followed by a whistling sound. Puffs of dust appeared on the buildings' walls and on the ground where Ada's defenders were gathered. Someone started to scream.

"Advance," called the gun crew chief. They moved up again.

A cloud of smoke erupted from a third story window on the building on the left. It was accompanied by the sound of gunfire. A gun crewmember fell to the ground moaning.

The crews reloaded their guns and raised one gun to aim at the window. The crew huddled behind the gun, waiting.

"Fire in the hole," the gun chief called.

The artillery piece boomed.

An upper part of the building exploded in a shower of dust. Masonry and bodies cascaded down onto the railroad tracks. People ran, barely visible through the dust and smoke. The second gun boomed, followed by the whistling sound of the flying metal shot. For an instant, no shots sounded. After that instance of quiet came the sound of screams. Again, shots rang out.

"I think they're retreating." Elroy lowered his binoculars and pointed. "They're heading into town." He turned toward the waiting warriors. "Platoons one and two, leapfrog advance."

The soldiers spread out into two parallel lines and ran for the smoking buildings. Beyond the buildings, the town was a maze of low brick structures. They paused and reformed. The leading group advanced, scurrying from doorway to doorway while their comrades provided covering fire. Once into position, they repeated the procedure and continued to advance. In the meantime, the artillery pieces fired at more distant targets.

From the west came a clatter of gunfire followed by the dull thud of the field guns. Smoke rose from the direction of the west side of the town. Small arm fire intensified.

"Damn," Chris said. "I wish those fools had taken my offer."

A horse whinnied loudly and she glanced in that direction.

A lathered horse lowered its head as a dust-covered man clad in brown slid off the saddle. "Beg yer pardon, ma'am," he wheezed. "Captain Sabich of the A and B battle groups sent me."

Chris beckoned an aide. "Get water for this man and horse," she said. "Well," she asked. "What is it?"

"Captain Sabich said to tell you our group has joined up with elements of the D and E groups." The dusty man gulped down some water from a leather bag. "We've got 'em bottled-up in the town. The scouts told Captain Sabich they don't believe any got away."

"Yes?" Chris asked.

"A group tried to break out, but them big field guns stopped them." The man grinned. "Chopped 'em up but good."

Right, Sabich the "Savage" would be good at that, thought Chris. *We're chopping up human beings when aliens are the real enemy. That poor messenger boy was dead when we got to him. How many will die before this is over? Too many.*

"All right. Return to your unit." She nodded for him to leave.

"Thank you, ma'am." The dusty man backed away, pulling on his horse's bridle.

Chris turned and caught Stanek's eye. "How's the rail crew doing?" she asked.

"They stopped when they got within the city limits," Elroy said. "They're afraid of an ambush."

"Keep 'em moving. Our people have swept the east side. We need the track ready for the Lima operation."

ॐ

By mid-afternoon, a dense cloud of black smoke rose from the commercial block in the center of Ada. A steady stream of people with white flags exited the town, surrendering as individuals. A small group held out at the grain elevator on the west side of Ada where the fighting concentrated. Whenever the Clan's soldiers encountered a strong resistance point, they brought up the field artillery and broke it open. They continued to advance, driving the remaining defenders into a tiny salient.

So far, Chris thought, *our casualties are light. Ten dead and thirty injured. I guess the Alliance forces have ten times that number. God,* she thought. *What a mess. We're slaughtering them and they still fight on.* Even as that thought crossed her mind, the guns grew quiet.

A foot messenger ran up, panting. "Commander Kucinski," he called. "The leader of the Alliance garrison is dead." The messenger paused to catch his breath. "His second-in-command has just surrendered the remaining Alliance forces."

"Thank you." Chris nodded. He must have been some hard-ass trying to make a name for himself.

She mounted her horse and beckoned to Stanek. "Make sure the cavalry screen stays on the roads between here and Lima. Second, get the train into town and onto a siding." She had scheduled a second train for early tomorrow. *It will bring supplies and more troops— former Fed guards,* she thought. *And damn good soldiers, too. Five more battle groups, some nine hundred more foot militia, along with five more artillery pieces. Should be enough,* she thought. *It has to be.*

CHAPTER EIGHTEEN

"What d'you mean?" Duncan Boggs asked. He had been in conference with his staff when a messenger burst in. "Ada's been captured?" His thin lips twisted tightly. "You say it's the Clan?" he said.

Over half of the Alliance's forces were in Dupont, ready to move out the next day for their attack on Defiance. "You sure?" He had not expected a Clan move from the east. He'd been sure the Central Ohio Union had no stomach for a war with him.

Boggs rose and put his hands on the highly polished table to lean forward and stare at the messenger. Six men in dark blue military uniforms at the table rose as well. "Well?"

"Yes, sir, Mr. Boggs." The messenger panted, swaying on his feet. Blood stained the side of his face and his clothes were caked with mud. "I saw at least two hundred of them. There was probably more. They just showed up out of nowhere and attacked us. They had big guns that smashed buildings." He caught his breath. "It was horrible. Colonel Smith kept fighting until he was killed. Then Lieutenant Schmiederer surrendered."

"Schmiederer surrendered?" Boggs's eyes narrowed. "He gave up to the Clan?" Most of the raiding parties he'd sent into the former Fed—now part of the Clan—had easy victories. Sure, one party got ambushed during a victory celebration, but those things happened.

The fact many farmers from the old Fed had joined their forces made him believe the Clan was divided and weak. "After we crush these invaders, Schmiederer will regret it to his dying day. And it won't be long coming."

Duncan Boggs turned to his officers. "I want a full mobilization of our remaining forces," he said. "I want to know what size force attacked Ada." He paused. "Our expedition to liberate Defiance will go forward on schedule. If the Clan has sent its forces down here, they can't be in Defiance. Make sure the crew in the watchtower is on their toes. This may be just the break we need. Let Beauvoir know what's going on." He sat down heavily. "I want his thinking on the situation." He pointed. "Jones, take care of it."

"Yes, sir." Jones was a younger officer who moved quickly, almost knocking his chair over. "I'll get messengers under way immediately."

"Get scouts into Ada. I want good information on the size of this raiding party. That is, if they're still there." Boggs sniffed, as though something smelled bad. "Even if Lima is impregnable, I always want to know what I'm facing."

"Beggin' your pardon, sir," the messenger said. "The Clan has horse-mounted patrols out on the west side of Ada, a lot of them. I had to hide a half dozen times."

Boggs stared at him. He'd heard how the Clan defeated the Feds but believed it was due to having crazy Billy Potato as its leader. *Sure, their horse-mounted soldiers were good, but my men are better. Still, it doesn't pay to take unnecessary risks.*

"Put the city on war footing," he said. "Prepare the positions along I-75."

Since the Clan's attack on Lima ten years ago, Boggs had built defenses around Lima to prevent such a thing from happening again. The old interstate highway that ran north-south on the east side of Lima now had a ten-foot high raised embankment tied into the Ottawa River fortifications and provided a strong defensive perimeter. He'd learned his lesson from an earlier attack and based his defensive strategy on it.

"I want to know the strength of this raiding force. In the meantime, I want security doubled. Send more men to the watchtower."

He pointed toward the lookout post on top of the old water tower by the reservoir on the east side of Lima. "No surprises in the middle of the night. Got it?"

"Yes, sir," the blue-clad men said in a chorus.

CHAPTER NINETEEN

Duncan Boggs squinted into the rising sun, staring at the dark stain on the horizon. It wasn't on east on Highway 81 from Ada—it was in the fields south of the road. He raised the binoculars again. From his vantage point on the lookout tower on top of the Lima General Hospital, he could see both the Ottawa River and the I-75 Highway. The dark stain on the horizon moved closer toward Lima.

"It's the fuckin' Clan," Boggs said. "Make sure all the gates are double-barred."

Less than one-third of the scouts sent out the previous day had returned; those that did were pursued to the edge of the city. None had discovered the size of the Clan's force.

Sunlight reflected off the ponds that once were Lima's reservoirs. Those ponds would make the Clan's force come between them and the river.

Maybe we could trap them there, he thought. *Where they couldn't use their cavalry. Maybe they'd make a mistake.*

"Send two regiments north of the river, parallel to the railroad tracks to get behind the Clan's forces," Boggs said. *If that force could drive the Clan against the perimeter, they'd be crushed.*

The wall on top of Interstate-75 had grown from a single row of concrete highway barriers to a ten-foot-high wall to protect Lima from attacks. Even after deploying the regiments, he still had over five hundred troops manning the city's defenses.

"Sir." A scout staggered up, panting. "The Clan's forces are at least eight hundred to a thousand warriors, sir."

"Shit," Boggs said. "It means they've brought most of their forces. There won't be many defending Defiance." An idea began to take shape. "Jones, recall those regiments just sent out."

"Yes, sir." Jones turned to leave.

"When the regiments get back, prepare them for a forced march to Dupont to join-up with Beauvoir's group."

"What about the Clan raid?"

"They won't take Lima," Boggs said. "I have as many soldiers as they have warriors." He smiled. "Cavalry isn't worth a damn against a high wall."

"Yes, sir."

"Get moving." Boggs pointed to the regiments moving east. "Get my soldiers back before they make contact."

ৎ

"Have you cordoned off the city?" Commander Chris Kucinski stared through her binoculars at Lima. It was a walled city bristling with defenses. All trees within a half-mile of its walls had been removed.

A month ago, she thought. *No, only a week ago, it would have been foolish to attack such a stronghold. With our new artillery, we should be inside by the end of the day. I pray it proves to be true. Maybe we can even get them to surrender and avoid a bloodbath.*

"Yes, Commander," Elroy said. "Cavalry's in position on the main roads out of town with artillery to make it binding. The areas between the roads are under patrol."

"Good." Chris's objective was to get the majority of the Alliance forces to surrender.

"I don't figure the Alliance foot soldiers will want to tangle with the roadblocks once they get a taste of our artillery." He liked using field guns against massed formations.

"Sometimes, Elroy, you're a little too bloody-minded." Chris raised the binoculars again to stare at the main east entrance to Lima. "Yes, that's where we'll go in."

The east entrance to Lima was a road that went under the old interstate highway. It had an opening that was fifteen feet high with two doors that came together in the center. The gate was made from white oak and was studded with steel bolt-heads. Brickwork filled the rest of the opening around the gate.

Chris pointed at the entrance. "Move the artillery up. Use it to reduce the defenses on both sides of the gate."

Fifteen minutes later the artillery advanced to within three hundred yards of the main entrance and took up positions. Each time a field gun fired, a section of the wall on top of the old highway shattered. The artillerymen targeted the wall above the entrance—an old overpass—and expanded outwards until about a hundred yards of wall on each side of the gate was down. It was just past nine o'clock.

"Cease fire," the gun chief said. He was a stocky, red-faced man with a loud voice. Some claimed he yelled a lot because he was partly deaf from firing the big guns; some said he just liked the sound of his own voice. "Move the guns forward."

Teams of militia pushed the artillery pieces closer to the gate. Other militia brought ammunition carts forward. The field guns took up positions on both sides of the road about one hundred yards from the main entrance. Each field gun had a framework covered with thick rough-sawn planks, behind which the gun crew crouched.

So far, the gate was untouched.

Gun crews raised the barrels of three of the five field guns to cover the remnants of the wall above the entrance. The two remaining guns aimed at the gate and waited for the order to fire.

"Load explosive rounds," the gun chief called.

The gun crew brought forward rounds wrapped in red cloth and carefully inserted them into the breeches of the two guns aimed at the wooden gate. Once the breeches clanked closed, the crews stepped clear of the carriage.

"Ready on the right," called one crew.

"Ready on the left."

"Fire," the gun chief yelled.

As the two guns boomed, they recoiled backward almost simultaneously. Explosions shook the wooden gate. When the smoke cleared, two sections of the doors were splintered but still intact.

"Again," the gun chief yelled.

The gun crews swabbed the guns' barrels, pushed in the explosive projectiles and their bags of black powder. They checked the aim and stood back.

"Fire."

The guns boomed. A hole appeared in one of the doors, a rosette of pale, splintered wood from which stamens of twisted metal rods protruded.

The gun chief shouted at the gun crews who repeated their dance. Two minutes later, the guns fired again. More holes appeared. One of the doors developed a list.

It took the artillery fifteen minutes to pound the doors into a mass of splinters and twisted metal. They shifted to the brickwork around their opening.

Within an hour, the east gate and underpass into Lima had become a four-foot high mound of rubble. When the defenders tried to pick off the artillery crew with both gun and bow, the three field pieces covering the highway responded with volleys of metal scrap.

The snipers' fire declined.

"Move 'em up," the gun chief yelled.

The artillerymen dragged two guns forward to within thirty yards from the opening and aimed each gun diagonally into the opening. From that position, they covered the whole area under the overpass.

From hiding places amid the rubble of the destroyed entrance, defenders fired sporadically at the artillery pieces.

"Load canister shot," the gun chief called.

The artillery pieces fired. The canisters struck the ceiling of the overpass and exploded, spraying hundreds of pieces of metal throughout the confined area of the overpass.

Before the smoke cleared, a Clan battle group advanced into the overpass. Several shots rang out. A platoon leader stepped out of the overpass and beckoned. A group of militia carrying shovels ran forward and began digging into the rubble, clearing a path for the artillery pieces.

"Well." Elroy lowered his binoculars. "We're inside Lima and it isn't even noon."

"We're not really inside until we get the artillery in place. Only then can we ask for their surrender." She glanced to the north and frowned. She raised the field glass and stared for a moment. "Take a look." She pointed north.

Elroy refocused his binoculars and stared in the direction indicated. "It looks like a squad of warriors with a prisoner," he said after a moment. "I wonder what prisoner would be important enough to bring back."

"Meantime," Chris said. "Make sure you get artillery on top of the overpass so we can target everything in Lima. Then, we'll ask them to surrender."

A platoon rode up with the prisoner within their midst. "Commander Kucinski," the platoon leader called.

The warriors were streaked with sweat and dust. The horses' flanks were wet with sweat and foam dripped from their mouths. "We caught this man on his way out of Lima. He was carrying this." He handed Chris a sheet of paper. "Captain Sabich thought it was important enough for you to see."

"You." Chris pointed to an aide. "Get water for these men and their horses."

As she read the words on the sheet of paper, her eyebrows knitted. She re-read its contents and then stared into the distance. "So, Boggs has an army on the way to Defiance." She handed the sheet of paper to Elroy. "We have to deal with that, too."

Chris approached the prisoner, who was barely a teenager. Blood trickled from his scalp and his left arm dangled limply at his side. Tear streaks lined his face and his lower lip trembled.

I hate doing this, she thought. *But anything to save lives.* "Son," she said in her most motherly fashion. "You're safe with me now. Why don't you and I have a little chat?" She smiled and led the prisoner aside. She glanced up to see the platoon leader still sitting stiffly in his horse, at a position of attention. She recognized him—he was a friend of her son, Stephan Stolz.

"Thanks, Stolz," she said. "Take care of your horses, then report back." *A leader-candidate getting his military credentials*, she thought. *I pray he doesn't get hurt.*

"Thank you, Commander." Stolz nodded his head. He raised the reins and guided his horse away.

Chris smiled at the prisoner. "Where were we?" She forced a smile. "Oh, yes. You're from Lima, right?"

The smooth-faced boy wiped his tears and nodded. "Yes."

"What's your name?" She put her arm around him.

"Charlie Holman." His lip quivered.

"Charlie, I'm Ms. Kucinski, and the first thing we have to do is get your wounds treated." She beckoned to an aid. "Get a medic over here for this lad."

"Yes, ma'am."

"Now." She put her arm around his shoulder and gently patted his back. "While we wait for the medic, why don't you tell me about Lima? Where you live, what goes on there, and so forth." She smiled. "Would you like something to drink? How about some sassafras tea?"

The blond-headed boy's lower lip quivered as he nodded. "Yes, please," he said. "I live on the west side of Lima ..."

After ten minutes, he had given Chris the information she sought. "I'll see you get back to your family after this is all over. Now, Charlie, don't you worry, everything will be all right." She motioned to the medic. "Take Charlie here and patch him up. Make sure he's safe."

"Yes, Commander," the medic said.

She beckoned to Elroy. "I think we can defeat the entire Alliance in the next couple of days if everything goes right," she said. "This is what we must do." She explained her plan.

CHAPTER TWENTY

Duncan Boggs stared out of the window. A column of smoke rose in the direction of the east gate. The Clan's big guns were silent. The rattle of rifle fire had taken over. "What's going on? Why did they stop firing?"

"Sir, they broke through the east gate," Captain Jones said. "We couldn't stop them. They used some kind of explosive within the confines of the gate. We lost sixty men in there."

Jones was in his early thirties, a tall well-proportioned man. His blond hair hung in limp straggles. Rivulets of sweat cut channels through the dust on his face. His blue uniform hung wrinkled and damp on his stooped frame.

"I moved men into the buildings opposite the gate and sent more along the embankment wall. But those damn guns, the big ones, are killing us."

"How did they get through the gate?" Boggs asked. "It's over a foot of seasoned white oak. How could anything get through that?"

He was sure their defenses were impregnable—he'd spent the last ten years making them that way. Now this officer was telling him the Clan had broken through in less than a half-day? From somewhere in the distance came a thud—the artillery had started again.

"It doesn't matter," Jones said. "They're through. Now they're in the city. They're chewing us to pieces. I don't know how to stop them." He shook his head in despair.

"You're relieved of command," Boggs said. "I can see you don't have what it takes to fight a battle." He turned and strode toward the door. "I'm taking control."

Jones sagged further and took a deep breath. "Believe me, we don't have a defense against those big guns—"

"Shut up," Boggs yelled. He put his head out the door. "Courier," he called.

"Yes, sir," said a lean, rangy young man.

"Take this message to Beauvoir in Dupont." Boggs scribbled on a piece of paper. "Tell him we need his troops to relieve us, and right away. Ride as hard as you can. Get this to him as soon as possible."

"Yes, sir." The courier saluted, turned, and ran down the hall. Before he reached the end of the hall, something flashed brightly and exploded. The blast blew out the windows. Masonry rained down and dust billowed, filling the air.

"What the Hell was that?" Boggs asked.

"That, sir." Jones rose and dusted himself off. "Was one of those big guns I was telling you about."

Just as he finished, another explosion rocked the building. Part of the ceiling collapsed. More dust filled the corridor. Someone screamed. There was a crash. The screams abruptly stopped.

Boggs staggered to the window, coughing and gasping for fresh air. In the distance, a group of men clustered around two dark objects on the embankment near the east gate caught his attention. "What the Hell's going on?"

Jones poked his head out of the window. Blood trickled from his head. Dust covered his face. He stared and sighed. "Those," he said, "are the Clan's big guns."

As he spoke, the gun fired, puffing out a cloud of gray smoke. At almost the same time, the world around them exploded.

In the instant before he died, Boggs saw the brightest flash of light in the world.

૨

Chris accepted the surrender of Lima from a badly frightened young officer who had difficulty believing he was now the highest-ranking member of General Boggs's staff. When the Clan artillery had bombarded the old hospital the Alliance used as its military head-quarters, no one had known most of the senior officers were still inside. An hour later, resistance was reduced to isolated pockets. The remaining forces gave up soon as the artillery was brought up.

"Elroy, your men did well," Chris said.

"Not my men," Elroy said. "They're under your command."

"We now control Lima," she said. "Now we have to deal with the other problem. How much action did the cavalry see?"

"Sabich." Elroy beckoned to the ranking officer of the Horse Soldiers. "Commander Kucinski would like to know how much action your cavalry saw."

"Commander." Captain Sabich nodded his head in acknowl-edgment.

He was a tall, muscular man with dark hair sprinkled with a trace of gray. He had a beard and a long face that looked like it would crack if forced to smile.

"There was an attempt at a break-out. A column of troops came out of Lima on the north road. We encouraged them to return with grapeshot. We pursued them right up to the north gate. Other than that, only a few people tried to leave. No real combat."

"Listen up. This is what needs to be done." Chris pointed to the map and explained their battle plans.

"It's two o'clock." Sabich stroked his beard. "If we move right away, I think we can do it."

"Good," Chris said. "I'm depending upon you."

Sabich's cavalry caught the Alliance armada floating down the Auglaize River at the village of Oakwood. To do that, they'd made a forty-mile forced march north to Oakwood. He left a trail of dead horses and men on foot, arriving with two-thirds of his original force fifteen minutes before the Alliance's armada floated down the river into the village.

He positioned two artillery pieces on the bridge where Highway 613 crossed over the Auglaize River. In the reflected moonlight, the boats drifted straight down toward the guns. At a range of one hundred yards, the artillery pieces opened fire. The surprise was complete. Less than one-third of the Alliance troops survived the ambush.

Missing from the casualties and prisoners was General Archie Beauvoir.

ૡ

Next morning, Sabich pushed north and caught the other half of the Alliance force as it attacked Defiance. The attackers were pinned between his cavalry and the city's artillery.

Sabich's men methodically slaughtered them. Only when the Alliance soldiers completely ceased shooting, did Sabich order a cease-fire. Almost half of the Alliance force died from the guns of Defiance and Sabich's battle groups.

When Sabich returned to Lima, he learned General Boggs and his command staff were dead. The battle at Lima, the ambush at Oakwood, and the massacre at Defiance had cut the military heart out of the Lima-Findlay Alliance.

ૡ

Taylor realized the Clan now controlled the northern half of Ohio— from the Indiana line to Pennsylvania.

It was just the first step. The aircraft Billy needed were further south—in Dayton—in the hands of Jamie "Pigseye" McFarland of the Columbus-Dayton Confederation.

CHAPTER TWENTY-ONE

"Captain Sabich," Ramsey said. "The Council of the Greater Clan congratulates you on your victory over the forces of the Lima-Findlay Alliance. Furthermore, the Council has passed a resolution promoting you to Commander of the seventh and eighth battle groups. Congratulations, Commander."

A rustle of voices went through the public section of the Council Chambers. They knew something was up, for Commander Kucinski had been commended for doing her job, but received no special honor or promotion.

The interior of the Council Chambers brightened and dimmed as puffy white clouds floated past. A breeze out of the northeast wafted through open windows. Even though the room was filled to overflowing, it was cool inside.

"You have also been chosen to garrison the territories of the former Lima-Findlay Alliance and guard the southern frontier against incursions from the Cee-Dee-Cee." The term "Cee-Dee-Cee" was commonly used within the Clan for the Columbus-Dayton Confederation that lay south of the Lima-Findlay Alliance territories. "The status of these territories is under study by the Council."

Now I understand, Taylor MacPherson thought. *They want to provoke an incident with the Confederation and Sabich the Savage is just the person to do it.*

Normally, Taylor was reluctant to promote military action; but in the case of the Cee-Dee-Cee, he felt it was justified. When Todd Sinkton had returned from his scouting expedition, he'd brought back vivid stories of semi-feudal conditions.

Furthermore, its leader, Jamie McFarland, would not meet with Clan emissaries to negotiate for any aircraft that might be at the old Air Force base.

"The next order of business is the third reading of the proposed merger of the Central Ohio Union with the Greater Clan." Sean Monahan raised his head, his reedy voice barely audible above the rustle of voices and shuffle of feet. "Their inclusion would be on the same basis as previous mergers, one of equals, with all property rights respected. If admitted, they shall elect four members to this Council, which is proportional to their population. However, they did request as a condition of joining the Clan, that transportation and communications be improved between Mansfield and Rocky River."

"That's reasonable," Ned Biehl said. "If we'd had better communications to the old Fed area earlier, we might have avoided some of the problems there."

"All well and good." Jon Beach struggled to his feet with the aid of a cane. "Are they willing to pay for it?"

Right, thought Taylor. *The people from the old Fed you previously tried to ban from Clan citizenship. Beach always seems to have the profit motive in mind.*

"Ah-um." Carver Washington cleared his throat. "As far as transport goes, seems to me we already have a pretty good railway line to Mansfield." He paused to clear his throat again. "As for the phone lines, isn't it in our own interest to know what's happening on the frontier?" He leaned forward to look at Ramsey. A trace of a smile crossed his dark brown face.

"Mr. Washington makes a good point," Ramsey said. "The merger of the Central Ohio Union with the Clan will add to our security. Their soldiers, while courageous and willing, are not as well trained or armed as ours. If they join us, and I hope they do, I'd make it my business to see their forces are brought up to Clan standards." He glanced at Beach as if expecting an argument.

In the public section, heads nodded in agreement with Ramsey's comments. Many had sons or husbands in the Clan's army and had an appreciation for what it took to be a Clan Horse Soldier. When no Elder spoke up immediately, a rustle of whispers swept the crowd in the public section.

"If there's no further discussion." Sean Monahan's eyes swung from side to side as he polled the Elders. "I call the question." He waited silently for an objection. "Shall the Central Ohio Union's application to merge with the Greater Clan, under the terms and conditions specified, be accepted? Those in favor raise their hand."

The public section became quiet. Eyes focused on the row of Elders sitting behind the long table on the elevated dais. One by one, seven hands rose.

"Those opposed?" In the silence, Monahan's thin voice easily reached the back of the room. Only Beach and Monahan voted against the measure.

"Thank you," Monahan said and wrote into the ledger. "The question is answered in the affirmative. The entity formerly known as the Central Ohio Union is now a part of the Greater Clan." He paused and stood. "I welcome the citizens of Mansfield and its surrounding areas into our democratic society."

ↄ

"When will I get electricity? These cockamamie portable generators drink fuel like mad and they're forever breaking down." Kevin O'Neil leaned across Joyce's desk, his smudged face close to hers.

"That question should be directed to distribution," Joyce said. "I believe Chip Wilson is the specialist in running power lines. My responsibility is to get generators running and provide power." She paused as she retrieved a file from her desk. "I don't believe we have excess capacity at this time."

Rain pattered on the windows of her office and water gurgled in the downspout outside. The office was large and tidy. Everything seemed to be in place. Her desk was clear except for two file folders and an engineering reference book. A cut-glass vase held a single red rose.

As O'Neil stepped back, his shoulders slumped. "We've got to do something." He sat down in the chair alongside the desk and put his head in his hands. "Why is it so difficult to get anything done anymore?"

Joyce leaned back in her chair to watch O'Neil. He had aged a lot in the last year. *Perhaps he's been working too hard. He doesn't blame me*, she realized. *He just wants help.* "Kevin," she said gently. "Why don't we talk to Taylor?"

"I thought he was out of the loop."

"Officially, yes." Joyce smiled. "He knows a lot of people and how to get things done. He still has a lot of power."

O'Neil rose slowly as though carrying a heavy weight. "D'you know where I can find him?" he asked.

Joyce rose and headed to the door. "Oh, yes. Follow me." She strode down the corridor, O'Neil in tow.

ॐ

"Well." Taylor leaned back in his chair. "I think the problem is two-fold. First, there are just not enough people who know how to run power lines. Second, the military aren't available as a source of labor at this time." He stared at Joyce and Kevin. *They were wet from the rain; they must have just come across campus.* "I'll talk to Ned Biehl on Council. He's a strong advocate for building infrastructure. Maybe he can shake something loose."

"We gotta do something." O'Neil sighed. "I just got another request from Sabich. He needs a locomotive to move a lot of materiel south. Problem is, all the easy-to-repair units were fixed and are in service. The only stuff that's left needs all kinds of parts."

"I see," Taylor said. "Your machine shop needs reliable power." *Yes,* he thought. *As soon as Kevin saw what the university craftsmen could do, he had to have his own machine shop and sent for machinists from Defiance to staff his locomotive repair facility.* "I believe I have to talk to Ramsey about your facility having reliable power and its contribution to our military strength."

"See?" Joyce had a wide smile as she nudged O'Neil on the arm. "I knew he would know what to do."

"Ms. Vargas," Taylor said. "They haven't said yes, yet." He paused for a moment. "Where do we stand with the fusion-powered generators?"

Joyce sighed. "A significant problem has cropped up." She crossed her legs. "We have the containment vessel, which isn't really a vessel. It's more of a combination of a magnetic and electric field containment system, which is pretty well worked out. Unfortunately, we're having trouble coordinating the electronic control and trapping system. At the expected high current flows, our switching gear is too massive and cumbersome." She sighed. "And too slow."

"So, there's no fusion-powered generation system coming soon." Taylor stared hard at Joyce. "Is that right?"

"That's correct."

Taylor pulled a tattered volume down from a bookshelf. "Let's see if there are any gas turbine generators nearby."

Joyce looked at O'Neil who shrugged.

"I thought so," Taylor said. "There are units all around here. Avon, Lorain, and some out in western Ohio." He made some notes on a sheet of paper. "Next, we need fuel." He stared briefly at the ceiling.

"We could get oil from Pennsylvania," O'Neil said.

"Too expensive for the volume required." Taylor snapped his fingers. "Natural gas, of course. There are old gas wells all over the place around here, and some are still productive." He stood and gathered the sheets of paper. "Let's go and see our Council members. Maybe we can get some action on this project."

Taylor directed the search for gas turbine generator units in good condition, which took them to Lorain and Bryan, Ohio, where they found mothballed units—perfectly preserved. Fortunately, both communities had rail lines, which simplified moving the units to Berea.

Taylor learned from an old engineer who had worked for the local gas company the existing underground gas distribution system was still intact and could be reversed to be a collection and transportation system.

With this knowledge, he found enough old gas wells in eastern Ohio to run the turbines. The project took months, even when given the highest priority. When the gas turbine generator came online, it provided power to the repair shops and the university.

As the engineers hooked more gas wells into the system, electricity became available first to the residents of Berea, then through a transmission line to the Hill.

Soon, more areas clamored for it.

CHAPTER TWENTY-TWO

When Todd Sinkton got assigned to Commander Sabich, he learned he had assembled an expeditionary force under secret orders from Council to invade the Confederation and remove Jamie "Pigseye" McFarland from power.

Todd's scouts discovered gangs of men under the supervision of Cee-Dee-Cee soldiers had removed the railroad track leading into Cee-Dee-Cee territory, even in some Clan areas. They also learned the town of Utica, some thirty miles due east of Columbus, had been raided and pillaged.

Todd accompanied Sabich to Utica. Sabich inspected the destroyed tracks. "McFarland's got a lot of nerve sending raiding parties into our territory," he said with a frown.

Every building in the town of Utica had been burned. A group of people watched from a distance as Todd examined the burned bridge and twisted sections of rail where it crossed a small creek.

"It looks like they put explosives under sections of the track." Sabich pointed to a dozen craters in the track, each with twisted or broken steel rail.

"McFarland can put a lot of men in the field. One thing the Cee-Dee-Cees has is a lot of people."

Todd had become a professional scout after raiders killed his wife during his absence. His family lived on the border with the old Fed and many of the locals knew of his service to the Clan. Some

suspected his farm was burned during the troubles due to his association with the Clan. After that, he saw no reason to settle down
again; he was a better scout than a farmer anyway.

"The Cee-Dee-Cees don't have much discipline and training.
They're just hordes of conscripts sent out to die."

"So where's the border, anyway?" Sabich pointed into the
distance where turkey buzzards circled. "Must be more dead."

"Good question," Todd said. "I always figured the border to be
outside the first town with a garrison of the ruling-types."

The Cee-Dee-Cee had a small ruling class composed of military
men with sworn loyalty to McFarland. The ruling-types maintained
control with an iron fist. They drafted people off the farms when
they needed manpower for their wars.

Todd pointed to the map and then down the road in a southeast-
erly direction. "That way. It's about fifteen miles to a place called
Johnstown."

The road was smooth and solid as it disappeared into the rolling
hills of the area. The valley bottoms had tilled fields surrounded by
hills covered with hardwoods. Even though it was overcast, the visibility was good.

"How big is this John's town?" Sabich asked.

"Johnstown is only a village. From there to the outskirts of
Columbus, it's another fifteen miles." Todd took a deep breath.
"Further west, the land becomes less rolling. Good cavalry country.
Not as flat as western Ohio, though."

"I've seen enough. Let's go." Sabich turned and strode north on
the track to a waiting locomotive. He called to an aide. "Hey, go tell
those people to get on the train. We'll take them back to Mount
Vernon and get them a place to stay. Let them know the Clan
provides assistance to people caught in a cross-border raid." It was a
Clan policy designed to ensure the loyalty of the people who lived
on the border.

"We'll be here until they get loaded." Sabich marched up the
tracks. "Todd," he said. "It's time to plan the campaign. Here's what
we're going to do...."

Over the next hour, he outlined his plans, eliciting information
from Todd about what they might expect.

෴

Sabich learned his tactics in the field and from reading military history. He knew fighting a pitched battle with the Confederation would be costly in time and materiel. He needed to finish this war quickly, in a similar fashion to the victory over the Lima-Findlay Alliance. He also knew his role in the war was far less than the politicians made out. He was too realistic to give in to the temptation to believe he was invincible. He knew he would need help.

෴

"Commander Kucinski." Sabich declined his head in respect.

"Commander Sabich." Chris smiled. "What can I do for you?" She leaned back in her chair.

The wall of her Spartan office held mementos of the campaigns she had fought: a broken rifle, a bow, a framed declaration, and in the place of honor, a stained leather motorcycle jacket perforated with a half dozen holes. These were the reminders of lessons learned with pain.

"I'm planning a campaign against the Cee-Dee-Cee," Sabich said. "I'd like to make a lightning strike into Dayton and take out its leadership. However, our scouts have found the Cee-Dee-Cee has reinforced the communities on the roads leading to Columbus and Dayton."

Chris waited. "Yes?"

"The way I see it, we need to threaten their assets so McFarland pulls forces away from Dayton," Sabich said. "I believe an attack on Columbus from the east would thin their forces around Dayton. Then we could run in a cavalry column with mobile artillery from Wapakoneta to Dayton. It'd take only a day or so." Wapakoneta was close to the border of the Cee-Dee-Cee. "Bypass the cities on the way to maintain an element of surprise."

"Who do you propose should lead the diversionary attack and the cavalry expedition?" Chris forced a smile. *Let me guess. He wants me to grind away at the Cee-Dee-Cee, end up with a bunch of casualties so that he can charge in and claim victory.*

"I thought it might be a topic for us to discuss." Sabich's poker face revealed nothing. "The cavalry expedition cannot just be a quick charge into Dayton. There have to be scouts out ahead to confirm there aren't significant roadblocks in the way." He raised his eyebrows. "All it would take is a hold up of one day and the column would never get to Dayton. So, I think who ever leads that expedition should be experienced in moving a column fast through hostile territory."

Chris waited. *Ah, and you're the one to do it.*

"The western Ohio experience taught me how to do this."

"How large a force did you have in mind?"

"At least five battle groups on horse," Sabich said. "And twice that number in the diversionary attack."

Lordy, Chris thought. *Seven hundred and fifty horses.* "That makes the logistics a little tricky," she said. "You'd have to carry a fair amount of provisions. And, mobilizing a force of that size on the frontier will attract attention." *Especially where you're hated, too.*

"I was concerned about that." Sabich pulled on his beard.

"How do you plan to keep your troop movements secret?"

"That is the nub of my problem." Sabich stared down for a moment. When he looked up, a trace of smile had cracked his face. "Commander Kucinski," he said softly. "How would you do it? Would you do it if I went to Council and requested I be put under your command?"

Chris took in a deep breath and raised her eyebrows. "Why would you do such a thing?"

"Because you're better at this than me," he said. "And I don't want this campaign to fail."

CHAPTER TWENTY-THREE

"Ready," Commander Sabich called. "Advance."

The battle group broke into a trot.

The rim of the horizon held the faint color of fresh peaches with the promise for a cloud-free day. The horses' hooves clattered and sparked on the stony asphalt of Highway 36. The gun carriages rolled smoothly, almost silent on their leather-bound rims, along the road lined with fields of young wheat.

At the gate to the city of Delaware, a small group of Clan militia rose out of the darkness to salute the horsemen. They swept through the open gate; past bloodied bodies sprawled awkwardly on the ground. The highway gave way to tree-lined streets filled with brick houses. The battle group clattered across the bridge over the Olentangy River and slowed as they entered the former Ohio Wesleyan University. As they rode on the grass, the only sounds they made were the thud of hooves, tackle jangling, and the creak of equipment.

Commander Sabich raised his hand. "Whoa," he called. "There." He pointed at a stately brick mansion.

Light streamed from several downstairs windows to backlight a surrounding wall. A metal-covered gate barred entrance to the building's compound.

"That's the local Cee-Dee-Cee headquarters," he said. "Platoons A and B to the rear. Commence action when in place."

Half the force peeled off and disappeared into the pre-dawn darkness. "Take position," Sabich said.

The riders dismounted and walked forward until they were about one hundred yards from the gate. The gun crew wheeled the artillery piece into position and released the horses from their harnesses. They set up the gun and aimed it. The dismounted cavalry spread out into a line that extended around the mansion. Birds started to make the first tentative calls of the day. It was quiet, almost too quiet.

From behind the mansion, a loud boom followed a flash. It was the artillery piece. Something flickered inside the mansion. Windows on the third floor began to glow as smoke streamed out.

"Fire," the gun chief yelled.

Flame leapt out of the gun's barrel and the metal-covered gate in the wall disappeared in a bright explosion.

The gun crew danced around the gun, swab flying in and out of the barrel as the breech clanged open. With rhythmic moves, the gunner pushed the shell and charge into the breech. The breech shut with a clank. Another tongue of flame ripped out of the barrel.

Screams came from the mansion. A gun fired. Voices called loudly. Bullets buzzed overhead. Flames licked out of the upstairs windows. Another crashing explosion and a cloud of dust rose out of the building as a corner crumbled and collapsed. A rapidly growing group of figures appeared at the gate and started to return fire.

"Platoon C at the ready." The line of soldiers flexed their bows as one. "Fire." Thirty-six yard-long arrows whistled through the air. "Platoon D, now." Another thirty-six arrows whistled into the crowd flowing through the gate. Ten seconds later, the soldiers repeated the cycle. Figures fell and the screaming started. Gunfire intensified as more figures appeared.

The artillery piece roared again. When the smoke cleared, no one remained standing at the gate.

More flames appeared at the windows of the building, soon engulfing the entire building. No one else came out.

"Retrieve platoons A and B," Sabich called.

A horseman rode off. Five minutes later, a column of riders rounded the building.

"Platoon C and D, mount up," called Sabich.

The two columns of riders merged and formed up. They trotted back toward the city entrance. Behind them, black smoke rose in a column, high into the sky. Faces, white and fleeting, appeared from behind red brick homes as the column swept past. No one offered any resistance.

"On the double." Sabich gave the hand signal for the column to increase speed. Ahead, a clot of people milled about the gate to the city. A row of guns rose.

"Fire at will," Sabich yelled.

Arrows arched into the guards at the gate. Guns flashed and two riders fell. More arrows flew, now flat and straight as the Clan Horse Soldiers thundered into the opening. In moments, the column swept out into the open and slowed to a trot.

Not bad, thought Sabich. *We wiped out another group of Cee-Dee-Cee ruling-types. First, Marysville, then Bellefontaine, and now Delaware. Soon McFarland won't have enough to maintain control, let alone fight a battle.*

$$\sim$$

"Do you see a pattern to these attacks?"

Jamie "Pigseye" McFarland was a slightly built man with thin, dark hair and sharp, angular features. He had gotten the nickname of "Pigseye" from the frequent use of the phrase, "In a pig's eye." Many, on first meeting him, made the mistake of underestimating his physical and mental capabilities since he spoke with the accent of the hills of West Virginia. He was gifted with lightning fast reflexes, a wiry strength that didn't seem possible in such a small frame, and a willingness to kill that was frightening.

"Well?" he asked.

The walls of his office were covered with stuffed heads of animals, hunting trophies. A window looked out onto the broad expanse of water that was the Mad River.

"They're just kinda jumping back and forth." Rufus Parker squinted at the map. "It looks like they might be opening up a way into Columbus." Sweat formed beads on his corpulent face. His massive frame overshadowed the smaller McFarland.

Standing quietly behind them was Archie Beauvoir, former advisor to General Boggs of the Lima-Findlay alliance.

"In a pig's eye. You remember them Clan boys who came down a couple of months ago nosing about for aircraft? Well, there's only one place they're interested in."

"Wright-Patterson."

"So, Archie, how, do you figure it?"

"I think they'll swing west again and go after ..." Beauvoir stared at the map. "Plain City, no, too small, too easy. It's gotta be Urbana or Sidney."

McFarland straightened up and smiled with all the warmth of a winter's day. "Get at least a thousand conscripts into both cities. I want to welcome them Clan boys when they come a-calling." His mountain heritage came out as he emphasized the twang of his voice. "They be fucking with me, not that dumb-ass Boggs." He smiled with oily insincerity. "No offense, Archie."

CHAPTER TWENTY-FOUR

Heat shimmered off the railroad tracks as Commander Chris Kucinski guided her horse through the piles of railroad ties scattered about.

Tall green grass waved steadily in the breeze. Puffball clouds drifted across a brilliant blue sky. To the east was the distinct mound where another road crossed the tree line marking Interstate 75.

"Captain Stanek," she called. "How far d'you get?"

"Commander Kucinski." Elroy Stanek touched his wide-brimmed hat and tilted his head. "We've repaired the rail line to the old Honda car factory at Anna. We're moving our base of operations there."

"Good." Chris dismounted.

Elroy took a deep breath. "You know, the local people are happy to see us. We're using some of them in the construction." He chuckled. "They're surprised we pay them to work."

"Any sign of Cee-Dee-Cee forces?"

"The cavalry caught a scouting party," Elroy said. "Didn't come close to us. It seems there aren't any ruling-types in the small villages. This area of Ohio is pretty empty. It'll be different when we get near Sidney, Piqua, or Troy."

"Maybe, maybe not," Chris said. "That'll trigger more patrols, maybe even a larger force. I'm sending for reinforcements." She noted much of the activity seemed to be focused on getting the camp packed up.

Right, she thought. *They're on the way south.* "Sabich has been chewing away at Cee-Dee-Cee towns around Columbus, trying to draw them out of Dayton. He'd like to make a lightning strike and get it over. From what I've seen of McFarland, he won't rise easily to the bait. I expect we'll get more attention soon. So, we push until something gives." She stared into the distance. "Are the phones working?"

"No. We're out of wire and haven't found the underground fiber optic link yet. We're using couriers to carry our reports back and forth until we do."

"The lack of a phone line concerns me."

"I've requested wire from Berea for the phone link. Nothing so far." Elroy shrugged.

"What about scavenging it from the roads around here?" Chris pointed west. "There's bound to be some."

Elroy plucked at his lower lip. "I suppose." He closed one eye. "Maybe I could use some of the scouting contingent—"

"No," said Chris. "If you need additional people, let your schedule slip. I'm not letting our scout coverage down for a single day. When we make our move, it's got to be a surprise. If the Cee-Dee-Cees show up, we may need reinforcements, and fast."

CHAPTER TWENTY-FIVE

"Forward." Commander Sabich spurred his horse on. It responded sluggishly.

It had been a long ride from Marysville. He planned to attack Urbana immediately. So far, the campaign had gone well; each time they attacked, they surprised the Cee-Dee-Cee military in its barracks.

This time, instead of a pre-dawn attack, they would strike at the end of the day, at mealtime, when people were relaxing. A change in pattern, he'd explained, a surprise.

The sentries at the gate to the city did not even offer token resistance. Instead they fled.

Sabich looked back. "Close it up." He gave the hand signal. Their destination was the old junior college on the southwest side of town that was now the Cee-Dee-Cee barracks. They had to cross through the center of the town.

It was quiet, almost too quiet for this time of day, he thought. *Good, we're going to surprise them again.*

As Sabich trotted into the center of town, among the tall brick buildings formerly housing stores, offices, and hotels, he saw the road ahead was blocked and bristled with guns.

"Halt! It's a trap! About face, retreat, on the double."

The battle group rotated with the precision that only comes

with experience to reverse their course. The horses broke into a canter.

A crackle of gunfire ripped a line of Clan Horse Soldiers from their saddles. Faces appeared in the windows above, along with more long-barreled guns opening fire.

Once clear of the center of town and its gunfire, a dark mass emerged to block the road before them that grew into hundreds of club and ax bearing men.

"Shit," said Sabich. "Look at all them fuckin' Cee-Dee-Cees!"

In unison, the Clan force unlimbered their bows and slowed their horses to a walk. "Platoons C and D, clear a path!"

The leading elements charged into the crowd and carved a deep notch in the Cee-Dee-Cee ranks, creating a trail of broken and bloodied bodies. Horses stumbled and fell as a sea of hands reached up to grab the riders. Clubs rose and fell with bone-crushing thuds. Blood splashed into the air. The mass of foot soldiers slowly digested the two platoons of Horse Soldiers with the remorseless swinging of clubs and axes.

Sabich reined his horse to a stop. "Halt," he screamed. "Load the field guns. Platoons A and B form a square. Protect the guns."

The Clan forces flowed into formation.

The two remaining platoons dismounted and formed into a block around the artillery pieces as their crews worked at a feverish pace to load them. They rained arrows down onto the horde of Cee-Dee-Cee foot soldiers.

Having consumed two platoons of Clan Horse Soldiers, the Cee-Dee-Cee foot soldiers now advanced with a hungry sound.

"Gun one ready," yelled the gun chief.

"Part ranks," Sabich shouted.

The Clan warriors parted in the middle to reveal a field gun pointed straight down the street toward the advancing mass.

"Fire."

The gun belched a tongue of flame and a load of metal ball shot. For a moment, smoke engulfed the Clan warriors.

As air cleared, Sabich could see a torn red swath through the center of the approaching mass of soldiers. The mass faltered, closed up, and then resumed its advance, slowly climbing over the dead and dying becoming a red, seeping barrier across the road. Arrows flew into the advancing horde.

"Gun two ready."

"Fire."

The second artillery piece roared.

When the smoke cleared, a trail of bloodied bodies ran fifty yards down the road. The remnants of the Cee-Dee-Cee force broke and ran into the trees and houses on the side streets. Gunfire from buildings continued. More holes appeared in the ranks of the Clan soldiers. Horses screamed and reared, hooves flashing blood-stained steel.

"Mount up," Sabich called. "Guard the artillery."

"Sir," called the gun chief. "Let me get one loaded." His face was black with soot.

"Goddamn it, hurry, man." As Sabich spoke, something struck him with a loud splat. He slumped in his saddle.

A platoon leader grabbed Sabich's horse's reins and urged it forward. Another Horse Soldier rode alongside holding Sabich upright on his horse.

The Clan force surged forward. The horses picked their way over the dead bodies in the road. Whinnying, heads tossing, eyes wide and foam flecking from their mouths, the horses' hooves thudded into broken flesh, cracking splintered bone and splashing blood on their flanks. The leather-clad wheels of the gun carriages splashed bloody grooves through the mass on the road.

Once clear of the battle area, the soldiers raced east on the main road. Thirty-some remaining soldiers reached the city gate. There, several hundred Cee-Dee-Cees lined up across the road.

The Clan soldiers halted about two hundred yards from the Cee-Dee-Cees. The human wall advanced toward them.

"Artillery, execute a reversal," called the gun chief. The team of horses pulled a field gun to the front of the column and turned in a circle. The field gun's barrel now faced the approaching Cee-Dee-Cee soldiers. The second gun, with only two horses left, made the same maneuver, only more slowly. "Hold your fire," called the gun chief. "Prepare to volley."

The Clan soldiers spread out in a line, each nocking an arrow in their bow. Horses snorted and stamped their hooves, moving rest-lessly. Riders released the reins.

The brown line was only one soldier deep.

The Cee-Dee-Cee troops approached within one hundred yards where they broke into a yelling, screaming mass. As they picked up speed, their glinting axes and clubs waved like ripe wheat in a summer breeze.

"Fire."

A flock of arrows rose. Both artillery pieces boomed. Smoke filled the air. The screaming began almost immediately. The smoke drifted away to reveal two gaping holes in the Cee-Dee-Cee line. The Cee-Dee-Cee soldiers stooped over fallen comrades. Less than half remained standing.

"Forward," yelled the gun chief.

The brown-clad warriors advanced. The horses moved first at a walking pace, then a trot. The gun carriages wheeled about and followed. Arrows continued to fly. The Clan column smashed through the broken line and trotted out of the city gate of Urbana. A trail of blood marked their passing.

$$\rightthreetimes$$

The next day, twenty-four Clan warriors returned to Marysville. They left behind ninety-six of their comrades. Commander Sabich died during the night. His and the bodies of thirty others were brought in on the backs of horses.

To speed their return and deny the artillery pieces to the Cee-Dee-Cee forces, they dumped them in a creek on the way back.

CHAPTER TWENTY-SIX

"That'll give the Clan second thoughts about raiding my cities." Pigseye McFarland had just learned the ambush at Urbana had worked. It didn't matter to him that over two hundred conscripts had died and another four hundred were wounded and likely to die.

What really mattered to him was that none of his military had been hurt and the Clan had been driven off. Six of McFarland's lieutenants stood in front of his desk, casting glances at each other.

Sunlight streamed in from the window overlooking the Mad River, lighting up the spacious office. Archie Beauvoir picked at his teeth while leaning against the wall behind McFarland.

"Mebbe so," Bucktooth Quinlan said. "I'm gonna need more workers come harvest time." Urbana was his territory and he had supplied the bulk of the conscripts for the ambush. "You gonna ship some in from Dayton to make up the shortfall?"

"In a pig's eye," McFarland said. "Just two weeks ago you was complaining about your population growing too rapidly." He smiled. "I just solved your problem."

"Well, I didn't need to lose six hundred workers in their prime." Quinlan turned away.

No one pressed issues with McFarland, who had an explosive temper and one of the few handguns with any ammo left. All had seen demonstrations of McFarland's marksmanship. No one had the desire to end up as target practice.

"How about some conscripts to defend Urbana in case the Clan comes back?" Quinlan frowned.

"You won't need them," said Beauvoir. "They won't be back. They don't like to lose that many from any one unit. It'll give 'em political troubles at home."

McFarland turned and pointed to Cranky Cutler, another of his lieutenants. "What's going on north of Sidney? I thought you sent a patrol out? Did they see anything?"

"I dunno," said Cranky. "Some of my boys didn't come back from patrol last week. Sometimes they find something good on the road and stick around for a couple of days of fun."

This was a common practice of the military ruling class when on patrol in rarely visited areas. They'd take a female who caught their attention and use her until they grew bored. It let the locals know who was boss. "Maybe they found something real good."

"What're you doing about it?"

"I dunno." Cranky scratched his butt. "Wait a little longer, and see if they come back."

"In a pig's eye." McFarland slammed his fist on the table. "Put together a patrol with a hundred conscripts. Send it north on seventy-five. When they get to where the creek crosses the highway north of Anna, have 'em chop up the railroad bridge but good."

"Yes, sir." Cranky leaned back in his chair. "First thing tomorrow—"

"In a pig's eye, today, Cranky, today."

༄

Todd Sinkton stood in the stirrups and stared south through the binoculars down the wide expanse of the old interstate highway. Grass grew from cracks in the road, giving the surface a hazy appearance through the binoculars. Even so, the dark stain in the distance moved, and grew larger. "I think it's a Cee-Dee-Cee force." Todd had been sent to the western frontier as part of the battle group to reinforce Commander Kucinski's group. Five hundred soldiers now occupied the old automobile factory at Anna.

"How many?" Captain Clarence Odum was a newly commis-

sioned officer fresh from training in Berea. He came from Mansfield
in the former Central Ohio Union.

"Hard to say. Maybe a couple of hundred." Todd lowered the
binoculars. "We should get off the highway so we can get a better
look at them as they go past." He gestured west, toward the willows
lining the creek that meandered under the highway.

"I think we should make a stand, here, at the creek," Captain
Odum said. "That way they won't be able to flank us."

"With all due respect, sir." Todd suppressed a smile. "I believe
our mission is to gather information, not fight them. We should ..."
He hesitated as he maneuvered his horse closer to Odum's. "We
should send a messenger back to Anna to let them know a Cee-Dee-
Cee force is on its way." He spoke quietly so that none of the
soldiers in the platoon could hear his words.

"Oh, yes." A touch of color suffused Odum's cheeks. "You're
right." He backed his horse up and raised his hand. He pointed
toward the creek. "Take cover behind the line of trees along the
creek," he called. "Williams, head back and let Commander
Kucinski know we've spotted an enemy force heading north. Tell
her we'll shadow them and keep her informed."

"Yes, sir." Williams, a small, slender red-haired man, saluted and
spurred his horse forward. He clattered north on the old highway
and soon disappeared from sight.

The platoon wended its way down the slope of the highway,
through the tall grass and across a ditch. They stepped single file
through the remnants of a wire fence that once bounded the highway's right of way. At the creek, the horses slowed to drink as they
waded through water that came up to their knees. The riders
clucked to their horses as they struggled up the slick, muddy bank.
The mature willow trees' branches drooped to the ground and
formed bowers that provided cover and shade.

The soldiers dismounted and hid their horses behind the trees.
One soldier climbed a tall pin oak towering above the willows where
he peered through an opening in the tree's dark green leaves at the
approaching column with his binoculars.

"There's about one hundred and twenty," he called. "Only a few
have guns, mainly hand weapons—no bows."

"We could take them. I know we could." Odum stared hard in

the direction of the highway as though he could see through the dense growth of trees.

"Maybe." Todd raised his eyebrows. "What if one of them gets away?" He knew that the whole concept of the campaign depended upon keeping it secret.

Reinforcements passed through Lima and Wapakoneta in sealed boxcars late at night without stopping to eliminate the chance spies would learn of the size of the build-up. The old Honda factory at Anna was large enough to completely conceal the forces and even exercise the horses. The key was the regular supply of materiel by the trains that came only in the night.

"You know what our orders are; no contact unless you have complete superiority and can guarantee not a single Cee-Dee-Cee gets away."

Captain Odum made a face.

Todd lowered his voice. "Look, if you want a career as a soldier, you follow orders." He looked around to make sure that none of the other soldiers could hear him. "There's a time and place for initiative. This isn't it." He paused. "Schliester," he called.

A bony young man with a prominent nose and hair so blond it was almost white stepped forward. "Yes, sir?"

"Take a message back to Anna." Todd made Schliester repeat his words twice. "Don't let the Cee-Dee-Cees see you. Stay on the far side of the railroad tracks on your way north."

ॐ

"Commander Kucinski." The red-haired rider reined his horse to a halt. Both he and his mount were sweat-stained and covered with dust. "Beggin' your pardon, ma'am, but Captain Odum asked me to advise you that he's spotted a Cee-Dee-Cee force coming north on the old highway."

"Where did he spot them?" Chris asked.

Other officers began to gather around the rider who slid off his horse.

"And what's your name?"

"It was two or three miles south of where that crick goes under the highway, mebbe six mile total," the rider said. "I'm Joey Williams, ma'am."

"All right, Williams," Chris said. "How many were there? Were they on horse or foot?"

"There were a lot of them, ma'am. They made a line all the way across the highway." He paused and his eyes rose to the sky as though trying to bring the sight back to mind. "I don't think they were on horse, at least, not most of them."

"Anything else?" Chris said.

"The patrol were gonna hide and watch them. He said he'd send another messenger once he got a count."

Chris turned to Elroy. "Who's the scout with that patrol?"

"Sinkton, Todd Sinkton."

Chris nodded. She turned to the messenger. "You can go now." She looked up at Elroy. "Mobilize a battle group of soldiers just in case it's a big force."

"Yes, Commander." Elroy hurried away.

Twenty minutes later, a skinny blond man rode through the gates of the old factory on a tall bay stallion. Schliester reported an accurate count and description of the approaching force.

"Take a platoon and make contact," Chris said.

Elroy stared at her. "You really want me to do that?"

"Get the Cee-Dee-Cees to chase you." She smiled. "All the way to Bellefontaine, if possible. They mustn't learn we're here."

The Cee-Dee-Cee force followed the platoon east until it reached the main road to Bellefontaine. The patrol continued east and the Cee-Dee-Cee force ceased following and turned southeast toward the town of Sidney. Two scouts shadowed them to the edge of town.

"I don't want to give McFarland any reason to think we'll come down seventy-five and attack Dayton." Chris's voice bounced off the walls.

The room, long and dim, had faded wallpaper from a previous era and could accommodate over one hundred persons.

She looked down the long water-stained teak table at her six officers. At her right hand was Elroy Stanek, long-time companion through many campaigns. Todd Sinkton sat behind Elroy, away from the table. The remaining officers had just arrived and would command sections of the invading force.

"If he does, we should expect the Cee-Dee-Cee to send hordes of poorly armed foot soldiers at us." She paused. "Quite frankly, I wish there were a way to avoid a bloodbath. I want to explore every idea that might cut this campaign short."

"Well, Commander," said Patrick Monahan. "We could draw them out, and give them the old run around. Wear them out, y'know." He was a cousin to Sean Monahan, the Clan Elder, and was believed to have political aspirations. "Use our cavalry."

"I wish it were that easy." Chris frowned. "Don't underestimate McFarland. He's experienced our artillery and cavalry. It's my guess he'll be difficult to draw out."

Elroy turned to Todd. "Give us an overview of the situation."

Todd stood and unfolded a tattered map. "Here's the way I see it." He reviewed his latest intelligence on Dayton and surrounding areas. "... As a result, the most direct route into Dayton is still straight down Highway 75."

"Oh, my." Chris sighed. "It's gonna be a bloody trip."

"We could bypass most of the towns 'cept Sidney," said Todd.

"Any ideas?" Chris looked around the table.

"I don't know if you know about the new artillery." Cal Majewski had just arrived from Defiance. His unit had tested the new guns produced in the Defiance ironworks.

"In what way, Captain ..." Chris hesitated for a moment. "Majewski. What makes them different?"

"They've got twice the range and more accuracy."

"Therefore?" Chris raised her eyebrows.

"My artillery teams can hit a house at two miles, usually dead center. All with the same ammo we've been using." Majewski's face briefly cracked a smile. His worn-out blond hair emphasized the brown color of his weathered skin. "They've got better optics and gun controls, too."

"How many of these improved guns do we have?"

"I brought down the six that were ready."

"I need to think about this," said Chris. "We'll meet here

tomorrow at the same time." She rose to her feet. "I want a tactical idea from each of you by then. Dismissed."

"Thank you, gentlemen, for your ideas," Chris said. "I will consider each carefully for our battle plan." She rose to her feet. It was a signal the meeting was over. "Prepare your units for departure. Our staff meeting will be at one hour before first light." She took a deep breath. "You'll get your individual orders at that time." She smiled briefly and nodded.

"Oh, Captain Majewski, may I have a word with you?"

"Yes, Commander." Cal Majewski stood and waited motionless. His face was taut, expressionless.

"Sit down, please." Chris gestured toward the chair adjacent to hers. "Can your long-range guns travel at the same pace as our other artillery?"

"Yes, Commander. There's little difference in appearance, except for a metal shield that protects the gun crew." Cal took a deep breath. "Defiance is building shields for the existing guns. They should be on the next supply train."

"Yes, gun crews take time to train. We've lost too many already." She glanced at the sheet of paper before her. "I want you to form a support group for these long-range guns so they can travel fast. You know, supplies, spare parts, all loaded on carriages that can keep up. As for backup personnel, take a platoon."

Majewski plucked at his lower lip. "I don't have any good archers in my battle group." He sighed. "Archery was never a strong point in the Fed. Can I borrow some?"

"I'll get you a platoon of archers, as well." She looked up at him. She was tired and the campaign had not even started. She got to her feet. "Have them ready to depart at first light."

CHAPTER TWENTY-SEVEN

Everything, Cal Majewski thought, *is going according to plan, and that worries me.*

The main Clan force of two thousand soldiers and militia was ten miles north, which had arrived by train that morning at the abandoned car factory in Anna.

The clatter of the horses' hooves made a percussive counterpoint to the gun carriages' creaking wood frames. The jingle of tackle completed the symphony of travel. Vapor rose from the horses' flanks as drizzle fell from a lead-colored sky. Muddy streams burbled down from young forests covering the rolling hills as flocks of birds flapped heavenwards.

Majewski had overseen covering the carriages' steel wheels with leather to silence them.

Majewski took his artillery squad south via secondary roads paralleling the old Interstate 75, accompanying the cavalry under the command of Captain Monahan. To the east, behind a thickly wooded ridge, was the town of Sidney. Clan horse soldiers armed with a mix of bows and rifles probed the roads ahead.

A rider came up the road from the south, both man and horse steaming damply.

"Sir." the man brought his horse to a halt. "The bridge over the Miami River is out. Captain Monahan asked me to advise you we must head east on the next road to cross I-75. It's the only bridge for some distance."

Right, thought Cal. *Like he's scouted the entire area. Bloody fool is spoiling for a fight.*

"Convey my respects to Captain Monahan. Remind him contact with the enemy must be avoided until we reach our objective. I trust there'll be an escort for us at the highway?"

"Yes, sir." The messenger saluted and spurred his horse. He disappeared down the road.

౨

In spite of Cal's fears, the day turned into a monotonous series of slogs on secondary roads. They zigged east around the town of Piqua and detoured west past Troy.

The drizzle turned to rain.

As the day began to fade, the rain stopped and the sky cleared. They made camp in an abandoned village. It was adjacent to a long body of water filling an empty valley where faded signs identified it as Englewood Reservoir.

౨

Cal woke chilled. Mist lay in all directions. He could see less than one hundred yards. Overhead, a pale moon shone wanly in a brightening sky. Dew dripped from the bushes surrounding the dilapidated buildings.

Thank God the powder is sealed in oiled leather pouches, he thought. *Otherwise we'd have a real problem. No wonder Commander Kucinski wants archers on an expedition such as this.*

The camp stirred. Voices muttered, low and sullen, punctuated by an occasional laugh.

A metal pan clattered and horses nickered with pleasure as their handlers put on feedbags. The rising sun turned the mist into a luminous veil. Sparrows chattered nervously in the still air.

Captain Patrick Monahan appeared, frowning. "We've got to close up formations," he said in an abrupt manner. "Too difficult to keep track of who's who if we're spread out."

"Good morning," Cal said. "How're you?"

"Er, fine." Monahan stumbled over his words. "When will you be ready to move out?"

"My men are binding fresh leather to the wheels right now," Cal said. "Maybe half an hour. I'm also having the gun crews load the guns with bags of rifle balls as a precaution." He took a deep breath. "Without primers, of course."

"That's a good idea, under these conditions."

"And where we are, we could see action today." Cal sighed. "I hope it goes according to plan."

"Sinkton has been here before. He knows, or should know, where McFarland's headquarters are." Monahan blew into his fingers, his breath steaming. "He reckons it's about fifteen miles to the Tongue."

He referred to the strip of land lying between the Miami and Mad Rivers that contained the former downtown Dayton. The city was accessible only over a heavily fortified interstate highway bridge. Most of Dayton had been burned sometime in the past. Upstream, the area between the two rivers had reverted back to a densely wooded swamp. Few people lived in the old city anymore.

A man wearing the insignia of a platoon leader walked up and saluted. "Excuse me, Captain Majewski," he said. "The guns're ready to roll."

"Thank you." Cal turned to Monahan. "We're ready when you are."

"Good," Monahan said. "Form up on the road heading south." He pointed and strode away without another word.

The mist thinned and the visibility grew to almost a quarter mile. Sunlight glittered off the dew-laden branches of the taller trees.

༄

Monahan's platoon followed the lake to a dam that held back the river. The valley, now with a winding river, had a mix of old oaks and dense thickets. Its few inhabitants fled as soon as they saw the column. After chasing and catching several—all of whom were on foot—Monahan decided to ignore the local people. He reasoned the column would arrive long before any word preceded them. The mist did not fully lift until late morning.

Monahan spotted a scout's signal on a distant rise. He recognized Todd Sinkton's lanky figure. "Halt."

The column rippled to a stop.

Interstate 75 lay about a mile to the east. The bridge into Dayton was four miles south. The scout trotted down the grade, staying on the grassy berm of the road.

"Sir," Todd said. "A force is moving north on the highway."

"What kind of force?" Monahan said in a loud voice.

"I didn't get a good count. I'd estimate that there were maybe five hundred men with guns." Todd made a face. "The rest, the conscripts, were like a horde. No discipline, no ranks, and impossible to count. I'd guess at least a thousand."

Monahan smiled. "I bet they're going to the aid of the towns on the highway." He nodded. "Good. Have a patrol shadow them. Keep me informed as to where they are. Also, send a message to Commander Kucinski the Cee-Dee-Cees are on their way."

Todd saluted and wheeled his horse about. He collected a squad and headed back up the grade. At the top of the rise, he dismounted and disappeared into the trees.

An hour later, a horse-mounted scout trotted down the road. "Sir, Mr. Sinkton sends his regards. The Cee-Dee-Cee force is continuing north on I-75. The gate on the bridge into Dayton is closed. The scout who saw it doesn't think it's heavily manned." The scout took a deep breath. "Scout Williams is on the way to our forces at Anna."

"Good." Monahan turned and yelled, "Form up and prepare to move out."

CHAPTER TWENTY-EIGHT

McFarland stared out the window at the street. Piqua was an old town, lots of red brick buildings tight against the Miami River. The part of Piqua that lay within a bend of the river had been fortified, but wasn't large enough to hold all his forces and provide them with a place to sleep.

"Don't let the Clan force you into a set-piece battle," said Archie Beauvoir. "That's how they beat Boggs."

"The Clan's got more horsemen than me. I sure don't want to meet them out in the open," McFarland said.

"Use your foot to swamp them, before they can bring up their artillery. Then your horsemen will be more than a match for them." Beauvoir nodded his head. "Move fast and catch them before they're ready."

"Where?"

"They're moving south on seventy-five. Bring all of your forces up quickly and surprise them when they attack Sidney." Beauvoir pointed at the map.

"Tomorrow," said McFarland. "We move on them."

McFarland knew it was easier dealing with rebellious farmers. *This damn Clan had cavalry as good as his own and maybe even better.*

The standard tactic of swamping his enemy with foot soldiers was costly in the face of the big guns of the Clan. He'd picked up three thousand additional conscripts figuring it should be enough to deal with another Clan raid. Still, something bothered him. He wasn't sure they'd learned their lesson at Urbana.

"Sir, I don't have enough food on hand to feed all your forces and pay my taxes." Hakim Salah's voice interrupted McFarland's train of thought. Salah was the overlord of Piqua.

"Think of my visit as an honor," McFarland said.

"What am I going to do?" Salah raised his hands in supplication. "It is months until harvest. My people will go hungry."

"If you can't figure that one out, maybe someone else should look after this area of the Confederation." McFarland smiled.

"Oh, no." Salah raised his hands and bowed his head. "I'll figure something out."

"Good." McFarland turned to the men lining the room. "What else have you learned?"

"The Clan just started an attack on Sidney, but didn't get very far." Johnny Cisternino's family controlled Sidney. He was a tall, dark complexioned man with a heavy beard and a trace of emerging paunch. He'd spent the night with a woman in Piqua, which had kept him from being trapped inside Sidney. "Apparently they didn't charge in like they usually do."

"We kicked their butts at Urbana." McFarland stared hard at Cisternino for a moment. He'd heard rumors about his weakness for women other than his wife. But, his family paid their taxes on time and supplied conscripts without complaint. "How many are there?" he asked. "How many big guns?"

"I don't know exactly." Cisternino spread his hands and shrugged. "Maybe five hundred horsemen, a lot. As for the big guns, I heard maybe six, seven."

"Did your father march the conscripts out to test them?"

"Naw, I don't think so." Cisternino knitted his brows together. "We don't have many conscripts in town. We keep them on the farm, raising food, kids, you know, being productive."

Idiot, thought McFarland. *He knows he's supposed to keep four, five hundred conscripts in town while there's a chance of a Clan raid.* "Didn't your father hear what happened at Urbana?"

"Yeah, but he figured they weren't gonna raid this area." Cisternino shrugged. "He figured living this close to Dayton made us safe."

McFarland turned to his men. "Tomorrow, we march for Sidney, straight up 75. Get the conscripts out front in a wide line so they can outflank any of those damn guns." He made a sweeping gesture with his arms. "Your boys will follow. Look to exploit any opportunities."

"What time do we start in the morning?" asked an older member of the military.

"We'll move our forces onto the highway an hour after first light." McFarland knew it would take time to round up the conscripts, some of whom would have a king-sized hangover.

CHAPTER TWENTY-NINE

A faint thud came from the north side of Sidney—it was an artillery piece firing.

Chris stared through the binoculars. Something was coming up I-75. She lowered her binoculars and glanced up and down the line.

Within the fringe of trees lining the Miami River flood plain were four hundred and fifty Clan Horse Soldiers, fifty militia, and six field guns. The highway was almost a half-mile away and ran parallel to the trees. In between was an open field. On the other side of the highway was another tree-lined road with a Clan force of the same size. Sidney lay about a mile north of their positions.

Another thud. The second army should have already arrived with more artillery. They had their orders to push in from the north and drive the Cee-Dee-Cees out of town and into the trap. If their timing was right, they would run into the force advancing from the south.

Chris smiled at the thought.

Several clusters of distant thuds sounded.

Yep, that's the second army, she thought. She glanced up and down the line.

Her officers watched the highway intently. The soldiers were off their horses, but still in formation. She turned back to the highway. With her binoculars, she could just make out the mass of the Cee-Dee-Cee army moving up from the south on the highway.

"Phew." She whistled. "That's a sizable force." It was bigger than Sinkton's messenger had reported.

A column of smoke rose from the town of Sidney.

"Elroy," she called. "Make sure our soldiers remain hidden. Before we act, I want the Cee-Dee-Cees pinned against the town." There was enough open ground between the old highway and the flood plain to make it cavalry territory.

"Right." Elroy hurried off.

The advancing force slowly crept past, a vast horde of people on foot followed by a sizable cavalry group armed with long-barreled rifles. In the center, surrounded by a dozen men in gray uniforms, was a small man on a black horse. The clatter of horses and gear mingled with the rhythmic thud of thousands of feet. It was primitive music that was the age-old prelude to war.

"Battle group one," Chris called out. "Prepare for action."

Behind her came the rattle of hundreds of pieces of horse tackle. Saddles creaked and horses whinnied as the force mounted.

"Battle group one ready," called Captain Odum.

"Seal the highway to the south," Chris called.

"Yes, Commander. Forward ho." Horse-mounted soldiers streamed from the cover of the trees. They formed up in lines and headed for the highway at a fast trot.

"Artillery," Chris called. "Target on the rear echelon of the force on the highway." She'd reviewed her preference in targets with the gun chiefs. They understood what she wanted.

"Artillery ready," the gun chief called.

As the Clan cavalry advanced, the Cee-Dee-Cee force on the highway came to a stop. With much hand waving, they underwent some kind of maneuver.

"Fire," called Chris.

Six guns spoke as one. Flame and smoke erupted on the road.

As the smoke cleared, the Cee-Dee-Cee force on the highway expanded like a disturbed ants' nest. People poured off the highway and flowed toward them like a stain. A distant barrage of artillery reports followed by more gouts of flame and smoke in the road told Chris the Clan group on the west side had joined the attack.

"Forward," Chris called.

The gun crews manhandled the guns forward until they were

clear of the trees. The two battle groups of mounted Clan soldiers emerged from the trees into the opening behind the artillery. Amid the field pieces, the militia raised their long-barreled rifles. The mounted warriors knocked arrows into their bows.

The artillery fired again. More mounted Cee-Dee-Cees dropped. Less than half remained on their horses.

A large clot of people appeared from the direction of the town of Sidney, streaming down the highway.

The flowing horde from the highway drew closer.

"Fire," screamed the gun chief.

Three artillery pieces boomed. Three openings appeared in the milling mass. A shower of arrows rose. A rolling rifle volley followed. Another shower of arrows.

An artillery piece spoke once more.

The mass of Cee-Dee-Cees continued to roll forward.

Two more artillery pieces bellowed out flame, smoke, and a storm of metal balls. Another artillery piece boomed.

Though full of holes, the horde came closer and closer.

"Lord," Chris said, "they're brave. Soldiers, advance."

A sea of clubs flowed over an artillery piece as clubs rose and fell on the artillerymen who began to waver.

Screaming "Clan, Clan," the Horse Soldiers advanced, sleeting a storm of arrows into the horde.

The club-wielding attackers faltered.

"Clan. Clan. Clan." The calls penetrated the sounds of battle.

The Clan Horse Soldiers thundered down from the highway. Odum's battle group attacked from the left flank, raining a volley of arrows on the milling mass of Cee-Dee-Cees. They halted twenty yards from the horde and formed up a line. The Clan Horse Soldiers began to volley arrows into the horde of Cee-Dee-Cees.

An artillery piece fired, followed by another.

Holes appeared in the horde. Caught between the massed Horse Soldiers and the artillery, the Cee-Dee-Cees turned and ran.

"Cease fire," Chris yelled.

"Cease fire," echoed up and down the line.

"Battle group three," Chris called. "Join battle group one. Return to the highway, and capture the enemy cavalry." It took less than a minute for the order to reach the furthest warrior.

The Clan soldiers trotted out and up the grade to return to the highway. More Clan soldiers appeared from the other side of the road.

Good, thought Chris. *They're on the same page.*

As she watched, there were more puffs of smoke and cracks from guns from the Cee-Dee-Cee cavalry. A line of Clan warriors fell from their horses. Bows flexed, and a cloud of arrows flew into the Cee-Dee-Cees. One-third of the Cee-Dee-Cee cavalry fell from their horses, including the small man on the black horse.

After six more volleys of arrows, the remaining Cee-Dee-Cee cavalry raised their hands. For a moment, voices stilled, broken only by the cries and screams of the wounded.

A horse shrilled in pain, thrashing helplessly on the ground. Guns became quiet. Distant artillery no longer spoke.

It's over, Chris thought. *Thank God.*

ว

By afternoon, the Clan controlled the town of Sidney. Chris's battle group joined up with the second army. Jamie McFarland and Archie Beauvoir were among the Cee-Dee-Cee dead.

"We've got to get a message to Captains Monahan and Majewski right away," she said. "There's no need for their mission now."

"Better get a battle group on the move, then," Elroy said. "Something that'll get through without falling to a sniper like that poor Williams lad." The scout had caught a lead ball on his ride and died during the night.

"Hurry," said Chris.

ว

On the second day after the ambush at Sidney, the battle group reached the remains of Monahan's force outside the Tongue section of Dayton. Cal Majewski was in command.

"We surprised them and took the bridge over the Miami River," said Cal. "It was all downhill from then on. They launched a pre-dawn counter-attack day before yesterday and almost pushed us off the bridge." He mopped his brow. His face was streaked with soot and sweat. "The archers saved our asses, but over half of them gave their lives to do it. That's when Captain Monahan got injured." He shook his head. "Finally, we got the artillery into action. The pebble shot inflicted tremendous casualties on the Cee-Dee-Cees during a charge. Once we drove them off, we built this barricade."

He pointed to a tangled mass of logs and rusty barbed wire stretching from one side of the bridge's railing to the other. The open area beyond was littered with hundreds of crumpled bodies covered with hopping and flapping black crows and vultures. Aromas of rotting flesh and spilled guts filled the air.

"We built these platforms for the artillery so we could bombard any building used by the Cee-Dee-Cee as a defense point." Cal gestured. Within a mile, many tall buildings exhibited holes, testifying to the volume and accuracy of his gunners.

"Haven't seen much activity lately."

Cal learned that over three-quarters of the expedition had been wounded. They couldn't have held on much longer; their artillery ammunition was about gone and the archers were down to three arrows each. The relieving battle group cleared a path over the bridge and advanced into Dayton. It was almost deserted except for a small force still holding on. It took less than one hour to eliminate the remaining opposition.

The word spread fast—Dayton had fallen.

Columbus surrendered two days later.

CHAPTER THIRTY

Mitch Doaks twisted his hat and took a deep breath. "Thank you for the pleasure of your company."

Noelle smiled. "It was a delight, thank you, Mitch. I rarely get a chance to eat lunch out." They had just returned from the Travelers' Inn. She stepped back from the doorway. "Please come in." She extended her hand toward him.

"Of course." Mitch stepped forward, took her hand, and followed her into the house.

Noelle carefully closed the door behind him. "Ms. Vargas won't be back until at least six. I hope you don't have to leave right away." She still held his hand as she looked up at him. "We rarely get to spend much time together."

Mitch took a deep breath. "Noelle," he said. "I don't know how to say this." His cheeks flushed. "I enjoy your company, no, it's more than that."

Noelle moved closer to him. "Yes, me too."

"What I mean." He hesitated. "I think we should—"

"Yes?" Noelle took a sharp breath.

"Well, I mean, I really enjoy being with you and want to spend more time with you, a lot of time." He closed his eyes and shook his head. "I don't know how to say this."

Noelle slipped her arms around his waist and laid her head on his chest. "I'd like to be with you all the time."

"I'm in love with you."

Noelle took a sharp breath. "Yes, I love you, too."

Mitch wrapped his arms around her. "Will you, will you marry me?"

"Mitch." Noelle pushed him away to see his face. "D'you mean that? D'you really mean it?"

"Yes."

"Yes, I do, I will, whatever." She lifted her face to him, eyes closed, and kissed him. "You take my breath away. Come." She pulled him along the cool, dark hallway, behind the stairs into a small bedroom.

"Is this yours?" Mitch asked.

"It's ours, or will be shortly." Noelle undid the front of her dress. "I can't wait until we're married." She began loosening the belt of Mitch's trousers.

᠎ ᠎

"Where the Hell are those damn planes?" Taylor MacPherson wiped the sweat from his forehead. He peered into a half-collapsed building that looked like it might be a hangar.

The former Wright-Patterson Air Force Base lay just east of Dayton in the flood plain of the Mad River. Around the buildings were reeds and rushes with clumps of willows and scrawny trees. There were weeds everywhere, marking the cracks in the concrete runways. It didn't look like an airfield anymore. One hangar was still intact, but empty. It was hot and it was almost suppertime.

Taylor had seen four planes, but they were either burned or vandalized. He'd heard there were intact aircraft stored at the airbase, which McFarland had seemed to confirm by refusing the Clan's access to them. So where were they? He swatted away a horse fly that sought landing rights on his head. He consulted a map of the area.

Okay, he thought. *The administrative buildings are—he checked the compass and looked up—over there.* A patch of straggly trees blocked his view. Sunlight glinted off water. *Crap*, he thought. *More water.* "Let's check the administration buildings, then call it a day."

Todd Sinkton nodded wearily.

They slogged through ankle-deep water, wading through a deeper section that at one time had been a drainage ditch. They squished through soft, sticky mud that formed pads on their boots. Reeds stuck to the mud, making huge wattle pancakes. Several times they had to stop and scrape the muck off. A shallow layer of water lay over a thin coating of mud that was like dark brown grease on the concrete apron fronting the administration building.

Todd slipped, his feet shooting out from under him. He fell hard, with a splash.

"Shit." He got up, hands coated with mud. "The sooner we get inside, the better." He rinsed the slime off his hands in the muddy water and continued on gingerly. "This stuff is as slick as ice."

Taylor and Todd poked their heads inside the administration building. Broken furniture lined the hallway; bird droppings stained the litter of paper, glass fragments, and dead leaves on the floor. They peered in through office doors to find ransacked filing cabinets, paper strewn all over the floor. They climbed up into the control tower.

Taylor glanced at a large framed map on the wall that caught his attention. He picked out several shards of glass to get a better view. "This is where we are now. That's where the hangars were." He traced a finger over the map and read the notation below.

Todd stood alongside him and peered at the right-hand side of the map. "This says something about an aircraft storage area."

"Let me see," Taylor said, crowding him.

"Here." Todd pointed.

It was in the eastern-most part of the base, an area with derelict buildings overgrown with young trees. It was also above the flood plain.

"It doesn't show the exact location." Taylor gently rubbed the surface of the map. "In fact, it's a label that was added." He quickly made a sketch on a piece of paper. As he placed the paper in a pocket, he glanced toward the window. The sun was low in the sky. "It'll have to wait until tomorrow," he said. "Let's head back."

~

The next morning, a squad of Todd Sinkton's scouts accompanied them to the eastern section of the airbase that held a jumble of old barracks.

Some had been looted; some burned, with their doors hanging open or roofs sagging amid several overgrown mounds. Trees and bushes grew everywhere. A concrete taxiway, still visible through the vegetation, connected the area to the main runway. By noon, they had been back and forth over the area twice, struggling through thick overgrowth.

"Another wild goose chase," Todd said.

"The taxiway does come into this area, though," Taylor mused. "We'd better take another look."

One of the scouts groaned.

Todd pointed at the top of a grass-covered mound. "I'll go there to see if any more buildings are out this way." He started to climb up the steep slope.

Something crunched, then clanged.

Todd yelled just as he disappeared.

Taylor scrambled up the slope. He stared into a rectangular hole into which vegetation dangled. "Todd, Todd, where are you?" He could see something slanting down below.

"Oh, man." Todd's voice was faint. "My ass hurts."

"Are you all right?" Taylor asked.

Todd groaned. "I'll survive."

There was a scrambling noise. He reappeared, covered with dirt and cobwebs. He was rubbing his buttocks.

"What happened?" Taylor asked.

"I stepped on something that gave way." Todd let out a deep breath. "I fell, maybe three, four feet before hitting ground. Then I bumped down this ramp. It could be stairs under all that shit. Whatever it was, it was slicker'n snot."

"What is it?" Taylor asked. "Somebody's hideaway?"

"I don't think so," Todd said. "It's too big for that. I couldn't see much down there. I need a light."

"You, you, and you." Taylor pointed to three of the watching scouts. "Cut some dry reeds and make torches, as many as you can carry. Hurry."

The scouts mounted their horses and trotted toward the flood plain. "You." Taylor pointed to a curly-haired young scout. "Go to the Clan camp in Dayton. Get at least two dozen candles and whatever oil lamps are available. Tell Captain Monahan I need another squad to help out."

"Yes, sir." The young man mounted his horse.

"The rest of you," Taylor said. "Clean out this opening and the stairs below."

Taylor realized Todd had fallen through a hole, which had been a doorway.

The remains of a corroded set of hinges hung off one side. Inside were steps. The missing door lay flat at the bottom of a short stairway that descended to ground level. A short corridor led to another door. The scouts used a battering ram to open the door into a short corridor with another steel door. Both had thick rubber gaskets around their edges.

The second door's lock broke more easily. It swung open smoothly on greasy hinges to reveal a dark and cavernous room. It had a dry, musty, fetid smell that made Taylor think of death.

"Bring the torches," Taylor said.

The reed bundles burned with copious smoke. Coughing, they made their way through the smoke-filled corridor into a dark cavern.

"What's that?" Todd called out.

Something reflected the flickering light of the burning reed torch. It towered over them.

Taylor stepped forward. It was a dark, camouflage colored surface curving away from him. He stepped to one side and held the torch higher.

A gaping maw stared back at him. Its diameter was big enough to swallow him. Inside the maw was a bright yellow disk filling its throat. Above was a smooth, rounded edge of a flat surface.

"Well, what d'you know," Taylor said.

"Oh, my God," said Todd.

Taylor swung his torch to his left. As his eyes grew accustomed to the dark, he caught reflections of stout columns descending from the rounded shape with rounded shapes below. "I do believe," he said softly. "We've found our aircraft."

Taylor's torch was almost burned out. In addition, the smoke made his eyes smart. He headed up the stairs, closely followed by Todd. "We'll wait until we get better lights," he said. "In the meantime, have your men spread out and see if they can find their way into the other mounds around here."

Todd saluted and turned away.

ૐ

By the end of the afternoon, they uncovered three more bunkers with aircraft that held Air National Guard Apache helicopters and C-17 aircraft. All of the craft appeared undamaged and had crates of equipment and spare parts. The bunkers apparently had been bunkers with dirt pushed up against their sides to disguise their appearance. And they had been tightly sealed.

The next day, Taylor entered a C-17. He checked the controls for some time, then turned on the main power switch.

Nothing happened. Its batteries were dead.

They found desiccated bodies, slumped-over mummies still wearing uniforms. Their clothing had insignia indicating they had belonged to the 179th Airlift Wing of the Ohio Air National Guard. There were no signs of violent death.

"I wonder if this was one of the places hit by a bio-weapon in the war that preceded the Collapse?" Taylor said.

Todd stared at him. "What did you say?"

Taylor glanced up. "Sorry. I was thinking out loud. I was wondering how all these military people died."

"Military?" Todd asked. "How can they be military? They don't have any weapons."

Taylor chuckled grimly. "Their clothing tells me they were part of the US Air Force. It was a military branch before the Collapse."

Todd raised his eyebrows.

ૐ

The next morning, Taylor discovered the bunkers had huge doors facing the taxiway. Netting and vines covered the doors. Even when they were removed, the sliding doors would not budge.

It didn't take long before he realized large electric motors moved them. Close examination showed the bunkers were well sealed and most of the material inside was clean, with only minor corrosion on steel items.

It was time to let Billy know they had found aircraft.

CHAPTER THIRTY-ONE

Taylor used the newly established telephone link from Anna to contact Billy. "Yes, these aircraft pre-date the Collapse." He listened for a while. "Well, they appear to be in good condition, but we have no power to start them.... Yes, there are spare parts in the bunkers with the aircraft...."

"Look, Billy, I wouldn't know how to fly one of these things even if I could get it started...." He paused a while. "It's not the same as the shuttle...." Taylor felt his eyebrows raise. "I see ... So you expect the same principles to apply? You really think you can fly one?" He smiled. "Well, then I guess the only problem is fuel."

Taylor took a train to Defiance and then on to Berea via Norwalk. It seemed a long way around, but it took less than one day. He realized it would have taken at least three days on horseback. He had plenty of company on the way back; warriors returning home, happy the war was over. Time went by quickly.

"Taylor, over here." Joyce waved her hand.

Families crowded the railway station platform greeting loved ones returning from Dayton. It was a happy homecoming, for casualties had been light.

"Taylor, I missed you." She threw her arms around him and kissed him.

"Mmm, me too." Taylor stroked her hair and held her tightly. "Gee, that feels good. What a great welcome for only being gone a couple of days," he said. "I wonder what it would be like if I were gone for a month."

Joyce pushed him away to hold him at arm's length. Deep lines appeared between her eyebrows. "You're not trying to tell me something, are you?"

Taylor smiled widely. "Gosh, no, I just wanted you to know how nice it felt to have you meet me." His grin faded. "Nobody ever met me before when I came back from a campaign."

"Not even that old bag—"

"Joyce, please." Taylor laughed. "Forget about her. You don't have to worry about her."

"I'm sorry." She leaned her head against Taylor. "I just don't want to lose you." She looked up, eyes sparkling. "Let's go straight home." A short while ago, she had given up her apartment and moved into Taylor's home.

"Why don't we stop at the Travelers' Inn and grab a quick bite? That way we don't have to sit around while Noelle fixes food. She always goes into a production when I return from a trip."

"Hah. I knew it. She does care for you."

"You want me to fire her? How're you in the kitchen? D'you like housework?" Taylor raised one eyebrow as he slipped his arm around her waist and steered her toward the road that led home. "I pay well, too." He chuckled.

Joyce remained silent, lips pressed tightly together.

"Did you hear we found an aircraft?"

"Yes. Billy's more excited than I've ever seen him," Joyce said. "He wants to get them flying as soon as possible."

"Really?" Taylor asked. "How'll he do that?"

"I don't know. Did you hear about the academics from Ohio State?"

"Yes, just the other day."

"Well, did you know that one of them, Leonard Vili, knew my father? He's an electrical engineer, a real electrical engineer. He's been a big help."

"So, what does this have to do with the aeronautical engineering skills needed to get a plane flying? Never mind finding pilots to go on a crazy expedition to the Bahamas."

"Everything." Joyce squeezed his arm. "You know the problem we were having with the electronic control and trapping system?"

They were on the bridge that crossed the river.

"Yes." The distance between Berea and the Hill seemed longer every time he made the trip.

"Well, Professor Vili thinks he knows how to solve it so we can directly tap the electricity generated." She sighed. "Not only that, he thinks he knows how to switch it back and forth from a direct discharge mode to a current trapping mode."

"Which means?"

"It's possible to make an aneutronic fusion power source that will generate both electricity and provide thrust for an aircraft or even a spaceship. How about that?" Joyce looked pleased with herself.

"When will you know if this Professor Willy is right?"

"Vili." She took a deep breath. "We're setting up a trial run tomorrow. If it works, we still have fabrication problems, but Billy doesn't seem worried about them."

They reached the Oxbow area near the Travelers' Inn. The road ran beneath tall locust and maples latching overhead. It kept the road cool and shady during the day and now, dim evening light filtered through.

Taylor slipped his arm further around Joyce's waist and pulled her closer. "I wish I'd met you sooner. You've changed the way I feel about life. I feel so much more alive than I've ever been, thanks to you."

"Oh, Taylor, I feel the same way about you." She kissed him and held him tightly. "You're everything I've ever wanted in a man, and more."

"Are you really hungry?" Taylor asked.

"Maybe later." She smiled. "Right now, I'm hungry for some loving."

"Funny, that's what I had in mind."

ॐ

The fusion reactor trial was a success.

Billy began working day and night with a group of technicians, showing them how to fabricate solid-state electronics components made from organic materials. Once they mastered the technique, it took less than a week to make the first set of controls for a large aneutronic reactor.

The initial trial popped the circuit breakers in the lab because the generator produced too much current. After Billy and his staff adjusted the reactor, they powered it up again. Bit by bit, they activated circuits in the university until all its lights were ablaze.

Once they accomplished that, amid a spontaneous celebration, they added the city of Berea to the power grid.

The technicians made a second set of controls. This time it took only two days. After that, they found they could produce controls faster than they could build reactors.

CHAPTER THIRTY-TWO

Taylor peered around the door into a laboratory. It was full of glassware and electronic equipment. It had a strange odor that reminded him of something out of the past. *Ah*, he thought. *It's disinfectant.*

"Doctor Encirlik, why d'you need more resources?"

Doctor Meltem Encirlik looked up from the electron microscope.

Gray streaked her long black hair and lines had taken up permanent residence around her eyes. Her small stature was thinner, to the point of emaciation. "You remember me telling you about the anti-aging information in the Billy download? You funded another technician for it?" She reached out with her hand toward Taylor as though to touch him.

"Yes." Taylor nodded.

"I now understand what was in Billy's download." Her eyes glowed brightly. "Now I know how to offset aging in humans. At least, I think I do." She paused as a frown crossed her face. "It'll take resources to put it into effect, so I'll need more funding. It also raises ethical questions. Where do we get the first stem cells, the ones to start growing the cultures?"

Taylor stroked his chin. "Stem cells?"

"To start, I need a source, fresh stem cells, so that I can use the techniques in the Billy download to grow more. The only source I have, at the present time, would be from a fetus."

Taylor nodded. "I see." *That would put the cat among the pigeons with some of the religious groups.*

"Tests with rats and rabbits have confirmed the fusion of modified stem cells with certain types of DNA can retard, perhaps even stop the aging process." Doctor Encirlik took a deep breath. "I believe this technique is transferable to humans. That's why I need an increase in my budget."

"I'll get you funding for additional facilities and staff," Taylor said. "Keep me informed as to your progress. But no human trials until after a full Council review."

Doctor Encirlik's face went blank. "Oh," she said slowly. "Yes, well, I see. Thank you."

ॐ

"What's going on?" Taylor looked into Tim Van Mihn's workshop. "I got your message you'd discovered something exciting."

Electronic equipment and wiring covered every surface. Tiny red lights blinked among black boxes with multiple wire leads. The wastebasket over-flowed. Something hummed.

Tim looked up and smiled crookedly; one side of his face mobile and the other side stiff with scar tissue. Broken teeth showed momentarily. "Ever since you gave me a ham radio, I've read up on radio communications. I even built an antenna system for it. We, that is, Sally Butterworth and I, have been monitoring a variety of frequencies."

An angular featured woman with a fierce crop of freckles sat behind the radio and nodded in their direction. She wore headphones that were barely visible in her thick red hair. Her bright green eyes were wide and curious. She stood. A long, light linen dress hung loosely about her thin frame. She smiled shyly as a flush suffused her features.

"Hi," she said.

"Sally, please check if anything is being transmitted on that military frequency. The one that has us puzzled," Tim said.

Sally bent down to the radio and tapped its keyboard. Numbers scrolled across the top of its monitor and a waveform rippled across the bottom. "They seem to broadcast about this time of day," she said.

The radio squawked briefly. "... Alpha-Bravo calling CINCPAC, do you read me?" The words came faintly through the hiss and spit of static.

"That does sounds like the military." Taylor peered forward. "Can we transmit on that frequency?"

"Sure," Tim said. "Now the antenna is hooked up, we should have enough power to cover most of the northern hemisphere."

"Have you talked to them?" Taylor asked.

"No, we haven't transmitted anything to them yet."

"I think it's time to give Alpha-Bravo a call," Taylor said. "Can you set up the transmitter so I can talk to them?"

"Sure," Tim said. "Sally, if you please."

Sally plugged in a microphone and flipped two switches. She tapped in the frequency on the keypad and handed the microphone to Taylor. "Whenever you're ready, just press the button."

"Alpha-Bravo, Alpha-Bravo. This is Taylor MacPherson of the Greater Clan of the Mid-West, located in the state of Ohio. Do you read me?" Taylor paused to listen.

The seconds ticked by before the radio squawked, "This is Alpha-Bravo, we read you loud and clear. This is a reserved military frequency. State your identity and business."

Taylor's eyebrows rose. "This is Taylor MacPherson in Ohio. I'm trying to make contact with any official representative of the US government...."

"Please repeat, did you say Ohio?"

"Yes, the Greater Clan is headquartered in Berea, which is just outside of Cleveland. We've established government in the northern half of Ohio."

"Are you a military unit?"

"No. We're a democratic form of government and we've started to reestablish some of the basic services—"

"How can you broadcast without power?"

"We've started to generate electricity, but that's not important yet. Who're you? What kind of military force are you? How many are in your group?"

"This is SSN-767, USS Hampton, at the Bangor Naval Base.

Our military strength is classified information. How do you generate electricity?"

"Why are you interested in our source of electricity?"

"That's classified."

"Suit yourself. Our power is generated ..." Taylor realized aneutronic fusion power was different from any pre-Collapse technology. He decided to fuzz his answer. "From, er, nuclear power."

"You've got nuclear fuel?" Alpha-Bravo's voice went up a notch. "I'd better inform Captain Mapes about this. Can you hold on until I get him?"

"Sure." Taylor swore silently.

Sometimes, he realized, *a little white lie becomes bigger and harder.* As he waited, the static hiss warbled up and down. It seemed to take forever.

"This is Malachi Mapes, captain of the USS Hampton. To whom am I speaking?" His voice was strong and well-modulated.

"This is Taylor MacPherson, in Berea, Ohio."

"Now what's this about having nuclear power?" The voice from the speaker demanded. "My officer said you claimed to be generating electricity with a nuke?"

"Yeah, sort of," said Taylor. "Enough for us. So, you're in Maine? That's almost close enough for us to send people there. What's the radiation like there? Has it diminished?"

"Maine? What do mean, Maine?"

"Didn't you say Bangor, Maine?"

"No, we're in Bangor, Washington. It's the Pacific center for the SSN and SSBN operations...."

Captain Mapes went on to explain the submarine base had survived a whopper mine attack. The main pulse or wave had gone down the Puget Sound, bypassing the Hood Canal. However, Seattle and Tacoma had been hit hard. Most of the waterfront and other low-lying areas had been swamped by the artificial tsunami.

As Taylor heard more details, he realized the military group was trying to hang onto their technology, but was running short of power. "How do you get your electricity?"

"We use the power plants in two Ohio-class submarines. We've cannibalized a dozen subs to keep them in fuel. If you could spare some fuel units ..." Captain Mapes paused.

"Sorry, can't help you. You're just too far away. Maybe when we get our aircraft flying—"

"Aircraft? Are you serious?" Captain Mapes said.

"Well, we found three C-17s in Wright-Patterson AFB," Taylor said. "Unfortunately, the batteries are shot and there's no fuel. And no one knows how to fly them."

"I see," said Captain Mapes. "Some of us do. We may be a little rusty. Some of us had a lot of hours under our belts."

"We may have need of your advice," Taylor said. "However, there is one of our people who thinks that he can get the aircraft operational. A very unusual individual."

Right, Taylor thought. *I'm not going to drop Billy's identity on these folks on the West Coast.*

"When I said we," Captain Mapes said. "I meant we're in contact with a military unit at Groom Lake. That's an old Air Force Base. Unfortunately, they no longer have fuel for their aircraft."

"Maybe we should contact them," Taylor said.

"I think you should be in contact with all of the military bases," said Captain Mapes. "We'll contact them first and let them know of your existence. Meantime, I'll turn you back over to Seaman Von Klaas who'll give you frequencies and other technical details." He paused for a moment. "We really do need to get nuke fuel units. If we run out of power, we'll lose the last of our subs." His voice softened to become almost wistful. "I hope you get your aircraft flying soon."

"We'll let you know when we do." Taylor meant it.

These people were the US military, the last official remnant of the government of the United States of America. It stirred feelings he had almost forgotten and offered hope of something he hadn't felt for a long time.

The memory of the alien threat flashed into his mind. "We need you, too, as much as you need us."

CHAPTER THIRTY-THREE

"TaylorMacPherson."

When Billy ran his name together into one word, Taylor knew Billy was excited about something. "Yes, Billy?"

"We must get aircraft operational. There was another attack by wild creatures on wrigglers last night. More died. This cannot continue." Billy waved his stubby arms. "We must fly aircraft and rescue Cha KinLaat and MinCha DuKaat."

"We're taking a trainload of supplies to Dayton in about ..." Taylor glanced at the calendar on the wall of his office. "Twelve days." Billy's team had studied plans of the C-17 aircraft and concluded to build aneutronic fusion units with the same dimensions as the Pratt & Whitney turbo-fan engines in the C-17s was impossible in the time available.

He sent a shipment of gold to Pennsylvania to get a railway wagon filled with lantern-grade fuel. As a result, Pittsburgh Pete wore a big smile these days. "Most of the equipment is ready. I'm still not sure if the railroad track into the base has been repaired."

"Use phone," Billy said. "Find out. I fear for the survival of my own kind."

Taylor stood. He recognized Billy worked hard and shared everything he knew with them. The Clan owed him. He made up his mind. "Let's find out what can be done."

ॐ

"Yes, yes, I see," Chris said into the telephone. "Well, put a couple more platoons on the rail line. Yes, I said platoons, not squads. Right. Call me tomorrow with the amount of track brought into service. Thank you, Captain." Chris carefully placed the phone into its cradle and looked up. "There, that should do it."

"Where do we stand on schedule?" Taylor asked.

"Oh, it's the usual case of someone making up their own priorities." Chris waved her hand as though swatting away a fly. "Monahan's back on duty and he decided the rail line repair could wait while he spruced up the barracks. He said something about a Council Elder's visit. Probably his uncle. Dumb shit. Anybody can clean, but few know how to repair tracks." She stared at them for a moment. "Sorry, I'm venting."

"When?" Taylor said.

"There's about six miles of track that needs rebuilding. It's going to take at least a week." Chris bit her lip. "I know, it should've been completed long ago. I just didn't check up on what was going on down there. Sorry."

Taylor stared into the distance for a moment. "All right, let's get the items on Billy's list loaded into box cars and schedule the first available locomotive to get down there." He smiled; it was completely without humor. "Maybe you'd like to come along for the ride." He smiled at Chris. "A little fresh air and a little exercise in ass-chewing is good for morale, y'know. Your morale, of course."

"I see." She shrugged.

"Let Monahan know there's a full train-load of supplies destined for the base and you expect the track to be ready. No ifs, buts, or maybes." Taylor stood and strode to the door where he stopped. "When you're in command, you command. Thanks, Chris. I appreciate your help. I really do."

ॐ

A week later, two locomotives, a dozen boxcars, and a tanker full of fuel rumbled into Wright-Patterson AFB. Two rows of brown-clad warriors lined the tracks in perfect formation. The wind blew hot and humid. Mountains of clouds towered in the sky. Lightning flickered in the distance.

As the train squealed to a halt, boxcars clanging, the crews jumped out shouting to the ground. The area alongside the tracks had been scraped clean of vegetation and the dusty red clay was pockmarked with hoof prints and ruts. Horse-drawn wagons lined up on a new track of rough gray stone curving toward the concrete taxiway. A mixture of tall reeds and scraggly willows formed a backdrop to the cleared area.

"Ten-Hut," shouted Captain Monahan.

The brown-clad warriors stiffened and raised their rifles alongside their bodies, faces rigidly facing forward.

"Present arms."

The warriors pushed their rifles forward in one concerted movement, erect, away from their bodies in a tight row.

"The eighth battle group welcomes you to Dayton and Wright-Patterson Air Force Base." Monahan turned and snapped a salute in the direction of the train.

"Afternoon, Captain Monahan." Chris beckoned him. "Get rid of this honor guard and get this train unloaded. I don't have time for nonsense. We'll discuss your priorities later. Now, move it." Her lips were a tight, thin line.

"Yes, sir, ma'am." Monahan almost tripped as he limped toward the line of warriors still at stiff attention. "Platoons A, B, and C, dismissed."

Hobbling fast, he veered in the direction of the line of wagons and the civilians. "All right," he yelled. "Let's get this train unloaded."

Taylor glanced at the sky. "Is there a place to put things under cover?" he asked. "If not, better leave it in the boxcars until we can get the main door of a bunker opened."

Taylor had found the large electric motors that moved the doors were corroded and had seized bearings because they weren't within the sealed bunkers. Replacements were among the supplies in one of the boxcars.

"I don't see anything close by. I'm sure that's beyond Monahan."

As Chris finished speaking, large drops of rain began to plop down, raising tiny clouds of dust. "Another mud-flavored adventure is about to begin."

"Send the repair items from boxcar number one to the closest bunker," Taylor said. "We need those things to fix the door-opening mechanism. Maybe we can get a generator inside and get the lights working."

"You, with the big ears." Chris pointed at a warrior alongside the boxcar who was trying to listen to their conversation. "Get me Captain Monahan." She snapped her fingers. "On the double."

"Er, who shall I say requests his presence?" The warrior's eyes moved over Chris as though seeking a clue as to her identity. There was a trace of a leer on his face.

"Commander Kucinski. Move it," she said.

"Yes, sir, ma'am," The warrior saluted, turned, and ran.

"I like your style," said Taylor.

Ten minutes later, Captain Monahan stood at attention in the rain outside the boxcar to receive his orders. He saluted smartly as he departed, slipping and sliding through the mud.

ౌ

By the end of the day, the repair supplies were in the first bunker where a crew of technicians worked feverishly under Billy's direction. The generators brought in from Berea powered temporary lighting and the technicians continued to toil through the night. By morning the rain stopped. The technicians powered-up the massive door-opening mechanism and with much squealing and clanking of metal, they rolled open.

The civilian workers completed unloading the train by noon and it departed. Billy switched his attention to the C-17 aircraft within the bunker. "That is not a safe craft."

"Why?" Taylor asked.

"It cannot land except at a high speed. That makes it unsafe," Billy said with finality.

"That's why we have airports, with runways, like the one just east of the Hill—" Taylor tried to explain.

"Aircraft should be able to land anywhere. This cannot." Billy pointed at the C-17's wing. "No supplemental lift generators." He gestured at the engines. "No variable thrust vector control. This aircraft cannot land where my people are," he said. "No airport there."

"Well, we can get you closer to them—"

"No," Billy said. "We must make this aircraft safe to fly." He paused and swiveled his head around. "It needs same capability as a Bird-that-Soars." He stopped and looked at the C-17 towering over him. He grunted something in his native language and stepped back, staring at the engines. "Same size," he said. "We use them."

"What are?" asked Taylor.

"Drive units. Must use them."

"What drive units?"

"Yes, the drive units in Defiance. They came from a Bird-that-Soars and have variable thrust vectors. We must use them to make this aircraft safe to fly."

"I thought we didn't have much time left to save your friends," Taylor said. "Now you want to completely change what is probably a working aircraft."

"You do not understand." Billy's voice deepened and his words came out almost as grunts. "Those units from Defiance came from a Bird-that-Soars. It has variable thrust vectors; no need for changes. The drive units have enough power to lift a Bird-that-Soars into space. This aircraft weighs less than a Bird-that-Soars. We replace engines on this aircraft in four days."

"Well," Taylor said. "What about the supplemental lift generators?"

"Do without on first aircraft. We start on engines tomorrow." Billy flashed a caricature of a smile. "Aircraft must be ready to fly in a week."

Taylor frowned. "You really mean that?"

"Yes."

"What about the electrical systems? And the controls for the flaps or whatever they're called, don't they need checking out?" Taylor crossed his arms and raised his eyebrows.

"The generators will provide electric power to the aircraft

tomorrow." Billy waved his stubby arms. "Then validate aircraft systems' operation. Not difficult, takes time and workers. I must go, there is much to do."

You've got that right, Taylor thought. *I'm damn glad I'm not going to be on this aircraft when it flies.*

CHAPTER THIRTY-FOUR

"Your body's like a young man's." Joyce leaned forward and traced a pattern on Taylor's chest. "You have no fat and your skin is smooth, unblemished."

A sheet covered the lower half of her naked body. Early morning sunlight danced a dappled pattern on the wall. The lacy curtains of the four-poster bed swayed in the warm breeze. Sparrows chirped busily outside the window.

"You say the nicest things." Taylor rolled over and reached for Joyce. "So young and ripe, ready for plucking." His fingers slipped onto her breast and found a nipple.

"Ouch." She flinched and moved away. "They're a little tender. I think you've had too much of them lately."

"Well, then let me find something else to touch." Taylor's hand slid down her back and between her buttocks.

Joyce sighed. "I hope you're not just teasing me. It seems all you have to do is touch me and I want you." She slid over Taylor and kissed him on the lips. Rolling onto her back, she reached for him.

"Oh, my, what an invitation." He nuzzled her breasts, tongue moving. His tongue and lips moved downward, brushing and kissing, over her stomach and past her navel. He pushed the sheet aside and it slipped to the floor.

Joyce placed a hand on his head, guiding him further until he reached the inside of her thighs. She grasped his hair and took a deep breath as his tongue found her. "Oh, Taylor," she whispered. "That feels so good." Her hips flexed and she widened her legs. "Oh, please." Her hands ran over his back, touching and kneading him.

He raised her legs and buried his face deeper.

"Oh, yes," Joyce said, head turned and eyes closed.

Taylor rose to his knees and moved over her.

Her hand found him and guided him. As he found her, she cried out, "Oh, Taylor."

"Joyce, my love," Taylor gasped and paused. He opened his eyes and smiled. "Yes, my love, oh, yes."

ॐ

"Order, order." The sergeant-at-arms banged his staff on the floor several times.

Slowly, the clamor of voices subsided within the Council Chambers. Every seat in the public section was filled and heads peered in through the crowded doorways. The murmur of voices subsided and the distant sound of crows squabbling in the treetops outside became clear. Voices ceased and feet became still.

"Is there a second on the nomination of Mr. Ned Biehl for Council Leader?" Sean Monahan asked in his thin voice.

"I second his nomination," called Pete Belamy in a booming voice. He had been the previous speaker in the Central Ohio Union Assembly and was now a Clan Elder.

"I move the nominations be closed," came quickly from a voice with a western Ohio accent.

Jon Beach hobbled to his feet. "Now don't you think we ought to have a couple of candidates to make this a democratic election?" His eyebrows, dark and heavy, were sunk in over his eyes. Everyone knew he wanted to be the leader but lacked the votes. "Especially someone from the Clan?"

A rumble went through the public section of the Council Chambers. Feet stirred and floorboards creaked.

Pete Belamy clambered to his feet and leaned forward over the raised table behind which the Elders sat. "Mr. Beach," Belamy's voice boomed. "Where d'you think Mr. Ned Biehl comes from? The moon? Or have you forgotten that the Clan no longer encompasses just you and your cozy little clique?"

"Now just a Goddamn minute," Beach said.

Several Elders rose.

The sergeant-at-arms pounded his staff. "Order."

"Ah-um," said Sean Monahan. "I believe your remark was out of order, Mr. Beach." He leaned forward. "The gentleman from Mansfield, Mr. Kozlowski has something to say."

A heavy-set balding man cleared his throat. "I'm Mike Kozlowski, representing the Mansfield District of the Greater Clan, which is an area that at one time was part of the Central Ohio Union, a great and noble ..."

"Yes, yes," Monahan said. "Please get to the point."

"Well," Kozlowski said. "I think Mr. Biehl would make a good Council Leader, even if he doesn't come from," he hesitated. "My area of the Clan. He's fair in the way he treats people, no matter their district." He sat down, chair creaking.

Another wave of chatter fluttered over the public section.

"Any other comments?" Monahan asked.

"There's a question on the floor, specifically a motion to close nominations." Belamy's voice boomed loudly.

"That is so." Monahan nodded. "I call the question. Those in favor of closing the nominations for Clan Leader, raise their hands." He carefully counted the raised hands and made a notation in his logbook. "So passed."

Whispering filled the public section.

"Those opposed?" Again, Monahan took the tally. "The nominations are closed. I call the previous question, the vote on the nominee for Clan Leader, Mr. Ned Biehl from Napoleon. Those in favor, raise your hand." He called the name of each Elder with their hand raised, noting their name in the logbook.

"Those opposed?" Monahan repeated the ritual name check and recorded the way each Elder voted. "Mr. Ned Biehl has been elected Clan Leader. Ten votes for and six votes opposed." The corners of his mouth turned down.

Several hands clapped and applause slowly grew. People in the public section rose to their feet and began to cheer. It was the first time in almost a year that the Council of Elders had elected a leader.

ॐ

Noelle fastened her dress. "When're you going to tell him?" She made a face at the mirror. "You mussed my hair." She reached up and shook loose a ribbon and began to brush it.

Mitch Doaks stood behind her and put his hands around her waist. "Soon, I promise." He kissed her on the neck. "You see, he's been very busy as of late. I haven't found the right time to tell him." His hands moved up toward her bosom, only to be met by Noelle's hand brushing his aside.

"We're not getting started again." She sighed and closed her eyes. "Not that I wouldn't like to. It's just I've got to get a meal ready for Mr. MacPherson and Ms. Vargas. Have you had any success in finding a place for us?"

Mitch sat down heavily on the edge of the bed. "I've looked at a lot of places, but everything has gotten so expensive. More and more people are moving here to work at the university." He shook his head. "Sure, I can find a room with a bathroom down the hall, but I don't want us to live like that."

"I only make one silver dollar a week." Noelle tied the ribbon in her hair and smoothed her dress. *There*, she thought. *Now I look better.*

She turned toward him. "I've saved some silver, but not enough to buy a place. I never saw the need to find any place else. Once my daughter, Martha, got married and moved to the western territories, I didn't see the need."

Mitch rose to his feet and headed toward the door. "I'll keep looking. When the time's right, I'll tell MacPherson about us and ask for a higher salary." He stepped toward Noelle and lifted her chin to kiss her on the lips. "Don't worry, m'dear, it'll all work out, you'll see."

ॐ

"Mr. MacPherson, thank you for coming." Ned Biehl rose to his feet and gestured toward a chair.

His office, which overlooked the Rocky River through a screen of trees, was large and well-lit. Papers covered an oak desk and files covered the matching credenza behind.

Biehl was a tall thin man with a long, narrow face and a thick head of hair with a sprinkling of gray. Beneath his bushy eyebrows, bright blue eyes twinkled on each side of a prominent nose.

"There's so many things that need to get done, I almost fear bringing them up in Council."

"That's nothing new."

"Yes," Ned said. "I certainly want to work with Council on questions of how we allocate our resources. However, I'm reluctant to encourage Council to get into the details of managing the re-introduction of technology."

He sniffed and leaned back in his chair. "I think you can appreciate that, perhaps even more than me. Some of the Council members are very hostile to new programs. They also have little or no understanding of what's required, or what the results might be." He stood and walked over to the window. "That's the problem."

"I'm not sure what you mean," Taylor said.

"Well." Ned chuckled. "The things you and Billy're cooking up just amaze me." He sat down and leaned forward, across his desk. "The benefits are almost impossible to conceive. I have this feeling there's more to come. However, I don't want Council tinkering with it and killing the goose that laid the golden egg."

"What d'you mean tinkering? You've got to involve the Council, we're a representative democracy—"

"Oh, don't get me wrong," Ned said. "I don't want to change our government. I just don't want it to get in the way of progress. Or, more correctly, I don't want my enemies blocking the technology needed to defend the Earth against the aliens."

"Ah," said Taylor. "You want to do some of this outside the overview of Council?"

"Not exactly." Ned reached behind him for a folder. "I need input from you on how to go about getting us, our society, up to speed, ready for the aliens. I want you and Billy to have sufficient funding so you don't have to keep coming back to Council. There'll be opposition to some projects, primarily political, because work or money doesn't get sent to certain home districts." Ned turned and the light caught his face, revealing bags under his eyes.

Taylor took a deep breath. "I think I understand. This has a price, doesn't it?"

"Well, I'd certainly appreciate any ideas you might have that would cause the Council to view favorably some of the costly expeditions of the past year." Ned smiled. "And what other bills we might have to pay in the future."

Taylor walked back and forth in front of the desk with his hands clasped behind him. "It's my opinion that the re-introduction of electricity will create more wealth than most people can imagine. In addition, we'll get benefits from alien technology in different areas. I'd guess we're also going to see a population explosion. Transportation and communications will grow very rapidly. In fact, they're expanding at an accelerating rate right now. Old factories will come back into operation, creating cheap goods for everyone."

"How does the Clan profit from it?" Ned leaned forward. "Can we use it to pay for the needed expenditures? If so, how?"

Ah, thought Taylor. *His problem is revenues.*

He sat down. "I think you should move to incorporate the Cee-Dee-Cee into the Clan. It's a large area, has a large population, and produces a surplus of food. Doing so will require improvements to transportation and communications, which will create jobs. Longer term, this area will be a huge market for goods produced in the longer established areas of the Clan. As for taxes, well, it makes for a larger base." He paused. "Once we start producing electricity in quantity, every town will have the opportunity to enjoy the lifestyle of Defiance."

Ned Biehl's eyes got a far-away look. "Yes," he said. "Defiance has all those lights and all those electrical gadgets that make life easy."

"It's my understanding the major towns will have electricity within eighteen months, with connections to the smaller communities in the following eighteen months. That should produce a substantial rise in the standard of living. Remember the boom in Defiance after Billy turned on the electricity?"

"Yes." Ned still had a far-away look.

Taylor smiled. "That, Mr. Biehl, is my vision of the future." He stood. "I hope it has something you can sell to Council."

"Yes." Ned still had a dreamy look. "Yes, I think it does." His eyes snapped back onto Taylor. "I have to think about how I want to say it. If you can put a budget together, I'll do my best to get it authorized. Don't think small; I don't want you coming back to me in six months asking for more."

CHAPTER THIRTY-FIVE

Taylor rolled the chair back to his desk and grabbed the phone. "Yes? You're kidding? You're not? Then I've got to go right away." He dropped the phone into the cradle and ran to the door.

Chris Kucinski had just left his office.

"Chris," Taylor called. "Billy's aircraft is down. I just got a phone call from one of his technicians at Wright-Patterson. Apparently, he just got into the aircraft and took off. He sent a radio message he had problems and was landing. As far as we know, he's somewhere north of Columbus."

Chris frowned. "Where d'you think he went down?"

"I don't know."

"Ma'am." The messenger in the doorway saluted and held out a piece of paper.

Chris glanced at the note. "It's a message from Billy. He's not hurt, and the plane has only minor damage. He wants his technicians as soon as possible." She raised her eyes to the heavens. "He said he landed near the rail line from Lima to Mansfield, in an open area, with a big runway."

"Thank goodness," Taylor said. "What happened?"

"It doesn't say. Only the plane has minor damage." Chris picked up the phone. "Priority call to Wright-Patterson AFB. No, not Dayton, the base, you know, where Captain Monahan is on temporary assignment. Thanks." She covered the mouthpiece and looked at Taylor. "I'll be glad when we get direct dial."

"Me, too," Taylor said.

"Monahan? Yes, I know. Listen, round up Billy's technicians and all the equipment and supplies they were using on the C-17 and put them on a train."

Chris listened for a moment. "I don't care which damn train you use. Get the first one available. This is important. Yes, and get it done by first light tomorrow. I expect the train to be on the line outside Mansfield by 9:00 AM. Got it? I'll see you then."

ೞ

Taylor saw the skid marks first. They pointed to the C-17 whose camouflage markings made it barely visible against the saplings lining the runway. As he walked through knee-high grasses, he realized the ground underfoot was relatively smooth. It was an old and long forgotten concrete runway.

Brush and grass lined each side of the runway. The plane had skidded off the end of the runway and its landing gear housing had a fringe of vegetation that looked like a green hula skirt. The engine on the right side was tilted and the door below the cockpit yawned open.

It was silent except for the sounds of birds singing and insects chirping.

"Hello?" Taylor called through the door. "Billy?" His voice echoed hollowly through the plane's interior.

"Ah, Taylor." Billy rose from the long grass beneath the plane's wing. There was a long dark mark down the side of his head. The front of his cloak had dark stains.

"You're hurt," Taylor said. "What happened?"

"I applied too much thrust. An engine mount bent. The engine's movement prevented me from using the thrust vectors, so I had to land the plane fast. It is very hard to control that way." Billy waved his hand. "Not a good way to land. This looks like the airport near Berea."

"What about your head?"

Billy reached up and fingered the dark stain. "Small cut. My biocomputer has applied localized pain deadeners and growth stimulants. Not a problem." He pointed toward the plane. "Must fix engine. Need a stronger mount." He swiveled away from the plane and cocked his head. A rumble in the distance announced the approach of a train from the south. "Are those my technicians?"

"I think so." Taylor stared up at the distorted engine mount. *Twelve-inch angle iron and bent. Wow*, he thought. "So, what made the mounts fail?"

"Testing aircraft," Billy said. "I tried to make it go straight up like a Bird-that-Soars. Not the same." He paused. "I will not do that again."

"Right." *Straight up?* Taylor thought. *How much power do those engines have, anyway?* "So, what fraction of the total power output did you apply?"

"One part in eight. It was too much."

That's for sure, Taylor thought. *Lemme see, this plane came with four fifty thousand pound thrust engines. That means these engines have more than one point six million pounds thrust. It's a wonder he didn't rip the wings off.*

"Well," he said. "Your technicians will be here soon. I'm going to head back to the tracks and get some soldiers down here. You'll need strong backs to build a platform and pull the engine."

CHAPTER THIRTY-SIX

It took five days of driving his technical staff and several platoons of soldiers before Billy was satisfied with the replaced engine mount.

The C-17 was ready. Billy got the plane airborne and flew to the old Cleveland Hopkins airport, which was east of the Hill.

He circled the airport twice and then glided the plane toward the runway just north of the old terminal. The C-17 lost its forward speed, howling loudly like a banshee and began to hover. It slowly descended to a runway bristling with weeds. The last thirty feet of vertical descent, the plane blew huge clouds of dust and leaves high into the air. Once on the ground, the plane's engines sighed into silence.

Billy's technicians used a team of twenty horses to tow the plane to a hangar where a workforce had been assembled.

The repairs had taken longer than he had anticipated due to the remote location and the need to haul in even the smallest part. Billy brought the technicians' tools back in the plane where they had been stored during the work. It was quicker than hauling them back to the railroad track.

Billy wanted to leave right away to rescue his people.

"I need at least a day to go over those engine mounts to make sure nothing will come loose." Kevin O'Neil had joined the repair crew. "They really should be castings, stronger than a temporary bolted-up girdle." Since he'd discovered a mothballed aluminum foundry at the old Ford plant next to the airport, he wanted to cast parts for the plane.

"You should plan your trip," Taylor said. "Figure out where you're going and what kind of supplies you need." He paused. "You'll need maps, food, and repair parts and tools. What about your friends? Will they need anything special? Think about it. Make sure you don't rush off unprepared. Even weapons."

"I want Captain Kerr and a squad of his men to come with me," Billy said. "He is very reliable."

"That's a start." Taylor pulled out a sheet of paper. "Tell me what you need."

After Billy dictated what he needed, he said, "Tomorrow, I get my people."

ᘓ

A covered wagon backed up to the plane, into which Billy's alien friends disappeared without the crowd at the airport catching a glimpse of them. Kerr's men continued to unload items from the back of the C-17 into more wagons. Billy poked his head out of the door under the cockpit.

"How did it go?" Taylor asked.

Billy clumped down the metal steps. "The flight there took about four hours," he said. "Another half-hour to find my people. We landed on a smooth area by the water. I went alone to look for Cha KinLaat and the wrigglers while Captain Kerr's men guarded the aircraft."

"Did you have any problem finding them?"

"No," said Billy. "It was difficult getting the wrigglers to board the aircraft because they had been attacked by many forms of Earth life. They are nervous about anything strange. When they saw Captain Kerr and his men, they tried to hide. I had to explain they were there for their protection.

"During the time I was gone, Captain Kerr's people unloaded supplies and prepared food. As we finished the meal, a long creature you call a crocodile appeared. When it went after a human, soldiers killed it with their black powder rifles.

"However, the noise startled the wrigglers. They fled their water tubs in the plane and sought to hide under things. It took an hour to get them back into the tubs on the airplane."

Taylor smiled at the image of them hunting down the tiny wrigglers. "Why didn't you come back right away?"

"Ah," Billy said. "Cha KinLaat and the others wanted to bring every last item that had been brought down from the Egg-that-Flies. That took time.

"By then, it was late afternoon, so I decided to wait until morning rather than try to return during the night." Billy looked around as Captain Kerr came up. "How much longer?"

"Oh, just a couple of minutes to get the immediate items," Kerr said. "We'll come back for the rest of the stuff later."

"So," Taylor said. "Where did you spend the night?"

"In the aircraft," Billy said.

Kerr smiled. "Kind of close quarters." He turned to Billy. "Your little guys have a distinct aroma." His smile widened. "They sure are cute, though."

Taylor could detect the rotting-vegetation smell typical of swamp water coming from the plane.

"The sun was hot and bright as soon as it came up. Unlike Qu'uda," Billy said. "Different than here." He turned his head to observe the loading of the wagons. More material lay behind them. "Captain Kerr's men prepared food. After we ate, we left. Once airborne, Cha KinLaat joined me in the cockpit to tell me what the females and the wrigglers had experienced."

"What was it like?" Taylor asked.

"It was terrible. Mata ChaLik BuMaru abandoned them with few supplies and no preparation. He showed no consideration for their condition. Like he abandoned me." He extended his claws as though raking an object. "I shall meet him one day. I shall have revenge. He may be a Defender, but I am not afraid of him."

"Mata who?" Taylor asked.

"Mata ChaLik BuMaru is the center of the circle of trained fighters called the Defenders on the Egg-that-Flies. He is the one who wants to return to Earth and destroy it."

"Excuse me," said Kerr. "We're ready to head to the university." He pointed to the wagons drawn up in a neat line. "Mr. Billy, perhaps you'd like to join your friends?"

"Yes." Billy hurried to the lead wagon. Their destination was the old Recreation building at Baldwin-Wallace University, which had a small swimming pool. It had been refilled and set up as the new home of the Qu'uda.

Behind a line of brown-clad soldiers, the crowd had grown to several thousand. The word had spread more aliens were coming. Even though it was known that they were allies, there was a nervous edge to the crowd.

Captain Kerr waited until the wagons began to move. "Y'know," he said, "I'm surprised to see how small these aliens are. Somehow, I'd assumed Billy was a normal-sized alien." He shook his head. "But these guys are little. They look like four feet tall green lizards that walk on their hind legs. You should see how thin they are. Every bone shows."

ꕥ

"Dr. Encirlik," Billy said softly.

Dr. Encirlik looked up quickly from the microscope and took a sharp breath. "Yes? What can I do for you?"

"My people are very sick. They eat but fail to gain weight," Billy said. "If something isn't done, I fear they will soon die. Their bodies are ill-equipped for this planet."

"How did you survive without problems?"

"I was modified before I came here," Billy said. "Even then, I became sick. They made more modifications. I am not like most Qu'uda."

"Do you know what these modifications are?" Dr. Encirlik stood and eyed Billy thoughtfully.

"No."

Dr. Encirlik took a deep breath. "I know so little about your biochemistry, I'd be afraid to try something without having specific instructions." She reached out and touched his arm. "I'm sorry. I just don't know what to do for them."

"There is something," Billy said. "You have a procedure for transferring body fluid from one person to the other."

"Body fluid? Which body fluid?" She narrowed her eyes.

"The main circulatory fluid."

"Ah, blood. We call that a transfusion." Dr. Encirlik nodded. "You want me to transfer some of your blood, I mean body fluid, to your friends, is that right?"

"Yes," said Billy. "As soon as possible."

"Let me get my equipment and a technician." She hurried toward the back of the laboratory. "I'll be there in an hour."

CHAPTER THIRTY-SEVEN

"This is a closed Council meeting for the purpose of reviewing the budget and plans of the university." Ned Biehl sorted through the stack of papers before him.

Rain beat against the windows of the Council Chambers and drummed on the roof. The room was warm and musty smelling. Chairs creaked as the Elders made themselves comfortable. They had been warned it would be a long session.

"Mr. MacPherson's request for funds is accompanied with several proposals and recommendations I believe should be examined by Council. Specifically, he recommends we incorporate the former Columbus-Dayton Confederation into the Greater Clan." He handed a stack of paper to Sean Monahan who sat on his left. "This is the economic analysis and justification for that action."

"Well, I don't know about that," Ramsey said. "It's a huge area with a lot of poor people. Not much benefit in adding an area that'll need a lot of help and money to bring it up to our standards."

"They don't have much to trade for our manufactured goods, either," Beach said. His district had many factories.

"I understand your concerns." Ned nodded. "However, with the coming electrification and industrialization, there'll be improvements in the living standard."

"Yes," Beach said. "I've heard that so-called claim."

"Mr. Beach." Ned stared briefly at Beach. "The change that took place in Defiance after electrification was significant. Everyone is wealthier. I don't think you want to debate that fact. Anything made in Defiance from metal costs less, right?"

Beach nodded slowly. His district had lost many jobs because it could not compete with the electrified factories of Defiance. "Sometimes I think we should ban electricity."

"Unfortunately," Ramsey said. "We need it to prepare for the aliens' return."

"Supposed return," Beach said with a sneer.

"Please," Biehl said. "This's getting nowhere." He raised a sheet of paper. "You have a copy of the economic justification for the incorporation of the Cee-Dee-Cee. This item will be discussed in an open meeting of Council next week. You have the analysis and the agenda.

"Next item is the request by Mr. MacPherson to set up a centralized electric power authority, separate from the university. He believes getting power to our communities has little to do with research and preparing for the aliens return."

"What did I tell you?" Beach said.

"Mr. Beach, may I continue?" Ned asked patiently.

"Sorry." His voice rang with practiced insincerity.

"He believes that it's more construction and engineering than research." Ned rose slightly in his seat to look at Beach. "In fact, he believes it should be done by soldiers from the barracks. After it becomes a part of the system, each community will repay the Clan for their services."

Since the Clan had defeated the Cee-Dee-Cee, word had spread about the Clan's new weapons. As a result, the Clan borders were quiet. Most of the soldiers had little to do.

"Sounds good to me." Ramsey nodded approval.

Pete Belamy raised his hand. "What if a community can't afford it? I can think of some farm areas that're mighty remote. It'd take a lot to get them into the system."

"Good point," Ned said. "If a community wants to provide the labor to build the system, fine. Even though we've got enough funds to finance this project, there are many other items that'll need our attention. I'm sure we can work those kind of details out."

"Well, who pays for the devices that'll make the electricity? And who's going to make them?" Belamy still seemed upset about something.

"That's one of the purposes of setting up the electric authority." Ned reached for another sheaf of papers. "You see, the university has no desire to become a manufacturer. The authority will contract with existing factories to make parts for the electric generators. Assembly will be done in a separate facility because no existing factory has the capability."

"Yes, some of the factories in my district could use some extra work." Beach's eyes brightened.

Ned smiled as though he'd just tasted something sweet. "Yes, I'm sure they'll be considered very seriously, especially since we expect the assembly facility will be at the old airport. So, local factories should get more work."

"Who gets to run this power authority?" Carver Washington leaned forward. "That sounds like a pretty high-level job."

Ned raised his eyebrows. "Mr. MacPherson nominated Ms. Joyce Vargas to head up the Centralized Electric Power Authority. She helped with Defiance's electrification and has an excellent under-standing of electricity—"

Beach leaned forward with a knowing leer on his face. "Isn't she MacPherson's, you know ..."

"Mr. Beach." Ned's voice echoed through the chambers. "Her technical qualifications are second only to those of Billy Potato. Her personal life is her own. If you know someone else better qualified, please feel free to nominate them for this position." He smiled at Beach. "After all, we want the best person to run this project."

"When d'you expect this project to start?" asked Monahan. "Will this be going to an open Council meeting, too?"

"The project's already underway." Ned reached for more paper. "The first generator will be sent to Defiance—"

"Now just a minute. They've already got electricity." Beach stood abruptly, knocking his chair over. "Why them?"

"Mr. Beach, please," said Ned. "It's to replace the units being used in the ..." He hesitated and looked at his notes. "Aircraft. Billy Potato needed them."

Beach picked up his chair and sat down. "Why do we need this damn flying machine, anyway?"

"We're reintroducing technology. They're an integral part of it."
Ned glanced at the other Elders. "May I finish?"

"Yes. Sorry." Beach's apology was without conviction.

"The nomination of Ms. Vargas to head the Centralized Electric
Power Authority is before this Council." Ned put his hands behind
his head. "Quite frankly, I don't know of anyone else who could
handle this job. She enjoys the confidence and support of Billy
Potato and Taylor MacPherson."

"I'll bet she does." There was a leer in Beach's voice.

"Did you wish to say something Mr. Beach?" Ned leaned
forward, a frown on his face. "Have you got something of importance to add to this discussion?"

Beach smirked but said nothing.

"I support her nomination and make a motion she be appointed
as head of the electric power authority, with a salary of five hundred
silver dollars per year—" Ned began.

"Five hundred." Sean Monahan gasped. "Why, that's ten times
the pay of a working man." His eyebrows creased into a frown.

"I know. It does seem like a lot." Ned nodded sympathetically.
"However, electricity will have a very powerful impact upon our
lives and must be done properly. Since it has the potential to make
all of us far richer, I believe the head of the electric power authority
should earn enough to be beyond temptation." It was an oblique
observation that some Elders had gotten wealthy during the course
of conducting Clan business. "Any other comments?" He glanced up
and down the row of Elders.

"Where'll this money come from?" asked Carver.

"This is specifically included in the budget submitted by Mr.
MacPherson—" Ned began.

"Oh, so he's the one that wants to make his girlfriend into a
high-priced, whatever you want to call it." Beach snickered.

"Beach, that's out of line." Carver pointed his finger at Beach.
"I'm getting tired of your snide comments. Besides, there's a motion
on the floor, which I second and call the question." He stared at
Beach as though daring him to speak.

Ned looked pleased. "Those in favor, raise their hand."

One by one, hands rose. Ned called names as he counted. "The
majority favors this appointment.

"Next item is the formation of the railway authority to restore rail lines throughout the Greater Clan. The railway authority will also build and repair locomotives, carriages, and other rolling stock. In addition, it will also operate the trains, maintain regular service and be available for use by the Clan's forces, should there be a need. Questions?"

"Who's going to run it?" Kozlowski asked.

"Captain Ed Kerr," said Ned. "He's been restoring railroad track from the beginning. He knows how to do it and he knows where the tracks go."

"Isn't he one of your former compatriots?" Beach pasted an innocent smile on his face. "From your neck of the woods?"

"Kerr was recommended by Commander Chris Kucinski for this position." Ned's face was expressionless. "Perhaps you'd like to review his credentials with her?"

Ramsey cleared his throat. "No need. I've talked to her already about Kerr. This is a good place for him." It was well known Ramsey resented Kerr's appointment to head a battle group and was happy to help him on his way out.

"What's this going to cost?" Monahan asked.

Ned passed out another sheet of paper. "The costs are broken into two parts: First is construction, which is significant; and the second is operations, which will generate income. If you'll look at the bottom section, you'll see this system will pay back all the construction costs by end of the fifth year. Recognize this assumes the Clan will grow and the volume of freight hauled will increase from year to year."

Monahan tapped the paper. "Let me get this right. This says the trains will produce a profit of one hundred thousand silver dollars per year at the end of the fifth year, is that right?" His eyebrows had risen.

"That's correct."

"Does that much silver exist?"

Ned took a deep breath. "Yes and no. There are plenty of gold and silver coins, because the Clan has a stockpile. However, not much has been stamped with the Clan's mark to make it legal currency. It's our expectation, as the economy expands from the introduction of electricity and increased trade, the Clan will intro-

duce more currency. That, fellow Elders, is where we get the funds
to pay for these projects."

No one said anything.

"That is also the reason why this is a closed meeting. To
preserve the value of the money in circulation, we cannot let the
general populace know we're making money. They work damn hard
for what little silver they get."

"So we really can afford these projects after all?" Ramsey asked.
"Will my men get paid for their work?"

"Of course." Ned smiled. "That's how we get new money into
circulation to meet the needs of an expanding economy."

ૐ

"Goddamn Biehl," Beach said quietly into the gloom. The room was
dimly lit, its windows shuttered, and the door closed. "He keeps
sending more and more work out of the Clan." He looked at the
shadowy figures across from him.

"Yes," came Monahan's reedy voice. "It's that damn electrical
power. Our water-powered mills can't compete and we're losing half
our population. Now Biehl wants MacPherson's bitch to give power
units to everybody."

"We'll have to do something to stop them, permanently." Beach
stood and limped to the window. "When the time is right." He
turned back toward the room. "Are you with me?"

Monahan took a deep breath. "Yes, and there are others who'll
stand with us, too."

ૐ

"How's my favorite engineer?" Kevin O'Neil peered around the door
into Joyce Vargas's office. He smiled and winked.

"Okay." Joyce did not look up.

"I need a favor, m'dear. I need line run."

"Right."

"Look," said Kevin. "I need power to the factory by the airport.
It has electric induction furnaces for both iron and aluminum.
That'll simplify making parts for the reactors."

Joyce looked up from a cherry wood desk over a stack of paper. "Get in line," she said. "Everyone wants their power yesterday. Submit a request like everyone else." She returned to writing on a piece of paper with a frown on her face. She winced and grasped her stomach.

"Joyce," Kevin said. "What's wrong?" He sat in the chair alongside her desk. "All I asked for was power for the production facilities so I can build you more fusion generators and you bite my head off. That's not like you."

Joyce straightened up. "I'm sorry."

"Apology accepted. So, what's bothering you?"

"My stomach's upset. I've had trouble keeping down food. All this work keeps piling up. Everyone wants it yesterday."

"I knew you weren't yourself," Kevin said. "How d'you feel? D'you have a headache, or anything else?"

"Upset stomach. I just feel something is wrong."

Kevin stood and nodded his head. "C'mon, let's go see Doctor Encirlik." He held out his hand. "Maybe there's something she can do for you. If not, at least she can give you an idea what's causing the problem."

"I don't have time—"

"Now, Joyce, you always have time for your health."

Kevin's attitude was that of a parent: Firm, almost commanding, with a gentleness that could only come from affection.

"C'mon. It'll only take a few minutes. She's in the next building."

"Oh, all right." Joyce threw her pen down and headed for the door with Kevin in tow. It took them less than two minutes to reach Doctor Encirlik's office.

"How long have you had this nausea?" Doctor Encirlik asked. "When did you last menstruate?"

"I've not been feeling well for a week or so."

Doctor Encirlik removed her fingers from Joyce's wrist. "Menstruation?" She reached for a battered stethoscope.

"I don't know. I don't remember."

"Are your breasts sore or tender?" Doctor Encirlik applied the stethoscope to Joyce's back.

"Why, yes. How did you know?"

"Well, it's possible you may be pregnant."

CHAPTER THIRTY-EIGHT

"Mr. MacPherson."

Taylor lifted his head. "Oh, Mitch, come in." He gestured toward a chair. "What is it?"

He delegated many of the routine activities of the university to Joe Del Corso and Mitch Doaks. This suited him just fine. He closed a file and pushed it aside.

"Can I to talk to you about a personal matter?" Mitch said. "I've been working at the university for over a year and I want to settle down, here, in this area."

"Good." Taylor leaned back in his chair and glanced out of the window.

Students hurried across campus over sere lawns. A glaring sun dominated the brassy sky.

Air conditioning, he thought, *that's what I need. This building is too damn hot in the summer.*

"You must like it here."

"I do," Mitch said. "It's different, though, from being a soldier. I don't have a barracks to live in. It takes all my money just to get by." He fiddled with a button on his shirt and examined the floor. "Well, what I'm saying is that I don't get paid enough to live on. I can't afford a real place to live."

"What's your pay?" Taylor asked.

"The same as I got as a soldier."

Taylor reached into a file drawer in his desk and pulled out a folder. "Let's see, you were listed as a platoon leader when on active duty." He frowned as he reviewed a column of figures. "Right, you're not being paid enough, especially for what you're doing." He stood and looked out of the window for a moment. "You should be paid more, in line with a senior administrator. Let me check and I'll get back to you."

Mitch remained sitting before Taylor's desk.

Taylor stared at him. "Is there something else?"

Mitch swallowed. "Er, yes, I, er, I want to get married."

"Congratulations. Who's the lucky woman?"

"It's er, it's Mrs. Smith."

Taylor took a deep breath. *Ah, now I understand. All those visits and the conversations that end when I come in.* He nodded slowly.

"I hope this doesn't cause any unpleasantness, being that she works for you and all that." Mitch's voice trailed off.

Taylor leaned back in his chair and put his hands behind his head. "This's why you need to find a place to live, right?"

"Yes." Mitch's face reddened slightly.

"Am I going to lose my housekeeper?"

"Well, we talked about that. We both like our jobs. I don't see how she can live in your home and be married to me." A pained expression crossed his face. "I wouldn't presume to move into your home." His face reddened.

Taylor chuckled. "So, I'm losing my live-in housekeeper." He glanced at the ceiling for moment. "Maybe we can work something out. Lord knows I don't want to get in the way of your and Noelle's happiness." *Besides,* he thought. *This solves the two-women-under-one-roof problem if it's handled carefully.*

Mitch's mouth fell open. "Then everything's all right? It won't cause a problem?"

"Absolutely not. I'm sure we can work things out." Taylor hesitated for a moment. "Look, you need to find a place to live, and you need a pay raise to do that. Assume your pay will be doubled. If I can do better than that, I will." *What's the phrase?* he thought. *Cheap at twice the price?*

Mitch's mouth opened wider. "Er, thank you, Mr. MacPherson,

thank you. That's very generous." He rose and turned as Joe Del Corso shot through the door. "Excuse me?"

"Sorry." Joe panted as he waved an envelope at Taylor. "I was told to get this to you right away, that it's urgent. I even had to stop doing the fall schedules."

"Thank you." Taylor took the envelope from Joe's hand and tore it open. His eyes narrowed as he read. "Oh, my God." He jumped up and ran out the door.

༄

Tim Van Minh stared at the fusion drive unit. It had been removed from the C-17 after Billy brought his fellow aliens back from Andros Island. *The unit seems small now that it's out*, he thought. The intense light from the LED lamps lit the concrete floor of the hangar where the unit sat.

Electricity, he thought. *It has improved the engineering facilities in so many ways. Machines, tools, lighting; every day there was something else that became available. Things that seemed daunting only a year ago were now routine.*

How, he wondered, *am I going to make another one of these? Even Cheronoff, the university's metallurgist, has no idea how to make copies of the titanium and ceramic parts in the thrust vector section of the drive unit.*

After he'd questioned Billy at length, he'd realized he didn't have the technology in his biocomputers because it was too specialized. It was time to take another tack.

"Well, Tim, what d'you think?" Kevin O'Neil asked. "Any ideas on how to make one?" He pointed at the drive unit.

"The basic drive unit, yes. The thrust vector control section, no." Tim straightened up. "Until we get to a higher level of materials technology, I think we should concentrate on making a straight replacement for the turbo-fan engines. That would be a modification of the basic power generator."

"Y'think so?" Kevin had commented making a small unit for the locomotives was more difficult than he'd first believed. The problem was how to scale-down the fusion reactor with an output suitable for a locomotive. To date, he hadn't succeeded.

"How much power d'you think you want from a replacement unit?"

Tim sniffed and reached for a handkerchief. *Allergies*, he thought. *Why am I cursed with allergies?* "I think we should go for a unit with twice the output of a turbo-fan, or about one hundred thousand pounds thrust. Use one drive unit to replace two engines. That would save weight, too. It would be equivalent to a forty megawatt-generator."

Tim talked frequently with Kevin, for the young engineer found he too, had a knack for mathematics and a strong practical bent.

Kevin nodded. "That's a good size for a power unit and it'd make a Hell of a train engine. I'd prefer to have lots of power units scattered around rather than a few large ones. Just in case."

"Yeah," Tim said. "Just in case." *Just in case the Qu'uda do bomb us back into the Stone Age.* "Okay. Why don't we do a joint design exercise to see if we can maximize the number of parts in common for both the drive and power units?"

Kevin held out his hand. "It's a deal."

Mitch knocked on the side door. The house's sandstone walls had weathered to gray. Moss grew bright green where water dripped from leaking gutters. The door was in a quiet, secluded alley, shadowed by an adjacent house.

The door opened quickly. "Well, what did he say?" A furrow creased Noelle's brow. "Was he upset?"

Mitch smiled. "Noelle, come here." He held his arms open.

"I want to know." She folded her arms across her bosom. "Right now." Her mouth was set in a thin line.

"Now, now, my sweet." Mitch's grin grew. "You're worrying too much. He wasn't a bit annoyed. In fact, he gave me a big increase in pay. Now we can afford a place of our own."

Noelle's eyebrows rose. "Really? Do I get to keep my position here?" Her hands unfolded and she reached for him.

"Yes, and yes." Mitch pulled Noelle to him and kissed her on the lips. His hand slid down to her buttocks.

"Now cut that out." She smiled as she brushed his hand away, glancing up the alley. "Somebody might see. Save it for when we're alone."

Mitch leaned back to look at her. "You make me feel like a young man. Every time I'm with you, I want you."

Noelle smiled and looked past him at the only window overlooking the side entrance. The curtains were still. "Well, come on in, then," she said. "No one's home."

ᕲ

Taylor stepped into Doctor Encirlik's office.

Filing cabinets with folders stacked high on top lined the walls. A battered metal desk held two neat piles of paper on each side of a large blotter pad and a glass vase with flowers. On the hardwood floor beside the desk was a small oriental rug. The credenza behind the desk was clear except for two faded photographs: One showed an older couple in a stiff pose; the other a handsome dark-haired young man in a medical coat.

The office was empty. He turned to go.

"Mr. MacPherson." Doctor Encirlik appeared silently. Her face was thin, drawn, with a grayish pallor.

"Dr. Encirlik, what happened?"

She smiled. "Ms. Vargas is pregnant."

Taylor sat down. "Pregnant? Joyce is pregnant?"

"You weren't intimate?" She raised her eyebrows.

Taylor felt a flush of heat in his face. "Well, yes, of course."

"Were you taking any kind of birth control precautions?" Dr. Encirlik's eyebrows arched.

"No, I never thought about it. For some reason or other, I didn't think it likely." He hesitated. "Joyce never had children. I thought ..." Taylor realized he'd never asked.

"Well, she is." Dr. Encirlik fiddled with her stethoscope. "She's had some morning sickness. I gave her something to settle her stomach. I suggested she might ease up on her work to reduce stress." She picked up a file folder and glanced at it. "Otherwise, I think she'll be fine."

"Good. Where is she?" Taylor asked.

"She's just down the hall," Dr. Encirlik said. "I've also given her some dietary recommendations. I'd like to see her on a regular basis. Other than that, she's free to leave."

"Thanks." Taylor turned to leave.

"I appreciate those additional resources. It really helps." A smile briefly lit Doctor Encirlik's face.

"You're welcome," Taylor said over his shoulder as he headed down the hall with long strides.

He stepped into an examining room where Joyce sat on a metal table. "Joyce, are you all right?"

Joyce made a wry face. "I feel better now. Kevin made me come here." She put her head in her hands. "I can't believe this happened," she said.

Taylor stood next to her. He gently lifted her head upright and pulled her close to him. "Joyce, it's the most wonderful thing that could've happened to us."

"Wonderful?" Joyce's voice quavered slightly. "I won't be able to do my job. It'll ruin everything."

"You're not listening." Taylor said. "You're even more precious to me. I've always wanted a family. Now it's happening."

Joyce pushed him away to look at his face. "What about me? You didn't ask me if I wanted a family."

"Do you want children?" Taylor asked.

"Well, yes, but not now. I'm not even married."

Taylor helped Joyce to her feet and pulled her close to him. "Well, let's get married and raise a family."

"Married?" Emotions ran across Joyce's face: Surprise, joy and then worry. "You're just telling me what I want to hear, aren't you?"

Taylor frowned. "I don't think so. Look, Joyce, I've been thinking about us getting married anyway." He hesitated for a moment. "You probably won't like the reason but I'm going to tell you: There have been some nasty comments made about your appointment and my relationship with you. Getting married will put an end to that." He took her hands and kissed them. "I want to protect you. Even more than that, I love you and don't want to lose you."

"Married." Joyce pronounced the word with an air of finality. "Married. So when will we get married?"

"If you want, we can do it this weekend." Taylor smiled. "That way, we'd finesse the demands for a big wedding and figuring out who to invite and who to offend." He kissed her hands again. "Besides, Dr. Encirlik thinks you should go easy on stressful activities."

Joyce wrinkled her nose as though she smelled something offensive. "She did say something about that."

"Well?"

"Well what?"

"Shall I make arrangements for a quiet wedding this weekend? Invite just a few friends and no politicians." Taylor's voice had become firm, business-like in tone.

Joyce sighed. "I don't know, I suppose so."

"Oh, by the way," Taylor said. "I just heard that another marriage is in the offing." He pursed his lips and waited.

"Who?" she asked.

"Noelle Smith."

"Noelle." Joyce's voice almost squeaked. "To whom?"

"Mitch Doaks, my assistant."

"Now I understand why he kept coming around. Why, that little sneak," Joyce said. "She's been carrying on with him under our noses. What nerve."

Taylor shrugged. "I don't know and don't care."

"You don't care she might have been—"

"Joyce." Taylor gently grasped her hand. "She'll be moving out. If she continues to work for me, and I hope she does, she'll only be there during the daytime." He lifted up her chin. "I thought you'd be happy about that."

Joyce nodded. "Yes, that would be better." She smiled. "We'll be alone at home, together."

Taylor touched her stomach. "Until the baby arrives."

ↄ

Ned Biehl rose to his feet and gestured toward a chair. "Please, have a seat." His large office overlooked the Rocky River through a screen of trees. File folders covered his oak desk and the matching credenza behind him. "Tell me about this proposal from the Pennsylvania communes."

Pittsburgh Pete stretched out his legs and put his hands behind his head. "Well, y'know I make deals with those folk in Pennsylvania all the time. In fact, only a month ago, I got a whole railroad tank car full of oil for the Clan—"

"Yes, yes," Ned said. "I'm well aware of that."

"Sorry," Pete said. "This's a new deal," he said brightly and flashed a smile. "They want to buy an electrical generator. They're willing to pay a hundred pieces of gold and a railroad tank car of oil for it—"

"Now, wait a minute." Ned frowned. "We paid a hundred pieces of gold for the tank car of lantern fuel, which by the way, is still sitting unused down in Dayton—"

"Right. They make money selling petroleum and coal," Pete said. "They also know electricity is the way of the future. They'd also be willing to form an alliance with the Clan, for mutual protection and benefit."

Ned stroked his nose. "I tell you what. I'll send a Clan delegation to meet with the folks in Pennsylvania to talk to them about this deal." He sighed. "There's more to electricity than just a generator. It takes a distribution system and equipment. What d'they plan to use the electricity for, anyway?"

Pittsburgh Pete waved his hand dismissively. "Oh, lighting and running equipment. Y'know, the usual stuff."

"How did they learn about it?"

"One of their traders visited Defiance—"

"Ah," said Ned. "The one who wanted to buy guns, right?"

"Well." Pete turned the corners of his mouth down in an almost-frown. "He might've wanted to buy a gun or two."

"If I remember correctly, he wanted to buy a thousand rifles," Ned said, nodding. "We'll never sell guns in that quantity to anyone who's outside the Clan." He stood. "Look, tell them we're willing to meet with them. Maybe I can get one of our Elders, perhaps Washington and the head of the electrical power authority to meet with them. They'll be able to define what's possible and what are their real needs."

"I'm not sure they're going to be happy about that."

"Try," Ned said. "We're not turning them down."

CHAPTER THIRTY-NINE

"Lordy," Joyce said, her voice breaking with each jolt of the horse. She clutched her belly. "I'd forgotten what it was like to ride a horse all day." Her hair straggled down damply over her face. She vainly swept at it for the umpteenth time. "If I'd realized how far this was, I wouldn't have come."

In front and behind, was a squad of Horse Soldiers. The narrow trail wound through never-ending maple trees whose branches latched overhead, hiding the sun. The air was still and humid.

Pittsburgh Pete turned in his saddle with the ease of an experienced rider. "They only wanted to speak with the boss about this electricity deal." He shrugged and turned back to keep his eye on the trail.

Damn and double damn, thought Joyce. *Why did I let them talk me into this? Washington should've made this trip, but Ned thought I could do as well as any politician. That was nice of him to say that. Getting married was a distraction even though the wedding was low key. It got me behind. I've got so many things to do now we can produce fusion power plants. Why am I wasting time with these rednecks in Pennsylvania?*

"It won't be long now," Pete said. "The meeting house is just over the hill." There was a Clan outpost on the border with Pennsylvania. "I sent a warrior ahead to make sure that you'll have a place to rest and get cleaned up."

"Thanks," Joyce said through gritted teeth. *I need a long soak in a tub to get the kinks out of my hide from this trip.*

The track leveled off and became less rocky. Ahead, the trees thinned. A trace of a breeze cooled her face.

She glanced left across the wide valley, and saw ridge after ridge of green hills rising to disappear into a faint, bluish haze.

The trail descended into a mass of maples and beech trees, once again becoming rocky and uneven. She smelled smoke and looked up. In the middle of a large clearing was a building compound that was surrounded by a man-high stone wall topped with a wood palisade. In the center was a tower that looked more like a lookout platform than anything else, from which several brown-clad men waved.

"This's it," said Pete. "The frontier."

"Where's the Pennsylvania delegation?"

"They won't show up until tomorrow, just for the meeting."

"What time will that be?"

"Early. An hour or so after first light." Pete pointed east. "That's their territory over there. There's a small village down by the creek. That's where they'll be coming from."

"I'm sorry, Mr. Krupansky, but it's Clan policy we don't sell our power generating units," Joyce said. *Lordy*, she thought. *Why can't he get it through his head we're willing to sell them power but not the fusion units?*

"Well, why not?" Krupansky was a large man with gray streaked stubble and long, stringy hair. His fringed brown leather clothing had a sheen of wear and dirt.

"We raised our offer to three hundred pieces of gold. That's a fortune. Surely it doesn't cost that much to make? Our people saw that unit in Defiance. It ain't that big. It ain't made of gold, either."

Joyce didn't like Krupansky. He needed a bath, and a shave wouldn't hurt either. He also had no idea what went into making the units; all he seemed to know was it wasn't large and he'd offered a pile of gold.

"Mr. Krupansky, there's a lot more to setting up an electrical system than a power generation unit. It'd be in both of our best interests if the Clan brought electrical power to the border, and provided a team of people to show you how to set up a system.

"We're willing to do this on the basis of you paying the cost of running a power line to the border, which would cost about two hundred pieces of gold. Then pay for the power and the cost of a team to provide instruction at the rate of five pieces of gold per month. This way you'll—"

"That's outrageous. You'll bleed us dry."

Joyce shrugged. "I'm sorry, but that's the way it is—"

"Look, girlie, you go on home and tell whoever's your boss you've managed to piss me off. It's obvious you don't have the authority to make a deal."

Krupansky stood and leaned forward, hands on the table. "You ain't heard the end of this. I'm gonna make a formal complaint to your Elders about your attitude. Sending a woman to negotiate with me instead of the boss man. I'm a member of the Brotherhood. I speak for the Pennsylvania communes."

He wagged his finger at Pittsburgh Pete. "Until I get more respect, no more coal or oil for the Clan, y'hear?"

Pete paled. "Mr. Krupansky." He raised his hand in a placating manner. "You gotta understand. She does run the electrical power authority. She's the head honcho."

Krupansky spat on the floor. "Bullshit. Women don't run things. Their place is in the kitchen or on their backs. I don't know why I even set down to talk to her in the first place." He jammed a hat on his head and walked out.

"Ms. Vargas, there's gonna be trouble with Pennsylvania over this." Pete shook his head. "Krupansky has a lot of influence in the Brotherhood."

Joyce put her papers into a satchel. "You ready?" she said. "I want to go home. I'm tired of this place and these people."

CHAPTER FORTY

Vapor rose from the indoor swimming pool's water surface. A yellow-green head crest emerged out of the water, followed by a long, flat face. The creature climbed out of the water with the peculiar gait that came from its reverse knee joints. It was about four feet tall, with scale-textured skin stretched tightly over a bony structure. It was almost man-like in form except for the stumpy trace of a tail and webbing between the digits on its hands and feet.

A multiple of tiny heads broke the surface and moved in formation toward the steps where the larger creature had exited the pool. One by one, they skittered up the steps, looking like miniature alligators without jaws. They scampered to a large box filled with reeds and climbed inside.

Billy stepped forward and held out a large blanket. "Here, Cha KinLaat," he said in the grunting language of the Qu'uda. "Put this on. It will keep you warm."

Cha KinLaat DoMar took the blanket and wrapped it around herself. "Today I feel stronger than yesterday," she said. "I feel more like myself."

Billy wobbled his head. It had been five days since he had given Cha KinLaat a transfusion of his blood. Two days ago he gave a transfusion to Yi MigLeek DuKuul, and this morning, to MinCha DuKaat. Both were too weak even to swim in the pool with the wrigglers. "Come," he said. "I want you to meet another alien." To date, the only aliens she had met were those who were in the flying machine and the "doctor" who had administered the transfusion.

"What is the point of it?" Cha KinLaat asked. "I cannot under-stand their squeaks. They do not understand me."

Billy bent his head. "This meeting may change that."

Cha KinLaat donned more clothing before they left the pool area. It was heated to temperatures comfortable for the Qu'uda and was too warm for the Earth aliens. "Very well."

"This human is called Tim Van Minh," Billy said. "He has built a device to help you learn their language. It is based upon the learning algorithm in my biocomputer."

Tim Van Minh hobbled forward with a metal box in his hands. He placed it on the table before them. His face moved to expose his teeth. He squeaked something.

"He greets you and bids you welcome," Billy said.

Tim picked up a set of headphones and placed them over his head. With exaggerated gestures, he demonstrated how their fit could be adjusted and then handed them to Cha KinLaat. He squeaked something. This time, he went on for some time.

"Put these on," Billy said. "Through them, you can hear the language learning algorithm." He helped Cha KinLaat to fit the headphones properly. "It will not be easy at first. Remember I learned to speak their language without any understanding of it. You will have an easier time. This is how you start it." He pushed a button.

Squeaks rattled in Cha KinLaat's ears.

Billy pushed the button again.

The squeaks stopped.

"Tell him," Cha KinLaat said, "I am grateful. Tell him I do not understand why his people do so much for us. And tell him I will say it to him in his own words one day." She bobbed her head in Tim's direction.

Billy relayed her words.

Tim's face moved and his teeth showed. Then he bent his head momentarily in Cha KinLaat's direction. He squeaked again, then turned, and left.

ॐ

"Taylor, are you awake?"

Taylor rose on an elbow. He struggled to free the sheet that had wrapped itself around his midriff. "What is it?"

"I couldn't sleep. I've got stomach cramps. They started right after I got back from that stupid Pennsylvania trip." Joyce moved closer to the bed and sat down uneasily. She felt under her night-gown. "I think I've started to spot."

"Oh, Lord." Taylor slid out of bed. "I'm going to get Doctor Encirlik. I won't be long." He struggled into his clothes.

The first trace of light was flirting with the eastern horizon when he returned with Doctor Encirlik.

"Let me see, Joyce," Dr. Encirlik said.

Without a word, Joyce folded back the bed covers.

Doctor Encirlik took a sharp breath. She bent over to take a closer look. "Roll up your sleeve," she said and retrieved something from her bag. "Put this around your arm," she said.

Joyce complied, saying nothing but watching every move the doctor made. "I don't feel well. I feel light-headed."

Doctor Encirlik pumped up the arm compress and stared at the gauge while she held Joyce's wrist. "Your blood pressure is depressed." She examined Joyce carefully and stared hard at the discharge. She took a deep breath. "I want you in my clinic." She turned to Taylor. "In the entrance of my clinic, there are stretchers stacked against the wall. Get one and a couple of strong men over here as soon as you can. I'll stay with Joyce in the meantime." She opened her bag and reached inside.

"How d'you feel?" Taylor asked as he held Joyce's hand.

Joyce's face was pale and still; she'd just suffered a miscarriage. The room had an odor that took him into the past. It was the smell of disinfectant and medicine. The metal bed was high off the floor and the sheets were real cotton. Someone must have found supplies long forgotten.

"I'm sore," she said. "And tired. Other than that, not bad." She sighed, and a tear came to her eye.

"I know." He stroked her hair gently.

"It's," she said, "It's that I'd gotten to like the idea of having a child." More tears appeared. "I hadn't wanted one before. When I got pregnant, it was such a surprise. After I got used to it, I wanted to have a child, our child." She closed her eyes. "I could've gotten out of that trip. I should've sent someone else." She grasped Taylor's hand and looked up at him. "It was my fault," she whispered, tears flowing. "I killed our baby."

"No." Taylor raised her hand to his lips. "It wasn't your fault." He stroked her hair. "These things happen."

CHAPTER FORTY-ONE

Technicians moved back and forth at the metal working machines inside the hangar at Cleveland Hopkins airport. The C-17 airplane loomed large, its long, drooping wings almost stretching from wall to wall. The inboard engines had been replaced with fusion-powered drive units that were bulkier and longer than the original turbo-fan units.

Kevin O'Neil and Tim Van Minh stepped back from a group of technicians to watch the preparations for the first flight with the new aneutronic fusion drive units. They had been extensively run on a ground test frame to develop the control parameters.

Taylor stared at the C-17. He had taken time off from the university after Joyce's miscarriage and gone with her to the Erie Islands for a vacation. The sailing trip seemed to have improved her spirits. However, he realized, something still bothered her. She wouldn't talk about it, and they hadn't made love for a long time. She worked long hours, harder than ever with the electrification project; often she came home late.

"Will it work?" he asked.

"Should," Kevin said. "We tested it four ways from Sunday." He scratched his head. "The new mounting cradle is a lot stronger than the old one and it fits the airframe perfectly."

"Right," Tim said. "Should be more than strong enough for the unit." He paused a moment. "We just had no idea of the power of the original drive units. It's a wonder that Billy didn't tear the plane apart when he tried to go straight up."

A technician with a green flag stepped in front of the C-17 and blew a whistle. The hangar became quiet for an instant and then everybody started to move at once. A team of twenty horses pulled the plane out through the hangar doors onto the taxiway. Once outside, the carters unhooked the horses and led them off.

A loud hum started which changed to a rumbling roar. Dust and litter flew up behind the plane. It eased forward. The rumbling roar faded, and the plane came to a stop.

Several technicians ran to the front of the plane and climbed in. The ladder folded up and the door clanked shut.

Taylor followed Kevin and Tim as they headed to the old terminal. "Where now?" He felt an excitement similar to when he was a child, like a memory of something fun from out of the past. His heart beat faster.

"Let's go on the roof over there." Kevin pointed at a portion of the terminal building extending toward the runway. "It's the best place to watch."

"Who's at the controls of the plane?"

"Billy," Tim said. "I've got three of my best students in the cockpit with him, observing and learning how to fly the aircraft." He hobbled forward and kept pace with them.

Taylor frowned. "Where did he learn to fly a C-17?"

Tim shrugged. "He did fly it to the Bahamas, but that was with vector thrust engines that let him take off vertically. Now he's aware of the fact these engines won't do that."

They climbed onto the roof and waited. A cool breeze came out of the northeast. It had a cold edge to it. *Winter isn't far off*, Taylor thought. *Even though the leaves have yet to fall. And my life has turned cold, too.*

A rumbling roar rolled across the airfield and then faded. The C-17 rolled down a taxiway to the west end of the long runway that ran to the northeast. The plane stopped at the end of the runway and remained stationary. Minutes ticked by.

"Is something wrong?" Taylor asked.

"I don't think so," Tim said. "We put together a long check list. Each student has to go through it."

As he finished speaking, the roar started again. The plane started to move. Clouds of dust billowed out behind it. The roar became louder and rose in pitch. The plane moved down the runway faster and faster. As it came opposite them, the plane's wheels lifted off the ground. The plane still flew parallel to the ground, faster and faster. Engines howled. The nose of the plane rose and the plane climbed steeply into the air. It disappeared from sight in less than a minute.

"Wow," said Tim Van Minh. "That was amazing."

Taylor took a deep breath. "That's the way it was before the Collapse," he said. "Except hundreds of aircraft took off from this airport every day." He stared at the horizon. He could hear something but didn't know from where it came.

Tim pointed. "He's on his way back."

"Is he going to land?" Taylor asked.

"Yes," Tim said. "We'll check everything. If there're no problems, they'll do it again. Then one of the students will give it a try. Take off; land. All day long until they have the feel for it."

"Did you get any pointers from those military types at Groom Lake?" Taylor asked.

"Yeah, Sally took dictation until it came out of her ears. I guess they read an instruction manual to her. She transcribed it. That's what the students have practically memorized. Billy still can't read well enough to use it." He pointed.

The C-17 descended toward the southeast end of the runway. It bobbled slightly then leveled out. The big plane slowly descended, and its wheels touched the runway. The plane bounced into the air and came down again. It wobbled and rolled to the end of the runway, turning onto a taxiway while still moving.

"Wow," said Tim. "I thought it was going to run out of runway. I'd better get going," he said. "I'm part of the team that'll check the plane."

༄

Joyce looked over a raised cup of hot sassafras tea. "Well, Mr. Biehl, thank you for meeting with me. I did want to explain what happened when I met with Krupansky. I'm not sure anyone could negotiate something that would please him and comply with Clan policy. I feel I owe you more than what I put in my report."

The small restaurant was almost deserted, and its staff was busy washing dishes and preparing food for the evening trade. Lacy curtains covered the windows that reduced the street traffic to vague passing outlines.

"I did read your report. There were some interesting insights on his personality and motivation. Nice job."

"Thank you," said Joyce. "It comes from studying people and getting to know them." She paused and took a sip of tea. "Like you. I find you fascinating, the way you manage people and how you get things done. I like the way you go about getting what you need." She raised her eyebrows and smiled.

"It's nice to know you take Clan politics seriously."

"I wasn't referring just to Clan politics." Joyce licked the rim of the cup. "I meant it on a more personal level, about you." She winked. "I like how you do things."

Ned swallowed hard. "Er, I'd like to think we're more than just fellow administrators."

Joyce put her glass of tea down and casually glanced around the restaurant. Satisfied that no one was watching. "More? You'd like us to be more, what?"

"Well, yes. I, er, find that you have a very good understanding of Clan politics and its various relationships."

"I think our relationship has a lot of potential, don't you?" Joyce slipped off her shoe. "On a personal level."

"Us?" Ned's eyes widened. He licked his lips nervously.

"Yes," Joyce said. "We could be more than, whatever."

"I suppose." Ned swallowed hard. "I'm not sure ..."

"For example." Joyce raised her foot and rubbed it against the inside of Ned's calf. "We could share something that isn't so obvious." She winked. Her toe rose higher. "Something personal, something very enjoyable, don't you agree?"

Ned gulped and slid his hand forward, across the table to cover Joyce's hand. "My, I think our relationship could be very interesting." He frowned. "What if your husband finds out?"

Joyce frowned briefly. "He won't. As much attention as he pays to that stupid university, he'll never notice." She smiled sweetly. "You're married. You know how it is."

Ned sighed. "Yes, something disappeared after the children arrived. They seem to get all the attention." He pulled on Joyce's hand and tried to lift it to his lips.

Joyce pulled her hand back. "Careful." She looked around. No one was listening. "Can you come to Columbus next week?" She lowered her voice. "I have a place there, a very private place."

CHAPTER FORTY-TWO

Cha KinLaat DoMar adjusted her headphones. "Mr. MacPherson," she said. "You want me at university teach?"

"Yes," said Taylor. "Teach us about Qu'uda."

"Not speak language good." Cha KinLaat cocked her head as though listening to something. "Need learn more."

Taylor wobbled his head. Billy had told him it was a part of their body language and meant acceptance. "Yes, you have learned much in little time." He waited a moment before he continued. "You'll learn more when you teach."

Cha KinLaat sat motionless for a moment. She turned to Billy and rattled off a series of grunts.

"Cha KinLaat feels honored you trust her to teach your young," Billy said. "She does not know enough words to say this yet. She did not understand what you meant about learning more when she would teach."

Taylor nodded. "There are some students who want to learn Qu'uda language. We teach you our language, you teach us yours." He moved his head up and down, Qu'uda style. There was a tremendous interest in learning more about Qu'uda since the arrival of the three aliens and their offspring. It had prompted many requests for lectures. "Cha KinLaat will be the center of attention as soon as she learns enough words to talk to the students."

Billy turned to Cha KinLaat and relayed the message.

She stood straighter and bobbed her head crest. "I teach students Qu'uda speak."

Taylor nodded again. "I'll make the arrangements."

~

Taylor looked up from the draft proposal and chewed on his pencil. It was eight o'clock. With the electricity on, he worked late on those days when Joyce traveled on the Central Electric Power Authority or CEPA business. She'd be out of town for most of the week.

If she'd only been affectionate when she returned from her last trip, I wouldn't mind, he thought. *It's been weeks, no, months since we've made love.*

"Hello, Taylor."

He looked up. Doctor Meltem Encirlik was at the door to his office. "Hi. C'mon in." He put the pencil down.

"Thanks." She slipped into the chair alongside his desk. "How's Joyce doing? She missed her last check-up."

Taylor leaned back in his chair and frowned. "She's been busy lately, the CEPA, you know. She's in Columbus until Friday, at the old university, again."

"I see." Doctor Encirlik got up and stared out of the window for a moment. She smoothed her smock and turned back to face Taylor. "Well," she said. "She's a big girl. She knows what she's doing."

Taylor realized something was different about Doctor Encirlik. *Ah*, he thought. *Her skin looks better. There seem to be fewer wrinkles, too. She must be using makeup.* Then he realized that the skin on her hands was smooth, The more he looked, the more he realized that she looked filled-out, healthier.

"Doctor Encirlik," he said. "You look, well, different...." He wasn't sure what to say.

"I've put on some weight." Doctor Encirlik stretched and put her hands behind her head. "There are other changes, too." She smiled and beckoned toward him. "There's something I must show you." She took his hand. "In my laboratory."

Taylor resisted her pull. "What's that?"

"My research." She pulled more insistently.

Taylor followed her to the laboratory.

"Look." She pointed at two cages of rats. One was filled with busy active rats; in the other, the rats huddled against the floor, barely moving. "They're both the same age, but these—" she pointed to the active rats, "were treated with stem cell-grafted DNA for the human growth hormone with a glycosylation end-product bond-breaker and other critical factors; I call it SC-DNA for short. From all appearances and cellular examination, the aging process has stopped, perhaps even reversed. I've raised two generations of offspring from the treated rats. Everything appears normal."

My God, Taylor thought. *What's she done?* He stared at her.

The lines in her face had disappeared; while her hair still had streaks of gray, it was glossy, healthy, and full. The age wrinkles on her hands were barely visible. She looked younger, healthier.

"Did you try this process on yourself?"

She smiled. "Yes, and it worked. I feel like celebrating." She grasped Taylor's hand. "Come have a drink with me, and I'll tell you about it." She led him across the hall to her office. She pulled a bottle from a cabinet.

"Hang on." Taylor frowned. "I thought you were going to review this with me and the Elders before you went any further."

Doctor Encirlik shrugged. "You were always too busy. The process I found in the Billy download worked better than my wildest dreams." She sat down on a faded leather couch. "The reason I tried it was a combination of the selfish and noble."

"You care to explain that?" Taylor asked.

"Sure," she said. "First, our drink." She brought over a bottle and two tall, narrow glasses. She poured a clear liquid into the glasses and handed one to Taylor. "The selfish part."

Taylor took a mouthful of the drink. A fiery liquid's vapor filled his mouth and nose. He gasped. "What's this?"

"Raki. It's authentic Turkish raki, otherwise known as lion's milk. It's similar to absinthe and priceless today. I've had it since the Collapse. This occasion deserves it." She took a sip and raised her eyebrows in appreciation. Her expression became somber. "I've got more than one reason to celebrate. You see, a year ago, I discovered a lump in my breast. That, and other symptoms, convinced me I had breast cancer. As I got weaker, I realized I was dying."

Lord, Taylor thought. *That explains why she aged so fast.*

"While working with the rats, I found that the SC-DNA also caused carcinomas to go into remission. Since I was terminal, I had nothing to lose. I didn't want to die. I also wanted to finish this work. I was desperate. I was afraid. When my weight dropped to seventy-five pounds, it was when I decided I had to do it. I was so weak I could barely push the needle into my arm." She raised her glass in salute and took another drink.

"Ten days later, I started to regain my strength and put on weight. That's when I knew it worked. In the past two months, I've made amazing progress. I'm alive, I'm well, and I feel wonderful." She smiled over her glass. "I've started exercising, and my weight is back to one hundred pounds. I'm alive and I'm prepared to live with those consequences."

Taylor realized he could not argue with what she had done. *I would've done the same thing.* He took another sip of the raki. *It wasn't bad*, he thought. *Better than the homemade liquors in the market.*

"There's the ethical issue."

"Yes," she said. "I haven't finished." She poured more raki in Taylor's glass. "The noble part. In any medical research, the step from animal trials to human trials is fraught with risk. So, I decided I'd be a human guinea pig. If it were going to kill someone, let it be me. I was as good as dead anyway." She raised her glass in salute. "I lived and it worked. The best of all worlds. I'm well, I'm fit, and I feel wonderful."

"How will this be used? Who'll get it? And what'll be the consequences? What're the side effects?"

Doctor Encirlik sat down next to Taylor. "Taylor," she said. "I've thought hard about those questions." Her knee touched his. "I know how to deal with the medical aspects."

Taylor looked closer at her. She did look younger now she'd lost the emaciated appearance of the past year. He realized she had a dark, almost sultry quality and very attractive, sexy.

Stop it, he thought. *I'm married.*

"Call me Meltem." She poured another glass of raki. "I want to hear how you pronounce my name."

"Meltem," he said.

"I love the way you say it." She sighed. "Where were we? Oh, yes, those ethical questions." She smiled and tossed her hair back. "Look, we can debate them all we want. Eventually they'll be decided by those political creatures we call the Elders, who I'm sure, will surprise both of us. Might even find a reason to sentence me to death, who knows?" Her hand descended lightly to Taylor's knee. "I'm not ready for that debate yet."

"You've discovered the elixir of life—"

"I don't know about that, which reminds me." She stood up and held her hand out to Taylor. "Come," she said. "It's time you got your treatment." She grasped his hand and pulled.

"Just a minute," Taylor said as he rose to his feet. "You can't go around treating people willy-nilly. The ethics—"

"Taylor, my dear. For such an intelligent man, you can be quite dense." She laughed. "I'd bet anything the Elders will include you in the group that gets it. I'm just jumping the gun a little." She took his hands and stood close to him. She looked into his eyes. "Look, when you started the Clan, you didn't hesitate to make hard decisions," she said. "You saved people's lives with action. You took me in, you saved my life." She lifted his hands to her lips. "I'm doing the same thing for you, my way."

"This is different—"

"Taylor," she said. "You're not listening. It's no different." She grasped his hand. "Come, I've got it all prepared." She dragged him across the hall to the laboratory.

"But, but ..." The idea was seductive. No, it was more than that; it was irresistible. Younger, what was the saying? Youth is wasted on the young? He made one last effort. "What're the risks? What about incompatibility problems?"

"There are fewer incompatibility risks for you than there were for me. Of that I'm sure. I used material from Joyce's miscarriage." Meltem said. "Sit down and roll up your sleeve." She got a syringe from a refrigerator.

"I don't think I should—"

"Taylor, sit down and shut up."

Taylor hesitated for a moment before sitting down.

"I don't think this is right—"

"Right or wrong, you don't have to get any older."

Meltem grasped his shirtsleeve and pushed it up. She swabbed his arm with a patch reeking of alcohol. She aspirated a hypodermic syringe.

"Hold on, don't I have a say in this?"

Meltem nodded. "I suppose." She straightened and cocked her head. "By the way, I discovered the Qu'uda encode their genetic information in DNA—just like humans."

"What? Are you sure?"

"When I did a transfusion between Billy and Cha KinLaat, I got a sample of his blood." A trace of a frown crossed her face.

"It was the perfect opportunity to find out something about their biology. When I got down to the molecular level, I almost fell over when I saw DNA structures. So, I did some quick comparisons between his DNA and mine. There are significant differences, but much of the structure was the same." She took a deep breath, about to continue.

"What does that mean?"

"Well, their DNA is less similar to ours than a dog's but closer than that of an earthworm. But it's still DNA and there has to be a connection."

"How?"

"Perhaps there's something to the panspermia theory after all." She shrugged. "Maybe the laws of chemistry and physics dictate certain chemical structures are essential to transfer the amount of information necessary to create a complex organism. I really don't know." She glanced at Taylor's arm and the small hypodermic syringe. "At the moment, it's just interesting information. They're still so different as to be completely biologically incompatible with us or Earth organisms."

As Taylor stared at the ceiling, lost in thought, she stabbed the needle into his arm.

"Ow." He flinched and turned as she withdrew the syringe. "You're done?" Any needle used today had been resharpened, he realized. None were truly sharp.

"Right." She pressed a piece of fabric on his arm.

"You tricked me." He felt both fear and anticipation. It was like the first step of a journey, one he secretly wanted.

"Yes, I did. It's for your own good." Meltem hesitated for a second. "The treatment works relatively slowly. The first results will take a week or two to appear." She put the equipment away. "There, done. Check back with me once a week." She looked at him appraisingly. "We still have some raki," she said. "Can't let it go to waste." She herded him back across the hall, and carefully closed the door.

Well, thought Taylor. *There's no one waiting for me tonight.* "I'm not sure if I should—"

"Taylor, if you don't, I'm going to scream." She put the raki on the coffee table and sat on the couch next to Taylor.

"All right," Taylor said. "What would you like to talk about?" He held out his glass for more raki. He could feel the alcohol beginning to work. *I could get to like this stuff in a hurry. This had better be my last drink.*

Meltem got up and wandered over to her desk. She held up a battered photograph. "This is Bulent. We were engaged to be married. A gang broke into the Cleveland Clinic and he tried to stop them. They killed him. I saw it happen." She put the photograph down and returned to the couch. "He's the only man who ever loved me. He was a good man."

"I'm sorry," Taylor said.

Meltem took another sip of raki. She glanced at Taylor. "When I came to the Clan, I was in mourning for a year as duty as a good Muslim. After you lost Franny—she was such a good woman, and nice to me, too—I used to fantasize you and I would get together."

"We'd get together?"

"Yes." She laughed. "We'd become lovers and we'd have lots of children." She smiled. "You were smart, important and I was an eligible female doctor. You were always nice to me. I thought you liked me. It seemed like the perfect match. It was obvious to me." She shook her head. "But no one else."

Taylor reached out and touched her face. A flush had livened her cheeks. "Meltem, if my heart hadn't been broken, I might've noticed." He sighed. "You know what happened. You were there. You were there for so many people." He looked down. "I never realized. Oh, yes, I knew you were a very giving person. I liked you, but I never knew how you felt. I locked my heart away, for every time I loved, someone died."

"Then you took in that young woman. Everyone knew how Noelle felt about you. I thought you felt the same about her."

Taylor shook his head. "I didn't feel at all."

"I think I understand. I was the same way after Bulent died. But life goes on." She kissed his hand. "Taylor, I still have feelings for you." Her hand dropped to his thigh. "I still like you, a lot. Please," she said. "A favor. Kiss me, please." She raised her face to him, lips parted, eyes closed.

Taylor sensed her nearness and longing. Something made him move his face close to hers. Their lips touched, gently at first and then with a fierce, demanding pressure. His hand slipped around her back and he pulled her closer. Their lips parted.

What am I doing? he thought. *This is wrong.*

He drew back.

Her eyes opened, dark and liquid. "Oh, no, don't stop now," she whispered. Her hand moved up the inside of his thigh, kneading with an insistent urgency. She raised her face to him again. Briefly, her fingernails bit into his flesh.

Arousal flared and consumed him. He kissed her again.

Her tongue entered his mouth.

He wanted her. His hand found an opening in her smock and reached through and found a breast, small and soft. He gently stroked her smooth skin. Pausing, he unbuttoned her smock and bent over. His lips found a nipple.

Her hand was against the back of his head, holding him; the other moved slowly up his thigh and found him.

Taylor came up for air. *Oh, God, what am I doing?* He pulled his hands away. "We shouldn't—"

"Yes," she said with a laugh. "We shouldn't, but we will. I feel like a teenager. I want you. Right now." She undid the buttons of her smock and slipped it off. There was nothing beneath the smock but smooth, soft skin.

Taylor took in her nudity: she was a small woman, almost diminutive, slim with small breasts crowned with dark cone-shaped nipples. For such a small woman, her legs seemed almost too long, but they were graceful and beautiful.

She smiled and reached out. "Come," she said. "Let me help you." She took him by the hands and pulled.

Taylor rose slowly to his feet.

She started with his shirt and unbuttoned it. As she slipped it off his shoulders, she worked her way down, pausing to touch and caress him. By the time she eased his trousers around his ankles, she had been over almost every part of his body.

It was beautifully exquisite torture. "Meltem." He gasped. "Please." He was fully aroused.

Meltem reached out for him and led him down to the floor. They sank onto the oriental rug, arms around each other.

The first time was rushed; the second was slower, more subtle, and infinitely more satisfying.

When done, she lay back and stared at the ceiling, a smile playing on her lips.

Meltem lay there for a few minutes. "That was so good." She laid her head on Taylor's chest. "I've always wanted a family. I dreamed of it from the time when I was a child," she said. "That vanished." She sat up and a smile filled her face. "Now that I'm well again, I've even started menstruating. I'm going to have a child. At least, I think I will."

"Oh? And who do you have in mind as the father?"

She ran her finger down his chest. "Oh, you."

Taylor sat upright. "Now wait a minute."

He became acutely aware he was sitting on the floor of her office without any clothes on. "What d'you mean? That I should leave Joyce?" *Someone could come in. Lord, what am I doing?*

Meltem closed her eyes and smiled. "Oh, no," she said. "I wouldn't ask you to do that. That's not necessary."

CHAPTER FORTY-THREE

Taylor stared over the pilot's head, through the cockpit window. His head pounded and his heart ached with guilt. *I shouldn't have done it*, he thought. *I'm married. I love Joyce.*

The idea Meltem might become pregnant came back. It had an illicitly arousing impact upon him. Children. The idea he could have children gripped him now he knew it was possible. He thought those days long behind him since Joyce's coolness dominated their relationship. He realized Meltem had planned the seduction. It wasn't just a quick roll in the hay.

He forced himself to think about how Billy's technicians had made dozens of practice flights, gradually extending their duration, gaining experience.

They had one close call on a hard landing when a tire blew out. That required cannibalizing one of the aircraft at Wright-Patterson. It made him realize more aircraft were needed. Two of the remaining aircraft were in the process of being fitted with fusion drive units. He returned to his seat and belted up.

A roar reverberated through the aircraft. A force pushed Taylor deep into his seat. *This is it*, he thought. *We're on our way to the West Coast.*

Contact with the submarine group at Bangor, Washington had led to this flight. Their doubt was obvious when he told them of the alien threat; their skepticism had come through even over the radio. It was time for them to meet Billy face to face.

The C-17 tilted back. The landing gear rumbled as it retracted, confirming they were airborne. He unbuckled and went forward to the cockpit. A cloud whipped past the window. The engines faded.

That must be the flaps, he thought. The engines grew louder. The clouds disappeared. The blue sky became darker and the plane leveled off.

"What's our altitude?" Taylor asked.

"We're at ten-thousand feet," said Charlie O'Connor. "We're under visual flight rules or VFR, for a checkpoint at the lower tip of Lake Michigan. Even if it's hidden by cloud, we'll still be able to head for the next checkpoint."

"Just get us there safely," Taylor said. *So*, he thought. *Young Charlie opted out of politics to become a pilot.* O'Connor had been a leader-candidate for several years. When the university had opened, he'd shown up to become a student. His quick intelligence and hard work had won him a place on the team of technicians chosen to become pilots.

"Yes, sir." O'Connor bent over the maps, checking the heading against the compass. He made a minor adjustment and leaned back. His eyes continued to sweep over the instruments.

Taylor stared out of the window. Through breaks in the clouds, green land stretched out endlessly. *What a great country*, he thought. *We're going to get it back.* After a while, he grew tired of the view and went back to his seat. The rhythmic vibration from the engines made him close his eyes.

ↄ

"... Mr. MacPherson?"

"Yes?" Taylor opened his eyes. He'd been in the middle of a delicious dream, traveling to, where was it?

"Lunch?" O'Connor asked. "There are sandwiches the galley."

"Thanks." Taylor's stomach rumbled from no breakfast. "Where are we?" He yawned and rubbed his eyes.

A quick frown of concentration crossed O'Connor's face. "We're approaching the Great Salt Lake VFR checkpoint. We'll verify our course when we cross it. From here on, the checkpoints are harder to spot."

Taylor unlatched his seat belt and rose. "What's our cruising speed?" he asked.

O'Connor blinked twice. "About four hundred knots. We expect to be over Puget Sound in about ..." The quick frown returned. "Ah, about an hour and a half."

"Thanks," said Taylor. He went to see what was in the galley. *I must have slept for quite a while.*

This is the dangerous part, Taylor thought.

The aircraft swayed from side to side and the engines' howl increased. The landing gear clanked, and the wind roar grew louder. The aircraft's nose rose, and the engines faded to a low whistle. He held his breath as the plane glided toward the ground.

The tires hit the runway with a screech and the entire aircraft shook. The engines bellowed in reverse and the aircraft decelerated. The tires thumped loudly, sounding through the fuselage as the craft slowed. The engines quieted.

I'd forgotten what landings were like, Taylor thought. *Those kids must have balls, flying this thing, using only written instructions, with no previous experience.* He unwound his clenched fist and offered a silent prayer of thanks.

The aircraft rolled along for several minutes, rumbling over cracks in the runway before coming to a halt. The engines faded into silence. Somewhere below, a door clanked open and folding steps clanged down. Voices rose and fell.

Taylor stared out through the open door.

Two long rows of camouflage-clad soldiers with M-16 rifles stood at parade attention. In front of them were a half dozen officers in khaki uniforms and peaked hats.

"Ten-hut," a voice cried. "Present arms."

The soldiers raised their weapons in one fluid motion. "At ease." The soldiers lowered their guns to rest on the ground and spread their legs. The officers saluted.

Taylor descended to the concrete and stepped forward. "I'm Taylor MacPherson from the Greater Clan of Ohio."

A tall, thin clean-shaven man in the center of the officers stepped forward, his khaki uniform pressed to a razor's edge. Time had etched lines into his walnut-brown face. His nose was long and thin, set above full lips.

"Pleased to meet you," he said and extended his hand. "I'm Captain Malachi Mapes of the SSN Hampton, stationed at Bangor Naval Base. We're sure glad to see you." He made a half turn. "I'd like you to meet my staff...." One by one, he introduced his officers.

"Why don't we go over to the terminal." Captain Mapes pointed to the building behind them. "We can talk there. Before we do that, what kind of service does your aircraft require?" His eyebrows rose expectantly.

Taylor looked back toward the plane. Billy watched from the doorway. Taylor beckoned for him to join them. He turned back to Captain Mapes. "Have your people talk to the crew. I'm only a passenger. There's someone else you must meet," he said. "We call him Billy Potato." He glanced back as Billy approached.

"Billy," Taylor called. "I'd like you to meet Captain Malachi Mapes of the SSN Hampton."

Billy ambled forward. "The honor is mine." He reached up to offer his hand. The wide-brimmed hat hid some of his face and his long ground-sweeping cloak concealed his body.

Captain Mapes stared at Billy's hand. Its three digits and opposing thumb were short and thick. "Er, pleased to meet you."

He shook his hand as though afraid it might electrocute him. "Yes, I think we should meet inside." He turned to his officers. "Make sure the airport perimeter is secure. Nothing happens to that plane. Get the flight crew what they need to service the aircraft. Dismissed."

༄

"I find all of this hard to believe," said Captain Mapes. "Alien invasion, fusion-powered aircraft, and Ohio the center of it all." He rubbed his hand over the last traces of hair on his head.

The carpeting on the floor was faded and stained. Paint flaked off the pale blue walls. He stared out through cracked windows at the runway where the C-17 was parked, surrounded by soldiers and visitors. Streams of visitors were going on board as others descended. Several horse-drawn wagons had pulled up alongside.

Earlier, a Lieutenant "Pip" Ryan had come in and given the captain a note. It had contained something that made him take the Clan delegation far more seriously. "Nevertheless, if you've got something that can power my boat, I'm interested."

"Look," Taylor said. "You've had an overview of the situation. What we want, no, what we need, is an alliance to defend the Earth when the Qu'uda return. You've got nukes, rockets, and connections with the remaining military." He rose and began to pace the length of the room.

Captain Mapes raised his eyebrows. "It takes an executive order with the right codes before I can deploy those birds." His full lips had tightened to thin, grim lines. "This all sounds too ..." He hesitated. "Hard to believe."

Taylor rubbed his face. "Billy, can we give them a fusion reactor?" Since learning of about Billy's DNA, he somehow felt that he was, well, less alien.

Billy cracked his mouth in a caricature of a smile. "One has just been finished. It depends upon what you and the Elders decide." His mouth tightened. "O'Neil and Van Minh set up the production facility. The only material shortage is boron. Soon, we will need more."

"All right." Taylor turned back to Captain Mapes. "Let's do this. You send some people back with us, including a pilot and an engineer and we'll provide you a fusion reactor with enough capacity to power your submarine." He wagged his finger at Captain Mapes. "That'll be our demonstration of sincerity. You get what you want, up front, with no haggling. You can see alien technology firsthand."

"That's mighty generous." Captain Mapes took a deep breath. "I don't think you understand my problem. I took an oath I'd protect those nukes and use them only with the proper authorization. You can't give me that and I can't release them to you." He rubbed his nose as though it itched. "Only the President in Washington can do that."

Taylor nodded. "If I take you or one of your people to Washington, DC so you see it no longer exists, will that be enough to release the weapons?"

Captain Mapes turned to the officer on his right. "Cy. You want to go with these folks and see what they're talking about?" It was more of an order than a request.

"Yes, sir. I'll go."

"You've met Cy Belasario, my executive officer, and he's a damn fine one, too." He nodded toward the short, stocky man with a thick neck. A large nose dominated his round face. "I'm trusting you with him. I want him back, understand?" There was a hard tone to his voice and his lips tightened into a thin line.

"Sir," Cy said. "We ought to see if we can pick up a pilot from Groom Lake. Maybe we can get Colonel Inez to go with us?"

"Yeah, good point." Captain Mapes turned toward Taylor. "You got any problem with making a pickup on the way?" He tapped his index finger on his lips.

"No. In fact, we'd like to visit these military bases while we're out here." Taylor hesitated. "Can we do that?"

Captain Mapes and Cy looked at each and raised their eyebrows. "Sure, if you're going to visit them, we'd like to ride along. We only know some of these folks from radio contact. We'd sure like to meet them face to face, too."

ॐ

Three days later, the C-17 lifted off the cracked concrete runway of the old Sea-Tac Airport and turned east. They had picked up Bud Inez from Groom Lake, a former Air Force test pilot who now sat in the co-pilot's seat. He and Charlie O'Connor worked together, exchanging information as they flew.

There were half a dozen passengers on board who chattered excitedly during the whole trip. Many had only spoken to each other by radio during the past twenty years.

CHAPTER FORTY-FOUR

Taylor opened the door to Joyce's office and peered in. He held a bouquet of red roses behind his back. "Joyce?" His heart pounded. His mouth was dry, like it was full of sawdust.

"Taylor, you're back." Joyce's eyes opened wide.

Taylor stepped in and placed the flowers on her desk. "These are for you." He studied her, waiting.

Joyce remained seated as she stared at the roses. "They're pretty." Her voice held little enthusiasm.

"I missed you." *Dear God*, Taylor thought. *Please bring her back to me. What made this happen? Does she know?*

"I missed you, too, Taylor." She looked away.

"I found your note. Last night when I got back."

"Oh." Her pupils dilated further.

"Why did you move out?" Taylor asked. "I didn't sleep at all last night, thinking about what it might mean."

Joyce rose and walked to the window, arms across her chest. "Taylor, my workload is unending." She paused and turned to face him. "I can't afford the time it takes each day to go back and forth to the Hill. So I got an apartment in town. I'll be home on weekends."

Taylor took a deep breath. "That's it?"

"Yes." Joyce turned to face the window again.

Taylor let out a sigh. "Why didn't you say so?" He moved behind her and wrapped his arms around her. "Joyce, I've missed you so much." As he held her, he realized that she had gained some weight. "What's happening with us?"

Oh, Lord, please make things right between us and I'll never look at another woman.

She leaned her head back. "Can you ever forgive me?"

"Forgive you for what?" He stroked her hair. "Joyce, I love you so very much."

She sniffed. "Our baby. It was my fault our baby died. I was careless."

"Joyce, please don't ever say that. It wasn't your fault. It just happened." Taylor squeezed her waist. "Whether we have a child or not doesn't change the way I feel about you."

Joyce nodded. Her eyes were focused on something distant.

"Blaming yourself and staying away from me won't help anything." He held her tightly. "Do you realize this is the first time I've held you in two weeks? I like holding you, I like being near you."

Joyce turned to face him. "Really?"

Taylor wiped a tear from her cheek with his index finger. "I love you, I miss you." He kissed her forehead. "I worry about you. Doctor Encirlik said you missed your check-up. She's concerned about you, too. She wants to make sure you have a complete recovery."

"Oh?" Joyce wrinkled her nose. "She was rough when she scraped me out. It hurt for a long time afterward."

"I don't think it was deliberate," Taylor said. "I've known her a long time. She's just a little direct at times." The memory of his encounter with her came flooding back.

Yes, she can be direct when she wants to be. Why oh why did I do it? "It'd worry me if you didn't go for your check-up." He paused a second. "After all, you still want children, don't you?"

His memory flashed back that Meltem did, too.

Joyce took a sharp breath and looked down. "I don't know. It was such a shock to find out I was pregnant. Then our baby became very precious to me. And I lost my baby." Her eyes watered. "I still feel it's my fault."

"Stop it, please," Taylor said. "It wasn't. Lots of women miscarry and then go on to have more children. Life's full of risks and losses. The only real measure of our success is what we do with what we've got." He took a deep breath. "All in all, I think you're doing great. I hear Ned Biehl thinks highly of you and your work."

Joyce looked up quickly and then laid her head on Taylor's chest. "I haven't been much of a wife to you lately, have I?" She ran her fingers over his shoulder.

"As long as we can deal with our problems, that's all that matters." Taylor stroked her hair. Her closeness and aroma awakened fond memories, memories of when they'd been together. "When are you going to show me your week-day digs?"

"Would you like to see them now?" A smile flickered over her face. "I made sure it had a double bed."

"Double bed? Hmm," Taylor said. "I think an inspection trip is definitely in order."

ॡ

"We should get Noelle to come over here during the week." Taylor glanced at their clothes scattered on the floor as he ran his hand over Joyce's back. Her skin was as smooth as silk. "Take care of the place just like our home on the Hill."

"It's hard to think about a housekeeper when you touch me like that." She looked over her shoulder at him.

Taylor smiled. For some reason, he felt full of energy and desire, more so than in a long time. *Must be abstinence*, he thought. *Then he remembered the time that he'd been with Meltem and felt a surge of guilt.* He forced the memory away. *I wonder if that injection did anything?* "Let me see," he said. "What does this do?" He moved his hand to her buttocks.

Joyce rolled over. "Don't tease me," she said, her eyes descending. "My, my, you weren't teasing." She reached out and beckoned for him to come to her. "That looks too good to waste."

CHAPTER FORTY-FIVE

The West Coast delegation and the Clan's technical experts sat around a large oak desk in Billy's spacious office. There were ten in total and the air was warm and humid. It was their first session to work out terms of the agreement. Coats covered the credenza in an untidy heap.

"Let me get this right," Cy Belasario said. "You're teaching engineering, based upon Cooter technology. Is that right?"

Billy waved his head. Ever since he had brought the rescued Qu'uda back to Berea, he had resumed using Qu'uda gestures and mannerisms. Some of his students had picked up his habit of wagging his head horizontally to indicate acceptance or agreement. "Yes. Some Qu'uda technology is more efficient than Earth technology. Therefore it makes good sense to use it."

"Which technologies have you focused on?" Cy asked.

Billy hesitated. "I do not understand your question."

"Let me rephrase that," Taylor said. "Which Qu'uda technologies do you teach?"

"Ah," Billy said. "Electric power and propulsion from nuclear fusion takes most of my time. Biotechnology for medical purposes is also taught." He paused. "There was much information downloaded from my biocomputers that is not understood." He waved a stubby arm in Taylor's direction. "He knows best what is taught at the university."

Taylor nodded. "We're playing catch-up. No one has studied anything for years. As a consequence, most of the course work is just basic studies. There's a tremendous need for engineers, technicians and teachers. We need to get our society back up to speed quickly. Research is conducted mainly by those people who had pre-Collapse training, with certain exceptions." Tim Van Minh immediately came to his mind.

"If the Qu'uda return and try to remove their technology, we want to be ready," Taylor said. "We plan to spread it far and wide."

"What if they nuke us?" Sweat glistened on Cy's brow. Damp patches grew at his armpits.

"Somehow, somewhere, someone will survive." Taylor took a deep breath. "It's not the nukes that really scare us." He paused. "If they really want to knock us back into the Stone Age or worse, they'll drop an asteroid on us."

No one spoke.

Outside, student voices rose and fell with words and laughter. Sparrows chattered in the bushes below the windows. Crows cawed in nearby treetops.

"A dino killer," Cy said in a voice that was almost a whisper. "A fucking dino killer."

"Right," said Taylor. "That's why we need your rockets and nukes as an insurance policy. We've got to meet them in space. Keep them away. If we don't, we could lose everything."

"We can't get into space," Cy said.

"Not difficult to get into space," Billy said. In the quiet of the room, the low grunting tones of his voice sounded harsh.

"Really?" Cy's jaw jutted forward. "How?"

"Use fusion drive units. Almost same design as power generator. Easy to build, even with Earth technology."

Cy looked at Taylor. "Is that right?"

"Everything Billy has told us has proved to be true."

Cy turned and stared at Billy. "Why're you doing this? Why d'you betray your own kind to help us?" His lip curled and his tone of voice implied Billy was a traitor.

"Here, I belong. My own kind cast me from the circle of our society and left me to die. Here, people show me I belong and accept me. I have a life." Billy raised both hands to his forehead, dropped them to his armpits, and dipped his head. "I am honored to be so close to the center, again important." He brought his hands together in a prayer-like motion. He did this when he talked about his elevation to the center.

The corners of Cy's mouth were still turned downward. "I don't know. It don't sound right to me." He looked at Taylor. "I'd keep a close eye on him, if it were me."

Taylor gritted his teeth and forced a smile. "Obviously our experience with Billy is longer than yours. We've chosen to make him the center of our efforts to build a technological society." From the corner of his eye, he saw Billy dip his head.

Good, he thought. *Billy knows his position with us is secure.* "We'd like to share his technology with you to prepare for the return of the Qu'uda spacecraft. Specifically, we're offering you a power unit for the SSN Hampton to replace the existing unit."

Cy raised his eyebrows. "Why?"

"To show how serious we are about working with you."

Cy grunted in a non-committal fashion.

"Correct me if I'm wrong," Taylor said. "The Hampton has a twenty-six megawatt generator." He paused.

Cy looked at Pip Ryan. "Well?"

"That's about right," Pip said. "We usually think in shaft horse-power, but that's roughly equivalent to our unit."

"Our standard fusion power source can put out up to forty megawatts," Taylor said. "We can make a unit available and get it to Sea-Tac within twenty-four hours. We're also willing to provide technicians to install it and train your people." He stood and leaned over the table, resting on his hands.

"Look, we need each other for common defense. Our original strategy was to spread technology far and wide, then hunker-down for their return. We now believe that's too risky. We want to stop them before they reach Earth. Are you with us?"

Cy stood and walked to the window and stared out. He put his hands behind his back. "I can't speak for the Captain," he began. "I know he views getting fuel for our sub as a high priority." He turned to face the group. "Instead of fuel, you offer us a whole reactor which you claim you can get to Sea-Tac overnight." He wiped his forehead. "That's hard to believe. Reactors are big and heavy.

Shielding makes them that way." His jaw jutted forward. "Besides, you didn't say anything about providing fuel for the unit."

Taylor drummed his fingers on the table for a moment. "Let me start by saying we have no fuel units for any uranium fueled reactor. None." He swallowed hard. "That's why we didn't offer them. Subject closed. As for the fusion power unit, it's almost identical in size to one of the engines on the C-17 that brought you here.

"It doesn't need any shielding. It's an aneutronic fusion reaction, which means no neutrons; thus, it has no secondary radiation. Therefore, no shielding is required."

"My pappy told me if anything sounds too good to be true, it probably is. I need my people to look this over." As Cy looked at Pip, his eyebrows rose and the corners of his mouth turned down as though he had tasted something bad. "That is, if you'll let us."

"When would you like to inspect your unit?"

"Convince me," Cy said. "Then I'll talk to the Captain."

Taylor forced a smile. He let out his breath. "Then why don't we go take a look right now?"

CHAPTER FORTY-SIX

Lieutenant Pip Ryan straightened up and ran his hand over the body of the power unit, which sat on a simple frame. He peered beneath it. "This isn't like anything I've ever seen before," he said.

A cast iron cage surrounded the copper windings that carried off the current generated from the fusion of boron and hydrogen. From the ends of the twenty-foot long cage, copper windings emerged from beneath the power coils. A simple unpainted aluminum box carried six gauges, which displayed the generator's operating parameters. A thin gray cable snaked over to a computer on a desk made from a weathered sheet of plywood on top of filing cabinets. It was the unit's controls.

Two thick rubber-covered cables rose from the power generator to the ceiling of the concrete block building to disappear through a hole in the wall. The generator hummed a resonant sixty-cycle note. The room was warm.

"It's got all of the attachments normal for a power source. It just doesn't look like one." Pip Ryan walked over to the computer and stared at the display for a moment. "Nine hundred or so amps at fourteen thousand four hundred volts. That's almost thirteen megawatts."

"Yes, sir." Freddy Crosby waved his hand. "Demand rises and falls, depending upon the time of day. This unit still has quite a bit of capacity left for this service area."

"How often d'you refuel this unit?" Pip asked.

Crosby rolled his eyes. "Other than providing water, I haven't had to put in any more boron. But then it's only been in service for a short while." He smiled as though hoping to have answered the question.

"At full output, we estimate ten kilos of boron should last about a year," Tim Van Minh said. "We need to find a source of boron if we're going to continue producing these units. Perhaps you could help us with that?"

Pip glanced at Tim. "I'd have to talk to some of our people. I don't know anything about boron."

"Lieutenant Ryan." Cy's voice was loud. "Can we use this reactor in the Hampton? It looks too small to be real."

Pip took a deep breath. "I need to figure out where the power terminal and regulator are to check it," he said. "The only problem I see is getting it inside the Hampton. That frame is too big to go through any of its hatches—"

"A cast frame is not crucial to the unit's operation," Tim Van Minh said. "Our first unit used a modular frame that can be assembled in place. It's in storage. However, the magnetic containment frame has to be iron."

Pip nodded and turned toward Cy. "Let me put a multi-meter on the line to verify its current flow."

∼

"... The Council of Elders unanimously approved the motion. The Greater Clan will enter into a mutual assistance agreement with the SUBGRU 9 of the Naval Submarine Base, Bangor, in the State of Washington, as spelled out in this document." Ned Biehl held up a package of papers. "Gentlemen, we look forward to working with you and making America great again."

The public section rose, cheering and clapping. Some stamped their feet and others whistled. After a few moments, the sergeant-at-arms banged the floor with his staff. "Order, Order." His voice was loud, but there was a broad smile on his face.

The public section resumed their seats and grew quiet.

"I might add I'm happy to be associated with an official agency of the United States government again." Ned extended his hand to Cy.

"This agreement will be beneficial to both us and the Clan. I look forward to the day when everyone can travel freely about the reestablished United States of America with all rights accorded to its citizens under the Constitution. Thank you, gentlemen." Cy sat down heavily and mopped his brow.

"The Council meeting is adjourned," Ned said.

Chairs scraped, floorboards creaked, and a rumble of conversation broke out as the people in the public section flowed toward the doors.

"Er, Mr. Washington, d'you have a moment?" Cy called.

"Certainly, Mr. Belasario. What can I do for you?" Carver Washington towered over Cy. He grasped Cy's hand with the practiced move of a politician.

"Well, Captain Mapes told me his wife had a cousin who moved to Berea, Ohio just before the war," Cy said. "A person by the name of Cedric Washington." He swallowed. "Since your last name is Washington, I just wondered if you knew anyone by the name of Cedric Washington?"

"Who be looking for Cedric Washington?" Carver asked.

"Captain Mapes's wife, LaTasha." Cy mopped his brow again. "If I remember correctly, she was originally from Detroit. Her maiden name was Foxworth. At least, that's what my wife tells me, and she's pretty tight with LaTasha."

"Well, I never." Carver shook his head. "This is the damnedest thing. I'm Cedric. I haven't gone by Cedric since I moved here from Detroit. Everyone here knows me as Carver. Don't ask why, it's a long story. LaTasha, my Lord, I haven't seen that skinny little girl since ..." He stopped, his eyes focusing on Cy. "I thought LaTasha was dead, killed in the war."

Cy raised his eyebrows. "LaTasha's very much alive. And she isn't a skinny little girl anymore. She's got three grown sons and a bunch of grandkids."

"Mr. Belasario, how'd you like to join my wife and me for supper?" Carver put his arm around Cy's shoulder and steered him toward the door. "I got of ton a questions, and I know my Ruby will have more."

~

"Er, Beach," Monahan called in his thin voice. "D'you have a moment?" He pointed toward a small conference room adjacent to the Council chambers.

Beach nodded and followed Monahan through the door, closing it firmly. "What is it?"

"Do you understand what Biehl is up to with this proposed alliance with these strangers?"

Beach shook his head. "I don't know what'll happen with this alliance, but I'm sure it won't be good for me or my people." He hooked his cane on the edge of the table and eased into a chair.

"I think it'll dilute our influence even further."

"How're you going to find out if that's so?"

"I've made sure Washington lets me know what happens when the plane goes out to the West Coast."

Beach's eyes widened. "How're you going to get him to do that?"

Monahan smiled thinly. "Oh, he owes me one."

~

"Hello, Taylor." A trace of a smile crossed Meltem's face as she leaned against the doorframe, arms crossed on her chest.

"Doctor Encirlik, Meltem, what're you doing here?" Taylor looked up from his cluttered desk, a pen in his hand. Through the window, distant lights glowed among the trees of the campus.

"I came to ask you a favor," she said softly. "I need to be on the plane tomorrow when it goes to the West Coast."

Taylor pointed to the chair alongside his desk. "Why?"

Meltem sat and crossed her legs. She straightened the edge of her white hospital coat. "I hear they have doctors and a hospital," she said. "I need to establish contact with them. I make too many decisions without having a professional colleague to call on for advice. I also have something they want."

"Which is?"

"I can show them how to make antibiotics."

Taylor frowned. "You can? Since when?" He had a feeling she had an ulterior motive; something didn't seem right.

"It's only been in the last few weeks I confirmed the replication technique works. It's something that came out of the Billy download." She raised her head and stared at Taylor.

"If you'd stopped by for your check-up, I would've told you. You appear to be well, but I can't tell without an examination." She sighed. "You've chosen to avoid me." She sighed. "Oh, well, I suppose that's understandable—"

"Stop it." Taylor felt his face redden. He rose to his feet. "That was something I shouldn't've done. What I did was wrong. I'm married." His anger faded. *She might have seduced me, but I was a willing participant.* "I'm sorry."

"Yes. I understand. It doesn't matter." She rose to her feet. "I really need to be on that plane tomorrow. Please arrange it." She headed toward the door.

"Can't it wait until we've firmed up our alliance with the West Coast?" Taylor wanted to make an excuse why she couldn't go, but couldn't think of a good one.

"I want to get the trip out of the way now," she said. "Before my pregnancy becomes advanced." She turned on her heel and headed for the door.

Taylor caught up with her at the entrance to the stair well. He put his hands on her shoulders and stared into her face. "You're pregnant?" It was more statement than question. "By whom?" He knew the answer even before she said a word.

She raised one hand to cover his hand on her shoulder and squeezed it gently. Her eyes moistened as she smiled. "Why, you, of course. There hasn't been anyone else. I don't want anyone else."

"But, but, we were only together that one night—"

"Yes." Her smile widened. "I believe it only takes once," she said. "Timing is everything. Now, I must get packed. I'll see you on the plane in the morning. Good night."

CHAPTER FORTY-SEVEN

The C-17 floated down to Sea-Tac's cracked concrete runway through cotton ball clouds and a rain shower. The plane touched the ground, raising circular clouds of spray as it carved tracks through the puddles. Once slowed, the droop-winged plane taxied to the terminal.

Moss, lichen, and ivy wove patterns on the terminal's damp, gray walls. Tiny conifers sprouted from cracks in its concrete apron. In addition to the uniformed soldiers standing guard, several hundred blue-clad men milled about, surrounding a large horse-drawn wagon.

Captain Mapes snapped an order. The blue-clad men flowed into formation and became silent. The rear doors of the C-17 whined open to reveal a large wooden crate surrounded by several dozen passengers.

"Welcome to Washington." Captain Mapes saluted. "How was your trip?"

"A little bumpy in places." Taylor extended his hand. "Finding this place in the rain was nerve wracking. I think our pilot is about done in. We brought more people along this time. Some will stay with the reactor. Others want to meet you. We also brought a doctor who's starved for professional contact. She also knows how to make antibiotics."

Captain Mapes eyes widened. "We haven't had antibiotics for years. Our medical people will be very interested in meeting this doctor." He grasped Taylor by the elbow and steered him toward the terminal. "Why don't we get out of the rain?"

ि

Taylor glanced at his watch and realized it had taken an hour to get the fusion generator out of the plane and onto a wagon. A short while later, the C-17 departed for Groom Lake in Nevada. The soldiers formed up around the wagon and they moved out in a long column.

"I hope we don't run into the Colville tribe," Captain Mapes said. "Last time they ambushed us, we gave them a good beating."

"Indians?" Taylor said.

"Oh, most of them aren't really Indians. The real Indians are east of the Cascades, the Yakimas and Umatillas," Captain Mapes said with a sigh. "The Colville's chief is the son of a used car salesman who originally came from the Philippines. One of our recruits knows his family." He shook his head in disgust.

"Recruits?" Taylor raised his eyebrows. "You're recruiting people?"

The column wended its way up a ramp that led onto an old interstate highway that headed north. The rain had ceased and sun peaked hesitantly between the clouds.

"Yeah, we try to get 'em young and train them right. Still, we're always under-strength." Captain Mapes pointed to a line of buildings being consumed by the advancing forest. "We were scavenging for supplies over there when we were ambushed last year. We used up a lot of ammo. Don't have much left."

On closer inspection, Taylor realized many soldiers' uniforms were threadbare. Not every soldier carried an M-16; some carried bows. "Where're we going?"

"To our base. It's a boat ride," Captain Mapes said. "Once we're on the water, we'll be safe."

The road rose up to a bridge that crossed a narrow body of water Captain Mapes identified as the Duwamish Waterway.

Collapsed buildings and debris were visible among the young conifers filling the land around the waterway. "The tsunami from a whopper mine pushed this far up the Duwamish. Really made a mess of the low-lying areas. Screws up getting around," Captain Mapes said. "It won't be long now. It's downhill to the dock."

It took a half-hour to reach a tongue of water that extended inland from the Duwamish Waterway, which was a concrete lined dock. As they arrived, a long, three-mast vessel whose sails were furled, eased up to the side of the dock. It looked like it might have been a steel barge at one time. A company of riflemen lined its rails.

"Look lively," Captain Mapes yelled. "Get everything on board double-quick time."

Taylor watched the sailors manhandle the wagon up a ramp and lash it down amidships. They herded the horses into stalls where they were blindfolded and wedged in tightly. Even though it looked like chaos, he realized the sailors seemed to know exactly what had to be done. Once everything was on board, the sailors disappeared.

The ship eased away from the dock. Taylor realized it had begun to move silently up the channel, toward open water. He leaned over the side. A row of long oars rose and dipped into the water with slow, smooth precision.

Well, I'll be damned, he thought. *No wonder they need so many sailors.*

As the ship moved away from shore, the swells increased. Along the eastern shore was downtown Seattle. Sunlight reflected off a perfectly mirrored skyscraper. The Space Needle looked undamaged. Other buildings bore dark, sooty stains and some were just bare metal skeletons. Conifers grew everywhere, invading the deserted city.

Sailors reappeared and raised the sails. The ship began to slice through the gray-green swells, away from Seattle and out into the Puget Sound. The wind was out of the west, clean and fresh, with a hint of the briny smell of the ocean.

It took about four hours to round the tip of Bainbridge Island and enter the Hood Canal. During the trip, Captain Mapes filled Taylor in on the history of the Bangor Naval Base.

The floating bridge on Hood Canal no longer barred the way in. It had broken loose when hit by the tsunami and they'd towed it out to deep water and sunk it. Six huge, rust-streaked submarines lined the docks. The sailors unloaded the wagon carrying the fusion reactor as the gloom of evening thickened. Lights flickered on around the base, but for the most part, tall conifers crowded out what little light showed.

Captain Mapes escorted the Clan delegation to a large, well-lit building where a row of uniformed people lined up in front to greet them. "This is the guest hall and will be your quarters while you're here. The staff will show you your rooms. Across the way," He glanced at his watch and then pointed through the trees to another, smaller building. "Is the mess hall. Chow will be served at nineteen hundred hours. Be there." He turned and walked out.

Doctor Encirlik appeared at his side. "What room did you get?" She raised her eyebrows.

Taylor glanced at his key. "I'm in B-6."

"Can I see you after supper?" A trace of a smile appeared.

"Meltem," Taylor said. "I don't think it would be right for us to be seen spending too much time together." He chuckled, trying to make light of his comment.

"You worry too much." Doctor Encirlik shook her head. "I'm going to freshen up. I'll see you at supper."

"My, that was good." Taylor leaned back in his chair. He had just finished a bowl of creamy oyster stew and plate of alder-smoked salmon, accompanied by a crisp, white Sauvignon Blanc. He sat next to Captain Mapes who had spent much of his time in deep conversation with Carver Washington. Captain Mapes had mixed his personnel among the Clan delegation according to similar responsibilities. It was his stated intention to help people to get to know each other and it appeared to be working.

Taylor's other companion was Mrs. Cissy Belasario who wanted to know all about Clan social life and what they did for entertainment. She was a stocky woman with thick gray hair and a slightly florid complexion. She was a gold mine of information about the trials and tribulations of the Bangor Naval Station.

"We have enough firepower to destroy half the world, but have problems controlling the peninsula where our base is situated," Cissy Belasario said, summing up her analysis.

"Really?" Taylor noticed Meltem had the attention of three serious-looking men, most of whom were in their fifties.

Maybe she'll find someone, he thought. He tried to convince himself it could happen. He wasn't sure he wanted that. "Perhaps that'll change," he said.

"Ladies and gentlemen," Captain Mapes said. "Our friends from the east have had a long day. Remember the time difference. I think it's only fair that we let them turn in early, at least, by our standards. I suspect they will be up far earlier than most of us. Good night, ladies and gentlemen."

Chairs scraped as people stood. Some left right away, others continued to talk. As Taylor headed out, he noticed Meltem still had two men in attendance, talking intently.

His room was large but austere; a double bed, which even had cotton sheets, and there was a dresser with mirror and a couple of battered chairs. A door led to a bathroom with a working toilet and shower.

All the comforts of home, he thought. *Nice to have a hot shower.* He stripped and took a long shower. As he toweled off, he heard something creak. He turned and became aware of eyes watching him. Through the bathroom's open door he saw Meltem sitting on the edge of the bed.

"What're you doing here?" Taylor hastily wrapped a towel around his waist and tried to tuck it in tight. He failed.

Meltem entered the bathroom. "If you won't come in for an examination, I guess I have to come to you." She lifted a stethoscope and placed it on his chest.

Taylor tried to brush it off.

"Now, now," she said. "It's just a quick check-up." She moved the stethoscope around several times before slipping it into a pocket. She returned to the bed, stooped, and picked up a black bag. "Blood pressure," she said. "Sit here." She pointed to a chair next to the bed.

"Can't you let me get some clothes on?" Taylor asked, continuing to hold the towel.

"What for?" she said. "There isn't anything I haven't seen before." She pointed to the chair again.

"I feel a little, well, awkward—"

"Nonsense. It makes the examination easier." She wrapped the cuff on his arm and pumped it up. She placed the stethoscope on his wrist and listened. "Good."

"Why're you doing this?" Taylor demanded. "If someone comes in, it wouldn't look very good."

"Tsk, tsk, Taylor, such a concern for appearances. I put the 'Do Not Disturb' sign on the door." She put the cuff and stethoscope into the bag. "Your blood pressure is good, even better than the last time I checked it. Your heart sounds fine." She lifted her head and raised her eyebrows. "How've you been feeling?" A trace of a smile lingered on her lips.

"Right now I feel a little awkward." Taylor adjusted the towel over his lap. "This isn't my idea of an office call."

"First answer my question. How d'you feel?"

"Actually quite good. I have more energy, more stamina." He hesitated. "And more interest in life."

"Excellent," she said.

Taylor stood and wrapped the towel more tightly. "This pregnancy, I need to know about it. How did it happen? And why me?"

"It's quite simple," she said. "I was ovulating, so I was fertile. We had intercourse. Twice. You impregnated me."

"Did you know you were ovulating?" Taylor held his breath.

"Of course." Meltem put the stethoscope away. "You really don't get it, do you? I literally came back from the edge of death. I realized I'd let a lot of things in life I wanted get away from me. Including you." She sighed. "If I can't have you, I'm going to have your child."

Meltem stood up in front of Taylor and took his hands. "I can't help how I feel about you. Don't worry, Taylor, I won't make a scene or try to break up your relationship with Joyce. I know you well enough to believe you'll come to see your child from time to time, and maybe even me. Discreetly, of course."

She moved close to him so that her knees touched his. "Like tonight." She stroked his damp hair. "I keep thinking about us the other night. Sometimes I get so excited I have to masturbate. I don't want to do that tonight." She leaned forward and pressed his face into her breasts. "I want it to be us, together, one last time."

"I can't." Taylor tried to push her away. Her aroma filled his nostrils. The memory of their previous encounter came flooding back.

He wanted her. No, he lusted for her.

As the memory returned, his body betrayed him. His erection grew, obvious under the towel. He bit his lip.

Meltem's eyes flashed downward and then back to his eyes. "You see?" She pushed her knees between his.

"No, don't." His legs opened. "I shouldn't," he said, as his hands advanced over her buttocks.

She leaned forward and their lips met. They kissed.

"Please, Meltem," Taylor whispered. "I mustn't." He felt her hand loosen the towel, then touch him. His knees felt like rubber. His resolve weakened as his desire rose. She pushed him back. He closed his eyes and lay flat on his back. *Oh, Lord.*

"First," Meltem said. "The light." She moved quickly to the room's entrance, clacked the security bolt shut, and turned off the light. Clothing rustled. "Ah, that's better," she said.

A moment later, Taylor felt the bed sag. Something dragged his towel away. A naked body covered his. A moment later, soft lips touch his chest and a cool hand caressed his face.

"Tonight," she whispered. "May be the last time for us. Every time may be the last time." She moved and her lips touched his chest again. "So we have to be especially good tonight."

CHAPTER FORTY-EIGHT

"We have military representatives from Fort Hunter-Liggett, Groom Lake Research Station, Fort Lewis, and Bangor Naval Station." Captain Mapes stood at the head of a long table in the room normally used as the mess hall. "We'd like to extend a special welcome to the observing representative from the Columbia River Valley Conference."

He referred to the political entity lying between the Cascades and Spokane that controlled the Columbia River's hydroelectric power. Bangor Naval Station had bought power from them previously, but as of late, they could no longer afford their price. "Mr. Johnny Bosworth of Yakima." He pointed to stocky middle-aged man wearing leather clothing. His long, brown hair framed a weather-beaten face.

"This meeting was requested by the organization known as the Greater Clan of Ohio, which is an amalgamation of city-states covering about two-thirds of Ohio." Captain Mapes glanced at his notes. "They contacted us and first visited us twenty days ago. They flew in from Ohio." He paused.

Johnny Bosworth's head turned quickly as the representative looked at the others present. His eyebrows rose.

"Initially, we were skeptical when they told us their aircraft, a C-17 transport, was powered by a nuclear fusion engine." Captain Mapes held up his hand. "I know, it sounded that way to us. So, we sent a delegation under my executive officer, Commander Cy Belasario, on a fact-finding mission. He and Lieutenant-Commander Pip Ryan, my chief engineering officer, came back after several days completely convinced."

"These nukes that power the plane have got to be dangerous," Colonel Ike Kolodny said.

He was small man, thin, with the leathery look of hard service. His narrow face was clean-shaven and dominated by a long hooked nose. He was a marine from Fort Lewis and had not been at the Sea-Tac Airport to see the C-17. "What about radiation?" He sat ramrod straight.

"That's a very good question we'll address in detail later. But a quick answer is no, they're not radioactive—"

"Then they're not nukes—" Kolodny said quickly.

"Please," Captain Mapes said. "We'll get into that later. We'll have a complete overview of the situation before we get down to details. There are even more astounding things you have to know." He paused to take a sip of water. "Let me introduce the people from Ohio at this time. Mr. Taylor MacPherson, representative of the Greater Clan."

Taylor stood briefly and made eye contact around the table. He was tired, a little sore, and felt very guilty from his time with Meltem.

"Mr. Billy Potato, head of the University of Technology."

Billy clambered to his feet, dipped his head, and sat.

"Mr. Carver Washington, Clan Elder and official Council representative who, I was surprised to find out, is related to my wife, LaTasha." Captain Mapes's head rose as he smiled briefly.

Carver raised his hand and nodded.

"There're other people from Ohio here, working with my technical staff to replace the S8G reactor in the Hampton with a nuclear fusion reactor that was a gift from the Clan."

"You've brought a nuke here?" Kolodny's voice had a hard edge.

"Yes." Captain Mapes's voice rose. "Mr. MacPherson will tell us what we face and what Ohio wants us to consider." He turned and beckoned for Taylor to rise.

Taylor walked to the head of the table. "Thank you for coming to this meeting. Let me say I'm very pleased to meet with you, as official representatives of the United States Government. After Washington DC was destroyed during the Collapse, we lost hope of seeing the Stars and Stripes again.

"Where to begin?" Taylor paused. "The Earth faces a threat to its existence. There is a real possibility Earth will be attacked by aliens—"

There was a collective intake of air.

"Aliens? What's this crap?" Kolodny shook his head.

"Listen." Taylor raised his voice. "And you'll find out." He smiled briefly as his voice softened. "About five years ago, an alien space-ship went into orbit around Earth. Something went wrong and it was disabled, stuck in orbit. Billy," He gestured toward him. "Was sent down to Earth to make parts for the space craft."

All heads turned to stare at Billy.

"Yes," said Taylor. "Billy is a member of the Qu'uda species. He has crossed interstellar space—"

"This is pure bullshit. Aliens, my ass." Kolodny rose to his feet. "You're either out of your fuckin' mind, or smoking—"

"You are wrong." Billy's voice boomed as he rose to his feet.

He removed his hat and cape to reveal a neck that flowed into a body without shoulders. Arms protruded from a body that was crossed with yellow-green scars, which accented his prominent breastbone and pear-shaped anatomy. As he raised his leg, his knee bent backwards, opposite to that of a human. "I am Qu'uda, not human."

The room's participants drew a collective breath.

Kolodny's sallow face paled and his Adam's apple wobbled.

Billy refastened his cloak and put his hat back on.

"Thank you, Billy," Taylor said.

"It is the only way to see the truth about me."

"Er, Colonel Kolodny," Captain Mapes said. "Let Mr. MacPherson finish his presentation first. There'll be plenty of time for questions afterwards."

Kolodny's face was ash white. He nodded silently.

"Billy came down near the town of Defiance in western Ohio. At that time it was the capital city of the Mid-West Federation."

Taylor continued with the history of the events up to the Qu'uda's departure and what Billy had learned, that led them to believe they would return.

$$\sim$$

"... So," Taylor said. "I propose we form a military council to establish a defense force to protect Earth from any attack brought by the Qu'uda against us."

"Who d'you propose for this military council?" Kolodny asked. "Who's going to be in command?"

"The Clan has nominated Billy Potato, Ed Kerr," Taylor hesitated momentarily. "Cha KinLaat DoMar, another Qu'uda and myself. As for command, the military council will set the direction and be responsible for obtaining resources from respective organizations. It is my hope that the existing military will supply the field officers."

"I see." Kolodny rubbed his chin. "Why such a large fraction of the council for the Clan?"

"From what I've learned, the Clan will be supplying a significant share of the technology and equipment to arm the defense force." Taylor sat down. "Our re-industrialization program is moving ahead. In addition, it's my understanding the Clan's population is the largest of the groups here." He paused for a moment. "With the possible exception of the Columbia Conference."

Johnny Bosworth, the delegate from the Columbia Conference, cleared his throat. "Our population is about fifty thousand souls," he said. "I can't speak for the Conference at this point, but I will make a report to the Conference of Cities on what I've heard here. Quite frankly, I find much of this hard to believe. It would make my task easier if there were some way to demonstrate a flying aircraft." His voice trailed off.

Captain Mapes nodded. "I'm sure that can be arranged."

Taylor tapped his pen on the table. "We're returning to Ohio tomorrow. If you like, we could fly you back. Where does your conference meet?"

Bosworth plucked at his lower lip. "They meet at Ritzville," he said. "Once a month. It won't be for a few weeks." He shrugged.

"You could take me back, but most of them wouldn't get to see you."

"If we made a radio available, could you tell them about what you heard?" Captain Mapes said. "Ask if they could call an emergency meeting so they could see the plane for themselves?"

Bosworth nodded. "No promises. I'm just a delegate."

Taylor frowned. "Where's Ritzville, anyway? I never heard of it." He looked up from gathering his papers.

"The junction of Interstate 90 and US 395," Bosworth said. "It's midway between Yakima, Walla Walla, and Spokane. It's used as a meeting location."

"I see," Taylor said. "Next meeting," he said. "When? How long will it take to get an answer from your leaders?"

He polled the table. It was agreed if the plane could provide transportation to the delegates from Fort Hunter-Liggett in California and the Columbia Conference, they would meet in ten days' time. "See you then."

The Columbia Conference agreed to an emergency meeting at Ritzville three days later. Bosworth assured them they would be safe and not harmed when they landed.

The C-17 landed on a dusty stretch of former interstate highway and came to a halt at an exit ramp. As they waited, tumbleweed rolled across the highway and disappeared into the straggle of sagebrush. A dozen dour men wearing leather clothing approached slowly to greet them. They inspected the plane, offering no commitment or opinions. An hour later, the plane lifted off and set course for Ohio.

CHAPTER FORTY-NINE

"Ms. Vargas." Ned Biehl looked over his prominent nose at her. "First we get a formal complaint from Krupansky of Pennsylvania that you insulted him and refused to deal with him, and now several border villages have gone up in flames."

His office held several Council Elders along with Pittsburgh Pete. Behind him, windows looked down upon the Rocky River, and in front of his desk, additional chairs had been squeezed in alongside the sofa in front of the overflowing bookshelves.

Joyce flushed. "Krupansky wants a power generator. That's against Clan policy. I offered to supply him with power. That wasn't good enough. Then he told me to go home and send my boss to deal with him instead of a woman, because it was an insult to him. You know this already. It was in my report." She waved her hand as though it would uncover the report.

A northeast wind rattled leaves against the windows.

She felt a chill. *What's this nonsense?* she thought. *I did my job. I lost my baby. And he's screwing me.*

"We don't want to send soldiers or militia into Pennsylvania after the Brotherhood. That would play into their hands. They're masters of ambush in those hills." Ned steepled his fingers. "No. We've got to open negotiations with the Brotherhood. We need to work something out."

"He won't respect you if you sue for peace," Pittsburgh Pete's voice came from the back of the office. "They're desperate," he said. "Ever since we quit purchasing oil and coal, they got a problem. They don't have money to buy food."

Ned looked at Pete. "I don't want to lose one soldier over Krupansky." He let out a sigh. "He's more of an annoyance than anything else."

"What about the border post and those three villages?" Ramsey said. "Don't they mean anything to you?"

Ned stared at Ramsey for a moment. "If you want to send an expedition into Pennsylvania, do it. I'll disavow it publicly, of course. You know what that'll cost you."

"Yes," Ramsey said. "I suppose you're right."

"Ms. Vargas." Ned took a deep breath. "We need you to apologize to Krupansky for the sake of the Clan." An obviously false smile flickered across his face.

"Apologize? To that smelly chauvinistic cretin? With all due respect, it was Krupansky who insulted me." Joyce's cheek flamed. *He's making me the scapegoat*, she thought. *Prick.*

Ned smiled thinly. "You don't have to mean it." He sniffed. "It would be," He hesitated, "purely for show."

"You mean politics." *Bite your tongue*, Joyce thought.

"Whatever." Ned resumed studying a piece of paper on the desk before him. "Pete, you'll take this message to the Brotherhood. The Clan would like a treaty with the Brotherhood, mutual protection, assistance, etc., some rubbish like that. If they're willing, we will resume purchase of oil at the same price as before. Also, we'll bring a power line to their border and supply them electricity at no charge for one year." He raised his head. "Oh yes, and it also has an apology from the 'girlie' in the CEPA." He smiled sourly. "My apologies, Ms. Vargas, but it costs less to wound pride than soldiers."

Pete took the letter and left the room without a word.

Joyce rose to her feet. "If it'd been a man, the soldiers would already be on the move—"

"Sit down," Ned said forcefully.

Joyce sat down. *I thought I was special to him. Bastard.*

"Priorities drive my decisions. The Clan doesn't need casualties while preparing to do battle with a much greater foe." Ned leaned back in his chair. "Personally, Ms. Vargas, I don't much like Mr.

Krupansky. I rather prefer your company to his. You're far smarter and certainly easier to deal with." A brief smile crossed his face. "This, as you said earlier, is politics. I believe with your help, the proposed course of action will save lives and gold." He sighed. "I hope you understand. Don't view this as a reprimand. Really, I know how hard you work for the Clan." His eyes caught hers and held them for an instance.

Joyce rose and reached across the desk and offered her hand. "I'm sorry that I blew up." *He's a smart, tough bastard*, she thought. *One who knows how to handle power.*

Ned stood and took her hand. "Thanks for understanding," he said. "I don't always like what I have to do or make other people do. Sometimes it's a necessity." He collected his papers and looked around. "Anything else? This meeting is adjourned."

As the Elders headed toward the door, Ned said, "a moment, please, Ms. Vargas." He smiled.

"Yes?" The last of the visitors drifted from the office.

"D'you have time to review the electrification progress?" Ned said with a brief smile. "Can we do it over lunch?"

Joyce stared at him for a moment. *I gave him a report on my work, so ...* "Why certainly," she said. "I'd be happy to." With Taylor away on a trip, it would a chance to slip away with Ned. She felt a rush of excitement and anticipation.

"Did you hear Biehl make a date with MacPherson's bitch?" Beach shielded his mouth with a hand. "D'you think something's going on between them?"

"I don't know." Monahan glanced up and down the corridor. "Biehl's married. If there is, we could make his life more complicated."

Beach's lips curled into a smile. "That'd be nice."

CHAPTER FIFTY

As scheduled, ten days later, the C-17 landed at the Sea-Tac Airport. It rumbled across the runway toward the terminal under a broken sky. The plane carried a tanker wagon of kerosene and six barrels of lubricating oil for Major Kolodny to get his mechanized armor moving again.

In addition, Doctor Encirlik had brought several cases of laboratory equipment and cultures to set up an antibiotics production facility.

"Good to see you, Mr. MacPherson." Captain Mapes extended his hand. "The meeting will be tomorrow with the same people present except for the Columbia Conference. They've declined to participate at this time. Something about internal politics."

"Nice seeing you, too," Taylor said. "Call me Taylor since we're working closely together—"

"Then call me Ki," Captain Mapes said. "We've got to get these supplies moved. Major Kolodny wants to secure the area between the Naval Station and Fort Lewis, including south Tacoma. Getting his armor running will make it a whole lot easier." They headed toward the terminal as teams of blue-clad sailors swarmed like ants in and out of the back of the C-17 carrying out boxes and crates.

Taylor saw the C-17 take off an hour later. It was on its way to Fort Hunter-Liggett, which was midway between Los Angeles and

San Francisco, and also to make a pickup at Groom Lake. *We need more aircraft*, he thought. *And soon.*

Soon after, the convoy set out for the dock on the Duwamish.

ༀ

"All right, ladies and gentlemen, let's get this meeting underway." Ki Mapes stood at the head of the long table in the mess hall. "We've got a lot to cover." He passed out a stack of paper. "Take one; it's our agenda."

Taylor mentally reviewed the participants.

Major Ike Kolodny of Fort Lewis, Colonel Ed Bates of Fort Hunter-Liggett, Lieutenant Colonel Bud Inez of the Aerospace Weapons Center at Groom Lake, Captain Mapes's officer staff and the contingent from the Clan. He glanced at the agenda.

Space access was the first item.

That ought to be interesting; how do we get into space?

"I'd like Bud Inez to bring us up to date on what's available and his ideas on reestablishing our presence in space." Ki gestured toward the balding round-faced man with the dark complexion and thick mustache. "Bud's an astronaut. He went into space on the shuttle."

Lieutenant Colonel Bud Inez stood. He was medium height with a stocky build and a bulging waistline. "Thanks, Ki. Well, I wish I could say we have something available, but we don't." He unfolded a map. "It's my recollection there were two locations where space shuttles might have survived. The first is Los Angeles and the other is Cape Kennedy."

Shuttle launches had been phased out before the Collapse in favor of commercial single-stage to orbit vehicles. "There may be another at Edwards, in the Mojave.

"It's my recommendation we check out these places first thing."

"Wait a minute," said Lieutenant Pip Ryan. "Even if they're still there, what do we do with them anyway?"

Taylor leaned forward. "Put them into service."

"How're we gonna do that?" Pip asked. "It takes a shit-load of stuff to get those birds ready to fly, never mind the solid fuel boosters, which don't exist." He threw his pencil down on the table. "I dunno. I think we're dreaming."

Billy clambered to his feet and then climbed on top his chair. "Not difficult to get into space. We have drive units that can lift shuttles to orbit and beyond. They are similar to drive units first used in plane. They have enough power to lift a plane to orbit except the airframe is too fragile to take thrust." His mouth widened as he attempted to imitate a human smile. "When I tried, I almost crashed. Bigger problem is to build a vehicle that is strong and airtight."

"D'you think it could? We're gonna need boosters and a support infrastructure to service the shuttle." Pip frowned. "I didn't see anything like that on my visit to Ohio."

"With fusion drive there is no need for boosters or large fuel tanks," Billy said. "Fusion drive can lift vehicle to orbit, perhaps further."

"What about radiation?" Major Ike Kolodny asked. "There's enough radioactives floating around. We don't need any more."

Billy swiveled his head toward the speaker. "No radiation. This is aneutronic fusion, no neutrons to transmute elements, therefore no radiation." His head swiveled in opposite direction. "Must find out if shuttle vehicles are space worthy." He stepped down off the chair and resumed his seat.

For a moment the room was quiet.

"I'd love to take a look at the shuttles," Bud Inez said. "I've got a ton of information on them back at the base."

He paused for a moment and then his words came in a rush. "Look, even after all this time, the mothballed shuttles just may be our best bet. They were in hangars. That should've given them protection from the weather." A flush crept into his face. "Their fluoropolymer seals won't deteriorate, at least, not quickly. The electronics inside should still be in good shape. It'd be great to go into space again." He looked at Taylor. "Maybe I could borrow a C-17 to go to Cape Kennedy ..."

Ki cleared his throat. "That," he said. "Is on the agenda." He looked at Billy. "You mentioned that there were two other aircraft being fitted with fusion drive engines. When d'you expect them to be operational?"

Billy stared at him for a moment. "The first should be ready in about twenty days." He paused. "These aircraft need special places to land and take off. Better if we had drive units with thrust vector control for safe operation."

"Right, Billy," Taylor said. "The next generation of engines will have thrust vector control. For that, we need advanced manufacturing. We'll get it, but not right away."

"What're you guys talking about?" Ki said.

"The Qu'uda shuttle could land and take off vertically. It has vectored thrust, sort of like the Brit's Harrier jump jet—"

"That's all well and good on something small," Bud said quickly. "We're talking about the space shuttle. That's a big mother. Way bigger than a jump jet."

"We're getting off the agenda." Ki raised his voice.

"Forgive me," Taylor said. "I've got to set the record straight. The alien shuttle was as large as a 747, maybe even a C-5B. Except, once airborne, it flew like a fighter."

The room became quiet. Eyes grew wide.

"How much power did you say these fusion drive units develop?" Bud had a far-away look in his eyes.

"Do not know how to convert into your units," Billy said.

"Based upon the fraction of the capacity of the engines Billy used while on the first flight of the modified C-17," Taylor said. "I estimated that each unit produces about a million pounds thrust. We need to get one in a test fixture."

"Whew." Bud whistled. "That'd make getting to orbit a lot easier. Put a cluster of them together and you could lift a battleship to orbit."

"Is battleship airtight with environmental controls?" Billy asked. "Drive units can be built larger and more powerful."

Ki leaned back in his chair. "So much for the agenda," he said with a chuckle. "We're miles ahead of where I thought we'd be. Doesn't matter," he said. "We're getting closer. Let me summarize what I believe is the plan." He picked up his sheet. "First, Ohio will provide a C-17 for Bud." He gestured in his direction. "He'll find out if there are any viable shuttles left. Then, it seems to me, fit one or more shuttles with a fusion drive. After that, everything gets fuzzy."

"What kind of weapons does the shuttle use?" Billy asked.

"It doesn't. It was designed for peaceful missions," Bud said. "Supposed to be a space truck," he said with a chuckle.

"Not safe against Bird-that-Soars," Billy said. "Egg-that-Flies has powerful weapons and a thick skin."

"What's he talking about?" Kolodny's irritation showed.

"Let me explain," Taylor said. "The Qu'uda mother ship, the Egg-that-Flies, is a very large craft. Maybe two miles long—"

"Two miles long?" Bud's mouth fell open. "You're kidding, of course."

"About two miles long." Taylor nodded without a smile.

"What kind of drive unit does that have?"

"It has a *nakra* drive," Billy said.

Into the resulting silence, Taylor said, "I believe that's a hydrogen-deuterium fusion drive system that's used only in deep space. The Bird-that-Soars is the shuttle, the one I described as being 747-size is a twin-engine craft that lands and takes off vertically. It also has some kind of energy weapon that fried two hundred or so Fed guards with one blast, very powerful. I got within a couple of hundred yards or so of that craft. It was unlike anything I'd seen before."

"So how do we defend against something like that?" Bud asked. "We can't put stuff like that into space—"

"Yes, we can," Pip said. "Didn't you hear him say that we can build even more powerful drive units? That means weight isn't a constraint on what we put up. Now we can use something that's big, strong, and armored, and still put it in orbit." He looked up and down the table. His eyes sparkled brightly and a flush crept into his cheeks.

"Where would we make something like that, anyway?" Bud asked. "I have no idea how to build stuff like that."

"Sounds like you need a shipyard," Ki said. "Heavy lift cranes, big metal forming equipment, lots of welders and workers. Back east, there used to be places like that, y'know, Groton Boatworks at Newport." He nodded his head.

Pip's face flushed. "I just had a really crazy idea." His eyes grew wide, almost staring. "How powerful can you make one of those drive units?"

Taylor turned to Billy. "How much larger can an aneutronic drive unit be built? How many times larger?"

Billy stared at the wall, face expressionless.

The room went silent. All eyes focused on Billy.

"About eight squared times larger." Billy swiveled his head toward Taylor and paused. "No need for larger units except in deep space. Fuel for *nakra* easier to obtain from gas planets and gaseous asteroids at fringe of system."

"Sixty times as large." Pip began to scribble furiously on the margin of his agenda. "Over sixty million pounds thrust. That ought to be enough."

"Ought to be enough for what?" Ki asked.

"To put a submarine in orbit."

"Now, just a damn minute," Ki said. "You're not thinking of putting one of my boats into orbit, are you?"

"Look," Pip said. "We need something big, strong, armored, and airtight." He paused. "That sounds a lot like a submarine to me." He began to nod. "It has environmental controls, air regeneration, the ability to function as a closed environment. Sure, it's going to need some modifications, but the basic structure and equipment is there."

"I'm not sure we should—" Ki said.

"Most of them are rusting away," Pip said. "What're we going to use them for? Fight the Russians? Attack the Chinese?" He let the question hang. "Right now, they're dinosaurs. Big and powerful with no role to play. This gives them a function—"

"Hang on a moment," Ki said. "How d'you figure on getting a sub upright to launch it?" He pursed his lips. "Dry weight for an Angeles class is sixteen thousand tons. There isn't a crane in the world that can pick that up. Never mind all the changes that would have to be made."

Pip frowned. "You've got a point there," he said. "I hadn't thought about that."

"Don't you launch your missiles underwater?" Taylor asked. "Don't you just kind of squirt them out and ignite them?"

Pip stared at him for a moment. "Right. We could do the same thing with the sub, 'cept we'd have to figure out how to get it pointed toward the surface."

"You mean keep my boats as boats, except with strap-on fusion drives?" Ki's face brightened.

"Not exactly," Pip said. "I'm still thinking about it. I need some time with the drawings and more info on the fusion drives, power output, service connections, dimensions, etc. Then I can put something down on paper and run the numbers. Then I'll have an answer as to whether it's feasible or not."

"All right." Ki picked up his agenda. "Something more mundane, but just as important." He turned toward Taylor. "We need more aircraft. If we find aircraft in good shape, can we get drive units for them?"

"Probably." Taylor took a deep breath. "Look, if we concentrate on C-17's, it'll go faster. Our people have designed a unit for it. So, if you know where there are more C-17s, they'd be the ones we could put into service most quickly."

Ki turned toward Bud. "Isn't there some place in the desert where there's a bunch of mothballed aircraft?"

"Yeah, in Arizona. Most of the stuff is junk, but there are a few newer birds, usually without engines." Bud rubbed his head. "Most C-17s were in the hands of the Air National Guard, the airlift and transportation units. I'd bet there's a bunch scattered around the country. When I get back to Groom Lake, I'll do some digging through the records to see what I can find. I'll let you know."

"Next," said Ki. "The Columbia Conference heard we're getting lubricants from Ohio. They want to trade power to get some. It seems to me we need to figure out what items we can use for trade. We've got a list of needs as long as my arm but we don't know what the people in Ohio need from us."

"At the present, don't worry about that," said Taylor. "I couldn't help thinking as we flew out this last time, we'll be reestablishing the United States of America. This has motivated our Council Leader, Ned Biehl, to make alliances with our neighbors to the east and the west. When that happens, we'll tie those areas into our rail and phone system." He paused. "Transportation and communications stimulates trade and prosperity, then peace. I'd recommend the same here."

"We've tried to link-up with the Columbia Conference, but they've always been leery about supporting us." Ki sighed. "With them having all that hydropower, they didn't need anything from us. Plus their agricultural areas are much better than ours." He shook his head. "The only things that they wanted were machined parts and seafood. And now, lubricants."

"Soon, a whole lot more," Taylor said. "I bet they don't have antibiotics, trains, phones, or planes."

"Excuse me," said Colonel Ed Bates. "Our folks at Fort Hunter-Liggett don't have any of that stuff. In fact, we're short of everything, including fighting men. We want to be a part of this, but I'm not sure what we can contribute."

Pip leaned forward. "Ed," he said. "If there's a shuttle at Edwards, we'll need you to get it."

"There's a tough bunch at Bakersfield in the way," Ed said. "They won't take it lightly if we cross their territory. It'd be a fight, that's for sure. The way south to Edwards is over Interstate Five, smack through the middle of their territory."

"If the shuttle is in good condition, we'll figure out some way to hang onto it," said Taylor. "You need troops?"

Ed looked up. "Me? Yes. There's less than five hundred soldiers fit for duty at Hunter-Liggett. We've got plenty of guns, some ammo, but no fuel for the armor. The Bakersfield bunch has thousands of men with few weapons, but they're tough and mean."

"I'll talk to our Council about this," Taylor said. "They might be willing to send an expeditionary force, especially if it's for the United States of America. There's just enough memory left of what that meant to our leaders they might act on it. The young people don't know or care what it means."

"The United States of America." Kolodny's voice broke. "Our United States of America." He stood, straight and rigid, and saluted, eyes shining wetly. "It's about time." He sat down slowly to a silent room.

"Last item on the agenda." Ki waited until he had their attention. "I'd like to send people back east to work with the folks there, with someone who can speak for me." He paused. "I think each of the military groups should do the same thing. Each of us does things differently. I like the idea of reestablishing the United States of America."

No brainer, Taylor thought. "Send anybody you want."

CHAPTER FIFTY-ONE

"Yes, Mr. Krupansky, the Greater Clan did have a good harvest." Ned Biehl glanced out the window of his office at the Rocky River far below. Leaves swirled in its current, making brown textured patterns. "We have no reason to give it away." His smile was cold. "Our farmers worked hard for it."

"Many of the Brotherhood are gonna go hungry this winter, all because you're not buying as much of our coal and oil as you previously did," Krupansky said.

"Then why did you authorize the incursion over our border?"

"It were a mistake. Those responsible have been punished—"

"That won't bring the dead back to life, nor re-build the homes of the survivors." Ned turned from the window. He stared at Krupansky sitting in the oak armchair before the desk. He had invited Krupansky into his office for informal discussions since the open meeting had gone badly. This wasn't going much better.

It was time for the offer. "If you want food," he said. "There may be a way to get it."

"Go on." Krupansky's eyes narrowed with suspicion.

"You can earn it."

"How?" The corners of Krupansky's mouth turned down as though he'd just tasted something bitter.

"Our allies need soldiers," Ned said. "Out on the West Coast. It would be for a year or so. They've asked us to provide soldiers under an enlistment contract. They'd pay in silver. Their rate of pay is about the same as what a laborer makes in the Greater Clan, which is one silver dollar a week." He sat down behind his desk and leaned forward, fingers steepled, tent-like. "I know you've got a thousand Brothers mobilized on our eastern border—"

"We done no such thing." Krupansky sounded offended. "They're farmers, they're hungry—"

"Please," Ned said. "This's a private meeting. Let's be honest. I know the disposition of your forces." He leaned back in his chair. "If you're not interested in joining the Clan or hearing what I've got to say, we might as well end this meeting." He stared at Krupansky without blinking, his mouth forming a hard line. "If you prefer war instead of food, we'll give you war. Total war. With aircraft, bombs, and heavy artillery. Burn every town. Instead, you could have an opportunity to earn silver."

"No," Krupansky said. "Tell me more about these allies of yours who need soldiers? Who're they?"

Ned took a deep breath. "It's the United States Army."

Krupansky's eyes narrowed. "Can't be. They was wiped out during the Collapse. There ain't no United States left."

"It's in California."

"California?" Krupansky said as though it were the end of the Earth. "You can't get there. Too far away. Too many hot zones between here and there."

"You know about our planes?" Ned looked down his long nose. "That we got from Wright-Patterson?"

"I heard something," Krupansky said. "I thought it was whiskey a talkin'."

"It's a fact. That's how we get to California. We fly there." Ned stood and retrieved a sheet of paper from a cabinet. "If you're inter-ested in providing five hundred enlistees for a term of at least one year, sign this document. It contains all the terms and conditions." He handed the paper to Krupansky. "Our allies want to move quickly on this." He watched from the corner of his eye. "We've got one group from the old Lima-Findlay area ready to go. Since you have a group near our border, it might be possible for you to send some." He handed Krupansky a pen.

"Now wait a minute," Krupansky said. "I need to talk this over with the Brotherhood before I send our Brothers off to war."

"I thought you were authorized to speak for the Brotherhood," Ned said in a voice ringing with mockery. "Have I been wasting my time with you?"

"What about food, clothing, and weapons?" Krupansky waved the piece of paper in the air. "Is that provided? How d'they get paid? Who handles the money?"

"If you read that contract, it's all in there." Ned picked up another sheet of paper. "Your men would cross our border without their weapons and board planes in groups of one hundred. They'll be processed at Fort Hunter-Liggett in California, then put through basic US Army training. They'll be fitted out and armed there. As for their pay, I thought you might act as agent to distribute the portion they send home." He smiled thinly.

Krupansky nodded slowly, as though he'd tasted something good. "Yes," he said. "That'd work." He looked up quickly, a smile starting. "You'd do it, in silver? How often?"

"In silver, once a month. We'd have to make arrangements for, er," Ned hesitated momentarily, "a delivery point. A place that's private, out of sight. To discourage bandits, of course."

Krupansky's smile widened. "Bandits, yeah, right." He placed the document on the desk and signed it. "Let's go back to the public meeting," he said. "We can tell them that we're working on a treaty. We don't have to say nothing about this here soldier deal, do we?"

As Ned rose to his feet, he smiled. "As you wish."

ॐ

Ned Biehl looked up from his desk and reflected on the past year. It hadn't been so difficult to persuade Krupansky to send two more contingents of enlistees out west, which had weakened the Brotherhood's capability for war. The Pennsylvania border was now peaceful and began to prosper from trade. Some of the enlistees' money had stuck to Krupansky's fingers, but most reached their families, who used it to buy food.

Ned derived great satisfaction when he learned Colonel Ed

Bates of the California National Guard had used the Pennsylvania enlistees in his battle with Bakersfield; the infusion of troops and fuel for his mechanized armor had left no doubt as to the result.

The stretch of California coast from Salinas to Santa Barbara was now under the Stars and Stripes. They'd found remains of a shuttle in Los Angeles that was too damaged to fly. All it was good for was spare parts.

Colonel Bates's forces crossed over the Coastal Range at Paso Robles into the Central Valley. After several battles, the southern end of the valley and its oilfields became secure.

Ned smiled at the memory of Colonel Bates's effusive thanks for the enlistees. Once Bates had an assured supply of fuel, he had moved north to gain control of the fertile delta area. After capturing Sacramento, Bates had declared the State of California reestablished and again a part of the United States. *Good*, thought Ned. *Even though it does nothing for us in Ohio.*

Ned found the reports of Major Kolodny's Marines opening Interstate 5 as far north as Bellingham and as far south as Eugene, Oregon, interesting but hard to comprehend. Kolodny's drive south slowed where conifer forests choked the highway to Roseburg. The mountains of southern Oregon and northern California were covered with fast-growing redwoods, which was a green curtain that swallowed all but the widest highway. Few could raise enough food to survive in those forests.

To the east, the Columbia Conference became an uneasy ally, tempted by the needed supplies but fearful of Kolodny's mechanized Marines. Assured they would not be invaded, they came under the Stars and Stripes and gained access to trade. Hydropower from the Columbia River fueled the northwest from Roseburg to Bellingham and its growing industrial activity. The once-devastated docks of Tacoma now hummed, where Pip Ryan's team worked on modifying two Ohio-class submarines, the Pennsylvania and the Maryland, for their role as the new space station.

Ned had learned Tacoma was now the terminus of the revitalized rail line extending south to the Columbia River, where it branched south and east. Trains ran through the Columbia River Gorge east to Spokane and south to Eugene. The flow of goods increased steadily over time. Trade made the region peaceful and prosperous.

Good, Ned thought. *We're making progress.*

CHAPTER FIFTY-TWO

"Look," Lieutenant Pip Ryan said. "It'll be easier once we get the boats into dry dock." The engineer looked up from a set of drawings and pointed to a sketch on the wall.

Faded green paint peeled from the walls of the small office. A window overlooked a chaotic boatyard. "This cradle will be ready in a month."

The cradle was a massive framework of girders that would support a submarine in the dry dock. A year had passed, and preparations continued without any work done on the boats.

"Well, it seems like we're still spinning our wheels, going nowhere." Captain Ki Mapes had seen his boat, the SSBN Maryland, towed with another Ohio-class submarine from the Bangor Naval Station to Tacoma over six months ago. They were still tied up at the same dock. "It reminds me of what government used to be like. More and more people doing less and less."

Pip sighed. "Soon you'll see some changes." He grabbed a sheet of paper. "Look," he said. "We found several cases of silicone RTV adhesive down in the Willamette Valley. They were just sitting in a warehouse."

Ki nodded. It didn't mean anything to him.

"We also got a shipment of welding units in from Ohio. Apparently there was a manufacturing facility, Lincoln Electric I believe, that made welding equipment. We've got to train people how to use them before we start on the boats. We've identified some old codgers who claim to have been welders from before the Collapse."

"Are you on schedule?" Ki's eyebrows rose.

"Ah, no." Pip made a long face.

"You know what you're going to do?"

Pip scratched his chin. "Kind of." He pulled over a large sheet of paper. "We've got the big picture pretty well figured out." He looked up with a wry grin. "Those damn details get me every time."

"Still plan to pull out the reactor and the drive system from those boats?" Ki looked as though he was about to lose a favorite toy. "And cut their tails off?"

"Yes."

Ki shook his head. "A waste of good submarines."

Pip shrugged. "There are four more boomers up at Bangor. In space, there's no need for a pressurized water reactor, a turbo-generator or electric motors. Taking them out gives us a twenty-seven percent increase in internal space." He pointed to the drawing. "That's where we'll put the air and water storage tanks, along with the fusion power source."

"Don't discard anything you remove," Ki said. "We might need them for the other boats."

"Sure." Pip pointed to the circled items scheduled for removal: sonar, towed arrays, ballast and buoyancy systems, auxiliary diesel generator, torpedoes and their launch equipment, hydraulic system, noisemakers—all items not needed to operate a space station. "There'll be a real pile of stuff coming your way. I figure that the boats will lose about forty-eight percent of their mass."

"You still think that itty-bitty rocket is gonna get it to orbit?" Ki pulled a drawing forward which showed a thirty-foot long fusion drive attached to the truncated end of the submarine. About sixty feet of the stern would be removed, with a reinforced steel plate welded across the opening, onto which the fusion drive unit would be mounted. "It sure doesn't look big enough."

Pip laughed. "It'd better be. The test data on the small units are very impressive," he said. "This direct scale-up should have more than enough power to get it into a high orbit. The beauty of the motor's size is the shuttle can bring it back to use for the second sub's ride up to orbit." He had persuaded the Defense Council the bigger missile submarines were far better candidates for the space station.

The big boats had more room inside and carried twenty-four Trident-2 missiles, each of which had seven three hundred-kiloton warheads. When both submarines were joined at their conning towers, the space station would possess a lot of firepower.

He had also made a case to spin the hulls and provide half-normal Earth gravity for its occupants. That would also even-out heat build-up from the sun's radiation. "Once they get to orbit, there'll still be a lot of work to do before they're spun-up."

"Speaking of orbit, did you hear the shuttle is ready to be tested?" Ki asked. "I was talking to Bud about more planes coming into service and he let that drop."

"I knew he was getting close. What a hassle it must have been." Pip shook his head. "Having to fight off crazies and dig the shuttle out of the hangar at the same time."

"Did you get to North Carolina?" Ki asked.

"No. Too busy here."

"The place must have been hit by a hurricane." Ki shook his head. "Pines, palmettos, and prickers, all tangled up every which way. Alligators creeping through the jungle, and bugs right out of a bad nightmare. Horrible place."

"I doubted he'd even get one shuttle put together," Pip said. "Then again, with a fusion drive, the shuttle doesn't have a bulky fuel tank and boosters hanging on it. Lower loads, less stress, and a more powerful motor is the way to go." He glanced at his watch. "Talking about going, I got to go, too, sir. With your permission?"

CHAPTER FIFTY-THREE

Ned Biehl rapped the gavel. The hall grew quiet. "I welcome you to the first meeting of representatives of the reestablished United States of America."

Behind him, a huge flag extended across the stage—it was the Stars and Stripes. The flag covered much of the faded stage curtain. The hall's windows were cracked and stained with age. The representatives sat on a mismatched array of rusted folding chairs. The wooden floor, once bright blond maple, was now scuffed and gray.

Applause started in the back of the hall and spread, until all present rose to their feet clapping. The hall, the former Strosacker Hall at Baldwin-Wallace University, was filled with men and women from several areas of the country. The Greater Clan, now extending from Pennsylvania into Illinois, had the largest contingent. California, consisting of the Central Valley and the coastal areas, was represented. Washington, Oregon and Nevada were present, too. Other Rocky Mountain States and Midwestern areas sent observers to see what this new USA was all about.

Ned raised his hand and gestured for the representatives to be seated. "Please, be seated."

Quiet returned to the hall.

"We invited you here for the formal re-establishment of the United States of America," Ned said. "As some of you may recall, its motto was; 'United we stand, divided we fall.' Today that is even more true. We're asking you to join us in the defense, not only of our country, but our planet as well. As you all know, we face the return of the aliens. I don't need to remind you what they might do to our country and our planet." He paused a moment. "All of us have been through difficult times and survived. We lived through the Collapse and a generation of darkness. We aren't going to let the aliens best us now."

The hall erupted into shouts and cheers.

"We must work together. All of you have seen some of the wonders of alien technology and how it benefits our way of life. We can build a new nation, richer, stronger, able to withstand anything that the aliens bring to bear against us ..."

Joyce slipped in the back door of the hall to observe along with the many others who had the same idea. She knew she would get involved in working out details of installing power facilities in the states that chose to join the reestablished United States. She glanced around, trying to locate Taylor. He was supposed to be here. There were too many people to spot him.

Joyce found her eyes drawn to Ned Biehl.

Mine, she thought. *He's mine. What was it he had said? The delegates have to see they're not alone in their decision to surrender their autonomy to the government of the United States.*

Joyce remembered how he'd taken her hand over lunch last year and said, "We have a glorious future ahead of us."

At the time she wondered if he was just talking politics. She found it exciting to speculate about it. She'd always admired men who held positions of power and Ned had risen to be the most powerful man she'd ever known. She felt the urge; she wanted him.

Later, she promised herself, *we'll go to my apartment*. They were very careful not to be seen, and even more careful about birth control.

ᘯ

Taylor gazed at the baby in his arms. *Other than the baby's bright blue eyes*, he thought. *Its red face and pudgy features provided no other clues to its parentage. My son*, he thought. My *very own son*. "He's beautiful," he found himself saying, overwhelmed by feelings not clearly understood.

"Taylor." Meltem's hand slipped out from beneath the bed covers to rest lightly on his forearm. "We made a beautiful, healthy child." She smiled weakly, her face puffy, with dark shadows under her eyes. "I named him Kemal after a great Turkish leader." She paused. "I was tempted to name him after you." Her eyes twinkled with amusement. "I didn't."

"How're you?" Taylor asked. "You look tired."

"It wasn't an easy labor. I'm small and he's a normal size. Not a good match," she said. "I'm really glad that Doctor Novotny came in from Bangor. Our midwives are good, but ..." She smiled. "Thank you for the flowers, it was a nice surprise."

The baby started to fuss and wave his tiny hands.

Meltem held out her hands for the baby. "Here," she said. "He wants to be fed."

Taylor carefully rotated the baby, hand behind its head, as he placed him in his mother's arms.

Meltem undid a button on her gown and guided a nipple into the baby's mouth. She stroked the baby's head as he began to suckle. She smiled contentedly. "I haven't had many visitors," she said. "Some of my staff and a couple of former patients. Then again, I didn't play up my pregnancy."

That, Taylor thought, *was an understatement.*

Meltem had concealed her pregnancy with baggy gowns, hiding her condition from all she could. When three military doctors had arrived from the West Coast, she'd given up her university role to concentrate on teaching them the production of antibiotics and other pharmaceuticals.

"Tell me," Taylor said. "Will the life extension treatment have any impact upon Kemal?" In spite of the guilty feelings from what he had done, he found he was drawn to her.

Now she has a baby, my son, he thought. *My very own son. I want to tell the whole world that Meltem gave me a son, a beautiful, healthy son.*

He knew he dared not.

Meltem shrugged. "I don't know. The only models for the treatment are the lab animals passing on the resistance to aging. I don't know whether it'll be true for human infants." She smiled briefly.

"He's as healthy as any child I've seen, if that's any indication. I'll test him to see if he has the SC-DNA present. It should be easy to pick out."

"I'm glad that you and ..." Taylor hesitated a moment, "our child are well." He stroked Meltem's hair. *There was something about her*, he thought. *I can't go there, I mustn't.*

"I have to go. I'm supposed to be at that US representatives' meeting." He leaned forward and kissed Meltem on the forehead. "Please take care of yourself," he said. "I will come to see you again."

"Soon, please." Meltem grasped Taylor by the shoulder. "I missed you." She pulled him closer.

Taylor resisted for a moment then allowed himself to be drawn to her, until his face was only inches from hers. His heart began to pound. There's something about her....

She raised her face to him. "Please," she said.

Taylor kissed her on the lips. "Soon," he said.

ৎ

"Are you sure?" Monahan wheezed. The small wood-paneled room had a musty smell from being closed up.

"Positive." Beech smiled triumphantly. "Biehl's very careful about sneaking into her apartment. He goes only when MacPherson is out of town."

"Does that old fart MacPherson have any idea what's going on?"

"I don't think so. He's always giving her flowers and other gifts. In public, they look like a real loving couple." Monahan went to the door and opened it a crack to glance out. He closed the door firmly. "Listen," he said. "Krupansky will help with this. That way, it won't be connected to us...."

CHAPTER FIFTY-FOUR

The distant star barely illuminated the two spacecraft. Fusion welding torches flickered at one end of a long, bulbous shape that was the future Little-Egg-that-Flies.

It will take a work period or two, Mata ChaLik realized, *for the workers to finish attaching the tail section to the newly-fabricated fuel tank for the Little-Egg.* He felt his headcrest engorge. As the most central of all on board, the leader of the Defenders, he knew it was his responsibility to lead this expedition to glory. *It has taken far too long to get this much accomplished, and much remains to be done. Those egg-sucking Home-Seekers are more concerned about protecting their stubby little tails than our home, Qu'uda.*

Fortunately, he thought. *I got the Bird-that-Soars repaired before DalChik DuJuga became difficult. As archivist, she holds the designs for the Bird-of-War hostage to get the Egg-that-Flies for her weak-willed Home-Seekers. What she needs is to be with Egg again.*

He turned toward the construction bay containing the framework of a Bird-of-War. Progress was slow; too many tools had to be made for its construction, tools that would have been readily available at any fabrication facility on Qu'uda. *Now,* he thought, *I have to meet with DalChik, to beg for another section of the plans to finish our warcraft.*

౨

DinKa BuLaat stared at the plans for the mounting plate in the propulsion system of the Bird-of-War. The plate was both the structural support that distributed thrust loads to the craft's frame and its fuel supply manifold. An advisory note in the plans recommended using a biocomputer-controlled high-pressure centrifugal caster to make the part. It even specified which caster. That equipment wasn't on board the Egg-that-Flies, for it had not been considered essential for their mission.

The basic mounting plate was straightforward, but the passages for the fuel and the electrical controls posed a problem. "Maybe we can run fuel lines on the surface of the plate," DinKa said.

"What about the flush-fit requirement called out here?" asked KliMah DuTri. "To eliminate point stress loading."

"We'll have to fabricate the mating surface so it form-fits." DinKa called up another holographic image of the bulkhead to which the mounting plate was attached. It was too thin for the necessary indentations to place the fuel lines on the surface of the mounting plate. "Looks like we'll have to machine grooves in the mounting plate."

Both knew it would take time to work the tough alloy used to mount the engines. That meant another slip in the schedule, which was sure to anger Mata ChaLik.

DinKa glanced up to see if there were any Defenders nearby who could overhear him. "Another Bilik story," he said. "Another delay pushing us ever further from the center."

"Bilik was right," said KliMah. "No one realized to what lengths he went to make the propulsion tube. We have become the Biliks of the Egg-that-Flies."

"At least there are a lot of us. We won't be left to die among the dry-land vermin like Bilik. Thank the Egg DalChik formed a circle for us to stand against the Defenders." DinKa referred to the recent gathering of those who wanted to return to Qu'uda. They had moved DalChik to its center due to her opposition to the ways of the Defenders.

Both KliMah and DinKa belonged to the Home-Seeker faction. It seemed they got a reprimand for falling behind schedule every day they worked on the warcraft for the Defenders. They were convinced Mata ChaLik had gone beyond the mission's objective.

KliMah wanted, no, longed, to return to Qu'uda. He was more than homesick; he was frightened. "We should be gathering fuel for the Egg-that-Flies and preparing to depart. If the Defenders want to stay, let them."

"Not until the Defenders get their own ship built, along with a Bird-of-War." DinKa started programming the forming machine to make the mounting plate. "They will not release the navigation data until they get it."

ॐ

"It is time to get fuel for the Egg-that-Flies," DalChik said. "We must make preparations to return." She stared with distaste at Mata ChaLik's holographic image. Podu trees with clinging vines, all dripping water, was a scene normally associated with erotic stories and aids for those who had difficulty mating.

It is very bad taste, she thought.

"There are many things that remain to be done to both the Little Egg-that-Flies and the Bird-of-War." Mata ChaLik moved, and water dripped onto his head crest. "Perhaps you should join me here, so that we may work out a schedule together?"

"I'm closer to you than I like," DalChik said. "We need to find ice-asteroids to get fuel. They are far apart in this part of the system."

"True," Mata ChaLik said. "As long as work continues on schedule, I have no objection to fuel gathering," he said.

They had argued earlier about schedule slippage and the need for the workers of the Home-Seeker faction to put in more time. "And there is no reduction in the workforce."

"This schedule of yours is an artificial construct." Anger crept into DalChik's voice. "What purpose does it serve to finish at any given time?"

"If there is no schedule," Mata ChaLik said loudly. "The ships will never be completed, do you not understand?" He spoke to her as though she was still a wriggler.

"Perhaps we should leave," DalChik said. Her claws extended visibly. "And take our chances among the stars."

"You will not leave until your workers have finished what they promised. That is an order." Mata ChaLik's head crest expanded in full engorgement. "Without the Little Egg-that-Flies and the Bird-of-War, the Defenders will keep the Egg-that-Flies."

"Even so," said DalChik. "The Egg-that-Flies can start preparations for the trip home. Fuel gathering does not require a full crew complement."

"If you choose to search for fuel," Mata ChaLik said. "Both craft will move together. I cannot let you take workers from me." That meant the Little-Egg would have to be attached to the side of the Egg-that-Flies and be towed along. He knew it would slow down construction even further. "You seek to delay our mission."

DalChik had heard this before.

ꝅ

The navigator sounded the alarm. "A messenger drone approaches," he cried. "News from home."

"Quick," said Mata ChaLik. "Release the codes." The messenger drone would broadcast its message as soon as it received a coded download signal on approaching the inner reaches of the planetary system.

"At once, Mata ChaLik BuMaru." The navigator used his full name in formal recognition of authority.

The message squealed in, a high-speed burst of information.

"Process the message and send it for my private reception only," Mata ChaLik said.

"As you command."

ꝅ

The message stated the Defenders on Qu'uda had detected radio signals of the Hoo-Lii aliens from the system of three suns.

Mata ChaLik paused. "Great Egg," he said. "That is the closest system to this one."

The message continued; the Defenders now believe this spacefaring civilization, the Hoo-Lii have spread out and may lie beyond Kota.

"So," he said. "They are closer to Qu'uda than previously believed."

He reviewed the message's contents several times and reluctantly agreed with the home-planet Defenders' reasoning. The message went on to instruct the crew of the Egg-that-Flies that it must not return to their home system for fear of leading the Hoo-Lii aliens to them and ordered the Qu'uda on the Egg-that-Flies to establish a settlement in the Kota system.

Mata ChaLik felt a tingle of triumph. *I was right. This message will bend DalChik DuJuga to my will. Now, I have authority from the very center of Qu'uda to destroy those dry-land vermin on the third planet.*

He read further; the Egg-that-Flies must not send back any message drones directly to the Qu'uda system. Any messages must be sent on a flyby basis, on a course for a far distant system to prevent the Hoo-Lii aliens learning Qu'uda's location.

This, he thought, *will be reason enough to forbid those cowardly Home-Seekers from taking the Egg-that-Flies back to Qu'uda. They will obey me.*

ᘒ

"I understand we must protect Qu'uda from discovery by the Hoo-Lii aliens," DalChik DuJuga said. "At the same time, however, we cannot risk damage to the Egg-that-Flies, or letting it fall into the hands of the dry-land vermin."

"You doubt the capability of my Defenders?" Mata ChaLik's voice rose. "You think those vermin are dangerous to me?"

DalChik touched a control. An image filled the air to show the recording recovered from the Star-Seeker's message drone. It showed the wrecked ship after the violent attack by those on the Hoo-Lii planet. "If they find us, they may do to us what they did to the Star-Seeker."

Mata ChaLik was silent. He knew of the damage inflicted upon the Star-Seeker by the fusion pumped laser of the Hoo-Lii aliens. Such a weapon was forbidden technology.

DalChik brought up a view of the Egg-that-Flies' propulsion

system after it had been damaged upon arrival above the third planet. "Your Defenders are not the issue. It is the unknown capabilities of the dry-land vermin. Bilik found their ability to learn and their understanding of technology far greater than any primitive culture should have."

Another image formed. It was the Bird-that-Soars after it had returned from its last trip to the surface of the third planet. The underside was pockmarked with holes and torn metal. "I trust you remember."

"Bah," said Mata ChaLik. "They won't surprise us again."

"Since the Egg-that-Flies cannot return to Qu'uda, it is now our home," said DalChik. "It must be preserved at all costs."

"Yes, but you must remain here, in this system."

DalChik's headcrest rose. "We choose not to accompany you and your Defenders." She hesitated. "However, we are loyal to Qu'uda. We, will not return home until it is safe to do so." She sagged, as though injured.

"The sooner these dry-land vermin are exterminated, the sooner we shall be safe." There was a note of triumph in Mata ChaLik's voice.

DalChik was slow to respond. "The sooner we may return home. We shall find a way."

CHAPTER FIFTY-FIVE

"I have fulfilled my obligation," DalChik DuJuga said. "You now have a fully functional Little-Egg."

It has been over five hundred sleep cycles since we received the message from Qu'uda, she thought, *a time we have labored unceasingly for these arrogant Defenders.* It had been a time of tension and hardship.

Mata ChaLik BuMaru stretched upwards; water glistened on his headcrest. Wet Podu trees framed his image. "The Bird-of-War is not finished. There are many parts which need to be made. I cannot let you leave with the Egg-that-Flies. Besides, where would you go? You cannot return to Qu'uda."

DalChik stared at him. *He has become more corpulent,* she thought. *He wallows in the material benefits of his position as the most central Defender.* "Your combat master, KaLik DuGan, cannot make up his mind what he wants. We do not know what parts need to be installed in the Bird-of-War." She paused. "As for the Egg-that-Flies, it needs fuel. It will take time to gather the amount we need for an interstellar trip."

"You cannot return to Qu'uda," Mata ChaLik said. "You heard the orders." His headcrest engorged.

"True," DalChik said. "However, I believe it prudent to bring the Egg-that-Flies up to full operational status in case we must flee with little notice. That is why I wish to commence the search for fuel."

And, she thought. *It will give my Home-Seekers a sense of mission, a feeling that they are one step closer to returning home.* "There is no fuel to spare for the Little-Egg."

Mata ChaLik scratched himself and moved directly under a limb that dripped water. "Perhaps you should concentrate on gathering fuel for the Little-Egg, enough to fill its tanks for our mission."

Not only is he vulgar, DalChik thought. *He also makes outrageous demands.* "Your ship is better suited to gather fuel from the gas giant planet than mine. And you will pass it on the way to the third planet. It will take less time than waiting for us to scour the cometary belt."

Mata ChaLik glowered at DalChik. "Do you not wish to obey the orders sent from Qu'uda?"

"They did not specify putting the Egg-that-Flies in danger. We have orders to settle on the third planet. However, you have chosen the strategy to exterminate its dry-land vermin first. And, I believe, you shall do so in such a fashion as to garner as much glory for you and your Defenders as possible."

"Who are you to critique the Defenders' military tactics?"

"If it were me, I would drop an asteroid on that world and leave. Take no chances with them."

"And disobey the order to establish a settlement?" Mata ChaLik drew up to his full height. "I know my mission. I shall fulfill it. You will provide me enough fuel to reach the gas giant planet. That is an order."

"I hear and obey, Mata ChaLik BuMaru." DalChik flattened her headcrest slightly. "Then I shall take the Egg-that-Flies to the edge of interstellar space, far away, safe from any danger."

༈

DalChik grew discouraged, for it took almost five hundred sleep cycles to locate enough icy comets to refill the Egg-that-Flies' tanks and provide the Little-Egg with enough fuel to reach the gas giant planet. Now she had to deal with Mata ChaLik.

"We shall keep radio silence during your absences," she said. "We shall watch for your return to this area of the cometary belt.

Only when we are sure it is the Little-Egg shall we open communications."

"How shall I find you out here, among the comets?" said Mata ChaLik. He knew the Egg-that-Flies, constructed from a metallic asteroid, would be impossible to detect at distance.

"Once we have filled our fuel tanks, we shall stay near the outermost planet and await your return." She indicated the tiny ninth planet that was in a binary dance with its moon.

ॐ

Far, far from the sun, at the edge of the solar system, the fabric of space-time began to resonate. A cubical framework of pale, glowing strings formed. From within the cubical construct, the fabric of space-time stretched and flexed. A long-stemmed object disgorged into normal space. The cube's luminous strings vanished with a kaleidoscopic flash. At the end of the object's long stem was a cylindrical section glittering in the light from distant stars. For long moments the craft drifted aimlessly without power, seemingly dead. The craft belonged to neither human nor Qu'uda.

It was Hoo-Lii.

One by one, tiny lights flickered on. Some time went by before the canister-shaped section of the craft began to rotate. At the opposite end of the long stem was a cluster of pods that looked like petals of an alien flower. They flickered into life with blue-white cones of energy. The craft began to move. It changed its orientation toward the sun of the solar system. The craft built velocity and rose above the plane of the ecliptic, heading toward the center of the system.

As the craft traveled inward through the cometary belt, its sensors sought out signs of anomalous radiation sources. The distant discharge of fiery plasma of a fusion flame drew the craft's attention to the gas giant planet of the system.

Something was there, something using a fusion drive system. Sensors found a huge vessel dipping in and out of the upper atmosphere of the giant gas planet.

The Hoo-Lii craft ceased all activities that generated radiation.

It became quiet and unseen to the huge vessel at the nearby the gas giant planet. The Hoo-Lii focused on the third planet of the system. It was the only one capable of supporting life. They set course for it.

CHAPTER FIFTY-SIX

Ned Biehl steepled his fingers. "So," he said. "You're satisfied with the progress to date?" The chair squeaked as he leaned backwards.

The credenza behind him was stacked with files. The in-basket on his desk was overflowing. Worry had etched lines between Ned's brows and the dark bags under his eyes had grown large.

Taylor took a deep breath. "We could do more if we had more trained personnel. That's the major bottle-neck." He frowned. "A number of people regard this effort as an opportunity to get rich. They're price-gouging and striking hard bargains."

"Out on the West Coast?" Ned asked.

"Much of it here, in the heart of the Clan."

Ned sighed. "I can imagine. Those with production monopolies from waterpower lost out when we got electricity. Then they discovered the value of their skilled tradesmen."

"So you know?" Taylor said.

"Yes. Beach and his boys." Ned made a face. "They're a real pain in the ass. Obstructionists."

"I don't know why. Electrification has raised living standards for everyone. Yes, taxes are high, but this is a war effort. We've got to support the military and get those subs modified. That means supplying them with trade goods for their neighbors, not to mention keeping both armies provisioned."

"Beach's faction resent sharing power with new areas of the Clan." Ned shook his head slowly.

"I had a similar problem with them." Taylor nodded.

"I can believe it. Anything new happening out west?"

"Yes, somebody from Bud Inez's group found a source of boron. Apparently there's an old mine not too far from Groom Lake. He used some of the Pennsylvania enlistees to get it going." Taylor chuckled. "That was pretty slick, getting the Brotherhood to send its army out west to fight for us."

Ned nodded. "Greed works every time. What else?"

"We've made progress in converting those submarines into space craft. It's really quite a sight to see how they've been chopped up and put back together. The first one should launch soon." Taylor chuckled. "Ki still doesn't like the idea of losing a couple of his boats."

"I've heard that. Anything that affects us?"

"Budget for next year. We'll need an increase for defense spending out west and university expansion." Taylor reached into a bag at his feet and retrieved a thick file. "It's all here."

Ned sighed. "Just add it to the pile." He gestured to the in-basket. "So, when're you going out west again?"

Taylor rose to his feet. "I'm not sure. I was hoping to have some time at home."

"Me, too. I plan to catch the fast train to Napoleon this evening. I haven't seen my family in almost a week."

"Yeah, I miss home when I'm away, too. By the way, thanks for taking Joyce out to dinner last week when I was gone. I heard you took her to the Travelers' Inn. That's one of her favorites."

"Er, yes," Ned said. "It was a, er, good opportunity to mix business with pleasure. Your wife is a very bright woman. I enjoy talking with her and I, er, get so much more from her in person than when I just read her reports."

Taylor smiled. "I can understand that."

౬

Whitecaps marched across the gray-green waters of the Juan de Fuca

Strait. Waves foamed over the bow of the Los Angeles class submarine Hampton as it headed west by northwest toward deep water off Port Angeles. Behind, rolling in the swells, in tow was the former missile submarine SSBN 735, the USS Pennsylvania. The former sub was soon to be a spacecraft. At the present it was a long, black hulk that lay low in the water. Its conning tower was almost gone; it had been cut down to minimize aerodynamic drag during its flight.

"I sure hope this works," Ki Mapes said softly. He peered from the Hampton's conning tower into the distance toward Cape Flattery. The weather report called for a high-pressure system to move in with better conditions. The sea still had a heavy swell.

If that nuke blows up, he thought. *We're done for. If it doesn't work, we're done for, too.*

"What was that, sir?" Pip Ryan asked.

"Are sure this is going to work?"

"It will. When we tested the drive unit at Groom Lake, its power output matched the design parameters." Pip glanced back at the rusty hulk yawing on the towline. "All it needs is eighty percent output and it'll achieve orbit in thirteen minutes." His voice quavered slightly.

"I'm damn glad I'm not going on that ride." Ki didn't really want to be here. Sure, they'd worked for years to get to this point. He knew there were no guarantees this screwed-up submarine with a nuclear rocket up its ass would work.

"Inez thinks it'll be the smoothest ride to orbit anyone has ever had. All that mass." Pip checked his watch. "Are we still on schedule?" It was a question he'd asked several times before.

Ki glanced at the navigation module. "More or less. We'll be on station in a few minutes. Then it's up to your people to get the boat flying." *If it doesn't blow up and kill us all. Well*, he thought, *I've done my duty*.

Pip took a deep breath. "It won't take long to flood the ballast tanks, and soon as the bird is vertical, it'll go."

"Just give me enough time to get well away. I don't much like the idea of lighting a rocket of that size near my boat. Especially a fusion rocket."

A seaman clattered up the conning tower's ladder. "Sir," he said.

"Sonar asked me to tell you we just passed the one hundred fathom depth contour."

"Very well," Ki said. "Dismissed."

The seaman disappeared down the ladder.

"This is as good a place as any," Ki said. He picked up a microphone. "All ahead stop."

The two boats coasted for ten minutes before slowing to a halt. Stopped, they wallowed in the waves as seaman scrambled around the deck, releasing lines. The former USS Pennsylvania drifted slowly away from the Hampton.

"Colonel Inez," Ki spoke into the microphone. "You're free and clear of the Hampton."

Somewhere a speaker crackled. "I read you loud and clear, Captain Mapes. Ballasting sequence starts minus ten at mark."

"Very well." Ki pushed a button. "Ahead at ten percent." A quiver ran through the boat and it surged forward.

Once underway, the boat became stable, rising and falling with the swells out of the Pacific as it headed further down the Strait toward open water.

"Damn, it feels good to be out again," he said quietly.

"What was that, sir?" Pip said.

"I'm just glad to have a boat under me." He turned and looked back at the Pennsylvania. It was a black shape low in white-flecked waters. He raised a pair of binoculars. "It's started the up-ending process. I can see the bow rising out of the water."

Pip keyed a hand-held radio.

"... seven minutes and counting," a voice squawked.

As Pip placed an earpiece in his ear, the radio went silent. "Better get your eye protection ready, sir," Pip said. "It sounds like they're ready to go."

"They've got balls," Ki said. "Lighting a nuclear rocket under water." He lifted off his hat and rubbed his head nervously. He took a deep breath. "After all this time, we're going back into space. I never dreamed it would be like this."

"No different than a Trident," Pip said. "Just bigger and hotter. Six minutes and counting."

The tiny black dot that was the bow of the Pennsylvania was

now completely upright as the ballast tanks filled. The Pennsylvania slowly vanished from sight.

"Five minutes and counting." Pip slipped on a pair of dark glasses.

"Bring us to a bearing of one-niner-five," Ki spoke into the microphone. The boat carved an arc through the swells until its bow pointed at the location where Pennsylvania had disappeared. "All ahead stop."

"T-minus thirty seconds and counting," Pip said.

Ki slipped on a pair of dark glasses and ear protection.

A small black fish-shaped object rose from the water on a huge ball of brilliant white fire and a giant column of steam. A white ring expanded from its base at tremendous velocity as the black object accelerated straight up.

A wall of noise hit them like a freight train. Both officers pressed their ear protection tighter until the sound diminished. The black object rose vertically until it disappeared, with only a fading point of light to show where it had gone. Slowly the roar faded.

Pip turned to Ki. "They've just passed through one hundred kilometers altitude," he said. "Velocity is seven point eight kilometers per second and increasing. Orbital velocity achieved. They're gonna make it." A grin split Pip's face. "We did it." He danced a little jig and raised a clenched fist into the air. "We damn-well did it, sir."

Ki felt a huge wave of relief sweep through him. *Thank God*, he thought. *Thank God it's over.*

"Let's go home."

CHAPTER FIFTY-SEVEN

"Er, Mr. Krupansky, d'you have a minute?" Beach said.

"What d'you want?" A scowl flickered across Krupansky's face as he paused on the stairs that led to the Council Chambers. He had become an Elder when the Brotherhood had joined the Clan but was openly unhappy with what he thought were restrictions on his freedom. Laws, he was fond of saying, were for those being ruled.

"You've probably noticed there's a group of us who don't agree with Biehl's way of, er, doing things."

"Yeah, you'n Monahan seem be at odds with him." Krupansky nodded. "Regular pissin' contest. 'Cept you ain't winning." He grinned and spat over the railing into the bushes.

"You're not getting your way with him, either."

"Ain't that the truth. You gonna do something about it?"

"There's more than us two." Beach beckoned him closer. "We're meeting for lunch in the back room at the Travelers' Inn. We'd wondered if you might like to join us an' talk about it."

"You buying?"

"You'd be our guest, of course." Beach's smile was forced.

"See ya then." Krupansky strode up the steps.

ح

"We have a leak," Bud Inez's voice crackled from the radio's speaker, static obscuring his words. "... left of air supply."

"Say again. Your last transmission broke up," Pip Ryan said into the microphone.

"We're losing about five percent of our air every hour. We'll be in hard vacuum within twenty-four hours."

Pip took a sharp breath. "Move into the command area and shut off the air supply to all the other sections. Take your EVA suits with you. I sure hope you don't need them."

"I read you loud and clear," Bud said through the static. "It's also damn hot up here. We're adsorbing too much radiation from the sun. That's not the only problem. We tried doing an EVA excursion and found the exterior hatches are jammed. Seems that they've got water in them. They're frozen solid. Since they're on the dark side, it'll take a while for the ice to evaporate. If we could get some rotation, that'd speed things up. Any ideas on handling this heat problem?"

"We'll get back to you on that," Pip said. "We'll have to step up the shuttle's schedule to get you out of there."

"I'll talk to you later. I've got to put supplies away. I'll contact you at twenty-one hundred hours Zulu."

❦

As Joyce finished buttoning her blouse, she looked over her shoulder at Ned Biehl tying his shoes.

Bright sun streaming through the curtains illuminated his face. Traffic sounds clattered up from the street below.

"If," Joyce said. "If you leave your wife, I'll leave Taylor." She stepped over to him and pulled his head against her midriff. "I hate sneaking around like this. I want to be with you all the time. I only feel complete when I'm with you."

The bed was untidy with damp stains in the center.

Ned gently disengaged Joyce's hands. "I understand." He took a deep breath. "It'll have to wait until the Qu'uda crisis is over." He stood and picked up a jacket draped over the back of a chair. "We can be together then."

"What?" Joyce almost spat. "Why not now?"

"If I leave my wife, next election, I'd lose my seat in Council. Her family is large and played an important role in my election. Leaving her could be the end of my political career."

"Surely you'd have a career without her and her family. You said you don't love your wife. That you haven't shared a bed with her in years—"

"True, but that doesn't mean we aren't partners." Ned took a deep breath. "She recognizes my position guarantees a good future for her children. Her family profits by association with me, even without favors or cutting special deals."

"Leave her, you can still lead the Clan."

Ned rolled his eyes. "No," he said flatly as he combed his hair and examined his appearance in the mirror. He had let his hair grow longer because, she'd said, it made him look younger.

"What am I to you then? A convenience?"

"Please, Joyce, you're very special to me. Don't you understand that I love you?"

"Well." Joyce sniffed. "You've got a strange way of showing it." She sat down on the bed.

"I would love nothing more than to cross the Hill with you on my arm, proclaiming to the world you're mine."

Joyce pursed her lips. "I don't know how much longer I can stand Taylor touching me. You've got to do something soon."

"Not now, please. I've got a lot on my mind."

"You can think of something."

Ned sighed. "I really don't have time for this. If you can't accept the realities of my position, perhaps we'd better end our relationship. Much as I want you, love you, I can't afford a scandal. You are, after all, still married to the most influential private citizen of the Clan. If he found out about us, well, I don't know what he would do."

Joyce rose and walked to a window. She pulled back the curtains and stared out at the busy square in the center of Berea. "It's ..." She hesitated. "It's just that I don't get enough of you. I want to be with you all the time."

Ned took a deep breath. "Right now, that's not possible. With the Qu'uda's return drawing near, it'd be foolish for me to turn the reins over to someone else."

"You don't have to give up your position."

"First election, it would be all over."

"It doesn't seem fair—"

"Life isn't fair." Ned put his jacket on and glanced at his watch. "I've got to go. There's a meeting in half an hour. I need to go over my notes." He put his hands on Joyce's shoulders. "Look, I'm sorry about the trap we're in. I wish I could just walk away from the whole damn thing with you on my arm. But I can't. It's part of my nature to be in the center of things. Like you."

"Yes, and you're good at it, too." Joyce rose and put her arms around him. "I shouldn't push you. I just want to be with you."

Ned gently pried her hands off. He turned away without another word and opened the door and leaned to look out.

A hand grabbed his hair and a large knife flashed.

Ned staggered backwards into the room. A knife protruded from his neck, blood pulsing out. His knees buckled.

Joyce tried to catch him but collapsed under him and fell to the floor.

A bandanna covered face appeared in the door opening for an instant before the door slammed shut.

Joyce screamed, "Ned."

She struggled from beneath him.

Ned's mouth moved but no words came out. His body shook in a convulsive spasm. He sagged, still twitching.

Joyce pulled the knife from his neck. Blood gouted out, splattering over both of them.

"Oh, Ned, what've they done to you?" She stared transfixed at her bloody hands and the dripping knife.

Feet pounded down the stairs, toward the street. "Murder. Murder," someone yelled. "Call the militia."

~

Taylor stifled a yawn and glanced out the window. Too many bodies made the room warm. Rain beating on the roof had almost a hypnotic quality. There was nothing new on the agenda. It was more discussion about what weapons to use on the Qu'uda.

Conifers swayed in the wind as veils of rain drifted across the opening.

Ugh, he thought. *What a climate, even more rain than northern Ohio.*

The door banged open and a dripping seaman burst in.

"Sir." The seaman went rigid with attention and snapped off a salute. "Beggin' your pardons, sirs. Urgent message for Mr. MacPherson." His hand held a limp envelope.

Taylor took the letter from him and opened it. As he read the contents, each word struck him like a body blow. "Oh, my God." He gasped and sat down. "I don't believe this."

Ki raised his eyebrows. "Anything we ought to know?" He half rose to his feet, concern creasing his face.

Taylor looked up. The room seemed distant. The words echoed in his ears. "Ned ... Ned Biehl is dead, assassinated."

"What? By whom?" Ki rose to his feet.

Taylor took a breath and looked up. "Joyce, my wife, Joyce, is the prime suspect." His guts felt like they were draining out of him. A coldness gripped him as the room became like a tunnel. He rose stiffly. "I've got to get back home."

The door burst open and a second messenger was in the room. "Sir." He was panting. "A problem's developed with the space station. It's leaking air." He reached inside his jacket. "This is a transcript of the last transmission from them."

Ki took the transcript and read it.

The messenger repeated what he had heard in the communications center. "... and they're over-heating from the sun's radiation, too."

"All right," Ki said. "This meeting is over. We need a plane for Taylor to go back to Ohio." He paused a second. "And we need to get a shuttle to the space station ASAP."

CHAPTER FIFTY-EIGHT

Taylor glanced out of the window. A steady procession of clouds revealed only glimpses of the land below. Chris Kucinski had given him a summary of the situation over the radio. A witness claimed to have heard Joyce and Ned quarrel and then saw her stab him as he tried to leave her apartment.

Why? Taylor thought. *Why Joyce?*

Learning she and Ned had been having an affair came as a shock. It chewed at him with a mixture of anger and sadness, even as he felt shame from his own infidelity. *Oh, God, what's happening to us?* On a cold, intellectual level, he realized the Clan had sustained a tremendous loss; who would take Ned's place?

"We've started our descent," a voice said. "Please fasten your seat belts."

Mechanically, Taylor complied.

It isn't in Joyce's nature to be violent if she doesn't get her way. She couldn't have killed Ned.

Damp stains in the apartment's bed confirmed Joyce and Ned had had sex shortly before the murder. Something didn't seem right. So many thoughts swirled through Taylor's head, he barely realized the plane had landed.

Taylor clambered down the steps toward a sea of faces. Some held barely repressed anger; most were blank, impassive.

Many called questions at him. One was Chris Kucinski. "Chris, please," he called. "Just get me out of here."

Chris beckoned with a finger. Six large soldiers carved a path through the crowd to escort Taylor to a horse-drawn wagon.

"Thanks." Taylor got in. "What about Joyce?" The wagon creaked into motion. "What happened?"

Chris's lips tightened into a thin line. "I'm not sure what to say other than Biehl's dead." She paused. "The Elders are at each other's throats fighting to elect their favorites."

Taylor took a deep breath. "What about Joyce?"

Chris's mouth hardened further. "Taylor," she said. "You aren't going to like what you hear."

Taylor nodded silently.

"Your wife was involved with Biehl, and for some time, too. A witness claims to have overheard them quarrel. He claims he saw Joyce stab Biehl."

"A witness?"

"Jeremy Blodgett. His apartment is next to Joyce's."

Taylor frowned. "An old lady lives next door to Joyce."

"Blodgett moved in last month. He came here from Pennsylvania looking for work. He said he was on his way out after lunch when he saw the crime." Chris frowned. "What puzzles me is how an unemployed laborer from Pennsylvania has the silver for an apartment in that building. However, he's not been accused of any crime, so I can't do much about that."

"You suspect something, don't you?"

Chris pursed her lips tightly. "We shouldn't be having this conversation, since your wife ..." She hesitated, "is the prime murder suspect." She glanced around as if to see if they were being followed. "Look, I hate to see this happen to you. There's no doubt in my mind Joyce was carrying on with Biehl. We found notes in the safe in his office. They were from Joyce, some almost a year old. I'm sorry."

Taylor stared at her. "Oh?"

"She's wanted to leave you for Biehl for a long time."

Chris's words picked at his wound like a sharp knife.

The shuttle inched closer to the long, dark shape that was the former submarine, SSBN Pennsylvania. The giant rusty cigar dwarfed the white and almost dainty shuttle. The shuttle's payload bay doors opened. Time passed slowly until two tiny figures in space suits appeared. A mechanical arm unfolded and lifted out a long cylindrical shape. The two tiny figures moved to each end of the object and busied themselves with it. As they moved away from the shuttle, a large, silvery sheet unrolled.

It took several hours for the figures to install the aluminum foil sunshade over the long axis of the former submarine. Only then did the payload bay doors of the shuttle close. The tiny figures returned to the shuttle and disappeared inside.

It was time for them to go home.

ॐ

"When d'you expect to get it completed?" Ki Mapes asked.

Ever since the crew had evacuated the submarine hull that was now the space station, Ki had ridden hard on Pip Ryan to get the second hull finished, including the modifications needed to prevent the same problems occurring.

Pip squirmed in his chair. "It's complete except for—"

"Then it's not." Ki rubbed his head. "What's holding it up?" He rose out of his chair and leaned over his desk toward Pip.

Outside the conifers shimmered in the bright sun. A steady stream of wagons filled the road.

"It's ..." Pip scrunched up his mouth. His face was drawn, and dark shadows lay under his eyes. "It's the retrofit package for Unit One." He had taken to calling the former submarine Pennsylvania Unit One. "Instead of just measuring it, we have to do everything from plans. Problem is, we have to make allowances for the temperature differences between ground level and out there. So, there's a lot of double checking going on."

Ki sat down and crossed his arms. "What d'you need to get this back on schedule?"

"Another construction manager, someone with experience."

Ki reached for the phone. "Mapes here. Get me a connection

with Taylor MacPherson in Rocky River." He leaned back in his chair. "I remember Taylor telling me about one of his project managers who was good with machinery. I believe his name was Kevin O'Neil." He leaned forward. "While we're waiting for that call," he said. "Let's see what else needs attention...."

The public section of the Council Chamber was packed. Heads and hands moved continually, and the hall buzzed with quiet conversation. The Elders began to take their seats, pausing to whisper into one another's ears before settling into their over-stuffed chairs.

"This Council meeting will come to order," Sean Monahan said in his high-pitched voice. "We will consider the nomination and election of a Council Leader. Are there any nominations?"

A chair scraped and Mike Kozlowski rose. He mopped his balding head and cleared his voice. "I nominate the gentleman from Wooster, Mr. Pete Belamy, former speaker for the Central Ohio Union." Kozlowski hitched his pants up over an expansive belly. "Mr. Belamy has a demonstrated track record of leadership and ability to bring people together. It is my opinion that he will lead the Greater Clan into a bright future." He cleared his voice and reached for a glass of water, a sure sign he was about to make a speech.

"Ah, thank you, Mr. Kozlowski," Monahan said. "Is there a second to this nomination?" He looked up and down the row of Elders, a quiet smile on his face.

"Er, yes," said Cal Majewski. He had been appointed as the interim representative from Napoleon to replace Ned Biehl. "I'll second Pete Belamy's nomination."

Monahan's eyebrows rose. "Er, thank you, er, Mr. ..." He referred to a roster before him. "Mr. Majewski."

"I move the nominations be closed," said Kozlowski.

"Now you just wait a minute," Ramsey said loudly. "I haven't had my chance to speak. I nominate Jon Beach for the position of Council Leader."

Beach nodded toward Ramsey and silently mouthed "thank you."

"Is there a second?" Monahan asked, his reedy voice barely audible. He glanced at Nick Krupansky.

"Yeah," said Krupansky loudly. "I second Jon Beach's nomination for Council Leader."

The public section of the Council Chamber stirred. There were many that remembered the conflict between Beach and Biehl. If Beach were elected, it would mean major changes in the policies of the past several years, policies that brought about a general increase in wealth. Beach was associated with the faction favoring the business and landed classes of the old Clan centered in Rocky River valley.

Monahan looked around with his eyebrows raised. "Are there any other nominations?" He pursed his lips. "Is there a motion to close the nominations?"

"So moved," Ramsey said quickly.

"Seconded," Carver Washington said.

"I call the question," Monahan intoned in rote fashion. "Those in favor, say aye."

A chorus of ayes followed.

"Opposed?" Monahan looked up and listened at the silence. "The ayes have it." He picked up a ledger. "I will now poll the Elders for their vote for Leader of the Council...." One by one, he called off each Council Elder's name and asked how he voted. He repeated the Elder's choice to obtain confirmation before writing the vote into the ledger.

As the vote came to a close, the buzz in the public section grew louder.

The vote was tied.

Monahan stood and raised his hand.

The room slowly quieted.

"Since we have been unable to elect a leader, Council is dissolved. Elections shall be held to determine the will of the people." He nodded to the sergeant-at-arms.

"This Council is now closed."

En masse, the public section rose to its feet and headed for the exits, chattering loudly.

ᘒ

Chris Kucinski looked up, a thick sheaf of papers in her left hand. Rain rattled against the window of her office. Around the battered oak desk sat Ed Kerr, Mitch Doaks, and Joe Del Corso. They were leaning forward, on the edge of their seats. "Are you sure of these facts?"

Kerr cleared his throat. "Yes," he said. "It was Joe who traced the silver Blodgett used." He paused. "Y'see, when we recruited troops from Pennsylvania for the West Coast, we had to find money to pay them. Well, we used a new source of silver coins. They had a small star punched into them as well as the Clan emblem. It was to find out their economic impact. Most stayed in Pennsylvania and were used for food purchases. Except for a few. Those that stuck to Krupansky's greedy fingers."

"Is it enough to use as evidence?"

Kerr frowned. "Probably not. But we're convinced Blodgett is Krupansky's agent. That makes Mrs. MacPherson's story more believable."

"I see." Chris stared briefly at the wall. *What a mess. That woman's behavior got the Clan's leader killed. Those letters, Taylor can never see them, they'd break his heart.* She took a deep breath. "Mr. Blodgett is far from a laborer, right?"

"Right," said Mitch Doaks. "Pittsburgh Pete has relatives in Pennsylvania. They did some digging around and found out that he's a commander in the Brotherhood's army, in a unit known for its dirty tricks."

"So, it looks like Krupansky placed an agent in an apartment next to the MacPherson's."

"We found listening holes in the walls," Mitch said. "There were patches on the wall next to Joyce's bedroom. I think they must've been watching Biehl and Joyce for at least a month."

"That's the period of time Krupansky and Beach have been buddies," Joe said. "Van Minh at the Travelers' Inn said they met several times." He paused. "Unfortunately, he didn't hear what they were talking about."

Chris nodded. "Figures," she said. "Beach likes to get others to do his dirty work." She leaned back in her chair. "So, Biehl may have been assassinated for political reasons, is that right? Looks like Joyce provided the opportunity."

The three men sitting opposite to Chris nodded.

"What do we do about it?"

Joe Del Corso leaned forward. "Er, I asked Dr. Encirlik if she had any drugs that would help make someone more, er, responsive while being questioned." His face reddened. "I explained this was a very, er, delicate situation." He swallowed hard. "I had to tell her it was connected with the Biehl murder before she agreed to help. She said she did have something that might help make someone easier to question."

"So?" Chris raised her eyebrows.

"Well." Joe's face was bright red. "I've had experience with Beach before. He doesn't play fair. It's time someone did to him what he does to others."

"We're not assassinating anyone," Chris said.

"No, I mean to get Blodgett to confess, then make the information public." Joe smiled. "Even if it isn't enough to hang Beach, he's done for, politically speaking."

Chris rose from her chair and walked to the window. "It may not be legal, but it'd serve justice," she said after a few moments. She turned to face the men. "Joe, you come with me. I need to talk to Dr. Encirlik. Kerr, keep a close eye on Blodgett; I don't want him disappearing."

Kerr nodded. "I've got a team of men watching him around the clock. Krupansky, too. They're not going anywhere."

"Krupansky. Yes, we need to deal with him, too."

～

In Tacoma, Pip Ryan was relieved the modifications needed to convert the second submarine into a space vessel had been completed. He was grateful to Kevin O'Neil who took over managing a second shift of workers. This vessel incorporated many of the changes needed to overcome the problems of the first. In addition, it carried parts and replacements necessary to repair the Pennsylvania.

He was thankful its launch went smoothly.

One day later, the shuttle arrived with its cargo hold filled with the components needed to join both submarine hulls together. Helium powered maneuvering packages nudged the two massive hulls into position to align the hulls at the stubs of their conning towers that were joined with a tubular section. Welding torches flickered for several days until the tubular section connecting the conning towers was sealed. This became a passageway between the two hulls.

Ten days later, the shuttle returned to orbit, bringing communications and sensors for installation on the exterior of the new space station. At the same time, crews sealed and insulated the passageway between the two hulls. Bit by bit, the station came to life as its equipment became operational.

The shuttle crew installed a spidery framework connecting both hulls at their ends. At the end of the framework was a platform and collar, which the shuttle used as a dock.

༄

Even though the small room adjacent to the Council Chamber was warm and stuffy, its door was shut tight. The Elders around the table stared attentively at Chris Kucinski as she summarized the findings in the Ned Biehl murder from a thick file.

"... and so," Chris said. "Once we linked the money to Blodgett, we got his confession, which was witnessed by Carver Washington. The statements of a disinterested witness substantiate Blodgett's account of the meetings between Krupansky and Beach when they planned the Biehl murder. Even if they did not wield the knife, they are responsible for Ned Biehl's death."

She handed the file to Washington. "Krupansky got away before we could apprehend him. Then we discovered Blodgett was dead. He'd been garroted." She shook her head and sighed. "I don't know how they got past Kerr's men, but they did."

"Mr. Beach, you've heard the evidence, what d'you have to say for yourself?" Washington's normally expressionless face was flushed, and his eyebrows crowded together like two thunderclouds. His anger was fueled from learning he had been used as an unwitting spy in this plot.

"It's all made up," Beach said. "My political enemies have fabricated this entire cockamamie story." He rose to his feet. "I don't need to hear another word of this farce." He limped toward the door. "Crap, pure crap," he said.

Two large brown-clad soldiers crossed their guns before Beach, barring his way.

"Get out of my way, you idiots," Beach said.

The soldiers did not move.

Washington glanced down the grim-faced Elders. "Well?" he said. "Do we let him get away with it?"

A chorus of "nos" rumbled from around the table.

"I say we hang the bastard," Cal Majewski said.

"Can't. He has legislative immunity," Chris said. "I say let him go. Let the people judge him. Release the evidence. Put it in the public record." He waved the file in the air.

Heads nodded.

Beach paled. "You can't release that material. This was supposed to be a confidential hearing. You're trying to destroy me with slander."

A thin smile rippled over Washington's lips. "Well, like you said, who'd believe this cockamamie story, anyway?"

CHAPTER FIFTY-NINE

Taylor stared at the paper on the desk before him, not seeing it. *Lord*, he thought. *I was such a fool. Why did this have to happen now?* He forced himself to look back at the desk. It was almost budget time again. *This time, there'll be no Ned Biehl to ramrod appropriations through Council.*

Joyce, oh, Joyce, why did it have to be you? She wasn't even sorry. It was clear they couldn't get back together. The memory strengthened and he was there, again, at the jail, as she was being released. He'd just learned that all charges against Joyce would be dropped and went to get her.

"... I couldn't help myself," he remembered her saying. "They were all like you, strong, powerful." Joyce bent forward, signing papers for her release.

"They?" Taylor asked. "Who?"

"I was drawn to Ned," she sniffed. "Just like the others. Like you." She sighed.

"Others?"

"Yes." She rubbed her hands in her eyes. "First it was Jimmy, Ol' Vic's boy. Y'know, the son of Vic Caputo, the boss of Defiance. He was the first."

"Joyce," Taylor said. "It really doesn't matter. I can let bygones be bygones. We don't ... have a problem there."

"It isn't just sex I'm talking about. There were others, but what I mean is those who were close to power. Just seducing the boss's son and introducing him to sex was fun. Being close to power turned me on." She sighed. "When he discovered he could have any young girl he wanted, I was out."

Taylor stared at her.

"People just treated me different when I was with him. I was special, people listened." Joyce said. "Then came Billy who knocked off ol' Vic. I never had sex with him, although I did try. After you defeated Billy, I found myself chasing after you. I was successful with you. When Ned became Council Leader, it was only a matter of time. I was attracted by what you represented—it's an addiction. I need men who are in power." She leaned forward and shrugged. "I've had time to think about it since I've been locked up. I thought about why I ended up with Ned. I just couldn't stay away from him. Yes, he wanted me, too. Poor bastard, locked into a loveless marriage and starved for sex. All I had to do was give him just a little bit of encouragement and he fell. Just like you."

Taylor began to feel uncomfortable. "What d'you mean by that?" His voice took a hard edge.

"You were easy," Joyce said, her voice muffled by her hand. "You were another influential, powerful man." She raised her head. "And you needed love."

"But ..." Taylor said. "You weren't political, you didn't seek to use the tools of power—"

"You still don't get it, do you?" Joyce laughed. "Being close to power turns me on, turns me on to the point that I get sexually aroused. And, most politically powerful men have strong sex drives. So, not only do I get turned on, I also get a lot of sex while turned on. It's a classic prescription for great sex. The only problem is that political power shifts. Since I'm addicted to great sex, I get drawn to the power."

"I thought that we had a good love life..." Taylor trailed off, realizing the lie of his statement. Since Joyce had lost her baby, their love life had been sporadic, strained. He saw a side, a hard, cold side he hadn't recognized before.

Joyce raised her head and stared at him for a moment. "You're kidding yourself. You've become a wimpy academic. Most of the time, I had to pretend you were someone else so I could do it with you."

Taylor recoiled as though hit. *She doesn't love me. I can forgive infidelity*, he thought. *But not her contempt.*

Shortly after, in a daze, Taylor had left the jail.

The next day, he filed for divorce, citing grounds of irreconcilable differences. As he'd signed the document, he'd felt a huge void within, as though the center of his being was gone.

He'd stared at the paper again. *I loved her. I've got to get back to work. I must.*

He forced himself back into focus. More items needed by the Defense Council for the first-contact platform. *Hmm, that shouldn't be too difficult.* One of many things needed for the space defense effort. He'd just shipped a telescope salvaged from the abandoned Case-Western University to the West Coast for the space platform.

"Mr. MacPherson," Joe Del Corso called through the door. "Visitors."

Taylor looked up.

Carver Washington and Pete Belamy stepped in.

"What can I do for you?" Taylor asked. "What brings representatives of the two main factions in Council here?"

Washington chuckled. "Oh, just an itty-bitty favor. And some news." He wasn't smiling.

Taylor grimaced. "Should I brace myself?"

"First, the news. We reinstated Joyce...."

"What?" Taylor stared hard at Washington.

"I'm sorry that things didn't work out between you and Mrs. MacPherson." Washington raised his hands as Taylor started to protest. "She's the only one who understands the electrical system and she did do a good job in the CEPA. The Council wasn't happy about it, but we need her back at work. I hope you understand. If it makes you feel any better, we've relocated her CEPA office to Columbus. So, she'll be gone from Berea. Look, she made you a happy man for a while. Just be thankful for God's gifts, even if they don't last forever."

"The CEPA's your game. You can do as you see fit." Taylor pursed his lips. "You didn't come to act as a marriage counselor," he said. "Especially with the honorable Mr. Pete Belamy. What's the favor?" He hardened his voice.

"We want you to run for Beach's seat, which you'll win, and then stand for Council Leader."

"Yes," Belamy said. "We can assemble a majority in Council for you if you do."

"You're asking a lot." Taylor took a deep breath. "Look," he said. "I've been there and done that. I'm a part of the old generation. I'm out of touch with a lot of things. I can't represent people if I don't know what their concerns are."

"Maybe so," Washington said. "We need someone to lead Council until this Qu'uda thing is over. Right now, Council is too polarized to accept anyone from either wing. We've got to get someone from the outside who'll keep things moving in the right direction. Then we can go back to the fun and games of politics. We can't afford that now. Other than Beach and Monahan, no one on Council really hates you. You're ..." He hesitated a moment, "an acceptable compromise."

"Thanks," Taylor said dryly. "That's your itty-bitty favor?" He shook his head. "You plan to turn my life upside down. Don't I have enough to do, running the university?"

"I always thought a good manager knew how to delegate," Washington said. "Don't you have a couple of good deputies?"

Taylor hesitated. True, Doaks and Del Corso handled much of the administration. *If I were involved with Council, I could stay in my home on the Hill instead of the apartment where ...*

The memories came back. For a second, his emotions threatened to swamp him. *Oh, God, maybe I do need a change.*

Taylor raised his head. "Y'say you have the votes?" he began. "Who specifically? What d'they expect in return?" It was like putting on an old slipper, dropping into the political mode of give and take.

The change had come.

℞

Snow covered the top of the distant Sheep Range Mountains. In the dun-colored flat that was Groom Lake, a crane slowly lowered a long, foil-covered bundle into the shuttle's bay. It was the telescope destined for installation on the space platform.

By the end of the day, all activity had ceased. The payload bay was full. The shuttle sat in a pool of bright lights.

"All systems are cleared for takeoff," the voice of the mission controller crackled from the speaker.

"Affirmative," Bud Inez said. "I've checked the systems and they're within parameters. We're ready to go." He glanced at the timer. Thirty minutes remained until they reached their launch window to meet with the space station. With the fusion drives, the shuttle would take off horizontally on a fall-away undercarriage.

The minutes ticked by slowly. Bud reviewed the checklist. He really didn't need to since this was his tenth flight up to the space platform in the last twelve months, but he always did. The remainder of the crew sat silent, busy with their checklists.

The space platform was huge. Soon it would have a crew of over a hundred. Just hauling water to fill its tanks took two trips. One more trip with radar and communications gear and the space station would be complete, more or less.

"... two minutes and counting," came the controller's voice.

Bud focused on the controls. He flicked the switch that started the fusion drive. He felt a vibration along with a rumble from the engine. The readout indicated normal parameters. A light glowed red indicating the explosive bolts cutting the restraint straps holding the rail undercarriage were armed.

As the fusion drive increased power, the vibration increased, shaking the shuttle slightly.

"... four, three, two, one, release."

Bud heard two loud reports and the roar of the fusion drive became an overwhelming wall of sound. He sank back into his seat as the craft shot forward.

In five seconds, the airspeed indicator showed two hundred knots and he raised the shuttle's nose. A light glowed green, showing the computer had taken over the flight controls. The mountains disappeared and blue sky filled the cockpit windows. The acceleration increased and the velocity rose to five hundred, then one thousand knots.

Clamped by three gees, Bud watched the instruments, body

heavy and frozen in his seat. The shuttle rose almost vertically and continued to accelerate. The velocity and altitude indicators changed scale to show kilometers. Outside, the sky had become black—they were in space.

The vibration from the engine eased as the drive throttled back. The shuttle began to rotate. The blue and white Earth appeared below.

Bud stared at the instruments. It was almost time for the computer to completely shut down the drive. They reached the space station's orbit and the engine fell silent. It was now a matter of waiting until they caught up with the station and then decelerate to match its velocity.

And, he marveled, *the shuttle still has more than ninety percent of its fuel left.*

Ahead, sunlight glinted on something. *The docking structure*, Bud thought. *Time to get this bird oriented properly.* The radar gave distance and differential velocities. He engaged the maneuvering thrusters several times.

"Shuttle, you're cleared to dock," came a voice from the speaker. "All systems are go."

"Affirmative," Bud said.

He always thought the space station looked like two cigars joined at the hip … if cigars had hips. The image became harder to maintain as the clutter of spidery structures and platforms at both ends became clear. One was for docking the shuttle; the other would be a space observatory. Both were motionless relative to the two long structures of the space station that rotated to produce gravity.

Upside down to the docking platform, the shuttle crept closer with its cargo bay doors open. Even at one hundred meters' separation, the closing velocity was below one meter per second and dropping. It was slow, delicate work.

Bud remained focused. *I haven't had a bad docking yet and I'm not about to start.*

Thirty minutes later, two arms from the docking platform firmly grasped the shuttle and rotated it into position to unload its cargo and passengers. A long tube extended from the dock and reached into the front of the shuttle's cargo bay. It was through this passageway the crew and passengers disembarked.

It was, Bud thought, *much easier than wearing an EVA suit. It's a big improvement over earlier transfers.* It was surprising how comfortable the station had become.

CHAPTER SIXTY

"Those opposed?" Sean Monahan's thin voice was barely audible above the sounds of restless feet, rustle of clothing, and whispered conversations. The sergeant-at-arms raised his finger to his lips and glowered at the packed Council Chamber. Faces peered in through the windows.

The Elders glanced from side to side along the dais. No one spoke. Frowns etched lines on several faces.

Monahan cleared his throat and looked up from the ledger. "Are there any opposing votes to the election of Taylor MacPherson to the position of Council Leader?" He swiveled his head in both directions. "Well?" he asked in a querulous tone, eyebrows raised.

For a moment the room quieted.

"Get on with it, Monahan," a voice called.

The corners of Monahan's mouth turned down. "Er, it seems MacPherson has been elected as the new Council Leader with twelve votes for and one vote opposed." He frowned. "Apparently there are six abstentions." He looked down the row of Elders.

Heads nodded.

A rumble swept through the public section as people began to rise and leave. A few faces held smiles and some had frowns, but most were blank. No one felt like rejoicing. Ned Biehl was barely in the ground and many still mourned his passing.

Taylor tapped a pencil against his lower lip. "Remember, I really didn't want this job." He tossed the pencil onto the desk. Several downstate Elders had threatened to bolt the voting bloc if they didn't get their way on legislation favoring their districts. "If you don't maintain the coalition in the Council, I'm resigning. Is that clear?"

The office's heavy furniture and thick rugs gave it a quiet atmosphere. Even though the desk had been cleaned out, Ned Biehl's personal pictures still remained on the wall.

I've got to send those pictures back to his family, he thought.

Pete Belamy squirmed in his chair. "Yes, we understand. But we don't speak for everyone."

"First vote that goes against any of these proposals brings my resignation," Taylor said. "Particularly the budget."

"You've got to be reasonable, though," Washington said. "You've got to give us something we can sell to our people."

"It'll be much like last year's, except bigger."

"What about funds for Pennsylvania?" Washington asked. "Since Krupansky resigned, he's reactivated the Brotherhood. He wants relief money to offset their manpower shortage. Not that they seem to have any trouble finding men for their ..." He paused. "Whatever they call that gang of thugs."

"The strong arm of the Brotherhood," Belamy said.

"No discretionary funds for them, that'd be trouble," Taylor said. "Maybe we need some kind of military along the old border with Pennsylvania. What about a contingent from the downstate areas? Ramsey should be here for that discussion."

"I'd like to get back to the budget," Washington said. "What's different from last year?"

"We need to increase the number of students in the university." Taylor picked up a piece of paper. "To hedge our bets if the Qu'uda defeat us in space. That means sending teams of instructors out to start universities throughout the US."

Belamy took a deep breath. "Why don't we wait until all the states vote on whether they want to join the restored US? Then we can tap them for funding."

"We have to start training the instructors now," Taylor said. "That takes years of preparation."

"You still plan to send a plane-load of machine tools and equipment every month out to the West Coast?" Washington asked.

Taylor studied a sheet of paper. "It's in the budget, but I'm not sure it'll continue at the same pace. Since both units of the space station are in orbit, the Tacoma shipyards aren't as busy. We may need to shift to a different product mix." He looked up. "They need so many things for re-industrialization our factories will be busy for the foreseeable future."

"And the money to pay the bills?" Belamy asked.

A trace of a smile flickered across Taylor's face. "As usual, through taxes."

꒜

The Clan mounted militia wended its way down the hillside on the narrow trail through dense forest on the Pennsylvania border. The militia's dark brown uniforms contrasted with the bright green leaves and the silver trunks of the beech trees. Hooves thudded on the gray-brown mud of the trail and provided a backdrop to the jingle-jangle of the tackle.

"Hold," called the militiaman in the lead.

The column halted. He stared at the ground. "Somebody just came by here." He pointed to a pile of horse dung. "It's still steaming." He looked around, trying to penetrate the gloom of the undergrowth. No birds called. Something had spooked them.

The lead militiaman turned in his saddle to the scout at his side. "How far to the PA border?"

"Maybe three miles," said the scout. "To the outpost."

The lead militiaman frowned. "Forward, on the double—"

A gunshot rang out, followed by a volley.

A third of the militia toppled from their saddles. The rest spurred their horses into a gallop.

A high-pitched warbling yell came from the woods. A mass of men in civilian clothing rose, firing guns.

Only a few militiamen escaped.

2

"This can't continue," Ramsey said, red-faced. "Militiamen getting slaughtered whenever they go near the border. That damned Brotherhood wants Pennsylvania as their private fiefdom."

"It has to be Krupansky," Taylor said. "He always was the big cheese in the Brotherhood—"

"Right, and they're demanding money to ease the conditions that are causing honest citizens to become criminals," Belamy said. "It's extortion, pure and simple."

Taylor glanced up at the two men standing before his desk. "I understand. Krupansky has discovered a very effective tactic of using people dressed as civilians to wage war. Once done, they fade into the population."

"So how do we deal with it?" Ramsey demanded.

Taylor shrugged. "You're the Elder in charge of the military, not me." He was more concerned than he cared to let on. Any large-scale mobilization would reduce industrial output.

"I recommend we mobilize a full army of Horse Soldiers. It'll take that many to run them to ground."

Taylor winced. Several thousand men taken away from production. "Let me talk to Major Ike Kolodny out west. We've done a lot for them. Maybe he can do something for us."

A flush suffused Ramsey's face. "You don't think my Horse Soldiers can handle Krupansky's thugs?"

Taylor raised his hands. "Please," he said. "Most of the soldiers have jobs in factories that're making things for the defense effort. Out west, there are units of the US Army that might be able to help." He took a breath. "Wouldn't you like to hear what these professionals think of the situation?"

"Well," Ramsey said. "Maybe."

2

"What's this all about?" Kolodny's jaw jutted forward in competition with his beak-like nose. He'd just arrived on the regular flight from the West Coast.

"Ramsey," Taylor said. "Why don't you give Major Kolodny a quick rundown on the situation?"

Ramsey cleared his throat. "We have a problem..." He gave an account of the troubles in the former border area with Pennsylvania. He spoke for almost a half-hour, stopping only when Kolodny sought points of clarification. "... So, we thought we might benefit from your experience."

"And, possibly, some of your forces," Taylor added.

Kolodny eased back in his chair for a moment. "Let me look at that map again." He leaned over the desk and stared hard at the topographic map. "Rough country," he murmured. "What about the locals?" he asked. "Are they friendly or hostile?"

"Scared, mostly," Ramsey said. "The Brotherhood isn't known for respecting civil liberties."

"Won't be easy," Kolodny said. "We need a way to corner them and make them fight."

"The Brotherhood's fighters are very good in the woods," Ramsey said. "They disappear any time they run up against a stronger force. Hard to pin down."

The grim set of Kolodny's mouth eased into a feral smile. "My men know how fight in the forest," he said. "It's like this around Puget Sound where we had to deal with the Colvilles. They're no longer a problem." The smile faded. "It kinda sounds like Afghanistan, 'cept there's no language problem. A bunch of nasties oppressing the locals." He gritted his teeth.

"Helicopters," he said. "I wish we had helicopters. It'd make it easier to trap them and force them into a battle."

"Helicopters?" Taylor stared at the wall for a moment. "There are six Apache helicopters at Wright-Patterson," he said. "They seem to be in good condition. No one here knew much about them, so we didn't touch them. You want them?"

"Damn right I do." A thin smile flickered over Kolodny's stony features. "I'll get some Groom Lake boys up here. They've got mechanics who've worked on helicopters."

Taylor pointed to the phone. "Ask the operator to make the connection. She'll call back when she has your party."

ᘒ

Taylor was daydreaming about his son, Kemal, when the phone rang. He picked it up. "MacPherson."

"Let's have dinner tonight," said a soft, feminine voice. "I can take the fast train and be there by eight."

Taylor's heart raced. "Joyce, I don't think we should." He closed his eyes and she was there. He imagined he could smell her presence, feel the warmth of her body ... The late arrival meant she would stay over; his body began to stir. Then her words from their last meeting came back and the wound opened anew. "I really don't think we should."

"Look," she said. "I'm sorry about what happened. I'd ..." she hesitated. When she spoke again, her voice was low, husky. "I'd like to make it up to you."

"Joyce, you agreed to a divorce. It's over between us. Let's not do something we'll regret later." *More like something I might do and regret later*, he thought. The words of an old phrase came to mind: Sin in haste and repent at leisure.

She chuckled. "Why, Taylor, I believe you're afraid of me."

"Not really." Taylor took a deep breath. "Besides, I have other plans for tonight." *There*, he thought. *A simple white lie should take care of it.*

"Well, I have to come to Berea next week for a meeting. Why don't I come a day early so we can have supper together that evening?" Her voice was almost business-like.

"My schedule is busy next week. I have a trip out west." Or will have by then. *You old fool, a voice jeered from the back of his head, she wants you because you're now the Council Leader. And your cock wants her.* "I must decline."

Joyce didn't speak for a moment. "Well, it's a case of realizing I miss you." She sighed. "I'll look you up when I'm next in town. 'Bye." She hung up.

Taylor put down the phone. *I have enough problems with Kolodny and Krupansky battling it out in Pennsylvania*, he thought. *Plus we now have a refugee problem with the Brotherhood's tactic of forcing non-combatants into our area.*

CHAPTER SIXTY-ONE

Taylor examined the multi-colored points glowing on the computer monitor screen that were images transmitted from the space station's telescope.

Shades at the window swayed and a breeze brought in the smell of freshly turned earth and flowers. In the distance workmen's hammers banged steadily in yet another university building. The room was warm, almost stuffy from the electronic equipment.

"So, this is what you'll use?"

"Yes," said Madeline Henderson, the university's astronomer who had set up the system to warn of the approaching Qu'uda spacecraft. "We'll add these data to those from our observatory. More stars are visible from the space telescope and any small, faint light sources will show up."

"Let me know what you find." Taylor turned to leave.

"Of course." Her smile revealed perfectly uniform teeth.

After leaving Hendersons' observatory, Taylor found himself at Meltem's laboratory. *I wonder how my son is doing*, he thought. *I've wanted to visit Meltem for some time and find out*. He took a deep breath and entered. "Meltem?"

"Oh, Taylor." Meltem looked up. "I didn't hear you come in."

She smoothed her hair. "How've you been? I heard your problems." Dark shadows lay under her eyes.

Taylor nodded. "Biehl's murder, and everything else." He stopped abruptly. "How're you? And Kemal?"

"He's started teething and fusses more lately. I've been assured he'll get over it. Other than that, he's fine."

"What about you? How d'you feel? You look tired."

Meltem sighed. "Oh, Kemal had a couple of bad nights. That means I did, too." She waved her hand toward a chair. "Please, stay and talk a while."

Taylor felt a moment of elation. "Thanks. Did you do any analyzes on Kemal? For the SC-DNA?"

She pursed her lips briefly. "It's there. However, the normal levels of human growth factor for a person of his age mask it. So, I'm not sure whether it'll be at the same levels we have. Have you noticed any physiological changes in yourself?"

"Hard to say. The demands of Council and defense preparations are never-ending. I'm always tired."

Meltem nodded slowly. "Do you think you could've carried this workload a year ago?"

Taylor cast his mind back. *Do this on four to six hours' sleep a night a year ago?* He shook his head. "Hardly." He paused. "Meltem ..." He reached for her hand.

She sighed and closed her eyes as his fingers found hers.

"I've been thinking about you."

She took a deep breath. "Me, too."

"I think about what happened between us." Taylor paused. "And now I think it might happen again."

"If you'd left Joyce for me, I would've taken you in an instant." She looked up. "But not now."

"Why not?"

"You're hurt, damaged by what happened. You need time, time to heal. I don't want you on a rebound, only to wake up one morning to an empty bed, finding I was but a shoulder for you to lean on while you got over your pain. I couldn't take that. I love you too much to have something like that happen."

Taylor nodded slowly. *Yes,* he thought. *She can declare her love for me without reservation, but my heart is filled with confusion. Both she and Kemal mean a lot to me. And my heart is still in turmoil.*

"You need time to mourn the loss of a love. I know you loved her." Meltem squeezed his hand. "Be patient. When the hurt is gone, you'll know. So will I."

Taylor took her hand and raised it to his lips. "Can I see you from time to time? You and Kemal?"

"Yes, I'd like that."

෴

Major Ike Kolodny stood stiff and erect before the Elders, his chin thrust forward. The private, wood-paneled room was cool and quiet. A chair creaked softly.

"You sure you took care of Krupansky?" Ramsey asked. "He's been reported dead before." He sniffed suspiciously.

"Sir," Kolodny said. "Would you like to see his head? Like a bounty hunter?" His lips thinned and turned down at the corners. Light gleamed off his freshly shaven chin. "I can dig him up and cut it off, if you insist."

"No," Ramsey said. "No, that won't be necessary. We just want to be sure, before your unit returns to the West Coast."

"Sir," Kolodny said. "I believe there's a task my unit needs to attend to prior to leaving."

"Oh?" Ramsey raised his eyebrows. "What's that?"

"Your soldiers need additional training before they become part of the United States military."

"Now who said my soldiers would join the United States army?" A tinge of red appeared in Ramsey's face.

"Er, Ramsey," Taylor said. "The Clan under Ned Biehl was the driving force to reestablish the United States government. I believe Major Kolodny has a good point. If the Clan forces become a part of the United States military, it sets a good example to the rest of the states."

Ramsey pursed his lips as though sucking on something sour. He looked from side to side as if gauging the feelings of the other Elders. "What d'you think, Monahan?"

"I don't think the Clan needs these other states," he said in his wheezy voice. "They need us more than we need them."

"Hold on now," Carver Washington said. "Don't y'understand we need to join together to face this outside threat? Biehl worked hard to move us in that direction." He turned his head. "What d'you think, Taylor?"

"Supposed threat," Monahan said.

Taylor tapped the side of his nose. "I agree with Major Kolodny. Even if the United States government isn't restored, our soldiers would benefit from training by a professional soldier, one who can teach them how to use modern weapons and tactics."

Major Kolodny stood a little straighter.

"Hmm." Ramsey closed one eye thoughtfully. "Maybe I ought to spend some time with Major Kolodny to see what he has in mind." He looked in both directions.

Heads nodded agreement.

"If that's the Council's wish."

"Mr. Ramsey, as the Council's military expert, I believe you would be the appropriate person to do just that," Taylor said. "Any objections?"

Silence reigned.

"Mr. Ramsey, the Council requests you consult with Major Kolodny on how to train the Clan soldiers to the standards of the US Military. That's all, Major Kolodny."

Kolodny saluted, pivoted on his heel, and marched out.

Taylor picked up a piece of paper. "Next item. It seems the Hendersons, with the help of Tim Van Minh, got a computerized astronomical comparator working. That'll help them find moving objects in space." He looked up. "Seems the solar system has more moving bodies than they initially realized. From orbit, they've discovered a lot of unidentified asteroids, none of which are heading toward Earth. They're adding them to the electronic files on all the objects in the solar system."

"Have they spotted the alien ship?" Pete Belamy asked.

"Not yet." Taylor looked down at the sheet of paper before him. "They've recruited and trained students to interpret the data. There was just too much for them to handle on their own. Which brings me to this item in the budget. Funding for the Astronomy Department at the university ..." He returned to the detailed review of the budget.

こ

"Hello, Taylor." A melodic voice cut through the muted chatter of the half-filled restaurant at the Travelers' Inn.

Reflexively, Taylor rose from his chair. "Joyce," he said. "I didn't know you were in town."

Joyce pulled a chair out and sat down. "Your secretary said you were having supper here." She unfolded a napkin and placed it on her lap. "So, I decided to join you."

"I'm meeting someone for supper," said Taylor. "Is there anything in particular we need to discuss?"

Joyce leaned forward and rested her chin in her hands. Her blouse was open to the point of revealing cleavage. She smiled. "How've you been? I've missed you."

Taylor took a deep breath. "Like I said, I already have plans for dinner, with an old friend."

"Then I'll join you. I know most of your friends."

Taylor forced a smile and glanced up. His smile broadened. "She's just arrived."

A frown flashed across Joyce's face before she turned in the direction of Taylor's glance.

"Doctor Encirlik, what're you doing here?" Joyce said.

The tiny doctor stood still, quiet. "Hello, Taylor." One eyebrow rose quizzically. "Ms. Vargas." She nodded.

Joyce turned toward Taylor, lines forming between her eyebrows. "What's she doing here?"

"Meltem is my dinner date," Taylor said. "I've been looking forward to this dinner with Meltem for some time."

Two spots of red appeared on Joyce's cheeks. She rose slowly. "I don't believe this. She's ..." She looked first at Taylor and then at Meltem. She shook her head and tossed the napkin on the table. Her smile was forced. "Some other time, Taylor. 'Bye." She strode out, head held high.

Meltem approached Taylor and offered her cheek.

Taylor bussed her cheek, then pulled back a chair for her.

Meltem sat down and smiled. "I'm proud of you," she said. "You didn't hesitate, not even once."

The New Year came with heavy snow and cold weather that disrupted flights to the West Coast. With their computerized comparator at the university, the Hendersons examined an ever-growing volume of space. The observatory staff, now several dozen, took turns checking out false alarms.

It was a student who spotted an anomalous point of light above the planetary ecliptic and brought it to the Hendersons' attention. As it got closer, it resolved into an elongated object, gleaming with fuzzy brightness. It had no trace of a tail; it wasn't a comet. It was too regular in shape and had too high an albedo to be an asteroid.

"I think it's them," Madeline said to no one in particular. Her best guess as to interception time was eleven or twelve months. That meant it was time for the Clan to move its weapons into space, weapons created by the alliance of humans and the stranded Qu'uda—Billy Pudjata, Cha KinLaat, and MinCha DuKaat.

"Bud," Taylor called out and he hurried down the pot-holed street that once had been a main thoroughfare in the US Navy submarine base at Bangor, Washington.

Conifers crowded the run-down buildings as alders threatened to take over the open space. A haze of rain obscured the Olympic Mountains in the distance. A breeze brought cries of seagulls, and the briny smell of the Pacific filled the air. It was chilly.

"Taylor, good to see you. What brings you out to the West Coast?" Colonel Bud Inez said.

"Same reason you're here. I brought a couple of guests to join in the discussions. Let's get out of this rain so you can meet them." Taylor followed Bud into a battered Quonset hut. Inside, the air was warm, almost steamy. A group of people sat around a battered table. Others milled about a counter at the side of the room, getting a hot drink.

"Bud, you've met Billy Pudjata before." Taylor nodded at Billy and then turned to an individual in the shadows. "This is MinCha DuKaat. He was a weapons specialist on the Egg-that-Flies before the Qu'uda abandoned him on Andros Island."

Bud hesitated for a moment to let his eyes adjust to the light to see MinCha DuKaat. "Er, pleased to meetcha," he said.

MinCha DuKaat grunted something in his native language, then offered a greeting in English. "The honor is mine, Colonel Inez. I have been looking forward to meeting you. You were not expecting me?" MinCha extended a fistful of claws. His long, yellowish-green face looked almost human except a lack of a nose and the rooster-like crest that flopped to one side.

Bud gingerly extended his hand. "You've got that right."

"MinCha has some insight as to what we are likely to face," Taylor said. "Let's get started." He gestured toward the table and dragged out a chair. "The Hendersons will give us an update on the astronomical data and the estimated time of arrival. Later, we'll link-up with Ki on the space station to fill him in on what's going on."

Slowly the group developed a consensus on how to deal with the approaching spacecraft. MinCha spelled out the dangers to be expected from any Bird-of-War craft. The news was not good for the space station. The meeting continued until nightfall.

Outside the Quonset hut, Bud grabbed Taylor by the arm. "Can we trust this alien?" Worry creased his eyebrows. "They look like ... a cross between a friggin' dinosaur and a man."

Taylor put his hand on Bud's shoulder. "Look, MinCha and the other Qu'udas almost died on Andros Island. If Billy hadn't kept in contact, they would've given up. When he rescued them, they were almost dead from malnutrition. Even so, it was nip and tuck, nursing them back to health. Since then, they've helped us understand Qu'uda technology. As females, they were furious about being abandoned at the most vulnerable point in their birthing cycle."

"Females? I thought you called MinCha him?"

"Yeah, well, they change gender. Don't ask me how, they just do. Something about stress and survival."

"Can we trust them?" Bud put his hands on his hips.

"Yes. The Qu'uda need, no, they must belong to a community. Our acceptance and care for them is greater than what they experienced in their own community. They've found they're more important, here on Earth, than on the Qu'uda spaceship. Something about being in the middle of things really motivates them. Besides, Billy and Cha KinLaat will keep an eye on them." Taylor hesitated. "You've got to meet Cha KinLaat sometime. She's something else. She feels so strongly about the way the Qu'uda abandoned her, she insists on being a part of the team that attacks the Egg-that-Flies. I guess it's personal."

"I'm still nervous about them knowing what we're doing."

Taylor chuckled without mirth. "I've got good news for you. MinCha will be posted to your facility in Nevada to help you make weapons. Feel free to pump MinCha about anything you like. You may be surprised at what you find out. Keep him involved."

Bud's mouth sagged open. "But, but—"

"Remember, the Qu'uda have to feel that they belong."

"But—"

"Make MinCha welcome." Taylor forced a smile. "You might be amazed at what you find out." He steered him back to the Quonset hut. Once back inside, Taylor announced MinCha's assignment to the Groom Lake facility in Nevada.

$$\curlyvee$$

"We can add radar ranging and an integrated weapons system." MinCha pointed at the drawing sprawled on the table.

"No, we've gotta keep the first-contact platform simple. It's a throwaway. It has only one purpose, even if the contact is peaceful and the lasers aren't used." Pip Ryan had the responsibility of transferring ideas into hard metal. And time was short.

Bud smiled at the debate but said nothing.

"It is but a metal tank with a small fusion drive and compressed gas maneuvering jets. It is so primitive."

"Listen, Minch ol' buddy. I don't care if they think we're primitive. We've got a spaceship with a fusion drive. That makes us equal to them," Pip said.

"Okay, guys," Bud said. "Forget doing the things the way you'd like to do them. We don't have time for anything fancy. We have to launch it within thirty days so we don't give the space station's posi-

tion away. Let me go over the basic requirements. Does the platform relay messages and accurately track the Egg-that-Flies'
position? Does it have enough protection to withstand a beam
weapon?" He counted off the points on his fingers. "Well, does it?"

Both Pip and MinCha said, "But—"

"Does it?" Bud said.

"Yeah, I guess it can." Pip knew when to quit.

"Narrow-beam radar would give us their position and limit the
chance of revealing our space station with incidental reflected radar
—" MinCha started to say.

"No." Bud shook his head. "We don't have time. Let's figure out
what we've gotta do before launch..."

The platform would have made Rube Goldberg smile. It was
built from salvaged materials: an old personal computer with several
terabytes of memory, servo motors, a radar unit from a sailboat, a
ham radio, a television, a handycam, and a set of lasers.

The shuttle carried weapons and supplies up to the space
station. The space station's crew added a second layer of metal foil
to the sun parasol above the space station to reduce leakage of electromagnetic radiation. It took three more shuttle trips to get all of
the parts of the first-contact platform into orbit, which they used to
complete the final assembly. Steadily, the visitor from outer space
drew closer.

ॐ

"... four—three—two—one—GO! We have a good start." The
fusion drive system of the first-contact platform came to life. The
platform operated on low power until system checkout. Then it
headed into an orbit near the moon before setting course toward
the oncoming craft.

ॐ

It was after New Year when the Hendersons made another discovery. A point of light stood out, a point of light showing movement
toward Earth.

"If I didn't know any better, I'd say this is another spaceship approaching the Earth." Lines creased Madeline's forehead. Seven months earlier, they'd been sure that they'd found the Qu'uda spaceship.

"It can't be," Butch Henderson said. "It's got to be some kind of natural object, a comet or a long period asteroid we don't know about."

The Hendersons reviewed their data and recalculated the new object's course several times. The data suggested it could be an asteroid. Its point of origin was from somewhere beyond the orbit of Mars, possibly from the vicinity of Jupiter. Its size and course worried the Hendersons; they estimated it was bigger than the Qu'uda ship, much bigger. It was moving faster, too. Even so, it would arrive about a month after the first ship.

They feared the Qu'uda might have pushed an asteroid onto a collision course with the Earth to knock Earth's civilization back into the Stone Age or beyond.

"We'd better tell Taylor right away," Madeline said.

CHAPTER SIXTY-TWO

"Good-bye, Meltem. I'll call again later." Taylor put down the phone.

I really miss seeing Meltem and Kemal. He'd found he now stopped by to visit them every day and sometimes twice. *If the Qu'uda destroy us, I'll never see them again.* He shivered.

For a moment he was torn between the desire to return home and his duty at the command center at the Bangor Naval Base. *We ought to win. We're prepared. We've got a first-class team on the space station. We've got to win. We've tried so hard to come back as a society; we must win.*

We've accomplished a lot in the past year. The western states of California, Oregon, Washington, Nevada, Utah, and the area under the Greater Clan had voted to reestablish the United States of America. Still, the union was more symbolic than actual. The laws of the local governments still prevailed. The local assemblies—all representative bodies, as required by the new Constitution—effectively ruled their local areas.

Columbus, Ohio had been proposed as the interim capitol city because it had survived the Collapse almost intact. The states cooperated in defense efforts against the return of the Qu'uda.

The Defense Council selected Ki Jones to command the space station. Analysis suggested the tactics needed in space were like those used in underwater warfare. Ki's struggle to keep his vessel and crew together was a testament to his tenacity and leadership skills.

The phone rang loudly, and Taylor snapped back to the present. "Hello?"

A woman's voice spoke, distorted and overlaid with static, "Mr. MacPherson?"

Taylor's heart leapt for a moment. For an instant, he thought, no, hoped, it was Meltem. "Yes?"

"This is Madeline Henderson, from the university—"

"Ah, yes, Madeline." Taylor cut off her explanation of who she was. "What can I do for you?"

"We've observed another body approaching Earth," she said.

Damn, Taylor thought. *I can barely hear her.* "What kind of body?"

"We believe it's a ..." A burst of static drowned out her voice. "... Its emissions are like a star, a new star."

"We've got a bad connection," Taylor said. "Repeat your message." The line crackled loudly.

"There's another one coming," she said. "Another ..." Her voice faded into the rasp and crackle of interference. "... have two different spectral signatures. That means that ..." Her voice faded. "... and it should arrive a month later."

"What's coming?"

"What did you say?" Madeline's voice squawked in his ear.

"Call me back," he shouted into the phone.

"I'll ..." The squeal of static grew louder.

Taylor heard a click and the phone went silent. *What the Hell was that all about?* he thought. *Someday, we'll get the fiber optic link reestablished. Bouncing radio messages off the space station didn't work well, especially whenever the sun acted up.*

A half a million miles from Earth, the first-contact platform used its gas jets to reverse its course to the alien spacecraft. Its fusion drive ignited and filled the sky with broadband radiation. The platform slowed its forward motion, seeking to match the alien craft's velocity.

The platform rotated again to place its ice-filled tank at the nose toward the approaching alien craft. Behind the tank, antennae emerged and focused on the alien ship. At the aft-end, communication gear aligned itself on the orbital space station.

The space station sent an IR laser pulse to the platform. The radio on the platform transmitted a greeting toward the alien craft in both English and Qu'uda languages, then went silent.

The only thing the radio picked up and relayed to the space station was the hiss of background emissions. Listeners on the space station heard nothing. The platform repeated its message, using a broad range of frequencies.

The alien ship remained silent.

ᘰ

Captain Ki Jones sounded frustrated. "We've been dinging them with messages for the past twenty-four hours. No response. Silent as a graveyard."

"How close is it now?" Taylor asked.

"It's within six hundred thousand klicks and approaching Earth at about two klicks per second," Ki said. "The platform is tracking the same course as the alien bogey. Their separation is about fifteen hundred klicks and closing."

Taylor did the calculation in his head. It would be in orbit around the Earth in a little over three days. "I guess it's time to up the ante," he said. "Be careful."

"Cha KinLaat is monitoring the frequencies used by the Qu'uda. If she hears anything, we'll know right away."

"All right. Just let me know what happens."

ᘰ

The platform unfolded a dish antenna that rotated toward the alien craft. Once aligned, it sent a radar pulse toward the alien craft in a manner that was analogous to a sonar ping in submarines. A few moments later, the craft's ghostly image showed up on the radar screen of the orbital space station.

Ki waited. Nothing. "They must be deaf and dumb if they don't hear that." He had hoped it would elicit a response. He was sure the alien craft must have sensors that could detect a radar pulse.

The spacecraft continued to approach. It remained silent.

A half a minute later, a radar operator called out, "Sir, we just got another reflected radar image." He paused. "Something else is out there."

"Yeah? Where? How far and how big?" Ki said.

"It's way out there. Must be, er, lemme see, about four million klicks or so. It's pretty big, too." The radar operator ran the calculation. "Geez. I've got a diameter in the range close to half a klick. I'd better re-check that."

"That could be the asteroid they warned us about, the one heading toward the Earth. We may have to deal with that sucker when it gets closer. Alert the missile boys and give them its location data." Ki had seen the calculations for changing the course of the asteroid with an explosion. It would take nukes.

꒳

Taylor didn't get another call from Madeline Henderson. When he tried to reach the university, he found its phone system down. *Damn*, he thought. *What was that call about?*

Taylor paced back and forth. "What's going on up there?" he asked.

Rain beating on the roof of the Quonset hut and the murmur of voices of the communications crew provided a steady backdrop of sound. Water steadily dripped off the conifers. Wisps of mist hung among the trees.

A young man looked up. "Not much at the moment. They're scanning the alien craft with radar. It hasn't responded. Just a sec," he said. "Something's happening." He bent over his radio and adjusted its controls.

"Well?" Taylor asked.

"They just picked up a radio signal," said the young man. "They're sending it down." He reached to the rack above the radio and snapped a switch. "I got it—it's being recorded."

A speaker came to life. "... received this from the bogey near the first-contact platform."

Something twittered from the speaker, then stopped. The automatic gain made the background hiss of static grow louder. A sound sang from the speaker that sounded like "Hooley." Immediately after came the same twittering sequence of sounds.

"That sounds like a bird," said a voice from the speaker and then another voice asked, "Where did it come from?"

Taylor recognized Ki's voice.

"I'm not real sure, sir," another voice squawked. "I think it came from the same direction as the bogey directly in front of our first-contact platform. Lemme check."

"Make sure that you got it recorded. Check to make sure command center has a good copy." It was Ki again. "Transmit the bird-call sound back to them and ask for their ID. Maybe we'll get a response." His voice contained a note of desperation.

"We got it." Taylor reached for a telephone. "Find Ulrich, the linguist. I need to speak to him."

"Sir," the radio operator said. "There's a new development." His eyes were wide and contrasted against his dark brown skin. He put his hands to his earphones and pressed them tight against his head. He frowned in concentration.

"What is it?" Taylor spoke over the phone perched between his ear and shoulder.

"There's something else out there," the radio operator said. "An asteroid ... no, wait, the asteroid's got delta-vee." The operator paused, listening carefully. "It has a fusion drive," he said. "That's a positive on the fusion drive."

"What?" Taylor said.

The radio operator glanced at Taylor. "A second alien ship, sir." His mouth remained open and his face took on a gray shade.

CHAPTER SIXTY-THREE

The radar operator swiveled in his seat "... we're gonna call the asteroid-thing bogey-two."

"Now, what about bogey-one?" Ki's voice had gone up a notch.

"Sir, bogey-one is pretty close to the first-contact platform. There's less than a hundred klicks separation between them." The radar operator continued to watch the faint images on his screen.

The command center on the space station was crowded and all its electronic equipment glowed with activity. "Bogey-one's course will take it toward the moon. My guess is it'll round the moon and then pass by us on the return leg."

"As soon as you have enough data, calculate its course, orientation, and altitude," Ki said. "Push the first-contact platform a little closer. It's time to use the optics. Low velocity change—do not flip it over to stop." He preferred to deal with one ship at a time, even if that meant shortening the schedule for first contact. *Never give the enemy a chance to assemble its forces if there was a chance of conflict. Tackle them while they're still divided; that was good military tactics.* Ki had a feeling this was leading to conflict.

"The maneuvering jets are on. We've got negative delta-vee."

"Take it in to about ten klicks and hold it there. Don't do anything fast." Ki made his voice sound confident even though his stomach had gone sour.

"Nice and easy." The image on the radar showed two blobs draw slowly closer together. "We're at ten klicks. We're matching velocities."

"Careful, don't overshoot it. Recompute and terminate thrust as soon as possible. Get it close, but not too close." Ki chewed on his lower lip.

"Yes, sir. We've got a precise course and velocity match. We'll confirm it once we get additional data."

"Are we close enough for a look-see at bogey-one?"

"Yes sir, maybe sir. It's out about ten klicks."

"Put it on optical."

"Yes, sir," a woman's voice crackled over the intercom. "Unfolding camera boom." Heads turned toward the video monitor. The control room grew quiet. "Video coming up."

As the camera oriented itself toward the approaching craft, pictures began to appear on a small monitor. Stars danced across the screen as the camera zeroed in on the approaching craft. A bright light swam into the middle of the screen and washed-out the image. The camera adjusted to the light and the glare diminished. A point of light centered in the screen. The telephoto lens dragged the point closer and closer, expanding it into an elongated smudge. The image shook in the screen as the camera adjusted its focus. The shape took form. It was a long, thin craft glittering in reflected starlight.

"Get this image to ground command immediately," Ki said. "I need feedback on this."

Over the intercom came the explosive guttural sound of Cha KinLaat's voice in her native language. A moment later she said, "Captain Jones, that is too small to be Qu'uda spaceship. And it is not a Bird-of-War."

"Then who or what is it?" Ki asked.

"Not Qu'uda. Aliens."

Ki shuddered as a wave of something cold swept through him and for a moment, his knees felt weak.

He hadn't slept much lately from the tension of waiting and preparing the space station for battle. Now, on top of all of that, there were alien-aliens out there. The sour lump in his stomach did a cartwheel. *Oh, shit, it's just got worse.*

"Sir, I've got a better image of that thing out there." The

woman's voice was steady. "I'm putting it on the large screen."

Ki swiveled in his chair.

The alien craft filled the screen. A scale on the bottom gave an indication of its size: Its main section was a stubby cylinder about three hundred feet in diameter and about one hundred feet long with a dome-shaped end. At the other end of the cylinder were six large spheres. Extending from between the spheres was a stalk about three hundred feet long with a cluster of pods at the far end. As the craft slowly rotated, it glittered like a jewel in the sunlight. Clinging to the side of the stubby cylinder were two structures that looked like wingless metallic cicadas, each about fifty feet long.

"My God," Ki's words came unbidden.

"Sir, we just received another radio signal," the radio operator called out. "It wasn't from bogey-one."

"Do you have a bearing?"

"Not yet, sir. It's definitely not bogey-one."

"Gimme something better than that."

"Sir, it came from the asteroid, bogey-two."

"Put it on audio," Ki said.

The sonorous grunting voice electrified the crew on the space station. All recognized the spoken Qu'uda language.

"Great Egg," Cha KinLaat's voice crackled from the speaker. "It's Mata ChaLik BuMaru. He has returned."

"What's goin' on?" Ki said. "What did he say? Where in Hell did it come from?"

"The Qu'uda have returned," Cha KinLaat said clearly over the intercom.

"What did they say?" Ki said.

"It was a communication between Huta Kah DaBuk and that stinking slime from a fetid pond, Mata ChaLik BuMaru," Cha KinLaat said. "He's out there, somewhere, giving orders to a Bird-of-War. It is on the way to Earth."

The radio operator looked up. "Sir, the transmission came from the vicinity of bogey-two, the asteroid-thing."

"Where the Hell is it?" Ki made his voice loud and demanding. "Goddamn it. I want answers. Where are the Qu'uda?"

"Sir," The radar operator said. "Bogey-two range is in excess of a million klicks, twelve degrees below plane of ecliptic, four degrees left of Saturn axis."

"What's its velocity?"

"Sir, bogey-two is approaching at about six klicks per second. It'll be here in about forty-eight hours."

CHAPTER SIXTY-FOUR

"Prepare for weightless operating conditions," Mata ChaLik BuMaru said. He remembered the earlier fate of the Egg-that-Flies. *I will not make the same mistake again by approaching too closely.* The Little-Egg-that-Flies had shed sufficient velocity to orbit Earth. "Orient the ship to face our direction of travel," he said.

"Mata ChaLik," KaLik DuGan's voice came over the comm-net. "The Bird-of-War is ready. Please open the outer doors."

KaLik, the battle tactics master, was in the Bird-of-War preparing to descend to the surface of the planet. The combat craft had multiple beam weapons on the tips of its stubby delta wings and short-range sensors intended for atmospheric scanning. He'd wanted to install heavy weapons, but Mata ChaLik had reasoned they were not necessary, sure the primitives on the planet below were no match for an armored Bird-of-War.

"The outer doors are open," said Mata ChaLik.

"Start the launch sequence," KaLik called out.

The Bird-of-War's computer communicated with the docking cradle to start the launch sequence. The cradle trundled the craft toward the outer blast doors of the dock. Behind, the airlock closed. The blast doors opened, and the Bird-of-War passed through into the star-lit void. Once through, the blast doors slid shut.

"Start the engines," KaLik said.

A low-pitched rumble went through the craft as its fusion drives ignited. Blue-white cones emerged from the twin engines to splash against the closed blast doors.

"Maneuvering thrust. Release from platform and launch."

The delta-shaped Bird-of-War eased away from the Little-Egg-that-Flies into the brilliant light of the nearby star. Even as it turned toward the sun and then the Earth, no light reflected from its stubby gray wings or its slabby surfaces. It ceased rotation and began to move away from the Little-Egg-that-Flies.

Inside the cockpit, KaLik and his combat officer, Huta Kah DaBuk faced the bulkhead that had a viewscreen with the image of the blue and white planet. Bright red lines showed their position and course vectors. Instruments and controls glowed orange in the console lying between them. The Bird-of-War was built for combat; its cockpit had no outside openings.

"KaLik DuGan," Mata ChaLik's voice had a sharp edge.

"Yes?" KaLik looked up from the controls.

"There's something out there. In front of you."

"Transmit your data to me." KaLik regretted not having deep-space sensors on board the Bird-of-War, but its primary mission was to exterminate the threat from the dry-land vermin below. There wasn't supposed to be anything out there. The viewscreen acquired a bright yellow spot.

The natives of this planet are primitive, he thought. "How can it be them? How could they have achieved space flight in such a short period of time?" he said.

"Perhaps it is a craft built by the Qu'uda who were left behind to guard our eggs." Doubt filled Mata ChaLik's voice.

"Why would they build a spaceship?"

"Remember, Bilik Pudjata mobilized Earth savages to build the fusion drive tube and we left four Qu'uda behind with more resources and greater knowledge. They had the benefit of his experience," Mata ChaLik said. "Maybe they did the same."

Those creatures on the planet are savages, dry-land vermin, KaLik thought. *What if they had built spacecraft in that period of time?* He remembered their difficulties in building the Little-Egg and the Bird-of-War. *No*, he thought. *It would be a formidable task.* "It would be difficult even for them."

"Then who is out there?"

"Suppose you are right, would they not answer you if you sent a message?" KaLik wanted to test Mata ChaLik's theory. *It is me that is out here, not him, facing them in a Bird-of-War designed for atmospheric service.*

"I'll greet them." Mata ChaLik paused and activated the transmitter. "This is Mata ChaLik BuMaru, spokesperson for the Defenders of Qu'uda. We have returned to fulfill our responsibilities. Identify yourselves, now."

ಲ

"Look, Cha KinLaat, we don't want to start a space war," Ki Mapes said. "We just sort of, er, need to convince them we're advanced enough to be treated as equals." He'd summoned Cha KinLaat to the command center of the space station after hearing the radio transmission in Qu'uda.

Cha KinLaat stared at Ki before answering. "Perhaps you are right. There will be time and opportunity enough to repay him for the way he treated us. I will enjoy that when the time comes." She flexed her hands. Claws appeared.

Ki nodded to a radio operator. "Hail them a couple of times. Then listen very carefully." He gestured for silence. The radar screens flickered. Bogey-two and its small companion continued to get closer.

A familiar voice broke in, "Space station, come in please. This is Butch Henderson. I've got important information for you." A burst of static accompanied his faint voice.

Ki looked at the radio operator and frowned. "What the Hell does he want? Doesn't he know what we're up to? Tell him to get off the air. We're busy right now."

The radio operator reached for the microphone but before he picked it up, Butch's voice came from the speaker, "Space station, we've confirmed the presence of two objects approaching Earth, two objects approaching Earth. Both are believed to be Qu'uda spaceships. Do you read me?"

Ki spoke into the microphone. "Butch, we read you loud and clear. We've already got them on our radar. We've received transmissions from both ships. One is definitely Qu'uda, the other is some other unknown alien species. Repeat, the other is an unknown alien species. Confirm message, please."

"Confirming message. One ship is Qu'uda, and the other is an unknown alien species. Omigod. The other is an unknown, repeat, unknown alien species. Over and out," Butch's voice quavered slightly as the carrier signal faded.

Ki stared at the wall and sighed. The whole idea of alien aliens scared him.

CHAPTER SIXTY-FIVE

"Mata ChaLik, did you hear that?"

"It is the dry-land vermin. We cannot allow them to go free and prey on our universe. We must drive them from space. Destroy them."

"I hear and obey." KaLik turned to his combat officer. "Huta Kah DaBuk, set course for the closest spaceship."

"Yes, KaLik DuGan." Huta unleashed a claw and touched several control pads.

The engines' output increased, and the Bird-of-War rotated into a new orientation. The vibration from the engines increased as thrust built. Once the ship achieved its new course, Huta tapped the controls and the engines shut down. Zero gravity returned. The craft shook with several clanks as armored shields covered all openings.

KaLik touched another control, eliciting more vibration as the Bird-of-War extended its sensors and unfolded two spindly beam weapons. In the viewscreen, a ship grew larger before them. It was a squat cylinder that rotated to present its dome-shaped end toward them. It was unlike anything he'd ever seen before. "Divert all power to weapon systems."

"I hear and obey." A hum filled the interior of the Bird-of-War as the fusion engines charged up the weapons.

They drew closer.

The ship was in range.

"Huta Kah DaBuk, fire at will."

Huta touched the controls. Once, then twice, narrow tongues of energy lashed out, gouging slices into the softly rounded shape in front of them.

Without warning, the Bird-of-War shuddered and rang like a struck gong. The viewscreen flared brightly and went black.

"Great Egg. What was that?" Huta said.

"Monitor your instruments. Activate auxiliary scanners, raise more sensors," KaLik said. "A powerful weapon hit us. Praise Egg, our armor held." A viewscreen glowed into life.

A grainy image of the ship grew before them. They were closing rapidly. More of the ship became visible. KaLik realized the Bird-of-War's course had changed. *Was it from the impact of the hit?* he wondered. *Their beam weapons had not penetrated the ship before them. Its rounded end must be a shield,* he realized. "Aim for the side of the ship," he said.

"Procedure calls for new beam weapons to be inspected before use," Huta said.

"Do it now before they rotate the ship. The round section at the front is a shield. Aim for the side. Now," KaLik said. *Now I know why this race of savages must be confined to their planet,* he thought. *If they can create a ship with armor and powerful weapons in the time since we departed, I fear for the entire universe. Mata ChaLik was right. They must be exterminated.*

"Hurry."

"Beam weapons ready," said Huta.

"Open fire, now." KaLik wondered. *Does Huta not recognize the danger the other craft poses to us?*

The Bird-of-War's energy beams sparkled against the side of the ship. Jets of gas appeared. A cloud of debris expanded and vanished. Two small structures detached and floated off, damaged like squashed insects. The ship grew to fill the viewing-scene and then abruptly disappeared.

"Where did it go?" Huta asked.

KaLik touched the controls.

In the viewscreen, the spacecraft with a dome-shaped end shrank as they drifted away from it. It did not resemble anything with which KaLik was familiar. Protruding from the cylinder was a long thin column terminating in what looked like a cluster of engines.

Strange, he thought. *Is it primitive or advanced? They are savages, so it must be primitive.* "We holed them. See the gas leaking out of its side?"

The computer squawked a warning.

KaLik touched a control. The viewscreen changed to a forward image. In the center of the screen was a bright speck of light. Below the image, a warning flashed.

"What is that?" he said and touched a control.

The image pulled in closer. It was a small, cylindrical spacecraft. "There's another." He opened a broadband communication link and called, "Identify yourself. This is KaLik DuGan, Defender of Qu'uda."

There was no response.

They slid steadily closer to the craft, closer and closer. "At extreme range for beam weapons, now," said Huta. "What shall I do?"

The craft grew large on the viewing screen.

"It refuses to respond," KaLik said. "Therefore it must belong to the dry-land vermin. Open fire."

The beam sparkled against the craft, lighting up its front. Geysers of gas spewed forth. The craft slowly tumbled from the force of the gas eruptions. It did not return fire.

"Stay alert, be ready to resume firing. It may only be damaged." KaLik watched the craft as they passed it. The dark shape disappeared among the background of stars.

"KaLik DuGan, report your status," Mata ChaLik's voice interrupted his examination of the space derelict.

"We have crippled two of the dry-land vermin's craft. One had a powerful weapon, an energy beam of some kind. It destroyed our primary sensors and a set of beam weapons. The second ship did not return fire at us."

"Show me," Mata ChaLik said.

"Prepare to receive the visual records of the contact." KaLik transmitted the recording to the Little-Egg-that-Flies.

"There is another ship in orbit around the planet," Mata ChaLik said. "It is about to go behind the planet."

KaLik touched the controls to expand the range of the sensors. Nothing appeared on the viewscreen. "Do you have its position?" he asked.

"Yes," Mata ChaLik said and paused. "Here are its co-ordinates and time of emergence from behind the planet."

"Transmission received." KaLik put the data on the viewscreen. Its orbit was close to the planet. "We must decrease velocity to match orbits with them." He reset the controls to rotate the Bird-of-War's orientation. He already knew exactly how he would deal with the third and last of the dry-land vermin's spaceships. He began to feel more confident about his mission. Even though it had not gone as expected, he had been successful. He started the fusion drive engines, filling the Bird-of-War with a low rumble.

Huta dozed off. There was nothing to do while they shed velocity to match orbits with the craft ahead. Tail-first they approached, the fusion drive's hot plasma licking around the body of the Bird-of-War, raising its temperature. While plasma bathed their craft, all external sensors were withdrawn to protect them. They were blind to anything approaching them.

CHAPTER SIXTY-SIX

"Holy shit. The sunnavabitches are killing each other." Ki stared at the images on the monitor coming from the first-contact platform.

The small spaceship that came from the Qu'uda asteroid ship had been designated as bogey-three. It had just opened fire on the unknown aliens' ship, making it sparkle with tiny points of brilliance. Without warning, bogey-three, the small Qu'uda ship, flashed into incandescence. The screen grew dark.

"What the Hell was that?" Ki looked at the radar operators. They were busy. None raised their heads.

"Sir," a woman's voice said from the opposite side of the room. It was the astronomer on temporary assignment to the optical scanning system. "Something made bogey-three very hot, very quickly." The young woman took a deep breath before continuing. "It looks like it was hit by a giant laser."

"Thanks." Ki couldn't recall her name.

The small Qu'uda ship continued to close on the seemingly lifeless ship of the unknown aliens. It angled past the aliens' ship. Tiny sparkles of brilliant light reappeared to light up the side of the aliens' ship.

"Damn, I don't believe it. Bogey-three survived the heat treatment. It's getting its licks in again. Gimme a close-up on bogey-one," Ki said.

The image swam closer, revealing a jet of dust emerging from the side of bogey-one. Two small clusters of debris cartwheeled away and disappeared. The jet faded as the debris scattered.

"Lemme see bogey-three from the platform," Ki said. The image of the small Qu'uda ship jerked onto the monitors. It had an angular look with no windows, hatches, or seam markings; it had small protuberances that stood out clearly. It looked as though it had been forged out of one piece of metal.

"Distance five klicks," a voice called out, indicating the amount of separation of the first-contact platform from the small Qu'uda ship.

"Keep the platform oriented head-on toward the Qu'uda ship," said Ki. "Retract all communications antennae. Hurry, if they take a pot-shot at it, I want its eyes to survive."

The image of the Qu'uda ship faded from the monitors. Two small, fuzzy specks of light replaced it. One of the specks bloomed brightly.

"Get me a close-up of the platform," Ki said.

The image of the first-contact platform rushed in, fuzzy and vibrating from extreme magnification. Its nose section was peeled open into ragged fingers of torn metal. A cloud of vapor dissipated rapidly. It looked like a damaged flower as it tumbled slowly, surrounded by an expanding field of debris.

Bogey-three was nowhere in sight.

"I think we're playing in the wrong league." Ki rubbed his bald head. He was more than a little worried. "That sucker's weapons are powerful."

"Sir, the platform's responding to our signal."

"Get it back online. We gotta see where bogey-three's heading." The platform vanished from the screen. White static lines started to run across the picture in the monitor.

"Why's the image breaking up?"

"Sir, it's our orbit. We're sliding behind the Earth. It's coming between the platform and us. We'll be occluded for about six hours."

"All right, give me visual on bogey-three."

"Yes, sir. We have about fifteen minutes before he's hidden, too," the woman's voice called out.

"Okay, let's use this time to get ready for our visitors," Ki said.

"First, de-spin the station. Once we reach zero gee, orient Unit One toward the approaching bogey. We'll use it as a shield. Move all personnel and portable equipment into unit two." He paused. "Missile section."

"Missile section here," said a voice from the intercom.

"Berkowitz." Berkowitz was the missile section chief. He had a soft Texas accent, which made him sound calm and relaxed. "Look, we got us a problem. Too many targets. Bogey-three is on a direct approach to us. It also has some nasty weapons. We need to divvy up the missiles between bogeys one, two, and three. I think it's prudent to save at least half our missiles for the bogey-two, the asteroid."

"Yes, sir," said Berkowitz. "How about floating half the missiles out in a radial pattern, y'know, a hundred or so klicks out? That'll make 'em hard to spot. There's plenty of helium in their maneuvering packages."

"Sounds good," Ki said. "You have my authorization to make it so." He tapped in his launch codes and glanced at the monitor.

Bogey-three had rotated its stern toward them and now glowed with a blue-white light as it approached. It was their last view of it as they slipped behind the Earth.

CHAPTER SIXTY-SEVEN

"Mata ChaLik, it will take one orbit to catch up with the savages' satellite. Then we can deal with the last of these dry-land vermin who dare to leave their planet," said KaLik.

"Be sure you destroy them," Mata ChaLik said. "I will contact you later." The Bird-of-War would be out of communication as it slipped behind the planet.

KaLik scanned the immediate volume of space before them and detected a number of small items. He remembered this planet had many dead satellites and other near-planet junk in orbit. The largest was the orbiting spacecraft.

Just junk, he thought.

A half sleep period later, when the orbiting spacecraft emerged from behind the planet, it shone a laser at them continuously. The power was low and did no harm to the Bird-of-War's armor. It was obviously some kind of communication signal, so he ignored it.

As they drew near the orbiting spacecraft, KaLik realized it was larger than the previous craft they had encountered. It had an unfamiliar configuration with two long, tapered cylinders joined by a column at the middle.

How, he wondered. *Were they able to build so many spacecraft in such a short period of time with so few resources? Did we underestimate them?*

"Huta Kah DaBuk, arm the beam weapons," KaLik said. With the Bird-of-War's reduced velocity to orbit around the planet. They were about to over-take the orbiting spacecraft. "Divert all power to weapons. Destroy the target."

The beam lashed out repeatedly, touching the odd-shaped craft. Each time the beam touched it, it sparkled brightly. Jets of gas briefly appeared and shiny flakes exfoliated off.

KaLik wondered if it would fight back.

The computer squawked a warning. Something had come within range of the sensors, something from behind them.

KaLik scanned the instruments and touched a control. The viewscreen changed abruptly to the rear view. It showed the blackness of space, sprinkled with the hard brilliance of many bright stars. He touched the controls again to enhance the image. The field of stars grew brighter. In the middle, one point of light brightened quickly. Something was closing fast.

"Huta Kah DaBuk, divert the weapons to automatic defense. Something approaches from our rear."

The object's velocity appeared on the screen. It was moving fast, very fast.

"What?" Huta asked.

"The object in the center of the viewscreen is attacking us." KaLik scanned the object. For a moment, he had the strange feeling he had seen it before. He glanced at his combat officer.

Huta worked at his usual pace, powering down the manual aiming system before turning on the automatics.

"Huta Kah DaBuk. Destroy the incoming missile. Impact time is imminent," KaLik screamed. He felt cornered and served by a mud-bound idiot. He glanced at the viewscreen. He recognized the petal-like protrusions on the front of the approaching object.

It was the second craft they'd attacked. He reached to activate the fusion drive.

CHAPTER SIXTY-EIGHT

"Are you sure you've made contact with the platform?" Ki asked. It was the second time he'd asked the radio operator the same question. The control room was crowded and the air had grown stuffy. *Damn ventilation system works better under gravity*, he thought.

"Yes, sir. Even without an antenna, I'm getting a signal from it. Not much of a signal, but we confirmed it on the oscilloscope."

"Does it still function?"

"The signal is too weak to monitor its operations. But we can send it commands," the operator said.

"Okay, get it moving. We've got enough data on bogey-three to plot its course. You know what's needed. Let me know when you've got enough feedback to tell if it's going to work." Ki was worried, no, frightened. The missile group had plotted the intersection points for their missiles with the Qu'uda ship. They'd have very high relative velocities and low probabilities of hitting their target unless they waited until the Qu'uda ship got closer. The problem was, in the clarity of space that was too close for comfort. A three hundred-kiloton nuke generated a lot of radiant energy—too much when it was that close. And several dozen would be way too much, even for a submarine's thick hull.

"Sir," the radio operator said. "I'm not yet positive, but the data show it's responding."

Ki felt a bleak ray of hope. *If this doesn't work, I'll launch the damn missiles, I have to. If it has to be done, I'll do it.*

"Lemme know when you've got a fix on it." He knew their chances of surviving the nukes' radiation were slim to nil. He felt a weariness unlike anything he had ever experienced before.

Damn, he thought. *I'm getting too old for this.*

Time dragged by. The space station slipped behind Earth and out of contact with the approaching spacecraft.

There wasn't anything Ki could do but wait six hours for them to arrive. There was nothing to be achieved in the control center. He went to his cabin where he lay down to rest. Somehow, he fell into an uneasy sleep.

ॐ

"... Captain Mapes, wake up, Captain Mapes."

Ki woke from a dream about his long-absent family. On the ceiling, directly above his bunk, was a picture of his wife. "LaTasha, baby, I'm coming home. I promise," he said. He closed his eyes for a second.

When he opened them, a bulb of ersatz coffee was under his nose. He missed the aroma of real coffee as he took his first sip. His cabin, cramped and austere, was all metal except for tattered foam padding on the sharp edges and corners. He swung out of the bunk and floated over to his desk.

"Sir, we estimate about fifty-five minutes until bogey-three is in range." The ensign hesitated. "We debated letting you sleep longer. We know you could use more rest."

"What about the platform?"

Ki sucked on the coffee. *God, this is a bad imitation of natural coffee. Maybe one of these days we'll have the real thing again.*

The ensign's voice brought him back, "Sir, it's on its way."

"What about its course?" Ki asked.

A trace of a frown crossed the ensign's face before he answered. "Sir, one of the missile people focused a communication laser on bogey-three and instructed the platform to home-in on its frequency. Seems to be working."

"Are you sure that it's not just coming home to momma?"

"The missile boys say not. Something about using both the bogey's IR signature combined with the laser reflection. That guarantees it's aimed at bogey-three, not us. The optics tech says it's heading right up the ass-end of bogey-three, if you'll excuse the expression, sir." The ensign flushed slightly. "Its drive is on full power. The final velocity differential will be at least three klicks per second. If it arrives in time."

Ki grabbed his gear and headed for the control room.

It was countdown time.

ʔ

The pace of operations had picked up and the control room was crowded. The radar operators set up several sets of antennae as back-ups for the primary system. They were ready.

A series of thuds vibrated through the station.

"Bogey-three just opened fire on us."

Lights flashed red on a control panel. More thuds and then silence. "Unit one is holed. No damage to unit two. Airlocks between units holding. Range ten klicks. Bogey-three closing at point one klicks per second."

"Where's the platform?" Ki asked.

"We don't know, sir. We lost our radar."

Another voice chimed in. "Laser's out."

"Deploying backup systems," a high-pitched voice called out.

More thuds vibrated the station. Another red light appeared on the status board. Somewhere a klaxon brayed. A breeze started blowing. A heavy metal door slammed shut.

"Unit two holed," came a voice over the intercom. "Leak located in forward torpedo bay."

"Releasing bubble-pack," came a higher-pitched voice over the intercom.

A bubble-pack was a mixture of expanded styrofoam crumbs, plastic peanuts, and foam balls that functioned as an emergency stop-leak.

"Leak under control."

"We have casualties in unit two. We need corpsmen, now."

"Pressure still dropping. Release more bubble-pack."

"Let's go visual," Ki called. "Unfold another camera."

"Done," the optic technician's voice called over the noise.

The thudding sounds started again.

"Two more leaks in forward torpedo bay."

"We have a leak in the missile section. It's a big one. God dammit, we need a patch...." Voices rattled over the intercom. Several more thuds. Somewhere, someone started screaming. More joined in to make a chorus of screams.

"Corpsmen. We need corpsmen. Goddammit, send the corpsmen, we've got casualties."

"Send over more bubble packs. We can't stop the leak."

Ki bit his lip and listened without comment. They knew what they were doing. They didn't need his orders. And they had every motivation to get it right.

If they don't make it, we'll die trying. He floated over to the optics section and stared over the technician's shoulder.

The optic technician tapped some keys and the large viewscreen came to life. It showed the blackness of space. Something was in the center, growing steadily larger.

"Will the platform get here?" Ki held his breath. "Do I have to launch the missiles?"

The course of bogey-three would take it past the station; soon they'd lose the shielding provided by Unit One. *Dear Lord, please don't be late.*

Red status lights flashed urgently.

"I don't know, sir. It'll be close."

No one spoke as Ki's hand crept closer to the red launch button. He hesitated.

All eyes turned to stare at the large viewscreen. It showed bogey-three, now a triangular shape. It was the Qu'uda ship. Its slabby, gray delta shape grew big on the monitor. Beams of energy flashed from the tips of its wings. Each time, something slammed the station hard.

From behind, a dark shape appeared, approaching it. It was a shape that grew large, very fast. It was the first-contact platform, battered and torn, but right on course.

"Hot damn, it arrived." Ki punched the air.

The screen flashed brightly.

The Qu'uda ship disappeared.

"Find out where it is, like now," Ki said.

"Sir," a new voice called. "Aft radar shows bogey-three and the platform on re-entry courses."

"Get it on visual," Ki said. He slipped the cover over the red launch button.

Two black objects appeared against the blues and whites of Earth, tumbling and getting smaller and smaller. In minutes, they started to glow and then flared brightly all the way down.

CHAPTER SIXTY-NINE

"KaLik DuGan," Mata ChaLik BuMaru called. "Answer me."

There was no response.

Mata ChaLik activated a circuit to trace the Bird-of-War.

Nothing, he thought, even after several tries. *I fear I will not hear from him again. Now I must deal with those savages.*

While Mata ChaLik felt safe from the weapons of the planet's dry-land vermin, the memories of the first visit lingered. *I will not go close to the planet. How did these primitives, who live in such squalor, get into space?*

"Set the course for a high orbit about the planet," Mata ChaLik said. He felt a vibration as the drive came to life. *Our beam weapons on the Little-Egg-that-Flies shall overwhelm their defenses*, he thought. *Even if they use projectile weapons, we are safe behind the ship's thick metallic skin.*

"Prepare the beam weapons. It is time to seek out the Earth savages. We shall destroy their spacecraft," Mata ChaLik said. "Activate all sensors, including active scanning."

ꙮ

"Sir, the big sucker, the asteroid, has changed course," said a voice on the intercom. "I mean bogey-two. It's now heading toward

Earth." The voice had gone up in pitch. "Approaching at two klicks per second with negative delta-vee."

Ki Mapes swallowed hard. "Radar, give me its course." His monitor flickered and displayed its heading. "What's it up to?"

"Sir, it could be a high orbit or a LaGrange point."

"Berkowitz," Ki called, his voice sharp and loud.

"Yes, sir," Berkowitz answered in his soft Texan drawl.

"Prepare a Big Boy for a strike against bogey-two. Target deflection mode," Ki said. *Half my crew is injured and there are eighteen dead. I want to smash those alien sunnavabitchin' bastards....* He tasted sweat on his upper lip.

"One Big Boy ready and waiting." Berkowitz's voice held a slight quaver. The Big Boy missile carried the eight nukes of 350 kilotons yield each normally found in a Trident's payload, all wired to explode simultaneously.

"Launch when ready."

"... three-two-one. We have ignition. Missile underway. It's tracking hot and true," Berkowitz's voice crackled over the intercom.

"On visual," Ki said.

"Yes, sir," the optics technician replied.

The missile appeared on the monitor's screen as a tiny sliver that rode on a bright spot of flame leaving a white trail clearly visible in the brilliant sunlight. Without gravity to hold it back, the rocket accelerated rapidly.

"They will see it coming," Cha KinLaat said. "They will destroy it before it reaches them."

The rocket engine's flame flickered out. The missile disappeared amid the stars.

The control room became silent, expectant. The backdrop hum of air circulating and the occasional chirp of automated equipment seemed loud as the crew held its collective breath.

A speck of light blossomed into a brief, brilliant existence, then faded from view.

"Damn," came a voice from the intercom. "Our missile got wasted before target acquisition." The voice hesitated for a moment. "Sir."

"It is a beam weapon of the collision defense," Cha KinLaat said. "It destroys anything that will strike the ship."

Ki turned toward the Qu'uda. He leaned back in his chair and put his hands behind his head. "Okay, Cha KinLaat, exactly how does it detect oncoming objects?" His jaw muscles worked. Lines creased his normally smooth face.

"Several ways. It uses something similar to your radar and it looks for heat, also." Cha KinLaat flexed her hands. Claws extended and retracted.

"Do they have to aim the beam?" Ki rubbed his bald head.

"No, it is under the control of an artificial intelligence, a biocomputer. The system wakes up when the sensors see something on collision course for the ship. The range of the beam is ..." she said. "In your terms, more than twenty kilometers."

"Berkowitz."

"Yes, sir?"

"How close d'you have to get a Big Boy to that ship out there to deflect it?" Ki demanded.

Lines furrowed Berkowitz's forehead and his eyes squinted momentarily. "Point eight-five klicks."

Ki stared at him, puzzled.

"Within point eight-five klicks, surface heating generates sufficient secondary thrust for deflection. The effect diminishes at the rate of the square of the distance. So, at two klicks, it would have one-quarter the effect as at one klick. Is that what y'all wanted to know?" Berkowitz asked.

"How about a single warhead?"

"Three and fifty hundred kilotons? Lemme see ..." Seconds ticked by. "Um, about three-tenths of a klick." Berkowitz sounded subdued.

"That close? I was afraid of that," Ki said. "Okay, listen up, this's what we're going to do." He sketched his idea on a piece of paper. The control center crew stared over his shoulder. One by one they nodded.

"That might work." Cha KinLaat wobbled her head crest.

"Okay. Let's do it."

Earlier, twenty-three Trident missiles had moved away from the space station in a radial pattern, driven by jets of helium from their maneuvering packages. The missiles were a thousand kilometers away from the station, parked in a circle at right angles to the course of the approaching alien ship. They continued to drift outward, maintaining their circular formation.

"Do we have sufficient angular separation?" Ki asked.

"Maybe." Berkowitz's voice was tentative. "I'd like a little more," he said. "It won't take long now. Bogey-two's close enough to make a contribution."

"Are you computing a course solution?"

"The trajectories? Continual updates."

Ki stared at the monitor. *Damn, it's big.*

Even though bogey-two was twenty thousand kilometers away, the telescope revealed its surface details. It no longer looked like an errant asteroid as it continued to approach. Though the front had the rough appearance of rock, it was clear that it was attached to some kind of shiny metallic structure. Small projections on the surface were barely visible. The scale at the bottom of the screen indicated that the alien craft was about five hundred feet in diameter.

"Attention please," Ki spoke into the microphone. "We're about to engage bogey-two. Secure all systems. Remember, we will never surrender. I expect you to do your best for this boat ... space station, and Earth. God bless you all." He put down the microphone.

Ki picked up a handset. "Berkowitz," he said. "Ready?"

"Aye, aye, sir."

"Optics," Ki called. "Gimme the big picture."

"Yes, sir."

The image on the monitor shrank until the alien craft was barely visible among the stars, seemingly motionless.

Simultaneously, a tenuous ring of tiny fingers of flame flickered into existence over a wide area as the missiles came to life. Each missile carried eight Maneuvering Re-entry Vehicle warheads. The missiles accelerated toward the alien craft until their rocket engines extinguished.

"Radar," Ki called, "Active scanning."

I hope this works, he thought. *No need to hide our presence now.*

A monitor glowed into life to show the image on the radar screen. Each of the twenty-three luminous dots simultaneously split into eight tiny traces, each diverged from the original course of its parent. Each missile had launched eight separate MARVs at the alien craft, each aimed at a different part of the oncoming alien ship.

On the visual monitor, something flashed brightly from the front surface the alien craft. A tiny trace glowed into luminosity like a firefly and disappeared. More flashes appeared. More fireflies flashed and vanished. The front of the approaching craft began to flicker almost continuously with flashes. The volume of space before it began to sparkle with multiple points of bright light. The cloud of fireflies descended closer and closer to the asteroid ship.

Shit, Ki thought. *It's going to kill every warhead.*

A point of light expanded and filled the visual monitor with monstrous brightness, lighting up the interior of command center before fading into blackness. The radar image dissolved into a hash of bright lines that faded into blankness.

"What happened?" Ki said.

"We got him," Berkowitz yelled. "We got the bastard with at least two nukes, maybe more. They must've got within three hundred meters."

"I want visual and radar, now," Ki called.

"One moment," came a female voice. It was the optics technician. "I've got to bring a spare photomultiplier online."

"Radar's gonna take a couple of minutes," a voice called. "One of the electronics' modules got deep fried. We took some serious radiation."

"I need to know what's going on," Ki said. He stared at the blank monitor used for the visual display.

It flickered. A sea of stars came into focus. The field of vision moved and contracted as the telescope zoomed in on something. It was the alien craft.

It looks different, Ki thought. *Smoother, not as rough-textured on the front.* "What's its course?" he asked.

"Er, don't have a good fix on its bearing yet," said a young male voice. "It's different than before. Doesn't look like it's on an orbit insertion trajectory. Its velocity is slightly different, too."

Ki stared as the image swam closer. The front surface of the alien craft was not only smoother, it was flatter. Took off an entire layer, along with all those nasty weapons.

"Berkowitz," Ki called. "I think your birds did the trick. Well done."

"Yes, sir, thank you, sir." Berkowitz sounded happy.

Ki turned to Cy Belasario. "Time to get the shuttle going." He picked up the microphone. "Boarding crew, report to the shuttle, immediately."

Now, he thought. *Let's see if we can capture that big sucker.*

CHAPTER SEVENTY

Ki watched the shuttle rotate and descend tail-first as it approached the front of the alien ship, decelerating to match velocities. The delta-winged craft appeared toy-like against the mass of the asteroid ship as it sank toward its surface.

"Captain Mapes," came the deep, sonorous voice of Cha KinLaat DoMar. "All the beam weapons on the front of the Qu'uda ship are destroyed, along with its docking entrance. We shall try the drive service access hatch at the rear of the ship."

"Okay," Ki said. "We'll let you know if we see any signs of activity. The Qu'uda ship's new course is taking it away from Earth. No detailed analysis yet as to where it might end up. Remember you've only got fuel and oxygen for thirty-six hours."

"Thank you, Captain Mapes," Cha KinLaat said. "We have access hatch in sight. I will join the boarding party."

"Good luck." Ki glanced at the technicians manning the monitoring equipment. "Any change?"

Heads shook. "No, sir."

ᘒ

Mata ChaLik felt awful. One of his limbs was broken and throbbed most painfully. He'd tried to protect himself as he slammed into a bulkhead. *It was difficult to see out of one eye.*

He touched his face. It was bleeding. Dim orange emergency lights showed silent bodies in awkward positions. The navigator lay crumpled against the bulkhead, quite dead.

The pain eased. *Must be that my biocomputer started the pain deadeners.* He found the situation appeared as though it were an impersonal recording.

Mata ChaLik touched the controls. The power level indicators showed all systems in emergency shutdown. The Little-Egg-that-Flies had only standby power. He couldn't find the energy to go through start-up. He activated the viewscreen and it flickered into life. He scrolled through the external sensors. Though few responded, none showed a forward view. He turned it off. The pain deadeners made reality distant; he needed rest. He gave up. There was nothing he could do. The last thing he remembered was lying down on the floor.

ᘓ

Mata ChaLik BuMaru felt a sharp pain.

A distant voice spoke. "... Ah, so you are alive," it said. "Good, I'll make you sorry you did not die."

Another sharp pain produced a rush of stimulation. Mata ChaLik opened his eyes. He saw a face he had not seen in many years. It was his former mating partner. "Cha KinLaat DoMar, what are you doing here?"

This cannot be, for she is guarding the eggs, or wrigglers, whichever, on the planet of the savages. She can't be here. His head felt like it was full of swamp-mud and his limb throbbed with insistent pain.

"I've waited a long time for this, Mata ChaLik. You see I didn't die. I survived with the help of the Earth savages. They took me in and I learned their ways, their savage ways. Now I know eight squared ways to kill you, all slow and quite painful."

Through his fog, Mata ChaLik felt a claw of fear touch him.

"I'm going to enjoy this. I've savored the thought of doing this for a long time—"

"Before you kill him, Cha KinLaat, he must tell us how to bring this ship back to life." It was MinCha DuKaat. "We have but a few hours to secure it, or abandon it."

Cha KinLaat looked up. "Yes, saving this ship comes first. And then ..." She wobbled her headcrest.

The boarding party on the space shuttle had expected resistance. They found the asteroid ship had only a skeleton crew, which apparently had been crippled by the shock from the nuclear bombs. They found dazed Qu'uda throughout the ship who had no fight left in them. There were many dead. The humans in the boarding party had come to take the Little-Egg-that-Flies as a prize; their Qu'uda allies wanted the crew.

"Mata ChaLik," MinCha DuKaat asked. "Refresh my memory on how to activate the fusion drive."

Mata ChaLik looked at him and then at Cha KinLaat behind him. He said nothing.

"It will be easier if you tell me. If I have to reason it out for myself, I will not have time to restrain Cha KinLaat," MinCha DuKaat said softly.

Mata ChaLik looked at the glowering Cha KinLaat, who flexed his claws. It was an easy decision.

"First," he said. "Make sure all power systems are locked out. Channel all power circuits to the emergency control center over there, behind the panel marked with a star." He pointed. "Run a test sequence on the fusion reactor's primary ignition system." He took them through the cold start-up sequence step by step.

It took several hours to restore the Little-Egg-that-Flies to life. Once they lit the fusion drive, they changed the ship's course and brought it to a halt at the LaGrange point above the Earth.

CHAPTER SEVENTY-ONE

"Look, you see how these sequences fit together? It's like they're trying to show us how their language is structured."

Ken Ulrich was a tall, bearded linguist from the University of Nevada who had been brought to the command center at Bangor. The recordings from the alien ship had been released to him. He almost jumped up and down with excitement. The sequence of messages, combined with other data transmitted from the Hooley ship, fascinated him. "Maybe I can figure it out."

"Okay, what does it say?" Taylor asked.

"Well, it's not something I can do instantly," Ulrich said, eyebrows raised. "It may take some time. This isn't Sanskrit, y'know. The mathematics will be dead easy. Then the physical substances should fall out of the linguistic analysis. However, understanding what they really mean will be more difficult. There are cultural differences, of course." He stroked his snow-white beard and said, "I'm guessing, but I think these Hooley people want something." He looked at Taylor over the top of a pair of glasses held together with a piece of wire from a paper clip and artfully tied thread.

"Really? Why's that?"

"Well, if they didn't, why did they come?"

"Don't know." Taylor looked away, as though staring at a distant object. "Better question is where did they come from? They don't seem to have any fuel tanks of any size, so their home base must be nearby. Or, maybe they dropped their fuel tanks. They also lost a lot of water and atmosphere." He shrugged. "Tell me what they're saying and we'll both know."

"I wish I could. We may need direct contact." Ulrich frowned. "You know, sit down with them and hold up items to establish a common frame of reference, and so forth."

"That's easier said than done. The Qu'uda attacked these aliens without warning. Then they witnessed us zap the asteroid ship with nukes. If I were in their shoes, I'd be damn cautious about who or what I let get near me. Hell, if it were me, I'd try to leave as quickly as possible. So, why haven't they left?" Taylor paused and scratched his head. "Let me know if you need anything to develop communications."

"You know ..." Ulrich grabbed Taylor's arm to prevent him from leaving. "If we send them something, that may help us get started with communications. Send them something that is universal, something basic and useful."

"Such as?" Taylor stared at the linguist.

"Oh, you know, the basics of life." Ulrich waved his hands. "Food, water, etcetera, you know, things that everybody needs."

"Scratch the food. Hell, we don't know if they're oxygen breathers or even carbon based. Forget about them metabolizing the same proteins and vitamins as us. That leaves just water. Is that a possibility?"

"Well, water could be a start." Ulrich nodded.

"You really want to try this?"

"Er, yes," Ulrich said. "Y'know, it's nice you take my suggestions seriously." A trace of blush touched his cheeks.

"I'll contact the space station," Taylor said.

"That could give us confirmation about what we think we know about their language," Ulrich said.

༈

"So you want me to send water to these Hooley-guys?" Ki felt his stomach wobble.

"Yeah, send them enough so they'll notice it, a full bladder. We'll replace it on the next supply run." Taylor's voice was breaking up in the radio transmission.

"Okay, we'll ship them the water, somehow." Ki already knew he would not let his shuttle get close to the alien ship. It was their only link with the surface. There was a lot of damage that had to be repaired for which he needed material and workers.

"We'll let you know when it's underway."

"Add lights and other stuff to make it highly visible," Taylor said. "We want them to see it coming. Okay?"

"Got it."

༞

The space station's crew watched the shuttle head toward the alien ship with a tank that contained a one thousand-liter bladder of water. They had added a video monitor and receiver to the tank, along with a gas maneuvering package. Perched on the tank was a video camera and transmitter to provide feedback.

"Velocity down to thirty meters per second. Range approximately ten klicks. Detaching tank. We have separation. Starting negative delta-vee now. The tank is tracking true." Bud Inez, the pilot, spoke quietly into the mike.

Brightly flashing lights on the stubby gray tank faded as it retreated from the shuttle.

"Reversing course." The relief in Bud's voice was audible. "We're coming back."

The image transmitted from the tank on the video monitor clearly showed the aliens' ship getting bigger and bigger.

"Maneuvering package braking at one hundred percent. Deceleration is according to plan," Bud said in a loud voice.

It wasn't necessary; data transmitted from the tank also reached the space station and relayed to Earth.

༞

Taylor stared at the fuzzy image in the monitor. It showed the cylinder-stem shape of the Hooley-alien spacecraft in harsh blacks and whites. The image slowly expanded as the water vessel drew closer. No lights showed on the alien craft; nothing moved.

"Starting instruction program," said a voice Taylor didn't recognize.

It was a picture sequence on a monitor showing how to operate the bladder's valve and finished with liquid discharging from a nozzle. The recorder would repeat the instructions until its batteries went dead.

The Hooley-alien craft filled the screen. As the tank craft drifted closer, details of the surface became clear. It had markings that looked like ports or doors, along with lines of metal steps or a ladder. Welded seams and patches made two large bands around the alien ship. The apparent motion between the two craft ceased. Nothing. Time ticked by slowly.

Something moved in the corner of the screen. The image jerked to the center of the screen and grew larger. A door opened revealing a cavity illuminated from within by dim orange light.

The image zoomed closer. It was a box with a long arm. Behind it was something bulky and dark. The box drifted out of the door directly toward the tank, growing large in the screen until it blocked out everything else. The image shrank.

Taylor stared hard at the dark bulky mass. It resolved into a long shape with ... Six appendages.

"Do you see that?"

"Ah, the guy with too many legs?" Ki's voice crackled from the speaker. "Yeah, I see it. I don't want to believe it."

The image in the screen shook and vibrated. It was obvious something was examining the tank closely.

The image began to move.

"They're taking it to the ship," a voice said.

"Just like a big lunker taking a plastic worm," Ki said softly.

The image moved through the door into a cubical chamber dimly illuminated by orange-red lights. The creature appeared. It was in a suit made of a silvery fabric or flexible material with an elongated helmet with a shiny gold coating. The creature stood motionless before the image, stooped low.

"Pressure has gone up, along with temperature," said a voice. "I think it must be an airlock. They probably closed the outside door."

"Do we have any gas analyzers on the annulus between the tank and the bladder?" Taylor asked.

"No," Ki said. "We didn't have any on hand suitable for deep space service."

"I think it just took a sample," a voice said.

The creature moved to a door that slid open, disappeared through it, and the door closed.

Nothing happened for almost an hour. The door reopened and the creature reappeared, pulling a hose, then stooped before the tank for several minutes.

"Ah, they're draining the bladder," said a voice. "Fast."

Four minutes later, the creature withdrew the hose and backed away from the tank, still holding the end of the hose. The creature disappeared through the door that then closed.

"The bladder's empty," the voice said.

"I wonder if they closed the valve?" Taylor asked.

"Yes, sir, it's closed," said the same voice.

The door slid open again and the creature reappeared carrying a small rectangular container. It approached the tank and then vanished from the view of the monitor's camera. Moments later, the tank began to move.

"They're putting it outside," said the voice.

The image showed the tank's retreat through the airlock door. The creature reentered the airlock and the door slid shut. Once again, the alien craft was dark, motionless and without light.

"We're getting a Hooley transmission," a different voice broke in. "I'm putting it on audio."

The now-familiar bird-twitter sound came from the speaker. It lasted for only ninety seconds and ended with "Hooley."

"The Hooley ship is moving," a voice said loudly. "It's rotating and accelerating."

The image on the monitor vanished to be replaced by another showing a faint and fuzzy outline of the alien ship. A pale blue glow grew from the petal-like pods at the end of the long stem. The ship began to move, accelerate.

"What's its heading?" Taylor asked.

"Ah, looks like it's away from the center of the system," a voice said. "Maybe on a course toward Saturn. Definitely not toward the space station or Earth—"

"Bud, get the shuttle moving and retrieve the tank," Ki said. "They put something on it. We need to see what it is."

"Captain Mapes," said Bud Inez. "What if it's some kind of bomb? Like a satchel nuke?"

There was a long silence. "Well," Ki said. "Figure something out. We gotta retrieve it. I don't believe they'd put it on the tank to blow it up. I'd bet on that."

"All right." Bud sounded deflated.

Ki put an edge to his voice. "That's an order. We need to know what those aliens left us, but be careful. Tow it in on a line. Have someone examine it. Check it with a Geiger counter. Whatever."

CHAPTER SEVENTY-TWO

"DalChik DuJuga."

"Yes?" DalChik recognized the navigator's voice. It distracted her from her search for additional asteroids, which were far and few between in the outer reaches of this system. She recalled the navigator had the responsibility to monitor the system while the Egg-that-Flies orbited a tiny gas world that was the outermost of the system's planets.

"Something strange happened. I detected an EMP."

"From a thermonuclear explosion?"

"Yes, it was near the position from where the Little-Egg-that-Flies last reported."

DalChik touched a control. A holographic image relayed from the navigator's station; the Egg-that-Flies appeared in front of her. She examined the image of the inner portion of the star system and the first four planets. A pulsing spot of green light indicated the origin of the EMP. It was very close to the third planet.

౭

"Something is coming from the third planet," the radar operator said. "It looks like a ship is heading in our direction."

"Enhance," DalChik said.

The size of the inner planets grew. Two faint yellow spots

appeared. One had a red vector line that extended from the vicinity of the third planet. The second yellow spot hung stationary, close to the planet, with a tiny green icon.

"What is that?" DalChik asked. "That which moves?"

"I don't know," said the navigator. "Its course will bring it near us. It could be the Little-Egg-that-Flies. Perhaps we should hail it—"

"No," said DalChik. "Not until we are certain. There is another spacecraft, near the third planet. Which is the Little-Egg-that-Flies? What is the other?"

"I cannot answer that question," the navigator said. "Not until it gets closer."

"Let us remain still and quiet until we know," she said.

↷

"Well, Ulrich, what does the last message from the Hooley-aliens mean?" Taylor asked. He ran his hands over three-day old stubble. He felt as though he hadn't slept in a week.

The long table in the center of the Quonset hut was covered with papers and file folders. The Defense Council had met to review the events of the past week, and in particular, what to do about the second alien species.

Ulrich stroked his beard with a blue-veined hand and frowned. "Well," he said. "Because of the items they left behind, I think they're saying they'll return." His frown intensified. "The last part of their message is puzzling. It seems like some kind of action verb, that they'll do something on their return." He sighed. "I wish I had more things to understand their culture, it'd make it easier." He had bags under his eyes and a nervous twitch at the corner of his mouth.

Taylor glanced at the other Defense Council members.

"D'you think it was a threat?" Carver Washington asked.

"From the words themselves, I can't say. However, in the context of what happened, I'd be inclined to say no."

"You're sure about that?" Carver said.

"Well, no," Ulrich said. "This is a totally new language and culture to me. It takes time to work these things out."

"What about the second item?" Taylor asked.

"Ah, yes." Ulrich pointed to the stack of thin metal sheets strung on four pieces of flexible wire between two plaques of engraved metal end plates. Each plate showed a six-limbed creature surrounded by something that looked like vegetation and insects. The metal had a sheen as though it were old and had been handled extensively.

"It's a long document, perhaps a history of their species." Ulrich pursed his lips. "There are sixty-four sheets and each one is covered on both sides with patterns of glyphs. I'm beginning to get a handle on the glyphs they use. One word is repeated throughout the document. If they're a religious species, I suspect that it is their word for God."

"And the basis of their religion?" Taylor asked.

"Well," Ulrich huffed, "it's a little soon to say—"

"Speculate," Taylor said forcefully.

Ulrich took a deep breath. "It may be ..." he hesitated. "This word may be the same word we've heard them utter so often, the Hooley-sound. That may be the name of their god."

"How would it be used?"

"Perhaps as a blessing ..." Ulrich pursed his lips. "Then again, if they're not religious ... The Hooley-sound might just be a meaningless greeting." He spread his hands. "I need more time with this and the recordings of all their sounds."

"What if the Hooley-sound is a challenge?" Washington asked. "An aggressive or domineering species?"

"Oh, I don't think they are," Ulrich said. "They didn't make any aggressive moves."

"True," said Taylor. "Then again, after the Qu'uda hammered them and blew away their shuttle craft, they might not have had much fight left in them."

"That doesn't seem reasonable," Ulrich said. "What about their laser—"

"True," said Taylor. "It's our duty to be suspicious. If they were friendly, why didn't they stick around to figure out how to communicate with us? Where're they going in a craft with such tiny fuel tanks?"

"Er, Mr. MacPherson," a tinny voice came from a speaker. "This is the space station. We've been tracking the Hooley-alien craft. It has started to decelerate. It doesn't look like the Kuiper belt anymore. Its course will take it near Pluto."

"Keep your eye on it. We need to know where its base is." Taylor turned toward Ulrich. "Keep working on the translations. We must find out what they said." He pointed at MinCha DuKaat. "What did you find out about the Egg-that-Flies?"

The short alien bobbed her head crest. "The remaining crew of the Little-Egg-that-Flies told us much. Cha KinLaat was very persuasive."

Yeah, I bet she was, Taylor thought.

Stories of Cha KinLaat raging through the captured ship had spread quickly. She had to be kept away from Mata ChaLik.

"What did you find out?"

"Another center formed with DalChik DuJuga at its hub. That center wishes to return to Qu'uda. They do not want to return to Earth. We found the Egg-that-Flies' location in the navigation computer. It's very close to the course of other alien craft. I think we should warn them...."

"What?" Taylor jumped up and knocked his chair over in the process. "They're meeting?"

"I do not think so. Only DalChik on the Egg-that-Flies can answer that," said MinCha.

"Should we contact them?" Taylor took a deep breath and looked at the people before him. "What d'you think?"

"Perhaps. She trained me and knows me well. We shared much time together. We bear no ill-will toward each other."

"I think we ought to find out where this Hooley-alien ship's going, and damn soon," Carver said. "An' find out just where the Qu'uda mother ship is. We need to keep an eye on 'em just in case they decide to come a-calling on us. No surprises."

"That wasn't my question," Taylor said. "Shall we contact the Qu'uda ship? I'm inclined to contact them."

"We should be able to beat them if it comes to a fight." Ki's voice came from the speaker. "Especially since we've now got two space stations above Earth."

"True," Carver said. "An' we've dealt with the war-like faction among the Qu'uda already. I say contact 'em."

"Well?" Taylor stared at the rows of faces.

Heads nodded slowly.

Taylor turned toward MinCha. "I guess that means you can call Dal-, Dal-, whatever her name is."

"DalChik DuJuga." MinCha's voice rolled her name out in deep, sonorous tones. "I will tell her what has happened. I shall warn her of the approach of the alien ship."

"Advise her to watch, but not interfere. We need to know where their base is."

♪

"DalChik."

"Yes?" She eased from her resting nest.

"I have received a laser message from MinCha DuKaat."

"Ah," DalChik said. "Then Mata ChaLik has rescued her from the surface of the savages' planet. How are the wrigglers?" Her egg had been among those sent to the surface.

"You should listen to the message. MinCha has become male again. He says he has joined with the dry-land vermin. They captured Mata ChaLik and his Defenders who suffered many casualties in a battle with the savages from the third planet—"

"What is this?" DalChik's headcrest engorged. "Transfer the message to me immediately." She heard a squeal from the comm-net and the familiar popping sound as the message opened.

"... from the third planet, this is MinCha DuKaat."

Yes, thought DalChik. *It does sound like him.*

"... were rescued by Bilik Pudjata-"

Bilik Pudjata lives? DalChik thought. *How can that be?*

"... the people of the third planet made us part of their circle and honored us. They saved our lives and those of our wrigglers—"

What? DalChik thought. *The savages saved our wrigglers?*

"... They treat us with respect, even kindness. They only wish to defend their home against the threats uttered by Mata ChaLik BuMaru—"

Mata ChaLik, DalChik thought. *Always seeking to use the claw of violence to solve every problem.*

"... the people of the third planet do not wish to bring war to you or Qu'uda. Their violence is only directed at those who threaten them. You will not be harmed if you do not threaten them—"

I hope he is right, DalChik thought. *I hope he is not being forced to say these things.*

"... now, another threat has emerged, another alien species, different from the humans, the Hoo-Lii in a spacecraft—"

"Great Egg. That cannot be," DalChik said.

"... which is on a course that will bring it close to you, in the Egg-that-Flies. We do not know if it is hostile. However, it was attacked by a Bird-of-War from the Little-Egg-that-Flies, which damaged it—"

Ah, DalChik thought. *The Defender mentality and its reliance upon force.*

"... it has small fuel tanks and may have a base somewhere near you. We want to know where it is. We want you to watch where it goes. Observe it with all your instruments, for it is far different than any spacecraft we know.

"DalChik DuJuga, please contact us. I long to hear your voice again. I have much to tell you, among which is that your little wriggler lives and thrives."

My wriggler is alive and well. DalChik lowered her head and gave silent thanks that her progeny had survived.

She raised her head and opened the comm-net. "Attention," she said, addressing the crew. "Secure the Egg-that-Flies for combat. An alien craft approaches. Its course will bring it near to us."

༚

DalChik stared at the holo image. The red line carried symbols indicating the alien ship was slowing. *Its course does bring it near, but not so near as to meet with us,* she thought. *Does it know we are here?*

"Lock all passive sensors on approaching craft," DalChik said. "Seal all internal passageways." She feared, no felt, attack was imminent. *We must take every precaution.*

The symbols in the holo image flashed to show change in status. The red line began to curve away from them.

DalChik stared. *It is changing course ... It is turning away from us....* "Computer, display distance to moving object."

Another set of symbols materialized, glowing, yellow.

Beyond range for even a fusion pumped laser, she thought. *What is it doing? Where is it going?*

The alien craft continued to reduce velocity as it changed course. The distance between it and the Egg-that-Flies increased as the alien craft's course straightened out.

"DalChik." The navigator's voice was filled with alarm. "My instruments show a gravitational anomaly in front of the alien craft." The navigator's voice quavered. "When I focus away from the alien craft, the anomaly is no longer there ..."

The holo image flickered.

"Great Egg." DalChik stared at the holo image. The alien craft was gone. It had disappeared. "What happened? Did it explode? Run a systems check, find out if there's a failure in the system. Go to optical backup."

"We have optical. It shows no trace of alien craft—"

"Run optical recordings up to point of disappearance." DalChik called. In the background, she heard voices rise and fall excitedly. Others had observed this strange happening.

"Recordings show a cubical structure appeared in the area around the alien craft, just prior to its disappearance—"

"DalChik," the navigator called. "The alien craft disappeared. It seemed to create a framework of luminous lines in that region of space. Then it went inside and was gone with a multi-colored splash of light...." The navigator sounded puzzled. "I need to look at other recordings," he said. "This doesn't seem possible."

"Computer," DalChik called. "Collect all data at the point the alien craft disappeared and show it on the holo-display."

Columns of data in red with sections highlighted in yellow replaced the image of the nearby planet. The change in values at the point of disappearance of the alien craft stood out.

There had been a massive distortion in space-time.

"This reminds me of what some theorists believe," came the voice of DuKlaat YataBu, the principal analyst for the Keepers-of-the-Egg. "An opening in space-time was postulated to allow faster-than-light travel—"

"Impossible," DalChik said quickly.

That dream had been pursued for years, a means to get off their crowded planet. That dream had faded. "They swam up that stream for many years and got nowhere."

"Nevertheless, my dear DalChik, the evidence is before us." His voice, often querulous with frustration of having no other theoretician to understand him, was rich with excitement. "Let me examine the data. Perhaps they will tell me something."

DalChik stared at the data. *We might have hailed that craft but for the warning from MinCha DuKaat, thinking it was the Little-Egg-that-Flies. We could have learned something from being close to them. Maybe we should contact them—*

"DalChik." It was the navigator. "There's still something odd about the place where that craft disappeared. It is a region with unusual gravity readings—"

"Transfer your observations to DuKlaat YataBu." DalChik said quickly. "This may be important." *Would DuKlaat be able to shed light on this? By himself? She knew that the old analyst needed the back and forth of intellectual debate to rise to his potential. Our ship does not have that....*

"Navigator, open a laser channel to MinCha DuKaat. It is time to talk with him."

ᘒ

"You're sure these data the Qu'uda sent are reliable?" Taylor frowned. "Absolutely sure?"

MinCha's voice rumbled from the speaker. He was part of the crew occupying the Little-Egg-that-Flies orbiting at a LaGrangian point. "Yes. She and I were close. There are so much data it would be hard to fabricate. They want to retrieve their wrigglers and then go home."

Taylor looked at Billy. "What d'you think?"

"If it were Mata ChaLik, I would doubt it. But DalChik DuJuga ..." Billy said. "I doubt she sends falsehoods."

"Our scientists have never seen anything like this," Taylor said. "It's not a black hole, but some other kind of gravity anomaly or construct into which the Hooley-aliens went. Not by accident, but deliberately. They postulate it might be an entrance or a shortcut through space-time. The emissions given off by the Hooley-craft give clues, but no answer as to how they did it. Or where they went. What now?"

"Sir?"

Taylor looked up. It was a messenger with an envelope. "Thanks," he said. He opened the letter. "Ulrich has confirmed his earlier translation. He's positive the Hooley-aliens said they will come back and do something to or for us." He looked up. "He's got an action word with an ambiguous meaning. They're coming back and there's only one way for them. Through the opening in space-time."

"Ulrich believes there's better than a fifty percent likelihood the action word is a threat."

"What're we going to do about it?" asked Carver.

"We're going wait for them," Taylor said. "We're going to be ready and waiting when they come back."

EPILOGUE

Even though it was a time of recovery, Taylor knew Earth faced an immense challenge. Once again aliens, this time the Hooley-aliens, were an unknown threat to humankind.

In addition, the existence of a mysterious rent in space-time was yet another challenge. Earth faced an unknown threat from an alien race with advanced technological prowess. For the immediate future, he focused on dealing with the Qu'uda.

The Qu'uda on the Egg-that-Flies came to Earth and got their offspring. By now, most of the wrigglers spoke English as well as their native tongue. They viewed humans the same as the three Qu'uda who took care of them; like adults only a little different. The majority of the wrigglers left Earth to join their parents on board the Egg-that-Flies.

A combined group of human and Qu'uda worked together to lift many tons of provisions and supplies to the Egg-that-Flies, along with a selection of items of human manufacture to replace those lost by the actions of the Defenders. Of special importance was the library, which showed the rich history of human civilization.

DuKlaat YataBu decided to stay behind on Earth to study the strange gravitational anomaly and learn more about these dry-land creatures called humans. Yi MigLeek DuKuul, who had never fully recovered from her ordeal on Andros and had strongly bonded with the wrigglers, chose to return to Qu'uda. The remaining Qu'uda—

Billy, MinCha, and Cha KinLaat—did not want to leave Earth, for it was now their home.

After six months of being in orbit about Earth, the Egg-that-Flies departed. It headed home with more Qu'uda on board than when it started. The message they carried from Earth was a request for peace with the Qu'uda.

Now, Taylor thought. *We have to prepare for the Hooley-aliens.*

DRAMATIS PERSONAE

(Major Characters denoted by *)

Clan Members

*Taylor MacPherson: First leader of the Clan.

*Billy Potato: Also known as Bilik Pudjata to the Deli Qu'uda. Highly modified and augmented. The former leader of the Fed, now the principal instructor in the University of High Technology.

*Joyce Vargas: University instructor and friend of Taylor MacPherson.

Kevin O'Neil: Engineer and construction boss for Greater Clan's projects.

Dr. Meltem Encirlik: A medical doctor trained in a pre-Collapse medical school.

*Joe Del Corso: 2nd son of Albert Del Corso.

*Tim Van Minh: Engineer specializing in electronics and communications; war injuries have left him crippled.

*Mrs. Noelle Sutton: Housekeeper to Taylor MacPherson.

*Charlie Ramsey: Elder, representing Horse People from the Oxbow.

*Jon Beach: Elder, representing the Between the Rivers District.

Sean Monahan: Elder, representing Indian Hill River Bottom District.

*Carver' Washington: Clan Elder.

*Todd Sinkton: Clan Horse Soldier, scout.

*Chris Kucinski: Commander in the Greater Clan army.

*Elroy Stanek: Military aide to Chris Kucinski.

Butch & Madeline Henderson: Astronomy instructors at the university.

*Ed Kerr: A leader of the Greater Clan's armed forces.

Slobodan Sabich, aka Sabich the Savage: a ruthless commander in the Greater Clan's armed forces.

FORMER U.S. MILITARY OFFICERS

Commander Malachi "Ki" Mapes: Captain of the Hampton (SSN 767), a Los Angeles class submarine.

Lieut. Pip Ryan: Engineering officer on the Hampton.

Lieut. Cy Belasario: Executive officer on the Hampton.

Col. Ed Bates: National Guard officer, leading a small remnant military group in northern California.

Maj. Ike Kolodny: A Marine officer who brings a remnant company up to strength from vigorous "recruiting."

Lt. Col. Bud Inez: An Air Force officer at the High Technology Aerospace Weapons Center, Yucca Flat, Nevada.

REGIONAL LEADERS

Jamie "Pigseye" McFarland: Leader of the Columbus-Dayton Confederation; a cold and brutal despot.

Duncan Boggs: Leader of the Lima-Findlay Alliance.

Pete Belamy: Elected Speaker for the Central Ohio Union.

Mike Kozlowski: Former mayor of Mansfield.

Duane Krupansky: Designated Speaker for the "Brotherhood" from Pennsylvania.

ALIENS AND THEIR EQUIPMENT

*Mata ChaLik BuMaru: Spokesperson for the Qu'uda committee on the Egg-that-Flies, which is known as the Keepers-of-the-Egg.

DalChik DuJuga: Principal archivist for the Keepers-of-the-Egg and leader of the "Home-Seekers" faction.

Cha KinLaat DoMar: Environmental analyst for the Keepers-of-the-Egg, abandoned on Earth by the Qu'uda.

MinCha DuKaat: Weapons specialist for the Keepers-of-the-Egg, abandoned on Earth by the Qu'uda.

Egg-that-Flies: The massive fusion-powered interstellar spacecraft made from an asteroid, belonging to the Qu'uda.

Little-Egg-that-Flies: A small asteroid with a fusion drive used as a weapons platform by the Qu'uda for their return to the Earth.

Bird-that-Soars: Fusion-powered atmospheric space shuttle; capable of interplanetary distances, belonging to the Qu'uda.

Bird-of-War: Fusion-powered battle craft; heavily armored; possesses powerful particle beam weapons and carries a squad of armed Qu'uda.

Suh-Joh: The Hoo-Lii Hive-Mother that sponsors the expedition to investigate EMP anomalies.

A SOCIETAL GLOSSARY

THE GREATER CLANS

Evolved out of post-Collapse semi-tribal units that originated from refugees on the shores of Lake Erie. They survived by becoming militarily powerful, ruthlessly suppressing gangs and bandits. The original Clan has expanded their territory from the borders of the former state of Pennsylvania in the east, and the state of Indiana in the west by assimilating the former Mid-West Federation. Their military strength originally came from horse-mounted warriors equipped with sophisticated recurve bows. With the rapid industrialization and growth of technology, their weapons are increasingly based upon black powder.

THE QU'UDA

A hermaphroditic egg-laying reptilian race inhabiting the Qu'uda planet and star system (also known as Epsilon Eridani). Their planet is close to a cool, red-orange star that emits very little ultraviolet radiation. The Qu'uda are an ancient civilization that has had space travel capabilities for many millennia. The race is very homogeneous and strongly oriented to conformity; the preservation of the ideals of the community is a very strong driving force within their civilization. Their government is by consensus; personal biocomputers link with the center of the community for real-time feed-back. Have long had fusion power and mine deuterium and hydrogen from the atmosphere of the gas giant planet of their star system. The Qu'uda sent a giant interstellar spaceship to Earth where it was damaged by an ancient orbital weapon. They have retreated to the outer planets to re-build their ship and manufacture weapons to return to the Earth.

HOO-LII

A high technology civilization which has colonized several star systems. Their society is matriarchal, with the majority of the popu-lace denied breeding privileges; a highly stratified totalitarian system. A Hoo-Lii planetary settlement was destroyed by the Qu'uda during an attempt to establish contact. Not much is known about the Hoo-Lii except they use digital signals to communicate with each other. They have faster-than-light drives for their inter-stellar ships and have been attracted to the solar system by faint, but anomalous electromagnetic pulses.

ABOUT THE AUTHOR

Malcolm Wood, born in England, came to the USA at age 14 and graduated from Aurora, Ohio High School and Kent State University with a degree in chemistry while working full-time. Three years later, he fulfilled a self-made promise and spent two years traveling around the world. After resuming a career in chemistry, he obtained a MA in economics. About thirty years ago, he became a registered professional engineer in two disciplines (petroleum and environmental engineering), leading to a career in finance, and later, environmental consulting.

It was about this time he resumed writing fiction while working for a company that prepared economic analyzes on specific industry sectors. Since these publications contained a significant element of fiction, it motivated him to start writing fiction. He attended numerous writing workshops and joined the Cleveland Science Fiction Critiquing group (also known as the Cajun Sushi Hamsters from Hell), which had such writers as Geoff Landis, S. Andrew Swann, Charles Oberndorf, and Maureen McHugh. Their critiques and comments pushed Malcolm hard to improve his craft. Almost twenty years ago, he formed the West Side Writers Fiction critiquing group, dedicated to writing at a professional level. During this time, he finished twelve novels and a biography of his travels.

His activities include obtaining a private pilot's license and a competition driver's license. In addition to writing, he has found time to ski, hunt, taste wine, and enjoy gourmet food.

IF YOU LIKED ...

If you liked Like A New Star, you might also enjoy:

Dawn

by M.B. Wood

Ignition

by Kevin J Anderson & Doug Beason

Alternitech

by Kevin J Anderson

Our list of other WordFire Press authors and titles is always growing. To find out more and to see our selection of titles, visit us at:

wordfirepress.com

OTHER WORDFIRE PRESS TITLES BY M.B. WOOD

Collapse

Stranger

The Blue Gem

Dawn

Our list of other WordFire Press authors and titles is always growing. To find out more and to see our selection of titles, visit us at:

wordfirepress.com